A Bounty of Evil

Markus Matthews

A Bounty of Evil

Tellwell Talent
www.tellwell.ca

ISBN
978-0-2288-1910-3 (Hardcover)
978-0-2288-1909-7 (Paperback)
978-0-2288-1911-0 (eBook)

To my buddy Mick for years of friendship
and making these books possible.

Chapter 1

Tuesday, April 11

I screamed like a little girl and may have peed myself a bit as Olivia jerked the wheel and made a hard right across two lanes of traffic. The tires squealed in protest, and I wasn't entirely sure all four wheels stayed on the ground. She missed an HSR city bus by inches, and the driver honked furiously at her.

"Christ, Liv, are you trying to kill us?" I asked as I white-knuckled the support handle on the upper frame of the passenger door.

"What? That wasn't even close," said Olivia. She laughed and hammered the throttle to the floor again.

"I'm pretty sure the bus's license plate is now embossed on the side of your car. You do realize that we are going to pick up Chinese food and aren't in the Daytona 500?"

Liv ignored my comment and kept driving. I noticed that she wasn't even wearing a seatbelt. My seatbelt was firmly buckled in, and at this point, I would have also enjoyed a helmet and a roll cage—or better yet, an ejection seat.

The lack of a seatbelt for Olivia made sense, since she was a vampire; even if we got into a head-on crash and she was thrown through the front windscreen, she would probably survive. Unless, of course, by some fluke she managed to impale herself on a white picket fence or take a tree branch through the heart. Actually, there was probably more risk of her dying wearing a seatbelt—if the car burst into flames, that would kill her.

We were approaching a three-way stop. There was a beige-colored Corolla in front of us that was slowing down to stop. I realized in horror that Olivia wasn't slowing down, and we had about two seconds before her new Audi TT RS and the Corolla became one fused ball of steel, plastic, and carbon fiber.

Liv deftly swung the car out to the oncoming traffic lane and blew through the intersection doing three times the posted speed limit.

"Those big red metal signs that say 'Stop' on them are there for a reason, you know?"

"Yeah—to get slow people out of my way," she giggled and continued to accelerate.

Being in a car with someone who had no fear of dying, didn't care about traffic laws, and had a love of extreme speeds was more than a bit disconcerting. The lack of care about traffic laws was mainly due to her vampire ability to mentally influence normal humans. If we got pulled over, she would just do her "These are not the droids you are looking for, move along" shtick, and the officer would let us go. Even if we got nabbed by an officer who was immune to her mental powers, she would just ditch the fake identity she was using and get a new one. Kind of hard to jail or fine someone who doesn't exist.

Actually, it wouldn't surprise me if she was looking for an excuse to drop this identity. It had been created by Sarah, the enforcer for the English vampire court, just over a month ago. Olivia and Sarah always seemed to rub each other the wrong way and were normally openly hostile to each other. As a result, when Sarah had created the IDs, she'd made Olivia's new name "Olivia Dick." Liv had fumed about that new name for days.

It probably didn't help that her best friend, Bree, and I teased her with lines like, "Liv, I'm sure you can handle a *dick*," "Stop being a *dick* and get over it," and, "C'mon, Bree, stop giving Liv such a *hard* time about her name."

I whimpered as we approached a sweeping bend at the end of the road. Olivia still had her foot firmly planted on the accelerator. We hit the curve doing Odin-only-knows what speed, and I felt the back wheels break loose. The tires screeched, and we left a trail of dark-grey smoke behind us as we went *slide*ways through the corner.

"Check it out! I'm drifting!" said Olivia as we slid around the bend.

I made a mental note to mention to Bree less *Fast and Furious* and more *Driving Miss Daisy* types of movies for Olivia.

"Wow, look at all that tire smoke," said Olivia as her hands frantically worked the steering wheel.

I ignored her, as I was too busy mentally writing my obituary for tomorrow's paper: "Yesterday, Zack Stevens, the former hero known as the Hamilton Hurricane, was killed in tragic automobile accident. He was thirty-three years old. He will be missed by his friends and family. Donations to the 'Ban Perky Vampires from Driving' fund would be appreciated."

Liv counter-steered out of the bend, and the car righted itself as we shot out of the corner.

Hindsight was a wonderfully tragic thing. I had never thought through the implications of Olivia asking if I wanted her to drive me to pick up the Chinese food in her shiny new yellow 2018 Audi TT RS. I wasn't really a car guy and didn't have a driver's license; as someone who had Air elemental powers and could use the wind to fly, I had never really seen the need to get one. When I was 2,000 feet in the air, cars all pretty much looked the same to me.

Sitting there in the driveway, Liv's Audi had looked fast with its huge tires, massive front grille, low aerodynamic lines, and narrow, angry-looking LED headlights. My only thought at the time had been that it would be sweet to check out some lovely German engineering, and I'd never taken it a step further and realized what I was getting myself into.

My attention was yanked back to the here and now as the Audi caught a small bit of air and Olivia entered the strip-mall parking lot. She slammed the car right, and we slid to a stop directly in front of the takeaway place.

In record time, I popped my seatbelt and practically jumped out of the Olivia death-mobile.

"I'll wait here for you," said Olivia with a happy smile.

"Don't bother. I will fly home."

"Why?" she asked with a confused look.

"Because the food will never survive the journey home the way you drive."

Olivia just laughed at that and said, "Okay, race you home!"

Before I could even answer, she and the car peeled away and left me standing there coughing in a cloud of tire smoke. She shouldn't have been able to squeal the tires; the traction control should have prevented that. My knees shook as it hit me that Olivia had probably had the traction control and any other safety/nanny features disabled when she'd picked the car up.

I walked into Wok to Go, and the attendant behind the cash register smiled at me in recognition. This was my fourth time here this month, and each time, I had made a sizeable order of food. I wondered if I was single-handedly covering his rent this month. Normally, a good rule to follow with Chinese food was to order a dish for each person, plus a fried-rice dish, and there would be plenty of food for everyone. This rule went out the window, though, if one of your diners was a Werepanther—at that point, triple everything, and you might get some food.

I paid and grabbed the three stuffed-to-the-brim bags from him, then headed out. I walked around the restaurant, and upon reaching the deserted rear of the building, used my power to control the wind to lift myself into the air, then flew home. I idly kicked around the idea of pushing it to make it home faster to see if I could beat Olivia, but decided to behave myself. The bags the Chinese food was in weren't the sturdiest, and with my luck, if I sped up, I would be bombing Hamilton residents with chicken balls. Coming home empty-handed when a hungry Were was expecting food would be a really bad idea …

I circled my four-bedroom house twice to make sure nothing was odd and no one was watching the place. It had been a month since all of us had been on the run due to a multi-million-dollar contract put out on Olivia by the French vampire court, and the paranoia I had developed during that time still hadn't diminished that much.

Satisfied that nothing was wrong, I descended to the front porch and let myself into the house. I did notice that Olivia's Audi was in the driveway and that she had, in fact, beaten me home. She greeted me at the door and was now wearing different clothes from earlier.

"Geez, it took you long enough. I've been home forever," said Olivia.

Bree rolled her eyes and pushed by Olivia, grabbing the bags of food from me. With her prizes in hand, Bree then turned and headed for the kitchen.

"Hey! That food is for all of us, missy!" I said to the back of her receding form.

Bree's head bobbed in acknowledgement.

I turned my attention back to Olivia. "By 'forever,' you mean less than the minute it took you to dash from the car, blur up to your room, change into that Detroit Lions jersey, and then sprint down the stairs again to make it look like you have been home for much longer than you really have been?"

Liv gave me a guilty smile, blew a playful kiss at me, and turned and walked away. I was amused, as Olivia normally moved so fast with her vamp speed that all I normally saw was a blur, but this time, she was purposely walking away slowly. She knew she looked good in that Honolulu-blue jersey and was tormenting me by letting me catch a glimpse of her lovely nude form under it. The tiny mesh holes that made up the fabric were certainly giving me an eyeful. Liv loved to tease me like that, and when she did it, I didn't know whether to be mad or grateful toward her—though, by the way the thin material clung to her lovely curves, I was certainly leaning toward grateful at this moment.

I took off my spring jacket and hung it up on one of the aluminum hooks by the door, then headed after the girls.

Bree was laying out all the food containers buffet style on the center island in the kitchen, and Stella and Blue were already standing there with plates in hand. Stella's small form made the two dinner plates she was holding look huge.

She waved one of the plates at me and said, "I saved you a spot, Zack!"

We have a house rule that Stella, Blue, and I get to build our plates first before Bree. If you lived with a Werepanther—or any Were—you would understand why that rule is in place, as with their hyper metabolism, they ate more than an NFL lineman after two-a-day practices.

Stella was the oldest of the five of us chronologically; she had been born in 1890, which made her 127 years old. To see her, though, you would guess her age to be about ten years old. Her youthful appearance was due to a side effect from the Hyde potion she'd been injected with by her evil adoptive father, Sir Reginald. Spending 108 years in a stasis chamber before Blue accidently rescued her also helped with the youthful looks.

Blue was the last member of our team. Besides having a first-class logical mind and warrior instincts that she had honed since almost birth, Blue also had the ability to travel anywhere in the world via the shadows. She could also transport people with her when she traveled.

I stepped in beside Stella and thanked her as I took one of the plates from her. She smiled, but I noticed she unconsciously stepped back to put more distance between us. Thanks to years with Sir Reginald, Stella had deep distrust of men. I couldn't blame her for that. She was getting better at being around me, though, and we were slowly building a trust between us, but it would probably be years, if ever, before she would be completely comfortable ...

Bree finished opening all the food containers. She saw the three of us standing there with plates in hand and said, "Hurry up, you three. If any of you take too long building your plates, I'm putting *you* on my plate, covering you in barbeque sauce, and eating you for dinner!"

The three of us laughed nervously at this—you never really knew if Bree was completely joking or not when it came to food—and quickly started heaping food on our plates.

"Which ones are the spicy ones?" asked Blue as she studied the mass of opened food containers.

I pointed to the Szechuan beef at the end of the counter that was probably so spicy I was surprised it hadn't eaten through the tinfoil container it was in. "That is your special dish," I said, then also pointed to the kung pao chicken that was also spicy but tame enough that I could put some on my plate.

Blue nodded happily, and my eyes watered in sympathy as I watched her fill more than half her plate with the Szechuan beef dish and all the angry red flecks it contained. Stella avoided that dish like I did.

"Tummy rumbling … You're all taking too long … You won't like me when I am hungry," said Bree as she eyed the food.

"Bree, stop being so dramatic. We'll be done in a minute," said Stella in a disapproving tone as she looked over at our famished blonde Were.

Bree eyed her for a moment, smiled, and said, "Screw it. Zack hand me the container of sweet-and-sour sauce. I'm just going to put Stella on my plate and have her for dinner."

Stella tossed a couple more chicken balls on her plate and quickly ran away laughing as Bree approached her with the plate.

Blue and I finished filling our plates and left Bree to it. I smiled as I noticed Bree was carrying two plates to the counter.

I grabbed a seat at the table and noticed Olivia was sipping on her pint-mug of blood. When we had first met, I used to get queasy whenever Liv was drinking human plasma from a donor bag or a pint mug from the Food-O-Tron. Now, I barely noticed. It was amazing what you could get used to. Now I was happy that she was being well supplied; the only thing worse than a hungry Were was a bloodthirsty vampire.

When we had been on the run a month ago, there had been too many times Olivia had looked at me like I was the last rice cake at a Weight Watcher's meeting. My elemental blood was in great demand by the vampire community. Sarah at the English vampire court had been throwing herself at me every time she saw me, offering sex in exchange for my blood. So far, I hadn't taken her up on it …

Now, with the Food-O-Tron working again, getting an unlimited supply of blood for Olivia wasn't an issue. The Food-O-Tron was an invention of Sir Reginald. Evil scumbag that he had been, he'd also been a genius. The device could perfectly replicate any dish that was added to it. It was located in his old secret lab that was buried underground in London, but with Blue's shadow-traveling ability, it was as easy to access as heading out to the garage. I had added human blood from medical supply bags to the machine recipe list, so Olivia could literally get a pint-mug of blood every minute from the machine if she wished.

"That is what I am talking about," said Blue with a satisfied smile after she tried a huge mouthful of the extra-spicy Szechuan beef.

Stella looked at Blue like she was crazy and shook her head at her friend's tolerance of peppery-hot foods.

Bree sat down, and we all went quiet as we stared at the two heaping plates of food in front of her.

"What?" she asked self-consciously.

"Stop staring, people. The girl needs her food, and with what I have planned for everyone tonight, you should *all* eat well, as you are going to need your energy, my pretties," said Blue with a smile filled with pointy white teeth.

By the playful flicking of her tail, I knew tonight would suck. Blue might look like one of the aliens from the movie *Avatar*, but in her role as trainer for the team, I was convinced that she was a demon from Hell sent to torment and punish us here on Earth. To be fair, I hadn't been in this good of shape since my teenage years. The mornings after one of her training sessions, I wasn't so grateful, though, as I usually woke aching and sore. There were times I hurt in areas I didn't know I even had muscles.

She was also training us to work better as a team, so we'd be more effective at taking down bounties together. The tactical exercises she'd put together were physically demanding and mentally taxing. The sessions were paying dividends, though, and we were all getting better at anticipating what each other would do in certain situations.

The training was also highlighting issues we had working together. The biggest source of friction in these exercises was between Bree and me. Before I had joined them, Bree had led the team, and now, that was my job. I had deep respect for Bree, and I knew she felt the same about me. The problem was that Bree's beast didn't have the same respect and felt that its natural place was being the alpha of any group it was a part of. I'd been trying to fix that issue for the last month, but so far, no luck ...

As I ate my dinner, I realized how natural it felt now to have the four of them around. I had been on my own for ten years as a hero and the last six as a bounty hunter and had had my concerns at taking them on as partners after our adventure with the French vampire court. Sure, there were adjustments, like Blue running me ragged night after night, putting up with Olivia and her slightly crazy and perky personality, dealing with Bree's moodiness and anger when the full moon approached, and being careful not to make any sudden or threatening moves around Stella, but at least things were never boring. I also found I was talking to myself less and less now, which, before they had shown up, was starting to be a real concern of mine.

We hadn't been out on a job together yet, as we'd been waiting for the ladies' UN-issued bounty-hunting IDs to come in. The UN bounty-hunting IDs had a number of advantages, but the two biggest were that they were recognized by law enforcement, and they granted the user tax-free status on any bounties collected.

The IDs had arrived last week, hence the reason why Bree and Liv had new vehicles parked in the driveway, as with their new IDs in place, I could transfer the ladies' share of the more than $2 million US in bounties we had collected while being hunted by the French vampire court.

With the IDs out of the way and all our paperwork in place, in the next couple of days we were going to start hunting down some scary fugitives—and hopefully make a tidy sum of money doing it.

Chapter 2

Tuesday, April 11

After dinner, Blue shadow-traveled us to our secret underground lab in London. The lab had become Stella's after she'd been left in stasis when Sir Reginald died. We stepped out into the main hangar. In the center of hangar, modular walls had been arranged to create a small building. The walls were built in four-foot-wide wheeled sections and could easily be rearranged so the "house" was different for each exercise. There were also mannequins inside the building that were painted in different colors; red ones were enemies, and yellow ones were civilians.

Blue would arrange the house and dummies in different positions. She would lay out a scenario, and we would have to figure out how to take down the enemies without having any civilian casualties. Blue would also pick the Enhanced abilities that the different enemies had.

Tonight's scenario was that a rogue group of vampires had bounties on them. They had taken an unknown number of civilians to feed from. Our job was to take down the vampires while keeping the civilians alive. The house was in an urban environment, so we also had to be concerned about keeping the damage to a minimum—including the imagined houses on either side.

We did these scenarios in two ways: full dress and walk-through. For the full-dress ones, Bree would be in her Werepanther form, and Stella would change to her Hyde form. Tonight, though, we were just doing them as walk-throughs, which meant Bree and Stella stayed in their usual human forms.

This scenario was turning out to be a real bitch. Try sneaking up on a group that had enhanced hearing and blinding speed. On most of the runs, the civilians were ruled dead before we even came in the front door. After a couple of hours, tempers were running short …

"Fail!" said Blue as we finished the scenario for the ninth time.

We groaned at this, but I had been expecting it. I knew at least one of the civilians had been killed on our last run-through.

Blue went over what we did wrong. Once she was done, she disappeared inside the "house" to rearrange the dummies again.

When she reemerged, I said, "Okay, people, huddle up, and let's do it right this time."

I modified the plan to correct the errors we had made last time, then started going over the new plan. After almost each point, Bree questioned or suggested different ways to do things. When she interrupted me for the sixth time, I'd had enough. "Okay, we are done. Blue, take Stella and Liv back home. Bree and I need to have a private discussion."

Blue nodded and walked to an area of the hangar that was in darkness, then opened a portal. Liv used her vampire speed and was gone in the blink of the eye. Stella hung back for a moment and glanced at both Bree and I. I knew she wanted to play peacemaker, but I shook my head at her and pointed to shadow portal. She reluctantly walked away and disappeared into the shadows, with Blue right behind her.

I turned my attention to Bree, who stood in front of me with her arms crossed and an annoyed expression on her face. The ladies had made me team leader due to my experience. I knew Bree respected that decision—and me—but I also knew that her beast didn't. I had two choices: I either could turn over the leadership duties to Bree or teach her beast who was in charge. My stomach tightened as I made my decision.

"Strip!" I said in a firm tone.

"Excuse me?" said Bree, looking at me like I had lost my mind.

"You have been questioning my authority all night." I held up my hand to cut off whatever she was going to say. "I know *you* don't have a problem with me being in charge, but your beast does. I think it has been playing with your emotions in the background and using you to challenge me. We are going to settle this once and for all. Go into the house, strip, and change. Let your beast take control and come after me. We are going to duel for the leadership role. You win, you are in charge. I win, and your beast respects me as its alpha."

A range of emotions flashed across her face. "No, I won't fight you. If I let the beast out, it will kill you."

I knew Bree wouldn't let the beast take over; her greatest fear was losing control of the beast and killing someone. I also knew this fight had to happen, which meant I needed to force the beast to come out, and there was only one way that would happen: I needed to make Bree mad.

I laughed at her. "You rate yourself too highly. I'm not going to lose to you. Heck, you couldn't beat an Earth elemental with Liv, Stella, and Blue's help. Your Were has no shot at winning against me by itself. Face it, Bree, you are the weak link of this team."

The look of hurt that crossed her face was like a punch in the gut to me, but I continued. "You will do this, or you are off the team. I can't risk you undermining my authority in the field. You hesitating or questioning my orders in combat could get us killed, and I won't allow that to happen."

Bree's eyes glowed for a moment as her beast rose to the surface as her anger flared. She took a deep breath to center herself and force the beast back. "I can control my beast," said Bree with gritted teeth.

"You can't, and that is the problem. It is manipulating you. It thinks I am weak and not worthy of leading. You either fight me, or you are off the team."

Another quick flash lit her eyes before she closed them and forced the beast back into its mental cage. She opened her eyes and gave me a pleading look.

I didn't want to fight her, either, but I knew we had to do this, or the beast would continue to push. Her beast was fighting to get free, and I needed to push a little harder, so I did something you should never do with a Were: I looked her straight in the eye and challenged her. "C'mon, let kitty out to play. I think your beast is chicken. Now that I'm calling it out, it's hiding behind you like the coward it is."

"Zack ..." begged Bree as another glow appeared in her eyes.

I started flapping my arms and making loud chicken noises.

"Zack, don't ..." said Bree, but her tone was deeper and more intense.

I knew the beast was near the surface now. I made fists to hide my trembling hands, as I knew I was playing with fire. I pushed some more. "Last chance. Fight me or pack your shit and leave—"

"*No!*" screamed Bree as her nails started to grow.

"Yes! Bring it, you oversized fleabag!"

Bree's growled deeply, and her eyes shone with menace. My sphincter tightened as the sounds of ripping cloth echoed around the hangar. Bree shredded her grey sweater top and sports bra, and seconds later, her track pants met the same fate. Her body convulsed in front of me, and I winced as I heard muscles tearing and bones cracking as she began to change.

Dark fur burst through from under her pale white skin, and I stepped back to put more room between us. Fifteen seconds later, Bree was gone, and in her place was more than 300 pounds of lethal feline killing machine. She had changed into her Werepanther form, rather than the standing hybrid form she usually used. The glowing ice-blue eyes looked at me with no sign of recognition behind them. I knew the beast and not Bree was in control. The panther opened its mouth, giving me an eyeful of the brutally powerful two-inch fangs, and let loose a deafening roar that shook the entire hangar.

"That's it, you magnificent bitch! Come get some!" I yelled back in challenge.

I had barely closed my mouth when it sprang at me. It closed the twenty feet between us in less than a couple of seconds. I just managed to call on my Air power as it leapt at me, and I lifted it over me. It was close enough that its back claws brushed through my hair when it went over.

In my haste, I'd applied much more power than I had intended. A loud *bong* reverberated in the air as the Werepanther ricocheted off one of the steel support beams in the ceiling. Gravity took hold, and it began to tumble back toward me. I caught it with my Air power, holding it suspended about ten feet off the floor.

"Whatcha gonna do now, little kitty?" I said.

It growled at me and swiped one of its massive claws at me. In my mind, I forced myself to refer to the Werepanther as "it" and not "she." I did this out of need—if I thought of it as Bree, I wouldn't be able to do what I needed to do.

"Do you yield?" I asked.

A short snarl of defiance was the reply. I steeled myself and began calling on my Electrical power. I pointed my right hand at it and let loose a small, sharp burst of lightning. The Werepanther let out a squeal of pain and convulsed as the electricity coursed through it. The smell of ozone and burnt fur lingered after.

"I am the alpha here ... I will keep this up until you give Bree control and change back," I said and shot another powerful burst at it.

I hated doing this but knew it needed to be done. I needed to have Bree's beast acknowledge me as the team leader.

It looked down at me with its intelligent blue eyes and flashed its teeth at me, then swiped a paw at me. I sent a huge blast of wind under it and rammed it hard into the ceiling. I winced internally at the distinctive sounds of bones cracking.

The Werepanther went almost instantly limp, and I worried I'd overdone it. I quickly lowered the Werepanther to the ground and started rushing forward to check if Bree was okay. I'd barely taken a step when it opened it eyes and stared malevolently at me.

Shit, not good. I jerked to halt as it nimbly sprang to its feet and charged at me. I frantically called on my Air power and barely managed to get in enough juice to push it away from me. The sound of fabric ripping echoed in the hangar as the Werepanther leapt by me to my right. It shot off into the far hallway and disappeared. I glanced down and saw four long gashes in the side of my T-shirt. Thankfully, it was just T-shirt. That had been way too close.

A loud roar of challenge came from deeper in the lab. It wanted me to come after it, but that wasn't happening. The three hallways that led from the hangar to the main lab were narrow and had too many doors and blind junctions in them. There was no way I was going to let the panther set the terrain in this fight.

I used my Air power to lift myself and rose to almost the top of the hangar. I flew backward, keeping my eyes on all three entrances until my back brushed up against the back wall. From this vantage point, I could see all the ways into the hangar and had plenty of open space between me and those entrances.

The panther roared again, and I smiled, as it sounded like it was getting impatient.

It was time to do what I did best: annoy the living shit out of someone. "Here, kitty, kitty, kitty ..."

Another roar shook the whole place, and I continued. "Stop hiding and come fight me, you big pussy!"

There was no response to that, so I started clucking again. I stopped my chicken routine when a loud crash came from the far right hallway. I turned slightly toward it, and out of the corner of my eye, a black blur of fur came bounding out of the left side hallway.

That was what made Weres so bloody dangerous: They weren't dumb animals—they had intelligence and cunning.

It had purposely knocked something in the right hallway to pull my attention, so it could sneak in from the left. Thankfully, being at the back of the hangar gave me enough time to deal with it.

I called on my Air power and lifted the Were off the ground. I lowered myself back to the floor of the hangar as I lifted the suspended panther higher. I hit it with a powerful blast of lightning, and it yelped and shuddered in pain.

I cut the power off to my blast and said, "Give up and change back to Bree, or there is more where that came from …"

It snarled defiantly at me. I sighed and hit it again. I hated every second of this. Bree was in there and no doubt feeling every bit of the pain the beast was experiencing. I stopped with the lightning and got another snarl. I increased the air pressure under the panther and smashed it hard into the ceiling again.

I spent the next ten minutes alternating between frying it with lightning and slamming it into steel beams in the ceiling, but it refused to yield. This was a problem, as with each passing second, I was draining more and more of my power. I was down to my reserves now.

It snarled at me again, and my gut tightened in fear. As much as I was trying not to think that this was Bree, I knew in my subconscious it was, and this kept me on a tight leash on what I could do. The problem was, the beast wasn't holding back, and if it got the chance, it would tear me into kibbles in the blink of an eye.

"Yield, you stupid brute! You can't win," I said as I shot another blast of lightning into it.

The strain of this was starting to show. I had sweat pouring off me now, and somehow, it knew I was weakening. As the lightning finished, it roared back at me again in angry defiance.

My power gave out for a moment, and the Were fell a couple of feet closer to me before I regained control and lifted it back up again. It was time to fish or cut bait. I could cut off the oxygen around it, which would knock it out, but that would only be temporary. I also had no idea how long it would be out for.

As I stood there desperately trying to figure out what to do, I caught the hum and crackle of the Tesla coils in the other room and smiled. I fired another massive blast of Air under the Were and bounced it off the ceiling again. This time, though, I didn't catch it and instead used my Air powers to fly out of the room. The sounds of splitting wood filled the hangar like a gunshot as it crashed down into the wooden mock house behind me.

A second later, a loud growl filled the room. I shuddered at the sound of triumph in that growl. I flew down the corridor as if Satan himself were on my tail. I heard the wood being smashed and had no doubt that the Werepanther was free now and coming after me.

I shot out of the corridor into the main area of the lab and barely cleared the two heavy workbenches between me and the Tesla coils. I stopped dead between the two arcing coils and almost moaned as the powerful electricity shot through me. I turned back toward the hangar, and the Werepanther shot out of the corridor like a black-furred rocket. It leapt up onto the table, sending test tubes and other lab equipment crashing to the ground. It didn't pause and bounded off the table directly at me.

I stopped it in midair using my Air powers. Its powerful maw gaped open and its razor-sharp talons were fully extended, but both were a good ten feet from me.

"You dumb beast, if I hadn't caught you, you would have fried to death in here ..."

It snarled again at me in response, and I laughed. "It's over. You can't touch me here; my powers are fully recharged, and I can keep frying you all night long. Submit and save yourself a world of hurt."

It growled at me in a tone that I could only take as "Fuck you." I sighed and extended my hand. It squealed as I poured lightning into it. We locked eyes as it shuddered and spasmed in front of me. This time, though, I didn't stop the lightning, I kept pouring it into the beast without mercy.

It was the longest two minutes of my life, and I almost cried as the hostile glow behind the menacing ice-blue eyes faded. I instantly cut off the flow of electricity and held the slow-changing form aloft. The claws and fangs retracted, muscles ripped, and bones cracked as the shift continued.

My relief at seeing Bree's sweaty, naked, and slightly battered form was intense. I lowered her shaking form to the ground and flew down and landed in front of her.

She stepped toward me and caught me straight in the mouth with a right hook that Mike Tyson would have been proud of. My head flew to the side from the force of the blow, and I tasted blood.

"You *son of a bitch*! You had no right to do that!" said Bree as she followed up with a hard left meant to catch me in the chest.

Thankfully, the left was high and caught me in the ribs. It hurt, but if had been a few inches lower, she would have knocked the air out of me. The shot with the left had also done me a favor: I had been in a daze from the first punch, and the pain rippling across my chest was enough to bring me out of it. I saw her right fist coming in low and just managed to step to the side and take it off my thigh. If she had connected with that one, I probably would never have been able to have kids.

Another left came in, but it was half-hearted at best, and I ducked around it. Bree looked at me and now had tears streaming down her cheeks. I stepped near her and pulled her into tight hug. She pounded my back a couple of times with her fists but with barely any of her strength behind it. She buried her face into my neck and sobbed. She balled her eyes out against me. I held her, stroked her hair, and whispered reassuring things. I smiled at the profanity that was murmured at me between sobs.

I knew she was upset at losing control and letting her beast ride her like that. As mad as she had been, she had pulled those punches.

I stood there quietly holding her for a long time. My lip was throbbing, and I was pretty sure at least two of my teeth were loose. I was also sure that I had a nasty bruise forming along the outsides of my ribs right now.

"You're bleeding!" said Bree as she broke our embrace and grabbed my chin to examine her handiwork.

"And you're naked, so fair trade, I think?"

She blushed, laughed, and rolled her eyes in the span of a few seconds. "Call Blue. I need clothes, and you need a healer …"

* * * * *

An hour later, I exited Marion's apartment. Marion, my healer, had been amused at my condition, and it had taken her no time to heal me. A fat lip, a couple of loose teeth, and a few bruises were probably among the mildest injuries I'd ever had her fix.

I didn't bother calling Blue for a lift, as she was probably in bed by now, and I had one stop I wanted to make first before going home. I had no doubt that Bree was probably still mad at me, and I wanted to pick up some extra protection …

Twenty minutes later, I landed on my front porch. I thought about trying to sneak in but figured there was no way I could be quiet enough that Liv or Bree wouldn't hear me. I unlocked the door and entered the house. The TV blared in the living room, and I guessed that was where Liv and Bree must be. I took a deep breath and headed to talk to Bree.

I made it to midway through the kitchen before Liv materialized in front of me. I swear, I hated vampire speed more than anything else in this world.

Liv had her arms crossed. She glared at me and opened her mouth to show that her fangs were descended. "You beat up my best friend!"

"That is between me and her. I would like to speak to her, if you don't mind?"

I tried getting around Liv, but she effortlessly mirrored my movements, blocking my path. "Look, Liv, let me through so I can apologize to Bree, okay?"

"No. She doesn't want to talk to you."

I sighed, but before I could argue, Bree yelled from the living room, "Liv, is he carrying coconut-topped German chocolate cake?"

"Yep!"

"Then let him though."

Liv stepped to the side, and I went to meet my fate.

Thankfully, Bree accepted my apology and my chocolatey offering. We talked, and she agreed that her beast had been manipulating her emotions and pushing her to buck my authority. She said this had caught her off guard. Usually, her beast was much more direct, and subtle was a new tact that she would have to watch for. She understood why I had forced the fight and surprised me by apologizing for giving me the busted lip and what have you.

The comments I had made to her earlier weighed heavily on my mind. "I also want to apologize for the things I said earlier. I only said those things to bring out your beast. You aren't the weak member of this team; you are one of the strongest. Your strength, conviction, and courage are the glue that hold this team together. I have no doubt in the next few years that it will be *you* leading this team, and I would be honored to follow you."

To my surprise, Bree put down her cake and got up and hugged me. She leaned in and whispered, "We are good, but don't you dare ever do that again!"

I felt another body press up against us as Liv joined the hug, and she said, "You two are the most important people in my life. The two of you fighting each other is like my worst nightmare. Do it again, and I will kick both of your asses. Understand?"

The moment was getting to me, and I felt my eyes starting to well up. I didn't want to be sniveling like a little girl in front of them and so said, "Tonight has been a very trying time for all of us, and I am feeling very close to both of you right now. We should move this party upstairs. I think us getting naked and working off all this stress together would be a great team-building exercise."

"Asshole," said Bree as she broke the hug. Her blue eyes twinkled, and she added, "You really think I am going to choose you over chocolate cake?"

Liv just laughed at both of us.

Bree sat back down on the couch and lovingly picked up the entire cake. Liv blurred off and returned almost instantly with a fork. Bree thanked her and she dug in. She moaned in almost sexual pleasure at the first bite.

"Well, as Bree seems to have found her love interest for the night, it looks like it is just you and me, Liv. I'm a bit stiff from the fight and could use a nice, hot shower. You want to make it hotter by joining me?"

Liv studied me with amusement for a moment and said, "Tempting, but we were going to watch *Clueless*, so I will take two hours of entertainment over two minutes that you might last any day ..."

I covered my heart and made a "You wound me" gesture at Liv's shot. I wished the girls good night and retreated upstairs for my shower. It was tempting to hang out with them, but tomorrow we were going to take on our first bounty together, and I had no doubt that it would be a long day.

Chapter 3

Wednesday, April 12

Blue and Stella were sitting at the kitchen table drinking tea as I entered.

Upon seeing me, they both got up, and Blue said, "Good morning. We were just going to use the Food-O-Tron to make some breakfast. What would you like?"

I kicked around the choices in my head. In the last month, I had added a number of new meals to the Food-O-Tron, but I decided to go with one of the first ones I had added. "Bacon and Egger. I'll set the table while you two are gone."

They nodded and walked into the living room, then disappeared into the shadows.

Five minutes later, they reappeared carrying three cast-iron pans from the Food-O-Tron, and each one had a couple of Bacon and Eggers in them. Blue dished out the pans to each of us as we sat down.

I was halfway through my first breakfast sandwich when a sleepy-eyed Bree wandered into the kitchen and said, "There better be some for me!"

We all surrendered our second Bacon and Eggers and dumped them on Bree's plate. Without a word, Blue got up and walked into the shadows, then disappeared. I knew she was hitting the lab again to get more.

Bree smiled as she sat down and inhaled her first Bacon and Egger. I was surprised she was up this early, as she usually stayed up until dawn to keep Olivia company and didn't surface until midafternoon. I wasn't sure if she was up early due to smelling the food or because today was going to be our first official day of bounty hunting. I was relieved to find that she seemed to be her normal self and hoped that meant she had put last night behind us.

Blue returned carrying three more pans, which was a good thing, as Bree had already killed her three and was looking for more. Once all the food had been handed out, and I finished my second sandwich, I turned my attention to Stella ...

Stella had her notebook open and was reviewing it. I asked, "What do you have for us?"

"Pixie infestation in north Burlington. No human causalities, but several family pets have gone missing. They are estimating the swarm to be over a hundred pixies, and at $500 per pixie, that is an adequate amount for our time."

"Pass. Next?" I answered with a shudder.

Bree laughed. "Are you scared of pixies?"

"I would rather stick my dick in a hornet's nest than get involved dealing with a pixie swarm."

"Why? Aren't they, like, six inches tall? How bad can they be?"

I took a sip of orange juice. "First off, they are fae, which means at least half of them are immune to my lightning attacks. They are also natural magic users with elemental affinity, so some of them would actually get a boost from me zapping them with lightning. They carry three-inch spears, half of which at least are going to be poison-tipped. They also have fangs and claws that, while tiny, are sharp enough to easily break skin. A swarm of pixies can completely strip a human to the bone in less than twenty seconds. They also cast spells, and while their magic attacks aren't individually that powerful, you have a hundred small fireballs, magic darts, acid attacks, frost spears, and electric attacks fired at you, and you're going to have a very bad day. Also, the bounty is per pixie, so the paperwork on that is also going to suck."

Stella piped up. "My Hyde form should be impervious to anything they can do."

"Probably, but pixies are also smart and can fly. Therefore, as soon as they noticed that they couldn't touch you, they would just scatter to the winds. Your Hyde form would turn any pixie it hit into paste, and photos of red splotches versus actual bodies are going to have the UN Bounty Commission questioning every claim we submit."

Stella looked a little crestfallen, and then Blue said, "According to the report, they have limited themselves to pets and wildlife. What if they move on to humans?"

Blue usually didn't say much outside of training, but whenever she did, it was usually insightful, and this was a classic example of that, as she had hit the main concern right on the head.

"As I said earlier, pixies are smart. By sticking to pets and wildlife, they realize they will probably be left alone. They know if they hit a human, then that will change. If they are listed on the UN bounty site, then they have probably been active in Burlington for at least a couple of weeks. I haven't seen any news reports of human skeletons being found, which means they haven't hit any humans, and I doubt they will change their pattern."

Blue nodded at this, and I turned to Stella and asked, "What else do you have?"

"The Rose assassin hit a Wall Street executive two days ago in New York. The bounty on capturing them is $3.5 million US. New York is practically in our backyard, and that type of money is certainly worth our time."

"Why did you call the Rose assassin 'them.' Is there more than one person doing these crimes?" asked Bree with a frown.

"May I?" I said to Stella before she answered. She nodded, and I continued. "The Rose is a shapechanger, and shapechangers are asexual, so 'they/them' singular is the correct pronoun."

"I take it, as you knew the Rose was a shapechanger, you were already aware of this bounty?" asked Stella.

I nodded and said, "The Rose assassin has been on the UN bounty site for almost ten years now. Bringing the Rose down would be quite the feather in our cap, but I think that might be shooting a bit high for our first team bounty. Lots of people over the years have tried to take the Rose down, but ten years later, they are still at large."

"Why are they called the Rose?" asked Bree.

"Every time they kill someone, they leave a single long-stemmed red rose on the body as their calling card."

After a moment of silence, Stella said, "I don't understand why this bounty is 'shooting a bit high.' With Blue's shadow-traveling ability and your ability to see auras of Enhanced Individuals, we should be uniquely suited for this type of job?"

"I agree with you that we would probably have a better chance than most other hunters, but the Rose is a pro. I have read their file a number of times, and their MO is always the same: They take the form of someone close to the victim—a good friend, lover, employee, or relative, someone the victim trusts implicitly—and then, when they are alone, the Rose kills them.

"A shapeshifter, by touching someone, can assume the person's appearance and memories. I'm guessing that the Rose, after the killing, changes to someone else completely and then leaves town. While the Rose might have been the victim's wife for the killing, probably no more than five minutes later they could be the building's janitor, a police officer, a random person who was walking by, or just about anyone. They never take more than one contract at a time in the same place. They could now be a school teacher in the Midwest, a businessman in China, a soldier in the Middle East, or just about anyone anywhere in the world."

"Can a shapeshifter take on someone's power?" asked Bree with concern.

I shook my head. "No, they only take on a person's memories and appearance. If they touched me, for example, they would look and sound like me and know what I know, but they wouldn't be able to cast lightning or control the air or see auras. There are power-absorbers and power-duplicators out there, but they only take *powers*, not appearances or memories. To answer your next question, a power-absorber steals your power, leaving you powerless for a period of time, and power-duplicators copy your power, but you still have your power."

Stella jumped in. "So you are saying that there is no point in going to New York, as the Rose is in the wind and could be anywhere in the world?" I nodded, and Stella continued. "If we were hunting the Rose, how would you do it?"

I thought about this for a few moments. "There are only two ways I can think of. The first is that we configure our phones and browsers to continually search for any news relating to the Rose and hope we get an alert immediately after they have killed someone. We'd shadow-travel there as soon as possible and then see if I can spot an aura I have never seen before. The other way is that we keep an eye on black-market hit contracts, and when a higher-end one pops up, we shadow the victim and hope that the Rose decides to take that contract, then we catch them in the act."

Stella pondered this for a moment. "I think it wouldn't hurt to configure a program on the computer to search for news on the Rose and send us alerts. I will set that up after this. But as that seems to be more of a long-term project, we need to find a bounty to work on *now*. The last one I found was related to killings up north. The UN bounty site doesn't have much detail on the perpetrator or perpetrators, as it lists the killer(s) as 'Unknown Enhanced Individual(s),' but there have been three attacks in the last ten days, with four bodies total. The bodies were savagely torn apart and partially eaten, and due to this, the authorities are convinced this is not a human predator. The bounty is $1 million US."

I whistled at the amount; that was a nice chunk of change. As this was in northern Ontario—and, therefore, almost in our backyard—the old hero part of me would very much have liked to see this killer or killers taken down. I wasn't so excited about not knowing what we were up against. I guessed that was why Stella seemed keen on this one, since she loved a good mystery.

"Rogue Were or Weres?" said Bree.

"Possibly. Stella, you mentioned three attacks and four bodies, so at one of the crime scenes, there were two victims?"

Stella nodded and flipped the page, then read out loud, " 'The second attack, a couple—Tammy Jamison, nineteen, and Dan Gilman, twenty-one—were killed at their campsite in the early evening. Their remains were discovered two days later when some hikers came across the site.' "

"Early April is a bit early to be camping up north, but it has been unseasonably warm. Did they have a tent, trailer, or RV?" I asked.

Stella looked through her notes and, after a bit, said, "Pop-up trailer. Blood was found outside the trailer, but the inside was clean."

"If it was a Were attack, then it was Were*s* plural," I said, thinking out loud.

"How do you figure that? One Were could easily kill two people," said Bree.

"Weres usually attack because they are hungry. If it killed the first victim, then it would begin eating immediately and ignore the second the person."

"Unless the second person tried to stop the attack?" countered Bree.

"Possible, but unlikely, since, as you well know, Weres are very efficient killing machines. If one attacked someone, it would tear the throat out or snap the victim's neck, killing the person instantly. Most people, seeing their companion killed like that, would realize there was nothing they could do to help and then get out of there. The fact that both sets of remains were together at the campsite makes me think they were both killed almost at the same time, which makes me think two attackers."

Another thought popped into my head. I turned to Stella and asked, "This attack was early evening, so it was after sunset. Were the other attacks at night too?"

"The first one was during the day. Thomas Martin, forty-three, had taken the day off from work to go bird-watching. According to friends, he was looking for bald eagles that might have been nesting in the area. He didn't return home that night, and his wife couldn't reach him, so she contacted police. The OPP found his car the next morning, and his remains were found about 200 feet from his car."

"You were thinking vampire?" asked Blue.

I nodded. "Or wights, zombies, or ghouls. The daytime attack rules out vampires and zombies. Wights or ghouls are still possible but unlikely; they can move around in the day but are pretty much blind due to the light, which makes daytime attacks rare."

"What other possibilities are there?" asked Bree.

"Some fae creatures would be strong enough to tear a human apart and would eat them, and can operate at day or night. A Tank-type Enhanced Individual like Stella's Hyde form would be strong enough but, unless they were insane, wouldn't eat a human. A demon would also fit the requirements. A yeti or sasquatch would certainly have the strength, though I don't remember the lore mentioning them eating humans. There are other supernatural creatures that would be powerful enough to tear a human apart and eat human flesh, but those are more obscure and not very likely. I think a small group of rogue Weres is probably the best possibility, but we will keep an open mind. What were the details on the third attack?"

Stella turned a couple of pages and then said, "Tamara Lightfoot, seventeen, went to a nearby friend's house after school and stayed for dinner. Decided to walk home by herself around 8:30 p.m. due to it being a mild night. Her parents got concerned at 10:00 p.m., as she hadn't gotten home yet and the kilometer-or-so walk should have taken much less time. The parents decided to go out looking for her by car shortly after that. They drove the route she would have walked and, at about the halfway mark, saw a pink runner that belonged to Tamara on the side of the road. They pulled over, found blood, and followed the trail for about twenty feet into the woods. They discovered their daughter's remains and called police. That was two nights ago."

The room was quiet after that, as we all dwelt on the horror of discovering your child's remains like that. There was something about this bounty that gave me an uneasy feeling, and I couldn't quite put my finger on it, but after hearing about Tamara, there was no way I was letting whoever had done this walk away.

"Well, it looks like we have our bounty," I said.

Stella and Bree gave me small smiles at this, and Blue simply nodded in agreement.

"So do we wait for Olivia to rise and hit the crime scenes for clues?" asked Bree with an edge of excitement in her voice.

"Nope," I said. "I'm going to call Ray Dunham. You and I are going to meet him and the alpha of the Barrie pack."

Bree's earlier excitement instantly turned to nervousness. I'd been bugging her for weeks to visit the Barrie pack. She had been a Werepanther for more than a year now and had yet to even meet another Were. She had continued putting me off on this and hadn't given me a reason why.

"You are thinking that if these are rogue Weres, that Ray and his alpha might be able to help or give us some information?" asked Stella.

I nodded. "The murders are quite a bit north of Barrie, and I'm not sure how far their territory runs, but they might be able to help or give us some direction. Ray's an EIRT officer and might have also been on scene and have some good insight."

EIRT stood for Enhanced Individual Response Team. Ten years ago, it had been called MRT, or Monster Response Team. They were part of the Royal Canadian Mounted Police (RCMP), which was Canada's version of the FBI. EIRT teams were usually made up of five or six officers, and at least one or two of them would be Enhanced Individuals. The rest were human, usually with SWAT training. If someone or something with powers was on a rampage, these teams were the ones called in to deal with them.

Stella nodded, as she seemed to see the logic, and then asked, "While you and Bree are being social, do we investigate the crime scenes?"

I shook my head. "No, we will do that all together later tonight after Bree and I are done, assuming we can meet with them tonight. In the meantime, find out everything you can about the four victims via the internet. See if they are connected or have anything in common. Map out the crime scenes and see if there is any sort of pattern. Use Google Earth to find the crime scenes and see what they have in common. Hit the lore sites and books in the office and see what else fits our killer's profile. Do some Google searches on missing people in northern Ontario. There might be other victims we don't know about. Check into the history in the area and see if there are any odd occurrences or local legends that might fit this. Basically, research, research, and more research. I want us to know everything we can before we hit those crime scenes. Use the whiteboard in the office upstairs to lay out your findings."

Stella and Blue got up, and Bree seemed to shrink down in her chair. I was concerned about Bree, but I would deal with that after I made my call to Ray. I found his number on the phone and was impressed that he picked up after only one ring.

We exchanged greetings, and I asked how Benny was doing.

Benny was an EIRT officer and also a telepath. He had been possessed by a demon the first time I had met him, Ray, and the rest of his EIRT team. My ability to see auras had tipped me off, as Benny's pale-green aura had had an extremely thick black outline around it. Thankfully, Demon Benny had crossed the line and tried to mentally probe me, and he had been arrested by Ray and his team. They had put a power blocker on Benny and, on their way back to headquarters, had stopped at a church after I had told Ray my concerns about Benny's aura. Entering the church had exorcised the demon, but demon possession was hard on someone, and it wasn't uncommon for the person not to survive the exorcism. Thankfully, Benny had survived and had been hospitalized immediately.

"Benny is doing okay. He is supposed to be back on official duty with us later this week. I'm guessing, though, you are calling for more than just to check up on Benny?" said Ray.

"Yeah, I would like Bree, our Werepanther, to meet you and your alpha as soon as possible ..."

"Is this a business or social call?"

"Both. It is more than overdue for Bree to meet other Weres, but we are also looking into the killings up north and hoped you and your alpha could help us out."

"As to the first part, Bree is more than welcome to come and meet the pack. Your timing is great, as tonight is our weekly meeting. I discussed Bree possibly meeting the pack with Shawn just after you and I met, and he was okay with it, but I will need to call him and make sure tonight is okay. As to the second part, I'm guessing you are thinking a rogue Were in these killings?"

I paused, as I didn't want to offend Ray with my answer. Weres tended to get a lot of bad press, and whenever something messy like this popped up, they usually were the first suspects. Most Weres, however, lived normal lives and integrated well with society. Normal people wouldn't have a clue that their neighbor was a Were unless it was a full moon. They were forced to change every full moon, but most Weres either locked themselves up for the night or found some place well away from humanity to roam for the night.

"It seems like a good possibility, but we are still looking at other Enhanced Individuals for this, as well," I said.

"The killings are outside our territory and are closer to the Sudbury pack's territory than ours. We have no missing members and haven't had any strays wander into our territory recently. I had Shawn call David, the alpha of the Sudbury pack, yesterday after the fourth body was reported. David is reporting the same: no missing members and no strays. If it is a rogue, then he or she is keeping a very low profile."

"Sorry for jumping to the Were conclusion then."

"Don't be. When I read the report, that was my first thought too. Let me call Shawn and ask about tonight for you and Bree. Actually, *you* are probably more of a problem than Bree; we usually don't allow non-Weres, other than spouses, to attend our meetings. You being an elemental and not just a human will help. Shawn enjoys meeting other Enhanced Individuals and feels that all Enhanced Individuals should work together and get along, for everyone's benefit."

"I appreciate this. Call me back when you find out if it is okay or not for both of us to attend."

"Will do. Talk to you soon," said Ray as he ended the call.

Chapter 4

Wednesday, April 12

Bree had gotten up while I was on the phone, and she returned with a bag of chips. The fact that she was barely eating them let me know something was up.

"Talk to me," I said.

"What?" replied Bree, not making eye contact and looking down at the table instead.

"What's your issue with meeting the Barrie pack? And don't say, 'Nothing.' You have been ducking me on this for weeks."

Bree went quiet, but I knew she was gathering her thoughts more than avoiding answering, so I waited.

"I'm scared, okay?"

"Of what?" I asked.

"That once I experience a pack bond I will want to stay with them. I can't leave Liv on her own; she needs me. I also am afraid I will kill someone in a dominance fight."

"Those are both valid concerns. Let me address the first one. The Barrie pack don't all live together with the alpha. They have regular lives and families, like most regular humans do. They meet once a week and get together on the night of the full moon and hunt together. So even if you bonded with them and wanted to be with them, it is really only Wednesday nights and the night of the full moon. I think Liv can get by without you for one night a week. On Wednesday nights and the night of the full moon, we can always send Liv to the English vampire court to hang out with Sarah."

Bree laughed at that and seemed to perk up when she realized that the Barrie pack wasn't a full-time commitment.

"As to your second concern, yes, dominance fights to the death do happen, but my understanding is, they are rare. Most times, it is just a staring contest. If it does turn physical, then usually it is just a straight fight and not to the death. In my talks with Ray, it seems like Shawn runs a tight ship, and he doesn't sound like the type of alpha who would encourage fights to the death. As alpha, Shawn would set the rules for the fight. Ray is the enforcer and Shawn's right hand, and Ray owes me, so if it does come down to a fight, I'm pretty sure I can set the terms." Bree nodded at this and seemed to be relieved, so I added, "If you do decide to pick a dominance fight, can I ask a favor?"

"Sure, what?"

"Pick it against a woman, okay?"

Bree got a confused expression on her face. "Why?"

"Well, if I get to set the terms of the fight, then I was thinking string bikinis and Jell-O would be my terms."

Bree snorted at this and shook her head at me. "Pig!"

"Actually, you know what? Don't worry about picking a woman. When Ray calls back, I will get *him* to pick who he thinks is the hottest woman in the Barrie pack and have him get her to pick a dominance fight with you—"

"Zack!" warned Bree, but it was softened with a grin.

"Shush, this is awesome. She will be Ray's champion, and you will be mine. That way, I can bet on this—"

"Zack!"

I didn't let her interrupt and jumped in with "Look, I know you are competitive and want to win. I know you can take whoever Ray picks. If anything, I'm worried you'll take her down too fast and not make it interesting. I've got it! Early in the fight, tear her bikini top off. She'll be annoyed about that and do the same to you. Once you are topless, Ray won't care if he loses money on the fight—"

"*Zack*!!"

I was on too much of roll to stop. "I know what you are going to say, and yes, I will split my winnings with you. You're my girl. Now, back to the fight: Once you are both topless, go for the pin, but make sure you roll around a bit in Jell-O and really shake those moneymakers. We are guests, after all, and want to make a good impression—"

A potato chip ricocheting off my forehead ended my fun. I looked over at Bree, who was trying to be mad at me, but a smile kept sneaking across her not-so-stern visage.

My iPhone vibrated, and I saw Ray's name on the display.

"Hey, Ray. That was either a quick no or a quick yes."

"You are good for tonight. Bring an appetite. Shawn has two pigs and a side of beef cooking on spits. The meeting starts at 6:30 p.m., but get there at 6:00 p.m. Shawn wants to meet you both first. I will be waiting for you both at the front gate."

"Sounds great. See you then."

* * * * *

Blue transported Bree and me to the woods that were just on the other side of the road that led up to the Barrie's pack compound.

"Call me when you want to come home," said Blue.

I nodded, and she disappeared into the shadows.

Bree looked nervous but composed. I head-gestured toward the direction of the roadway, and she nodded. Blue had done a good job picking our spot; we were less than ten feet from the gravel roadway that went past the main gate.

As we stepped out onto the road, I noticed Ray's lean form standing by the gate, with two larger men flanking him. They all turned their attention to us. Ray held up a hand to have them wait there and moved quickly across the road to intercept us.

It was odd seeing Ray in casual clothes, as I'd only seen him in uniform. He was wearing a cream-colored Stetson, a leather jacket with a grey flannel shirt under it, blue jeans, and brown-leather cowboy boots that looked worn-in and comfortable. I found this outdoor casual look seemed to suit him better than his EIRT uniform.

I was ahead of Bree and smiled and held out my hand as Ray reached us.

He shook my hand. "Zack, good to see you again."

"Thanks for having us. Speaking of 'us,' this is Bree."

I moved to the side, but neither of them spoke and just locked eyes. The hairs on the back of my neck went up at the sudden change in both their demeanors. They were both dead-still, and Bree's eyes almost seemed to glow. She brought her right hand up, and her fingers lengthened, her nails turning into razor-sharp talons. Black fur sprouted and quickly covered her hand. The whole change happened in less than ten seconds.

Ray dropped his eyes. Bree nodded and shifted her hand back to human form. The tension in the air instantly disappeared.

"Sorry," mumbled Bree, and Ray held up his hand and cut her off.

"Don't apologize for something that is perfectly natural. That was an impressive display."

"Thanks," said Bree with a small smile and held out her hand. "I'm Bree. Nice to meet you, Ray."

They shook hands, and Ray said, "Shall we get off the road and get inside?"

Ray led, and we followed him to the gate. There was a long, wired high fence that ran down the compound side of the road on either side of the main gate. There were lightning-bolt warning signs posted all along the fence. There were also larger metal warning signs on the fence that read, "Wolf Sanctuary: Private Property. No Trespassing." I smiled at the sign, as it was pretty close to the truth and, I assumed, discouraged people from hopping the electrified fence. I could sense the current running through the fence, and part of me was tempted to go rub up against it for a quick recharge, but I managed to resist the urge.

There was a driveway that came off the road for about fifteen feet and then stopped at the main gate. At the front gate was a small guard station. The two large men I had spotted earlier with Ray were waiting outside the hut. Both were wearing dark-blue jackets that had "Security" written in large, glowing yellow letters. Neither was armed, but both had walkie-talkies on their hips.

Both men were Weres. The smaller one had a purple, brown, and silver aura like Ray's, so he was a Werewolf, but his aura was much smaller than Ray's, and therefore, he hadn't been a Were for that long. The larger of the two had a purple, brown, and green aura, which meant he was a Werebear. The aura was larger than his companion's but smaller than Ray's; I guessed he'd been a Were for around fifteen years.

As we approached, Ray said, "Daniel, Bear, this is Zack and Bree. They are my guests for the night."

I held out my hand to Daniel, who was the shorter of the two but still had a good four inches of height on me. He had thick brown hair and brown eyes and was built like an NFL linebacker. He nodded and shook my hand—he damn near crushed it, too, with how hard he gripped.

This pissed me off, and almost instinctively, I shot a decent dose of electricity down my hand. He let go of my hand like it had bitten him, which it sort of had. Daniel growled, and his eyes changed slightly, becoming more wolf-like.

I arced a large and showy amount of electricity from my right hand to my left that had large light-blue sparks dripping of it and warned,

"If you change, only one of us will be leaving alive, and it will be me. You were a dick with the Captain Crunch handshake, and I returned the favor, so the way I see it, we are even ..."

"Daniel! Stand down. These are my guests, so even if you by some miracle beat an Air elemental—who can fly, by the way, which will make it a very one-sided fight—I will take offence, and you will have to deal with me, too," said Ray in a firm tone of voice.

Daniel growled at this, and Ray shot him a stern look. His shoulders slumped, Daniel then stepped back and held up his hands. "Sorry, Zack, I was out of line with the handshake."

I nodded and shifted my attention to Bear, who smiled and shook my hand in his own massive one. Bear was every bit of 6'6", had to be easily over 300 pounds, and probably qualified as one of the biggest men I had ever seen. That weight wasn't fat, either; he looked like he could bench press a truck. His handshake was firm, but it was obvious he didn't have anything to prove.

Bree locked eyes with Daniel, who dropped his gaze not even a second after meeting Bree's glowing blue eyes. They both nodded at each other, and Bree turned her attention to Bear. Bear lasted about three seconds and then dropped his gaze. This puzzled me, for his aura was larger than Bree's, and Werebears weren't known to be afraid of much. It was almost comical to see a man who had a good foot of height on Bree's 5'4" size—and easily had double her weight—deferring to her.

I guess I shouldn't have been too surprised, as Ray had deferred to her, as well, and his aura was stronger than Bear's. I was starting to figure out that dominance with Weres wasn't so much about raw power but more about *will*power, and Bree had a spine of steel.

"Nice to meet you, ma'am," said Bear with smile and a deep, rich tone of voice.

"Good to meet you, as well, Bear," said Bree with a grin of her own.

The two of them made eye contact again for a few more moments, and it dawned on me that there was something about Bear that Bree was attracted to—and by Bear's demeanor, it was mutual. The smile never left her face, and she was idly playing with her blonde hair with her right hand. Bree had also leaned forward ever so slightly, and from Bear's vantage point, he must be getting a nice glance at her chest in the V-neck sweater she was wearing.

I grinned as Bree licked her lips and continued staring at Bear like he was a perfectly cooked medium-rare beef tenderloin.

Ray gave me an amused glance, as all of us could sense the romantic tension between them. I called her name twice, but she ignored me. I blinked at that and decided to have some fun.

I theatrically glanced at my watch and said, "We are a little early, so if you two kids want to retire to the guard shack and get to know each other a little better, we have the time. The shack looks a little small, but Bree is tiny, and the confined space will allow her to demonstrate how flexible she is ..."

Bree's cheeks went crimson at my comment, and she exclaimed, "Zack!"

I took an elbow to my gut for my trouble.

Ray and Daniel both brought up their hands to hide their amusement.

Bree glanced again at Bear. "It was nice to meet you, Bear. Hopefully, I'll see you again."

Bear smiled and just nodded his head firmly in agreement.

Daniel hit the button for the motorized gate, and Bree, Ray, and I silently walked up the long gravel driveway. There were thick trees down both sides of the driveway, though by its length, I was starting to feel like it should be called a road. Once on the trip, I caught a flash of purple, brown, and silver aura shining out from deep in the trees and knew there was at least one Werewolf in beast form out there.

As we got closer to the main building, I caught a whiff of some really good-smelling barbeque in the air. I knew Bree had caught it, as well, as she had that "Mmm, food!" expression on her face.

We came around the bend, and the pack's lodge came into view. The place was impressive and at least ten times the size of my house. The main building was a three-story-tall section, with a peaked roof that opened toward us. There were two symmetrical wings that connected off the main area, but these were only two floors high, and their green metal-peaked roofs were perpendicular to us. The whole building had been made from timber logs, and the wood had been stained in a clear coat.

There were modern white-plastic-framed windows all over the front of the building that would let in lots of natural light. The two side wings both had second-floor balconies that ran the length of them.

That wonderful aroma of grilled meat was stronger now, and I noticed thin tendrils of greyish smoke rising from behind the lodge.

"This place is stunning," said Bree as we approached the front entrance.

"Yeah, it is much nicer than our old one. About eight years ago, the original lodge burned down due to a grease fire in the kitchen, and we had to rebuild. The fire sucked, but no one was hurt, and it actually worked out, as we were really outgrowing the old location anyway. We used insurance money and members' funds to build this one," answered Ray.

" 'Members' funds'?" asked Bree.

"All pack members pay dues. The dues cover the food provided, the upkeep of the lodge, land, taxes, and other expenses the pack incurs. The dues are usually between 5 to 10 percent of their earnings."

Ray held one of the two main glass doors open for us, and Bree and I entered the lodge. The main room was huge, and even though this area was three stories in height, there were no floors directly above us, just massive high, open ceilings. There were at least fifteen eight-seater tables in the center of this hall area. The back wall was mostly glass and had doors that opened to the back outside area of the lodge. I could see three fire pits from here, and each one had meat slowly turning on spits. Midway down the right wall, there was a small raised stage with a podium and microphone. There were several doors on both the right and left walls that led to the left and right wings.

"This is our main meeting area that also doubles as our main dining area," said Ray. "The entire first floor of the left wing is our kitchen and food-prep area. The first floor of the right wing has Shawn's main office and other smaller offices and meetings rooms, as well as a couple of holding cells. The second floor of the right wing has Shawn's and his family's living area and a couple of smaller living areas for the few staff who are here full-time. The second floor of the left wing has guest quarters. I will take you for a tour later if you wish, but Shawn wanted to meet you both before everyone gets here."

He strode toward the closest door on the right. It led to a corridor, and there was a set of stairs against the wall on the right. We went left, and the first door we stopped in front of had "Shawn Woods" etched in a plastic silver nameplate on the solid wooden door. Ray knocked, and a deep, rough voice said, "It's open."

Ray opened the door, and I followed him in, with Bree on my heels. A purple, brown, and silver aura radiated out to almost a foot from around the man sitting behind the desk.

Shawn got up from the desk as we entered, and while his aura was impressive, his physical form was a bit of a letdown. He was probably about 5'9" and somewhere around 160 pounds with his lean and wiry form. Short brown hair with a hint or two of grey around the edges and his weathered-and-tanned face made him look like he was in his late thirties or early forties, but by his aura, I was sure he was probably over a hundred years old. The wise and calculating ice-blue eyes that studied us also made me suspect he was older.

Shawn's furnishings in the office caught my attention. The desk looked like something rescued from a thrift shop. It was one of those teacher desks with the stainless-steel legs, a thin metal casing around the outside, and a fake-wood laminated top. The chairs were the stainless-steel framed ones, too—the type that are the cheapest ones you can find at an office supply store. There was a worn-looking four-drawer filing cabinet in the corner. With how impressive the lodge has been up to this point, I'd been expecting something more lavish for the alpha.

The walls, though, were more interesting. Directly behind Shawn, there was a superb painting of two wolves in a snow-covered forest with white-capped mountains in the background. On the far left wall, there was a mounted buck's head that had an impressive set of antlers. The right wall had several large mounted fish.

He offered his hand across the desk to me, and we shook. His hand was warm, calloused, and rough. The warmth was a side effect of Shawn being a Were; their body temperatures always ran hotter than normal humans. His grip was firm but not challenging. I found myself staring directly into his piercing blue eyes, and then realized I was unintentionally challenging him and immediately dropped my gaze.

He smiled at this. "No need to drop your eyes; you are not a Were, and I am comfortable enough in my status that I don't take a non-Were making eye contact as a challenge."

I thanked him for having us by this evening and then realized Bree was directly behind me. I introduced her as I moved out of the way.

They made eye contact with each other and went deathly still. After a long ten seconds of this, Bree slowly brought up her right hand, and I cursed to myself as I watched her change it. The hand sprouted black fur, and her feminine nails morphed into wicked and deadly black talons. The process again took less than ten seconds, which was an impressive—if not poorly timed—display of her power.

Only Bree would be brazen enough to keep challenging a freaking alpha in his den with his entire pack about to arrive in twenty minutes.

I had assumed she would meet his gaze for a moment and then drop her eyes in submission.

Shawn raised an amused eyebrow at Bree's display, and he gave a nod of begrudging approval. A moment later, he brought his own right hand up in a loose fist. He opened his hand, and in that short eye-blink of time, he'd already transformed it into something much deadlier. White-grey fur covered his hand, and his fingers had extended into lethal-looking claws. The sheer speed in which he had done this left me in awe.

Despite this, Bree stood firm and didn't drop her gaze. The longer this went on, the more dangerous it would get. At this point, I was already watching Ray out of the corner of my eye and trying to figure the best way out of here if things went south. Ray, however, just stayed still and calm, and wasn't reacting or even showing much tension at the test of wills between his alpha and Bree.

Finally, after the longest minute of my life, Bree dropped her gaze.

"Hot dog!" said Shawn with a smile. "It has been too long since someone gave me that much of a contest. I do love a woman with a fire in her belly. That's why I married my Izzy. She, too, is a firecracker who bends for no man. Damn glad to meet you, Bree."

He lowered his right hand, which instantly turned back to human form, then held it out to Bree.

Bree seemed amused at Shawn's reaction to the challenge, and after taking ten seconds or so to change her hand back, shook Shawn's hand warmly.

"Please, take a load off. Ray, please check on how dinner is coming. I would like a few minutes alone with our guests," said Shawn.

Ray nodded and left. Bree and I sat down while Shawn took his own seat.

The deep knot of fear in my stomach was starting to unwind from Shawn's friendly and down-home type of attitude. I'd read quite a bit about Were lore, but other than Bree, hadn't spent much time with Weres. I did know that Bree seriously challenging an alpha on his home turf was a big no-no. Anytime Weres met for the first time, there would be a dominance challenge. The protocol, though, when meeting an alpha in their den was to briefly meet their gaze and then instantly lower it. I silently kicked myself for not mentioning this to Bree beforehand. A lesser man might have taken this encounter in a much different direction than Shawn had. A fool might have taken

Shawn's actions as weakness, but I knew this was a sign of strength, and for that, he had my deepest respect.

"Ray has told me your story, and I must say, you are quite a remarkable young lady," said Shawn.

"Thank you, Mr. Woods."

" 'Mr. Woods' was my father. Please, call me Shawn."

Bree nodded.

He continued. "I also have no doubt in my mind that your sire was Ricardo, the former alpha of the Buenos Aires pack. I met him eight years ago at a Were conference in Las Vegas. I wasn't a huge fan, as he was brash and arrogant, but the guy did have a massive set of brass ones on him; he neither feared nor bowed to anyone. Only a child of Ricardo's would be bold enough to challenge an alpha when she is barely past being a yearling."

Bree lowered her eyes but didn't say anything.

"I'll apologize on her behalf. As Ray must have explained, she has not had any exposure to the Were community and only did that out of ignorance and instinct. You have my deepest thanks for showing us the mercy you have," I said.

Shawn waved his hand as if dismissing the whole challenge thing. "As I said earlier, I do love a woman with fire in her belly. Speaking of bellies, mine is starting to rumble, and our time before dinner and tonight's meeting grows short. Tonight, both of you are here as my guests. This means anyone who challenges you is challenging me directly. I do ask that you both refrain from starting challenges or fights with anyone, and if either of you strike the first blow, they are in their rights to challenge you directly. I have a good, stable pack and don't expect any issues, but putting down ground rules never hurts."

We both nodded, and Shawn continued. "Ray informed me that you were looking into the killings up north. That is well north of our territorial limit and west of the Sudbury pack's limit. It is currently an open and unclaimed area. Neither of our packs have any unaccounted-for members. Ray showed me the EIRT report, and if it is a Were, I suspect you are looking at two Weres minimum. I also don't think whatever is doing these killings is a Were."

I raised an eyebrow, and Shawn said, "Usually, if a Were goes rogue and gets a taste for human blood, they head toward civilization—unless they are being hunted by a pack. These killers seem to be keeping to sparsely populated areas, and that doesn't feel right to me for rogue

Were. On the other hand, rogues are usually not too mentally stable, which means anything is possible."

I couldn't fault his reasoning, and even before this meeting, I had been beginning to doubt the killings were Were-related. "If not a Were, any thoughts on what might be behind these attacks?" I asked.

Shawn rubbed his chin and had a faraway look on his face as he thought about this for a bit. "Nothing is jumping out at me, but whatever it is, it is either timid and weak or clever and dangerous. The area is wide open, and it is picking victims who are either alone or in pairs, and avoiding groups. It's the vast area it is operating in that has me concerned; it is going to be very hard to track down this creature due to that. The question is, is the creature picking off stragglers because it is afraid of taking on bigger groups, or is it doing this to keep a low profile and staying to isolated areas to make things much harder on the authorities?"

Chapter 5

Wednesday, April 12

The discussion with Shawn wrapped up shortly after that. A low rumble of voices echoed from the main hall, signaling that the rest of the pack had started to arrive. Shawn led us out of his office and to the main hall. He gave various people a nod here and there. Bree and I got a few curious looks as we passed by.

Shawn led us directly to the podium. He got on the stage and turned on the mic. Not even a second after that, the hall went eerily and almost unnaturally dead-quiet. All the faces in the hall turned and gave Shawn their full attention. If I thought about it, the reaction made sense: If I had an alpha, I wouldn't want to piss him off by not shutting up when he wanted to talk.

"Thank you all for coming to tonight's meeting. Dinner will be served shortly, but I have one quick announcement to make. Zack and Bree, beside me, are here as my guests. Please be sure to extend your full courtesy to them. Enjoy your night."

Ray popped out of the crowd, and Shawn turned to us and said, "There are matters I have to attend to before tonight's meal. I will leave you in Ray's capable hands. I will add, however, that Bree, if you are looking for a pack, we would be happy to add you to our ranks."

"Thank you, Shawn. You are too kind. I'm not sure if I'm looking to join a pack at this moment. Also, I'm living in Hamilton. Wouldn't that be in another pack's territory?"

"That would be in the Six Nations pack area, but I doubt they would be interested in you joining them."

"Is that because she is a Werepanther?" I asked.

Shawn laughed and shook his head. "No, it is because she isn't a Native. There is a pack, however, in Mississauga, and they would probably be interested in you joining them. Those two packs have an agreement between them: Natives who live in the Mississauga pack's area can join the Six Nations pack, and non-Natives in the Six Nations territory can join the Mississauga one. I'm sure the Mississauga pack would love to have you, but I'm not sure you'd want to join them.

They've had four different alphas in the last ten years, and I can't say I am huge fan of Ahmed, who is their current one. They meet on Tuesdays and Fridays, and if you like, I can get you the number if you wish to attend one of their meetings?"

"I don't think that will be necessary. Would either of the packs have an issue with me living in Hamilton and joining your pack?" asked Bree.

"It is Six Nations territory, and as I said, they wouldn't be interested in you joining them. And since it is outside the Mississauga pack's area, they have no say in things. If you are serious about joining us, I would have to call Jim, the alpha of the Six Nations pack, and get his blessing, but I don't see him making a big issue about it."

Bree frowned and asked, "If the Six Nations doesn't taken non-Natives, why would you need Jim's blessing?"

"Because it is still his territory, and he has first right of refusal. It is really just a courtesy call, but small things like that help defuse any possible tension between our packs."

Bree nodded. "Can I take some time to think about this?"

"Of course. We aren't going anywhere. If you want to attend a few more meetings after this one as a guest to get a better feel—or even come out with us on the next full moon—you are more than welcome," said Shawn.

Bree thanked him, and he headed off toward either his office or his living quarters.

Ray asked us to follow him and led us to a table that had just two people sitting there. They stood as we approached. By the way they stayed close to each other, I suspected they were a couple. They both looked like they were in their late teens or early twenties, but by their auras, I suspected they were older than that.

The female caught my attention first for two reasons. The first was that her aura was purple (Were) with a red (cat-type Were) and orange (tiger) outline. I recalled Ray mentioning that their pack had a Weretiger from India, and as she was Indian, I figured this must be her.

The second thing I noticed was that she was stunning. She was only an inch taller than Bree but had more of Olivia's long-and-lean type of frame. What really made my breath catch was her face. It was like she was a Disney princess brought to life: huge deep-brown eyes that had a real twinkle to them, and this dainty nose, and full lips, all framed by flawless light-brown skin and long, sensuous black hair. She really was a sight to behold.

I leaned in to Bree and said, "Our earlier discussion about a female opponent? We have a winner!"

This got me another elbow to the ribs. It was a real shame that Bree wasn't more adventurous, as I was sure that her Jell-O wrestling my newfound opponent would have gone over really well in this testosterone-filled environment.

Ray gave us both a questioning look, and I just gave him a "Don't worry about it" wave in response.

The Weretiger's male companion almost was unnoticeable beside her. His aura was interesting, though, as purple with a green-and-brown outline meant he was a Werebear. Recalling Bree's earlier interest in Bear at the gate, I wondered if cat-type Weres were attracted to Werebears or if this was just a coincidence. The male was shorter than me but had a gangly awkwardness to him that had me thinking *nerd*. The pockmarks on his skin and the black Star Wars T-shirt also seemed to back this up.

"Zack, Bree, this is Sabina and Brent. As Sabina is our only resident cat-type Were, Shawn thought you might like to meet her," said Ray.

I shook hands with both of them, and Bree did the same. They both met Bree's eyes only for a brief second before submitting. I wasn't sure if they were naturally submissive, if they sensed Bree's extraordinary willpower, or if, as we were Shawn's guests, they were showing respect for Shawn by not starting any type of dominance game with Bree—or some combination of all three.

We all sat down at the table, and Brent said, "You aren't a Were; your hand was too cool, and my beast didn't sense a challenge from you. But something about your scent doesn't come across as normal human either. Do you mind me asking what you are?"

Brent's voice was a touch high-pitch, which rolled in nicely with my *nerd* assessment earlier, but there was something genuine and kind about him that I instantly liked. I also appreciated his body language toward Sabina, as he was being protective of her but not smothering.

"Air elemental."

"No way! That is awesome! We have an Ice elemental, Dave, who lives in our building, and he is a great guy. He isn't super powerful, but he makes the coolest ice sculptures; the details on them are amazing, and they seem so life-like. He made me a scale ice model of the Death Star for my birthday last year. I was crushed when it didn't fit in our fridge's freezer. Do you control air or electricity or both?" asked Brent, practically bouncing in his seat with excitement.

Sabina leaned closer and lightly elbowed Brent. "Please excuse my mate; he gets a bit carried away at times. The only thing he is into more than Star Wars is the Enhanced community."

Sabina caught me off-guard a bit when she spoke, as I had expected a strong Indian accent, but there was barely a trace of it. Her voice was also as lovely as she was, and I loved how strong yet feminine it sounded.

"Honestly, it is fine. And to answer his question, both air and electricity."

Brent's eyes damn near popped out of his head at my answer. "Oh my God, both abilities. You are just like the Hamilton Hurricane! Can you fly like he can?"

Bree smothered a laugh beside me at Brent's question, but I just ignored her and nodded.

"That must be completely rad to fly through the air like that. Maybe one day you could take me up with you?"

"We'll see," I said, not wanting to commit to anything.

Sabina nudged Brent again, then asked us, "Do you two live in the Barrie area?" as if trying to change the subject and tone down Brent's excitement. Unfortunately, that was the wrong question to ask.

Bree grinned and said, "No, we are actually from Hamilton and just visiting due to a case we are working on."

Brent looked at Bree and then turned toward me, and then it all came together for him. He went dead-still and just stared at me open-mouthed—and, for a couple of long seconds, stayed that way. He opened and closed his mouth twice, but no words came out.

I just nodded in answer to his silent question and made a zipping motion with my hand across my mouth.

Brent winked and gave me two thumbs up.

It took Sabina a couple of seconds longer, but she, too, caught on that I was the Hamilton Hurricane. I could tell by her expression that she was absolutely mortified that she had indirectly outed me.

"Don't worry about it," I said, "but if we could change the subject? As I'm very much aware that everyone in this room has hear-a-pin-drop-at-a-thousand-yards type of hearing. I know you probably have many questions, Brent, and I would be happy to answer them for you at another time. Maybe the four of us could get together for dinner sometime?"

The expression on Brent's face was like it was his birthday, Christmas, and his first sexual experience all rolled into one. I pulled out my iPhone and brought up my cell number on the screen, then handed it to him. He whipped out his phone and entered my number like it was the Holy Grail. He passed me my phone back and was already frantically typing out a text to me.

Thankfully, the food was brought out shortly after that—nothing ends a conversation with a group of Weres faster than heaping platters of barbeque.

Both the pork and the beef were truly exceptional; the meat fell off the bones at the lightest touch of a fork. The barbeque sauce that both were slathered in was sweet yet tangy, with a hint of smoke and heat. Sides of homemade coleslaw, potato salad, grilled vegetables, and fresh-baked cornmeal muffins were served with the main course. All of it was so amazing that I stuffed myself to the gills and had to decline even trying a bite of the tasty-looking triple-chocolate cake that was served for dessert.

At the end of the meal, it was announced that there would be a thirty-minute break before the meeting started. I was surprised that a good third of the hall cleared out, and I asked where everyone was going.

"Smokers out to get their fix," said Sabina with a look that made it clear she didn't approve.

Brent rolled his eyes at Sabina and said, "There is no health risk to them; if they want to waste their money, who are we to judge?"

I must have had a slightly puzzled expression, because Brent then added, "The Were healing factor fixes any damage a cigarette does almost instantly."

Sabina rolled her eyes and asked, "You said earlier that you were here due to a case you were working on ..."

I nodded. "Yeah, we are chasing the bounty on the four murders that took place up north."

Brent's eyes widened. "You think it's a rogue Were doing the killings?"

I tentatively nodded, and he continued. "When the first murder happened, that was my thought, too, but when the couple were murdered, that theory went out the window."

"Why's that?"

"If it was a rogue Were, it would have killed the first person and immediately started eating. The other person would have been easily able to get away. So that means it is either two rogue Weres or something else. The problem is, having two Weres go rogue at the same time is extremely rare. I've never heard of that happening before. When a Were goes rogue and develops a taste for human blood, they are totally insane and just guided by instinct. If that happened for two Weres at the same time, they'd be much more likely to kill each other than to work together."

I silently kicked myself as Brent finished speaking. I'd dealt with rogue Weres in the past, and they'd been totally feral. Brent was right: The chances of two of them working together were slim to none.

Brent had obviously given these killing some thought, and I was keen to learn what ideas he had and asked, "So what do you think is doing the killings?"

"A Super-class Enhanced with strength and a blade—or claw ability. The Super is either insane, or maybe it was experimented on or abused by humans and hates them, and this is its way of getting revenge."

Sabina rolled her eyes again and said, "I swear, those comic books you read are rotting your brain! I still think it is a rogue Were doing the killings." Brent was about to argue, but Sabina held up her hand to cut him off and added, "The couple that was killed could have easily been the same Were. It killed the first victim, and the other victim attacked the Were to try and save their lover. The Were would have killed the second victim for interrupting its meal."

Bree was about to ask a question, but feedback from the microphone echoed throughout the hall as Shawn turned it on. The hall went quiet as Shawn spoke for the next ten minutes. He covered surprisingly mundane stuff like the pack's finances, different fundraising events and gatherings that were coming up on the calendar, an engagement announcement, and other topics that would be covered at a company's Christmas party or a local charity meeting. The only thing that made it Were-centric was the announcement that the full moon was two weeks away.

At the end of the speech, Shawn announced that it was time to break off into smaller support groups.

Three females came up to our table shortly after that and flocked to Sabina. By their auras, two of them were Wererats, and the other was a Werebear. The Werebear, Jolene, was Brent's cousin.

"Bree? Normally, Jolene, Tammy, Diane, and I have an all-ladies support group and discuss our problems or just gossip. But there is something I really need to talk to you about," said Sabina.

Bree's expression was one of curiosity, and she looked at me as if to ask, "Do we have time?"

I nodded in response to her silent question.

Bree smiled, got up, and joined the women, and they headed off.

I was a bit nervous letting Bree out of my sight. I liked and trusted Ray, and Shawn seemed solid, but there were a lot of strangers here, and while everyone seemed great, it only took one bad apple to cause a problem.

Brent must have sensed my uneasiness, as he said, "Relax, Zack, they are just having a hen party. Bree will be fine. I usually join one of the support groups at this point, too, but I think tonight I will stay and keep you company. It's a nice night. Do you want to go for a walk around the property?"

For early April, it was unseasonably mild, and with all that food in my belly, a walk sounded pretty good. It also beat sitting around and dwelling on Bree.

Brent and I ended up outside, and I let him lead the way in the darkness. I knew Brent was anxious to talk about my Hamilton Hurricane exploits, and once we were far enough away from prying ears, I told him we could talk about it but that I also wanted to hear about what it was like to be a Werebear.

He and I spent the next hour chatting about Were- and hero-related topics, and time flew by. Brent was extremely knowledgeable about Weres and Were culture, and I was amazed at how much I learned. I also found I really enjoyed talking to him, especially when we were heading back to the lodge and we got onto Star Wars, video games, and books—I was stunned at how many favorite games and authors we had in common. I made his night by using my Air power to float him back to the lodge.

We entered the building, and Sabina and Bree were waiting for us. Bree gave me a tentative smile as we approached, but I could sense the worry coming off her in waves and wondered what was up. We said our goodbyes to everyone, and I thanked Ray and Shawn for having us. Bree said she would consider joining but wanted to attend a couple more meetings first and try a full moon with the pack. Shawn didn't have an issue with that and told her to come back next Wednesday.

The two of us walked to the gate. Once we were away from the main lodge, Bree said in a shaky voice, "Sabina told me about something called 'the Heat.' Female cat-type Weres go into the Heat like a house cat does. Or, at least, Weretigers and Werelions do. I was the first Werepanther she'd met, so she doesn't know if this affects Werepanthers or not ..."

My first reaction was amusement, but I smothered that due to Bree's obvious fear and concern. My humor then disappeared when I imagined a 300-pound Werepanther with deadly claws and fangs jumping some poor guy while looking to get laid—that scenario had deadly consequences. I told Bree my concerns.

She shook her head and said, "The Heat doesn't force someone to change. If it hits, I stay in my human form, but the beast would be fully in control."

I was relieved at that, but even that meant the situation could still be dangerous. Bree in her human form was easily twice as strong as a normal human. If her beast approached someone and was turned down, things could get ugly fast.

Bree turned to me with tears in her eyes and said, "When it hit Sabina for the first time, she ended up in an alley having sex with multiple men ... I don't want that to happen to me ..."

I grabbed Bree and pulled her into a hug. I stroked her hair and said, "Shush, that won't happen ... You learned to control your beast's rage; you'll learn to control this too."

Bree sobbed quietly against my shoulder for a bit, and then she broke the hug, wiped her eyes, and said, "You're right. Sabina said the Heat usually occurs for the first time two to three years after the first change. I have at least nine months to figure this out. I will talk to Blue and Stella about this when we get home. My first plan is to lock myself up in the cell in the lab if it hits. If I can't get to lab, then you are my fallback plan. I will use you to get through the Heat."

I was about to make one of my usual lecherous comments to lighten the mood, but Bree cut me off. "And don't make a smart-ass comment here. I'm serious. Can I count on you if this thing hits?"

My humor died with that comment, and seeing how tense Bree was at the moment, I realized this was no time for flippancy. "Bree, I promise that if you need me, I'll be there for you."

She seemed to relax at this, and the tension that had been gripping her small form lessened. "Thank you," she said quietly with a small smile.

Chapter 6

Wednesday, April 12

Blue picked us up and brought us back to the house. Bree took Blue upstairs to talk with her and Stella about her concerns about the Heat, and I made a beeline for the kitchen. My early morning start, combined with the huge meal earlier, had me yawning. I needed a coffee pick-me-up, as I knew we still needed to visit all three crime scenes this evening.

Armed with a mug of caffeine, I joined the rest of the team upstairs. The room went quiet as I entered. I was pleased to see that Bree's expression had returned to its usual determined-to-get-things-done look.

My jaw hit the floor when I glanced around the office, which had been transformed from my office to something I'd see on those forensic crime shows. I took in all the pictures, diagrams, and maps on the walls and whiteboard. There were vivid and bloody crime-scene photos pinned up on the wall in three clusters. In the center of the cluster was a full-size color map of northern Ontario with three colored pins, each with a taut piece of red yarn that connected back to each of the picture groups. I stepped closer to the map and realized that Stella and Blue had marked each murder site on the map, and the strings led back to the photos of each crime scene.

I had no idea where Stella and Blue had gotten the photos. I knew they weren't included in the bounty information on the UN bounty site. I suspected Blue, with her shadow-traveling abilities, had probably lifted them from either local police or the EIRT, and I decided I really didn't want to know where she had gotten them.

"Looks like you have been busy while we were gone," I said, still taking in everything.

The place looked like a conspiracy nut's wet dream, and I was truly impressed at the details they had gathered in such a short period of time. I was drawn to the crime-scene photos and studied the first cluster of pictures of Thomas Martin's murder. The sheer savagery and brute strength involved in the killing was shocking. You tended to forget how much blood a human body contained until you saw the vast amount of it strewn over a smaller area. His right arm and left leg had been separated from his body; whether they had been torn off or chewed off, I couldn't tell. Half his throat was missing and so was one eye. The chest cavity had the ribs pulled open like they were cupboard doors, and his heart was missing. There was also a gaping hole where his genitals used to be. On the ground beside the body was a pair of wire-frame glasses, and one of the lenses had been smashed.

There were teeth and claw marks all over the body, and whoever had done this had had a simmering fountain of rage driving them. The teeth and claw marks, the consumed organs and flesh, and the brute force required certainly were the hallmarks of a rogue Were, but something didn't feel right here. I studied the picture, and that nagging feeling grew. I was missing something but couldn't pin it down.

"What do we know about Thomas Martin?" I asked.

"One moment," replied Stella as she opened a file on the computer. "Thomas Martin was forty-three years old. He worked as a civil engineer for a medium-size private firm. He was married to a Camille Davis, who is forty-five—his first marriage, her second. Camille works as an elementary school teacher. There are two kids from the wife's first marriage: Dylan, twenty, and Brad, eighteen. Dylan is in his second year of university, and Brad is finishing his last year of high school. Thomas was the treasurer of the Ontario Birding Society."

"Any of them have a connection to the Enhanced community?"

Stella gave me an odd look. "Why?"

"The rage in this killing is extreme, and I was wondering if it was personal."

"Nothing we could find. He did take a supportive stance on a Humans First Facebook article that was posted by one of Dylan's university friends. Thomas and Dylan argued back and forth in posts a bit before they both moved on to other things," replied Stella.

Humans First was a worldwide anti-"monster" group that believed all Enhanced Individuals were a threat to humanity and should either be killed or sent away to well-guarded reservations. The group had been popular after events of World War II had brought "monsters" out of the shadows, but its popularity had diminished in the sixties. It had made a comeback in the last ten years, though, after most Western governments had passed laws giving more rights to Enhanced

Individuals and banning the term *monsters* in favor of the more PC term *Enhanced Individuals*.

That Dylan as a university student was anti-Humans First wasn't a shock; youth and college students were the big supporters of the rights bills for Enhanced Individuals and had been the driving force behind getting them passed in the first place. It also wasn't too out of the ordinary that Thomas, being older and more conservative, would have seen some value in the message that Humans First was putting out; there were a number of Enhanced Individuals walking around out there who were as dangerous as a nuclear bomb, and it was easy to see how this might make people nervous.

"Did it seem like either one was being super radical about the issue?" I asked.

"Not really. Dylan thought Humans First was a racist terror organization, and Thomas argued that Enhanced Individuals, with their great powers, needed *more* restrictions on them, not less. But neither seemed to get out of hand with it."

Olivia had been standing quietly beside me, looking at the photos. "Did you notice the claw and bite marks?"

"Yeah, there were a ton of them. Why?"

"Not the amount, but the bloodstains around them. He was still bleeding when they were made and, therefore, was still alive," said Liv.

Trust our resident vampire to notice something like that, but I could have kissed her for that observation. Those bloodstains were what had been nagging at me earlier. "Shit. You are right. I am not sure this was a Were attack, then—or if it was, it was an odd one. Weres tend to kill quickly, as their main goal is to feed. Whoever did this played with their food first."

I studied the shots again and moved on to the second group of pictures. The second attack was Tammy Jamison, nineteen, and Dan Gilman, twenty-one, who were killed while out camping. Dan's body was in fairly good shape compared to the mauling Thomas had taken; his throat was torn out, and there was a large hole in his chest where his heart used to be, but other than those wounds and a couple of small scrapes, that was it. Tammy, on the other hand, had died hard—she had the same blood-smear wounds Thomas had. More of her body had been eaten too. Like the other two victims, her heart was gone as well. She had also been decapitated. There were wrecked clothes, boots, and gloves scattered around the kill site. My eyes lingered on what looked like a woman's fur boot. The fur was white, but the fur had these odd designs on it in a dull reddish-brown color. My eyes widened as it dawned on me—that wasn't a funky pattern but dried blood.

"It looks like whatever killed this couple hit the male first and either tore out his throat or heart and killed him instantly, and then it moved on to the woman and took its time," said Blue, standing beside me.

I nodded and moved on to the last group of photos. I was surprised these shots weren't making me queasier than they were. I think the extreme violence and gore involved actually helped; they made the pictures seem unreal somehow.

The last group of photos were of the latest victim, Tamara Lightfoot, seventeen. She, too, had died hard and was covered in bloody claw and bite marks. Her heart was missing as well.

The missing hearts were also odd for a Were attack; their favorites were the liver and kidneys, as those were more nourishing than a heart.

"Did the other three victims have any connections to the Enhanced community, or did the four of them have anything in common?" I asked.

Stella looked up from the computer again. "The couple were into the outdoors and members of a number of environmental groups, but nothing I could find in their histories showed any connections to the Enhanced community. Tamara was a huge *Twilight* fan and had an obsession with vampires, but I couldn't see any connections to actual vampires. She and her mom had a number of heated Facebook disagreements when she was thirteen to fifteen, but the last couple of years, they seemed to be getting along better."

"What girl doesn't fight with her mother at that age?" said Bree.

"I didn't," answered Liv.

"Yeah, but your parents were super chill. It is hard to rebel when you have nothing to rebel against," argued Bree.

Bree was the oldest of seven kids, and her parents were conservative and strict. Olivia's only sibling was an older sister, and her parents were more modern and easy-going. Their discussion reflected the differences in their upbringing.

I turned my attention to the map. Thomas, the first victim, had been killed near Nipigon; the couple had been killed near Armstrong, which was a good 200 kilometers north of the first sight. Tamara had been killed near Hornepayne, which was 500 clicks southeast of

Armstrong. That was a heck of a lot of territory to cover, and with only three sites, it wasn't like there was a pattern or anything to go by.

I opened up the discussion to theories and ideas, but in the end, nothing really significant came out of it. We had three kill sites, four victims with nothing in common, and no clue where this creature would strike next.

We also still didn't know exactly what we were dealing with, and that probably concerned me the most. A rogue Were made the most sense from a commonality standpoint, but there were too many things that didn't fit for a Were killing. The more I thought about it, the more I started leaning toward some sort of dark fae creature. The area was mostly open wilderness, which the fae would be comfortable in. The cooler climate fit, too, as the dark fae were ruled by the Winter court. Human hearts were used in many dark fae spells and rituals. The fae couldn't stand iron, so being away from large cities would be a plus for them. They'd also be vicious enough to do this kind of carnage. The problem was, there were at least ten different fae creatures I could think of that could do something like this. Those options ranged from "This will be an interesting fight" to "Anyone have a nuclear bomb handy?"

I thought about some of the creatures from the deadlier end of the fae spectrum and shuddered. I was starting to think we should have gone with the pixie bounty instead …

Chapter 7

Wednesday, April 12

Blue transported us to the first murder site. We emerged out of the shadows at the side of a single-lane paved road with trees around it and into the darkness. The half moon flittering in and out of the clouds barely cast enough illumination to hold off the blackness. The leafless trees arose from the ground like skeletal fingers reaching into the night.

I was not an outdoors person and had been an urban dweller all my life. The utter silence felt unnatural to me, as I missed the constant hum the city had to offer. I tentatively reached out and readied my powers in an attempt to lessen my anxiety due to the foreign environment. I found this whole area creepy and figured the only thing it was missing to make it complete was a madman in an old-school hockey mask holding a machete. As we were investigating three sites that had a total of four mutilated victims, I figured I might as well add hockey-mask guy to our list of suspects; he was as likely as some of the other monsters we'd listed as possible suspects. In a strange way, I found the thought of adding a psychopath from fake horror movies as a suspect to our bounty case funny and felt my nervousness lessen a bit.

With a word, Liv and Blue took the lead. They both could see as equally well in the dark as they could in the day. Stella and I stumbled along behind them, and Bree, who had better night vision than either of us, took up the rear.

There was a small clearing at the side of the road with just enough space to park a couple of cars. Off from the clearing, there was a narrow trail that led into the woods. According to the file, the kill site was about a hundred feet down the trail. As this was ten days after the killing, there was no police tape or anything that made the area stand out. The only evidence that something had happened here were several tire tracks in the dirt clearing that indicated there had been substantial traffic coming and going at some point in the recent past.

Even though it had been ten days since the killing, when we got to the trail and proceeded single file into the foreboding dark woods, my heart rate picked up, and my adrenaline surged. My senses were hyper alert, and I again started to pull on the edges of my Electrical power in case it was needed.

I wasn't too hopeful on this first site being that useful. The police would have been over the scene with a fine-tooth comb, and there had been a light dusting of snow and two rainy downpours since the murder. But with Blue's travel ability, it had only taken seconds to get here, and I figured spending twenty minutes to give the place a look-over wouldn't hurt. Maybe the sites themselves held something in common.

"We are here," said Liv as we reached a small clearing in woods just off the trail.

"You sure this is the place?" I asked as I looked around and saw nothing that interesting or remarkable around us.

She nodded. "There is the faint smell of blood in the air, and this is the strongest source of it."

Vampire senses never failed to amaze me. The fact that Liv could still scent blood that had been spilled over a week ago—and three storms had been in, washing the area clean—was truly impressive. Or frightening …

Liv moved to the left side of clearing. "Where I am standing is where Thomas was probably killed."

A single car drove past on the roadway outside the forest, and I barely heard it. With this place being so isolated, Thomas could have screamed, shot off flares, or fired a cannon, and nobody would have noticed—especially this time of year, as anyone driving by would have had their windows up and their heaters on. In short, our killer had picked an ideal time to hit Thomas when he was alone and vulnerable.

Stella and I stood still while the other three wandered around and searched the site for anything that might help us.

"Liv? Bree? Do either of you smell anything that isn't blood- or forest-related?" I asked.

"I'm getting the barest trace of something funky-smelling, but I can't pin it down," answered Bree.

"More like *skunky* than funky, but it is faint and hard to detect through all the other scents I'm picking up. It, too, is strongest where the blood scent is," added Liv.

They tried working out the mystery scent for another minute but couldn't describe it any better.

Blue was gazing around and looked deep in thought, so I asked, "What are you thinking?"

"That the victim never had a chance."

"Why do you say that?"

"A middle-age male, probably out of shape and excited to be out birding. It was daylight, with no one around for miles. He would have had his guard down. The density of the trees and the lack of dried leaves or twigs on the ground meant the killer could easily get within twenty feet of the victim without being noticed. The victim would be looking to the treetops or the sky. All the killer had to do was wait until something caught Thomas's attention, and then he'd be able to strike. I'd bet the victim was wounded before he even realized something was wrong ..."

I thought about it and couldn't argue with anything she'd said. We'd barely made a sound walking in here, and we weren't even trying to be quiet. Blue was right: The poor guy would have been bleeding before he even knew there was a threat.

We hung around for another few minutes but decided there was nothing more the area could teach us. Blue used the shadows to take us to the next site.

This was another place I wasn't overly hopeful about, as it had been a week since the two murders had occurred here, and two heavy rains had hit this area as well. We stepped out into a much wider clearing, and I could instantly see the appeal of why Dan and Tammy had been camping here. There was a small lake to my right, and the spot was surrounded by woods and seemed to be miles away from everything. The spot had a tranquil feel to it that instantly made you feel at one with nature.

The ground had a bunch of tire tracks from the emergency vehicles that had been here a week ago. Liv pulled us over to the right side of the clearing and pointed out where both bodies had been killed. She was pretty sure the closer one to us had been Tammy, as the scent of blood was stronger there than at the one about six feet away. As Tammy's body had been mauled to a much greater extent than Dan's, I figured Liv was probably right.

"Liv, are you getting that same faint skunky smell here, as well?" asked Bree as she closed her eyes and focused on what her nose was telling her.

"Yeah, it is there in the background, but the blood and other scents are still masking it."

They both struggled to describe the scent, but both agreed it was an aroma that shouldn't be here. The lack of detail on the scent was annoying, but in an odd way, it was also a relief. The fact that the same smell was at both locations meant the same creature had done both killings; having two different brutal killers out there would have been much worse.

Blue was looking at a black spot on the ground about eight feet from where the bodies had been. I raised an eyebrow at her, and she said, "Remains of a campfire. The couple were roasting marshmallows or snuggling in front of the fire. They, too, would have been easy prey. The fire would have impaired their night vision. The killer could have crept up almost on them before they realized he was here. Add in that they were probably drinking, as well, and they had no chance. They were probably sitting in lawn chairs, which was another disadvantage. The killer runs in and slashes the male's throat, killing him almost instantly. The female would be in shock for more than long enough for the killer to be on her. Her being seated automatically gives the killer the edge. By her wounds, he took his time with her. She could have screamed nonstop, but with no one around for miles, it wouldn't have helped. They didn't have a chance."

Blue's comments had me clearly picturing the scene in my head, and she was right again: The couple hadn't had a chance.

After a few minutes of fruitless searching, we decided to move to the last kill site.

We stepped out of the shadows at the side of the road near Tamara's murder location, and both Olivia and Bree faltered.

"Oh my God, that smell is awful!" gagged Bree.

"It is like rotten eggs!" exclaimed Olivia with a grimace fixed on her face.

I couldn't smell what they were picking up, but I had always been practically nose-blind all my life. My stomach sudden knotted up as one of mom's lectures came flooding back to me and I knew what we were dealing with.

Everyone but me was starting to walk toward the yellow police tape that was fluttering in the breeze, and I said, "Everyone freeze! Stella change now!"

I called on my power and lifted myself about ten feet into the air to get a better look at the area. Stella was already gone, and in her place stood her hideous Hyde persona in all its powerful glory. Blue had her sword out and was in a defensive stance but was smart enough not to ignite the flames on the blade, as that would have cost all of us our night vision. Bree had her coat open and had gone clothing-free under it in anticipation of having to change into her Were form. I was pleased to see that all four of them had huddled up in a defensive formation, and each of them was watching and guarding all the different approaches.

"Bree? Liv? Can either of you sense anything near us?" I asked as I did a slow turn in the air, searching frantically in the darkness.

"There are some deer north of us, but they are the only thing in the area besides us," said Olivia.

"I'm not sensing anything near us, but the stench of the blood and rotten eggs is overpowering my nose at this moment," replied Bree.

"What is going on, Zack?" asked Olivia.

"Our killer is a demon—and not the weaker possessing-a-human type but the full-blown avatar-on-Earth type. Whenever a demon uses its powers, a side effect is a strong sulfur smell. Sulfur smells just like rotten eggs," I explained as I lowered myself into the center of the defensive circle.

My heart was pounding in my chest, but I was starting to calm down. If Liv or Bree couldn't sense anything nearby, chances were that the demon was long gone.

"Do we investigate the site or go home?" questioned Bree.

The police had probably been over the site in detail and picked up anything that might have been related to the murder. I doubted we'd find anything useful. The attack had been two days ago, and the demon was long gone. The main goal of visiting the sites was to try and figure out what we were dealing with, and now that we had, I didn't see much point in continuing.

"Let's go home and regroup," I said.

Chapter 8

Wednesday, April 12

We actually ended up back at our secret underground lab, as Bree was hungry and wanted to access the Food-O-Tron. I was glad to be there, as well—500 feet underground in another country and a secure place that had no exits or entrances did wonders for my nerves. A full-blown demon was nothing to mess with or take lightly. I was really starting to feel nostalgic for bloodthirsty rogue Weres as our main suspects.

After Bree got herself a spicy chicken sandwich, fries, and a lemonade from the Food-O-Tron, the rest of us took our turns. Olivia had it replicate a pint glass of blood, Stella and Blue both got a tea each and a tray of chocolate chips cookies to share, and I just got a Coke. We retired to one of the empty workbenches and began discussing the case.

Bree asked, "Zack, I don't understand why the bounty site lists the killer as unknown? I mean, that sulfur stench was awful. Surely they would have detected it …"

"*I* couldn't smell it," I said with a shrug.

Bree's eyes widened, and she turned to Blue and Stella. "Could you two smell it?"

Stella shook her head, and Blue said, "Only after you mentioned it, and then only slightly."

Bree went quiet for a moment and added, "Okay, but the killing was two days ago, so the scent would have been even stronger then. I still don't understand how the cops missed that?"

I explained, "Murder scenes don't have the nicest of aromas. Most cops wouldn't be inhaling deeply, trying to get a good whiff of the scene. In fact, a number of them would dab a little Vaseline under their noses to avoid it entirely. You also have to remember that normal humans don't have your incredible sense of smell. Also, between the blood, voided bladder, and decomposition of the victim, that sulfur smell would have been hard to notice."

Bree's shoulders slumped a little, and she nodded in agreement.

Blue said, "We know it's a demon. How do we kill it?"

The one thing that I always loved about Blue was her direct-and-practical warrior manner.

"That is getting ahead of the first question. Now that we know it is a demon, the smart thing to do would be to contact the EIRT, tell them our findings, and let them deal with it. I have a simple rule when it comes to major members of the God class of Enhanced Individuals: avoid them at all costs."

The original five classes of Enhanced Individuals had been defined by Charles Darwin about eight years after he wrote his *On the Origin of the Species*. Unlike his more famous work on evolution, *Five Classes* hadn't seen the public light until just after World War II, as the British government had confiscated the copies of it. The book had been privately published and sent to other governments around the world, but the general public had been unaware of it. The policy of all governments at the time had been to keep things that went bump in the night secret in order to prevent public panic. After World War II, as the Nazis had enlisted Enhanced Individuals like the dark fae and demons, the cat came out of the bag, and *Five Classes* was finally released to the public. In the sixties, a UN commission had updated it to seven classes to include the new Super and Alien/Unknown classes. Of the seven classes, the God class was the most powerful.

I groaned internally at the facial expressions I got from my statement. Stella looked like I had kicked a puppy or something. Blue had her normal neutral poker face, but by her upright twitching tail, I could tell she was upset. Bree had a look of determination and outrage on her face, and Liv was giving me a confused look.

"I don't understand. You helped Benny get rid of his demon. Isn't that a demon too? Why is this one different?" asked Stella.

"Benny was possessed—he had a power-blocking collar and silver-spelled cuffs on and, therefore, wasn't a threat to anyone at the time. There is a huge difference between that demon and this one. Humans possessed by demons are stronger, faster, and don't feel pain, but really aren't that much harder to deal with than a zombie. They are a minor player in the God class, like imps, cherubs, and succubae. This is a full demon and, therefore, a major player and not something to take lightly."

"What is so dangerous about a full demon?" asked Stella.

"Full demons are exceptionally strong and tough. They can use glamour, just like the fae, to appear human, but they are really covered in dark-colored scales with small horns and glowing red, orange, or yellow eyes. This form isn't their true form and is really just a shell. They heal incredibly fast, and they are telekinetic. They can hit you or pin you by using the telekinesis. They can also teleport, though the teleporting seems to really drain them, so they will only use that power a couple of times a day. Their blood is toxic, like acid, which reminds me—Liv, do not drink from a demon."

I glanced over to her, and she gave me a small nod. I continued. "Their blood will make you immensely powerful, but it is pure evil and will take you to a very dark place that you don't want to go. The shell form can also turn its fingertips into sharp claws and sprout vampire-like fangs as well. If they use telekinesis, teleport, or sprout claws or fangs, you will smell sulfur. The glamour they use doesn't cause the sulfur smell.

"To kill a demon, we need to hit the shell with enough damage to overwhelm its healing capabilities, at which point the shell will crack open and the demon's true form will manifest completely on Earth. The good news is the teleporting and telekinesis abilities will be gone; the bad news is the demon will physically be even stronger and tougher. It will be probably ten to twelve feet tall and weigh easily over 1,000 pounds. It will also be immune to fire in both forms. Religious/blessed items and silver are the most effective way to harm a demon in either form," I finished.

The room was quiet for a moment, and then Bree said, "This demon is killing people and needs to be stopped. The bounty is also $1 million, which is a good chunk of money that I don't want to walk away from. This is also our first bounty together, and I don't think walking away from it sets good precedent."

Bree brought up good points, and by the determined tone of her voice, I doubted she'd let this one go. I prayed that the others would be more open-minded and that I could persuade them over to my side. "Yes, it is killing people, and that is why I think we should turn it over to EIRT. They are professionals, and once they learn it is a demon, they will pull out all the stops to take care of this thing. The $1 million is a nice chunk of change, but not if we aren't around to spend it."

"Are you ordering us to drop this and move on to something else?" asked Bree.

"I would if I could. I am team leader, but that only applies during combat. Outside of combat, we are all partners, and therefore, this gets decided by vote—and majority rules." I paused for a moment as I noticed that all of their expressions picked up. I knew how this vote was going to go. "Look, I know you all want to stop this thing, but we are bounty hunters, not heroes, which means our primary goal is to make money safely. There is nothing remotely safe about taking on a full demon. I beg of you, let this one go. We will find something else, and EIRT will deal with the demon."

"You done?" asked Bree. I nodded, and she continued. "All in favor of taking down the demon, raise your hand."

Bree's hand went up as soon as she finished; Stella and Blue were right behind her. To my surprise, Liv kept her hand down.

"Three to two. It looks like we are going demon-hunting!" said Bree.

I nodded reluctantly in acceptance. "Liv, I am curious why you voted against it?"

"You said not to drink demon blood. My fangs and the ability to drain someone are my best fighting abilities. I didn't want to take on a bounty where I wouldn't be useful."

The one thing that always kept me on my toes with my new teammates was their ability to surprise me, and Liv's comment caught me off guard. Olivia was usually flighty, easy-going, and unpredictable. Her answer, though, was a well-reasoned one, and that almost seemed out of character for her.

"Olivia, I think I have solution to your lack-of-fang problem." Liv perked up with interest at Blue, and Blue continued. "We have been training with the Kendo wooden swords for the last few months together, and you have improved quite remarkably in that time. I know Sarah owns a couple of blades that have silver edges that she uses when dealing with Weres. I will ask to borrow one. We can also get the blade blessed, which—between that and the silver edge—should make it a fairly good demon blade."

Liv smiled at this. I had to admit that the idea of her vampire speed and an edged weapon together was something I wouldn't want to take on. Another idea struck me as I thought about Liv using weapons. "I was also thinking of Nerf guns filled with holy water for you, me, and Blue."

Holy water against demons was like spraying them with acid. The thing I loved about this was that you could hit them at range. The holy water would be safe to use around Liv as well. With vampires, holy items only hurt them if the vampire meant the user harm and the user was a true believer. With demons, however, neither of those things applied, and all religious items worked like a charm on them.

Stella found a pen and paper, and we started making a list of all the things we would need to take this demon down, but Blue once again got to the heart of the matter: "I am all for gearing up to take this thing down, but the bigger problem is going to be finding it in the first place. The demon can teleport. Therefore, after it kills someone, it will most likely jump out of the area, which means we have no trail to track."

"There is a bit of good news there," I said. "Unlike your ability to shadow-travel, the longer the distance, the more effort it costs the demon, which means it likely has a base of operations in the area. The bad news is that these killings have been hundreds of kilometers apart, which means this base is in a fairly big search area."

Blue scratched her chin as she considered the issue. "I believe the quaint human expression 'Like searching for needle in a haystack' sums up things nicely. We need to find a way to track this thing, or else there are going to be more bodies stacking up. Stella and I can check with our contacts at the English vampire court tomorrow. They employ a range of Enhanced Individuals besides vampires, and they may have some ideas on how to find a demon. Zack, can you call your wizard friend who set up your wards? He may have a spell that we can use. In a couple of weeks, if we haven't found a way to track it, maybe we can use the Barrie pack."

I must have had a confused expression on my face, because Blue added, "It will be a full moon then. I was thinking I could use my shadow-traveling to dump the whole pack in the center of the search area and send them out to each of the four compass points. I have to think that wherever this demon is hiding out, it must reek of sulfur, and with a Were's olfactory senses, if any of the groups get near it, they will pick it up. Weres in beast form can travel exceptionally long distances, and they would be able to cover a lot of the search area."

The Were idea was intriguing—assuming, of course, Shawn would be up to helping us out like that. Northern Ontario was open territory and wouldn't be violating another pack's backyard. The area was sparsely populated, which meant there wasn't much chance of them running into humans. I wasn't sure, though, if the pack could be disciplined to stay on a set direction all night; a deer running across their path would probably pull them off course. The other problem was whether they could remember the exact location the next day when they were human if their beast had actually found the spot. But even if they couldn't remember, at least we could narrow down the area, and maybe we could use Bree in beast form to find the hideout.

"Can a demon teleport someone else besides themselves?" asked Stella, breaking the silence.

"Probably, but it would require more effort and lessen the range they can travel. Why do you ask?"

Stella said, "I don't understand why the demon wouldn't take its victims back to its home base. It obviously likes to take its time when tormenting them, and while the areas it has hit are fairly isolated, there is a risk of it being discovered. This would also not leave the bodies around for people to find and, therefore, not bring as much attention to what it is doing."

I thought about this for a bit. "I'm guessing it figures it isn't worth the effort to teleport them, and if it was discovered, it would probably just kill whoever stumbled upon it. If the scene got too risky—like an EIRT team showing up—it would just teleport out. As to leaving the bodies, that is actually smart: If the people were missing, then search parties would be out combing the woods and might find its lair. Demons also love causing chaos and fear, and a string of bodies certainly does that."

"What would it use as its home base?" asked Bree.

"An empty cabin in the woods, an abandoned mine, a cave, or even just a random clearing somewhere. They don't feel cold or heat, so it would be no issue for it just to hang out just about anywhere."

We spent a few more minutes kicking around different ideas and thoughts on how to find and deal with the demon, but then Blue smiled and said, "As our night of bounty hunting was cut short, we still have time to get in a workout session."

We all groaned at this, but Blue opened a shadow portal to the house. We got changed and headed out for our workout.

* * * * *

"C'mon, ladies! Pick up the pace!" taunted Blue and glared at me at the rear of the group.

We ended up in the Mojave Desert, which Blue had picked for tonight's workout. For the last hour, she'd had us jogging in full packs up and down freaking sand dunes. My legs were on fire, and my dinner was arguing with me on whether it was coming up or not. At least the temperature was nice, at 12° Celsius. Despite the milder temperature, I was still sweating like a pig as we continued our journey from hell. My earlier thoughts about her being a demon and not an alien from another world were ringing true.

"I'm suddenly getting the urge for alien blood," muttered Olivia just ahead of me as Blue yelled at us again.

"What was that, maggot?" barked Blue.

"Nothing," answered Olivia.

"That is what I thought I heard. If you can still talk, then I'm not pushing you slackers hard enough!"

The five of us had ended up watching a lot of movies in the past month during our downtime. Being the only guy, the choices the ladies had made of romantic comedies, historical dramas, and mystery/suspense movies had killed me. So when I had gotten to pick my movie, I had wanted something super manly as payback ... and had gone with *Full Metal Jacket*. Unfortunately for me, Blue had thought the drill sergeant in the movie was fan-fucking-tastic and thought emulating him during our training was a wonderful idea. It had been funny at first, but the novelty of it had long worn off.

I will give her credit: She never directly used a line from the movie but instead came up with her own unique personal brand of insults that still kept true to the spirit of the film.

Anyone who saw us might wonder how a vampire like Olivia, who had super-human speed and strength, was barely keeping ahead of me. I'd like to claim it was my great physical prowess, but the truth was that Liv had a 500-pound knapsack on her back versus the 60-pound one I was carrying. Bree, as she was in her human form, had a 150-pound one. Stella, since she was in her human form, had a 25-pound one. What really pissed me off was that Blue had 120 pounds on her back and ran like it was nothing.

Twenty minutes later, I collapsed onto my knees and puked up my dinner all over the once-pristine sand.

"Squad, halt! Congratulations, Stella, you aren't the biggest little girl in this desert tonight, as Zack gets that honor!" gleefully taunted Blue.

"Thank God!" said Olivia, who plunked herself down with sigh on the sand. I noticed she picked a spot that was a good ten feet away from me and my mess.

"Zack's reward for tapping out tonight is yard pickup tomorrow," said Blue.

I almost smiled in relief at that but ended up dry-heaving instead. Blue always pushed us until someone tapped out or puked, and then assigned that person "shit detail," which was usually something that needed cleaning or fixing around the house. Yard pickup was a light task that I didn't mind doing. I had figured I'd be getting toilet- or floor-scrubbing. I was guessing—as I'd kept going until puking, rather than just saying, "I quit/I'm done"—Blue was going easy on me for a change.

Once I'd finished yakking, Bree came over and helped me to my feet, and Blue shadow-transported us back to the basement of our house. We all gratefully dumped our packs in the corner and headed upstairs, except for Blue, who casually said she was going to get her sword practice in. I rolled my eyes at this, as we had just spent the last hour and a half doing brutal exercise—and Blue still needed more?

Stella excused herself, as she was going upstairs to have a hot bath and then go to bed. We wished her a good night, and Olivia, Bree, and I headed for the kitchen. I grabbed a bottle of water off the counter and collapsed down in a seat at the kitchen table. Liv joined me at the table with a pint-mug of plasma she had chilling in the fridge. Bree was at the counter, making herself a sandwich that could feed a small nation.

"Hey, Zack, do you want me to make you a sandwich? I'm guessing you're hungry, since you just made room!" teased Bree.

My stomach chose that moment to make some unhappy noises, and I politely declined her offer by giving her the finger, to which she laughed and, I assumed, took as a "no."

"Zack, you are the leader of this group. Why do you let Blue torment us like this?" asked Olivia after taking a deep pull of her glass of blood, the sight of which wasn't doing my delicate stomach any favors.

"Three reasons. The first is, it is her job in her role as team trainer, and as much as I hate it, I can't argue with her results; I haven't been in this good of shape in a while. The second reason is she reminds me of my mother when she was training me as a teen, though Blue is a kinder, gentler version of my mom ..."

Liv laughed at this last one. "You really did have a messed-up childhood, didn't you?"

"Mom took training as life-or-death serious."

Bree joined us at the table. "What is the third reason?"

I smiled. "The third reason is that one of these days, you are either going to make good on the debt of multiple babies that you owe me, or Liv is going to finally succumb to my charms and get into bed with me, and if either of those things happens, I want to make sure I am in great shape so that neither of you kill me in the process."

Bree rolled her eyes but smiled, and Olivia laughed. The baby-owing was an ongoing joke between Bree and I, as each time I introduced her to new foods she loved or I saved her life, she would add a baby to the total that she owed me. The count was currently at four.

Bree tucked into her sandwich as Olivia drained the last of her glass and then stood up. "I'm going to have a shower. I have sand in places that sand shouldn't be."

My eyes were drawn to the white crop top Liv was wearing, as it was extremely obvious that she wasn't wearing a bra under it. The black yoga pants that clung to her lovely, long shapely legs caught my attention next. I glanced up and noticed Liv had busted me checking her out.

She smiled at this. "If you like what you see, you can join me in my shower and see more ..."

"Liv!" admonished Bree.

"What? There are two bathrooms upstairs, and Stella has taken over one, so am I just being practical," argued Olivia.

A lovely visual of Liv and me in the shower together popped into my mind, and my shorts began to get less comfortable. I cocked my eyebrow at her and considered her offer, as Liv was bold, but this felt like there was catch somewhere that I was missing.

"C'mon, Zack, it will be fun. I will even soap you up ... though I may take a small nibble for my services," said Liv, giving me a coy smile and slowly licking her top lip.

"Hey, Sarah has offered me mind-blowing sex for 'just a nibble,' and all you are offering is that you will clean me?"

Sarah was the enforcer for the English vampire court. She was also smoking hot and a dead ringer for the dark-haired actress in those vampire vs. Werewolf movies ... well, other than the dueling scar on her face, but I thought Sarah's scar made her hotter, as it gave her face real character. Sarah and Olivia also got along like oil and water.

"She is old and has lower standards than I do," said Olivia.

"Pass."

"Your loss," said Liv with a shrug.

She turned and walked to the stairs, which let me check out her amazing ass in those pants. I knew she did this on purpose, as normally she moved faster than the eye could see. As I drooled over her lovely assets, part of me was regretting not taking her up on her offer.

Bree cleared her throat. "Stop checking out the slutty vampire."

"Hey! I heard that!" yelled Liv as she disappeared up the stairs.

"Good!" yelled back Bree with a laugh.

I smiled at the two of them and took another pull on my water, trying to get fluids back into me while Bree continued attacking her sandwich with gusto.

A few minutes later, I heard the shower go on upstairs. Bree put down her sandwich and said, "You do know that if you went up and joined her and she did feed off of you, she probably would do much more than just clean you?"

I nodded at this. "Yeah, I know."

"Then why are you hanging out here with me?"

I grinned and gave Bree a leer, then said, "Maybe I'm saving myself for a certain lovely, curvaceous blonde who loves me and wants to have many beautiful babies with me. Also, since you all made me team leader, I'm not sure if sleeping with Olivia is a good idea. Now you, as second in charge, would probably be fine, as we are both 'management,' so for the good of the team, how about it?"

"Well, if it is for the team, just let me finish my sandwich, and then you can ravage me right here on the kitchen table," said Bree with enough sarcasm in her tone that my sarcasm meter damn near exploded.

She paused for a moment. "Honestly, I don't understand you at times. You flirt with us both nonstop and can be a total pig, but Liv just offered herself up, and you turned her down. And don't give me that 'team leader' crap. We are all partners, and therefore, we are all 'management,' as you put it."

"Bree, twenty minutes ago I was puking my guts out in the middle of a desert, and I can barely feel my legs at this point. I'm not sure I could keep up with Liv on my best day, but if I do get the chance to be with her, I at least want a sporting chance, which certainly isn't right now."

Bree was already back to her sandwich again, as very few things came between a Were and her food, but she gave me a nod.

"Since you are asking probing questions, let me ask you one: If I did take Liv up on her offer, would you be cool with that?"

Bree finished her mouthful, and I could see the wheels turning in her head as she pondered my question. "You are both consenting adults. What you do together is your own business."

"That is not an answer. You and Liv are best friends, and I'd like to think we are pretty good friends too. If I took Liv up on her offer, you wouldn't have a problem with it?"

Bree went quiet as she thought about it, and I decided to try a different tack. "Actually, don't answer that. Answer this instead: If I slept with Liv, does that end any shot I had at sleeping with you?"

Bree's eyes widened, and she didn't answer for a moment or two. "I think it is pretty safe to say if you slept with Liv that your chances with me would go down dramatically. Are you really holding out for me?"

"Sort of. As I deeply respect your friendship with Liv and with me, and I realize that sleeping with either of you might cause issues with your friendship, I have decided that there is only one route I can go …"

"Abstinence?" said Bree in a shocked tone of voice.

"What? No. The solution is obviously a threesome! Think about it—it is the perfect solution. Neither of you would get upset at each other for sleeping with me first, and I would get to be the gooey cream filling in a Bree-and-Olivia sandwich. Win-win for everyone."

Bree burst out laughing and shook her head. "You are such an asshole."

I finished my water and yawned. "And on that note, I am going to bed. I'd ask you to join me, but as Liv is still in the shower, we are missing the third piece of our sexy puzzle. I will just wish you good night instead."

"Dream on—and don't forget to set you alarm earlier, as that yard isn't going to pick up itself," said Bree with a smile.

I stood up and was pleased to note that my legs didn't shake too badly, then headed upstairs to bed.

* * * * *

My alarm buzzed at me loudly, and I groaned as I reached over and fumbled for the snooze button. Ten minutes later, it went off again, and I pulled myself out of my warm and comfy bed and decided to face the day. There was a dull ache in most of the muscles in my body from yesterday, but it wasn't as bad as I had feared it was going to be.

I stepped into the shower and almost moaned at how great the scalding-hot water felt as it magically helped lessen the sore muscles.

Twenty minutes later, with a coffee in one hand and a garbage bag in the other, I stepped out onto the front porch. The nice thing about snow was it covered everything with a nice, pristine blanket of white; the downside was when it melted, you were left with a brown lawn, and all the garbage and crap that had littered the lawn all winter was exposed.

I sighed and got down to work picking up the debris. It actually didn't take that long, and as far as Blue's punishments went, this was definitely one of the lighter ones. I dumped the half-full garbage bag in the bin.

I then joined Stella and Blue in the kitchen for lunch. Blue had shadow-traveled back to the lab and hit the Food-O-Tron, returning with our food. After lunch, we discussed our plans for the day. Stella and Blue were going to hit the English vampire court this afternoon, as it would be evening in London, and get a sword for Olivia. They were also going to take care of picking up Nerf guns and holy water. Blue again asked me to call Walter, the wizard who had set up my wards, to see if he had a spell to track the demon.

* * * * *

"You want a spell to track down a full demon? Are you nuts?!" exclaimed Walter over the phone.

"Hey, I voted to drop this bounty, but I was out-voted by my partners. I agree with you that the smartest play is to avoid demons altogether. The question is, can you do a spell that will let us track one?"

Walter hemmed and hawed as he thought about my request. "Maybe. I can enspell an item that will point toward the strongest source of evil, which, since this demon is up north in an area that is sparsely populated, should lead you to it. Though, if you happen to run across something worse than a demon, that is your problem."

I shuddered a little at the thought of running across something more evil than a demon, but figured the chances were remote. The next concern I had was the item's range—too long, and it might pick up something other than the demon; too short, and it would take us a ton more searching to do. "What type of range can you put on this thing?"

There was another pause as Walter kicked my question around in his head. I knew he was thinking about the too-long and too-short issue as well. "Fifty kilometers?"

"Any chance of a one-hundred-kilometer range? We have a lot of area to search," I countered.

"Yeah. That will take a bit longer, but it's doable. This will cost you $10,000, and it will take me about a day to make."

I agreed to his price, which was less than I had been expecting; it had cost me $40,000 the last time he'd recharged the wards on the house.

He said he would call me when he was done, and we ended the call.

With that out of the way, I decided to spend the rest of the afternoon doing research into demon lore in the hopes of finding something else that could help us.

Chapter 9

Thursday, April 13

That night, I'd barely taken my first bite of dinner when Blue gleefully announced, "Eat up, my pretties! I have something extra special planned for tonight's training exercise, which will commence right after Olivia gets up and has her breakfast."

I didn't think it was possible to take the enjoyment out of a Philly cheesesteak, but Blue had managed to do just that. Doing one of her forced marches with a full stomach was going to suck at an epic level.

Wanting to focus on something else, I changed the subject. "Did you get all the stuff we discussed?"

"Yes, it is all in the garage, other than this beauty," said Blue as she lifted a sheathed katana from its resting place against the table beside her.

I held out my hand, and she passed it to me. I admired it. The scabbard, guard, and hilt were all in midnight black. There was no elaborate decoration, but there was no doubting the sword's quality. It was elegant in its simplicity and perfection. I drew the blade out about six inches and studied it. The leading edge was a slightly darker hue than the rest of it, and I assumed that was the silver edge. It certain looked lethal and dangerous. Combine that with vampire speed, and I was happy I was not the demon.

I resheathed the blade and handed it back to Blue.

Ten minutes later, the door to the basement opened and Olivia lurched out from the darkness. We all wished her a good morning, and she waved us off and made a beeline for the fridge. She removed the pint-glass of blood that Blue had left for her and drank it down in one long pull.

Olivia wandered over to the table, and Bree excused herself to go get changed into her workout gear.

"I have a gift for you," said Blue.

Olivia perked up at this. Blue handed the borrowed katana to Stella, who passed it on to Liv.

"Oh! Pretty!" exclaimed Olivia.

She removed the full length of the blade from the scabbard and placed the empty sheath on the table, then held the blade out in front of her in a fighting stance. "It's heavier than the wooden practice swords but feels easier to handle."

She made two slow slashing motions in front of her, trying to get a feel for the blade.

Blue said, "That is because the katana has better balance than what you are used to. My Keetiyatomi blade is the same—heavier but easier to handle due to the balance. Speaking of that, Zack, you said demons are immune to fire, right?"

I nodded, and she continued. "Therefore, the flame feature of my sword won't be of much use against the demon. I wonder, though, if it would be considered a blessed item. Keetiyatomi was given to my ancestors by a god-king who ruled our lands. The god-kings were similar to Egyptian pharaohs in that they weren't just rulers but considered gods on Earth as well."

I pondered it for a few moments and said, "It would fit the description of a blessed item, but I am not sure if a god/religious figure from another world would have the same effect on a demon as one from Earth. I guess we'll find out soon enough."

Liv started getting more aggressive in her swings, and now the blade was moving fast enough that it was barely a blur in front of my eyes. She continued her display, and the swings got wider and more dramatic. A cloud of white foam stuffing exploded into the air.

"Oops!" she said, bringing the blade's motion to a stop.

A good chunk of the back of the black leather Ikea Henriksdal chair Bree had been sitting in earlier fell to the floor with a dull *thud*.

"Sorry," said Liv as she hurriedly reached for the scabbard and sheathed the blade.

"No problem. That chair was, like, super old at six months and was due to be replaced soon anyway. Also, Liv, when we go into combat against the demon, your new spot is directly beside Blue, since she trained you," I said, still starring opened-mouthed at the now-deceased piece of quality Swedish engineering.

"I didn't mean to," said Olivia with a sad pout on her face.

"It happens," said Blue. "Thankfully, it was only a chair. When I was a young girl, I was practicing with a live blade in my mother's sewing room against a mannequin that happened to have my mother's prized embroidered evening gown on it. That gown was for the god-king's festival, which was one of our most sacred holidays. My mother had spent months making it. I got carried away in my blade routine and cut the dress and the mannequin in half. My parents were both furious, and to this day, I can still clearly remember the beating I got for it. All swordsmen make this type of mistake once; learn from it and move on. There are a number of swordsmen whose first mistake was against a sibling or servant who happened to be in the wrong place at the wrong time."

Liv seemed to cheer up at this.

Stella's iPhone chimed at that moment, and she pulled it out. As Stella read the text, the amused expression on her face instantly disappeared. "There has been another attack. This time, the victim was an OPP officer who was out driving on patrol."

"Any more details than that?" I asked.

"The attack was on Highway 11, about thirty kilometers east of Longlac. The bounty site doesn't have any more information than that and is listing more details as 'pending.' "

"Alright, Liv, tell Bree to get changed into her sweats. We are all going to gear up and head out. As this attack was on a police officer, it probably didn't happen that long ago. We may get lucky, and the demon might still be in the area. Blue, break out those Nerf guns you bought and fill them with the holy water and then help Liv figure out a way to strap that sword sheath on."

I whipped out my iPhone and looked up Longlac on Google Maps. It was northeast of Thunder Bay, which meant it was out in the middle of nowhere.

It took twenty minutes, but we were loaded for bear and ready to go. Blue led us through the shadows, and instantly, we were standing out in the rain on a dark strip of road with the flashing lights of numerous police cruisers all around us. There was a line of flickering red flares running down the length of the damp road.

"Put your hands on top of your head and get facedown on the ground!" was barked at us a moment later.

Not a second after that, there were more guns pointed at us than I was comfortable with. I thickened the air in front of us as a precaution; it would only take one officer to get a little jumpy, and the bullets would start flying. I groaned as I saw we were less than twenty-five feet from a cruiser covered with a blue tarp, and I realized that Blue had warped us directly inside the perimeter of an active crime scene.

"Liv? Bree? Is the demon in the area?" I asked quietly, knowing either of them, with their enhanced hearing, would pick it up.

There was no way I was getting all of us prone and vulnerable until I knew the answer to that question.

"Last warning! Put your hands on top of your head and get facedown on the ground," ordered a stern voice from the darkness.

"It was here, but the smell isn't getting any stronger, so it is gone," said Olivia from somewhere behind me.

"Agreed," added Bree.

If neither of them were picking up any active signs, then the demon was probably long gone.

"Do as they say, and do not resist," I said as I slowly moved my hands up in the least threatening way possible.

I didn't relish getting down on the cold, wet pavement but didn't see that we had much of a choice. As soon as we were on the ground, we were swarmed by uniformed officers. They kicked the Nerf guns away from us, and my hands were quickly and not-so-gently cuffed behind my back.

"Is EIRT on site? Can I please speak with the team leader?" I asked.

I got no response and tried another tactic. "In my back pocket is my hero ID, and all five of us are registered UN bounty hunters. We know what has been doing the killings, and we are in the process of tracking it down."

No response, but at least I felt the officer pinning me down grab my wallet.

A few moments later, a voice behind me said, "Bounty hunter, hero, or whatever, Mr. Stevens, this is an active crime scene, and you are interfering with a police investigation. We are going to take you into custody and keep you on scene until the EIRT decides what to do with you."

A couple of officers hauled me to my feet and marched us farther away from the attack site. Near the site, I spotted two auras and figured both must belong to EIRT team members. One aura was made up of green and brown that filled more than half of the aura with a good-size chunk of blue and two smaller slices of yellow and red. The plethora of oddly spaced colors meant this was a human mage; the brown and green meant it was a mage whose primary specialty was Earth and nature magic. The mage was also decent with Water/Ice spells due to the large blue area, and dabbled in Air and Fire. The aura was also a good size, as it extended a good six inches in all directions, which meant this was a fairly powerful mage.

The second aura was orange with a dotted red-and-white outline surrounding it. The orange outline meant the person was a Super, and the dotted red-and-white outline meant a Tank. Tanks were Enhanced Individuals who were exceptionally strong and could take a lot of damage. Stella's Hyde persona would be classed as a Tank, and this was why she had a dotted red outline that covered the left side of her aura.

I saw a police van parked fifty feet away and figured that was where they were taking us. They jerked me and the rest of my team toward the two snarling and barking German shepherds across the road that were part of the K9 unit. I figured this was their idea of giving us a little payback and trying to scare us for crashing their crime scene. A moment later, both dogs stopped barking and darted behind their handlers with a few whimpers.

"What the hell?" muttered the cop behind me.

I smiled to myself, as I knew what had happened: The puppies had scented Bree, our Werepanther. Now the puppies knew they weren't the toughest thing on the block anymore.

The officers stopped screwing around and led us directly to the van. They made us get in and made a point of cuffing our ankles to the floor. The door slammed, and we were left alone.

I sighed. "Blue, in the future when transporting us to a crime scene, please make sure you drop us *outside* the perimeter. Cops get very touchy about having civilians mucking about inside their investigation area."

"Noted," answered Blue.

"Are they going to charge us with something?" asked Bree with concern.

I pondered this and figured they wouldn't, as they had left Blue and Olivia with their swords. If they had been serious about charging us, there was no way they would have done that. They were probably going to hold us here for a while to make a point. After that, they'd have the EIRT team leader talk to us and let him make the call. The feds wouldn't be as touchy about us crashing the crime scene, and they'd probably let us go. I explained all of this to Bree and the others.

"Any chance it's Ray Dunham out there?" asked Bree.

"Nope. I saw auras for a mage and a Tank, and I haven't met either before."

We sat back on the hard metal benches and tried to get comfortable, passing the first twenty minutes in silence. The silence was a blessing, but then Olivia got bored and started asking, "Are we there yet?" every minute. It was cute for the first five minutes, but then it became annoying.

"This sucks!" said Bree as she awkwardly shifted in her seat.

"It's not so bad and could be worse—if we weren't stuck in here, I'm sure Blue would be marching us uphill over some brutal terrain she thought would be fun for us to train on," I said.

"At least we would be doing something," added Olivia.

"We could do that now if you want ...," said Blue.

Bree looked at Blue like she was crazy. "How much exercising can we do? We are handcuffed and bolted to the floor in a paddy wagon ..."

Blue's tail playfully fluttered around with excitement behind her, and I knew this meant she was amused. She smiled, revealing her sharp, pointed white teeth, and she brought her arms up, then held them wide apart. Her cuffs were gone.

"Zack, I can get us all free. There is no reason for all of us to stay here. I will take Bree, Liv, and Stella out training, and you can deal with the local constabulary—unless, of course, you want to get in your training, in which case someone else can stay."

I knew the cops would be annoyed at the ladies for leaving, but since the cops had been dicks, I didn't really care about that too much. There was no point in all of us wasting our time here, and I gave them my blessing.

I also didn't know how long the cops would leave us here, and it wouldn't be long before Bree started getting hungry again, which would just make a bad situation even worse.

"Go for it. I will call you when I need transport back to the house," I said.

Blue leaned forward and used a thin piece of metal to pick the lock on her ankle cuffs. It took her less than a minute, and she was free. In about ten minutes, she had the rest of us uncuffed and then used the shadows at the back of the van to transport the rest of the team out of there. It was a relief to have the cuffs off, and I spent the next few minutes rubbing my wrists and getting the circulation going again.

Not having Olivia asking, "Are we there yet?" was also an improvement, but the silence in the back of the van was odd. I had been on my own for sixteen years, ten of those as a hero and another six as a bounty hunter. But for the last couple of months, I had been part of a team. It shocked me that I found being on my own like this as weird as I did.

I pulled out my iPhone and was going to kill time surfing the internet, but the internet out here was nonexistent. In the end, I took off my coat and rolled it up as a pillow, then stretched out on the metal bench and tried to get some sleep …

"Wake up!" being barked at me in an unfriendly voice roused me from my slumber. There were two unhappy OPP officers leaning over me. I sat up and grabbed my phone, seeing that it was coming up on 11:00 p.m. I clutched my phone harder as it dawned on me that they had left me in the van for over three hours. That was three hours that could have been used tracking or searching for the demon and putting a stop to its murder spree. Three hours would have also had Bree dangerously hungry.

"Where are the others?" asked the shorter of the two cops.

"They got bored and left."

I was rewarded with two looks of confusion, and I shrugged. I unraveled my coat and put it back on, then stood up—or at least got to my feet in a hunched-over position, due to the height of the van.

"Where do you think you are going?" questioned the same cop as before while reaching for his baton.

"If you two are here, it is because EIRT wants to talk to me and you were sent to fetch us. I want to apologize for popping into the middle of your crime scene. That was a mistake on my part; I should have told my shadow-traveler to put us outside the perimeter. I would also like to express my condolences for the loss of your fellow officer. Most of all, though, I want to nail the SOB who did this, which is what we all want. You have made your point with the handcuffs, the perp walk, the attempt to intimidate us with the dogs, and leaving us … well, *me* stuck in this van for over three hours. So can we stop screwing around and take me to EIRT, so I can help?"

I hoped that apologizing would be enough, but I guess emotions were running high. Shorty pulled out the billy club from his belt.

"Don't," I warned and let an impressive and showy amount of sparks drip from my hands.

His eyes went wide, and I added, "I have been patient, but that patience has run out. If you swing that club at me or if your partner keeps reaching for his weapon, I will fry you both, and it will make being tased seem tame. Let's all be smart here, and you can both exit the vehicle and take me to EIRT like you were ordered to, okay?"

Shorty paused for a moment, and I briefly thought I would have to follow through on my threat, but he wisely holstered the nightstick, and his partner carefully lifted his hand away from his gun. They turned and awkwardly exited the van, and I followed them out into the night. Threatening a police officer like I had just done was a crime, but as one of them had been about to give me an illegal beatdown, I doubted either would try to press charges.

They turned and headed across the road, and we passed five cruisers before coming to two unmarked black SUVs that I recognized as standard EIRT vehicles. The mage was standing in front of the second SUV, talking to a senior OPP officer. There was no sign of the Tank I had spotted earlier or any other members of the EIRT team.

The senior OPP officer turned to address the two OPP officers who had been sent to collect me. The senior officer's eyes widened when he saw that I was no longer cuffed, and I assumed he was also wondering how a party of five had become one.

The senior OPP officer was whipcord lean and trim and stood a good six feet tall. The buzzed grey hair that showed from under his cap had been trimmed with military precision. He ripped into the two officers about me being not being cuffed and why there had been five people taken into custody, yet there was only one standing in front of him now. His face was a deep, ruddy red, and I could actually see the veins at his temples and neck throbbing as he continued dressing down the two unfortunate officers. I was seriously starting to get concerned that he was going to stroke out or have a heart attack.

As he paused in his rant, the mage spoke up. "Superintendent, while discipline is important, maybe you can hand it out later. Why don't we interrogate the suspect first?"

For a brief moment, the superintendent went even darker at being interrupted, but then he composed himself and gave a brief nod. He dismissed the two officers and made a pointing gesture at me.

The officers fled as I stepped forward and took over the spot they had been standing in.

I took a moment to study the mage. Physically, he was unremarkable: He was a couple of inches shorter than I was, with dark hair that was short and neat, and no facial hair. This was odd for a mage; many of them tended to go for the long hair and beard like they were the second coming of Merlin. The other odd thing about the mage was he was in EIRT tactical gear. Usually, they wore the full robes they had been awarded upon finishing their schooling. The nameplate on his uniform read "Lieutenant Buckingham III." His appearance put him in his early thirties, but mages had longer lifespans than normal, and I guessed his age at probably closer to fifty.

Both men were studying me. The superintendent was radiating rage and barely controlled anger, which I could understand; one of his officers was dead, and the feds would be in their rights to take over this crime scene from him and the OPP. The mage, however, was giving me a look that pissed me off: The grimace on his face was like one made when stepping in dog crap by accident. I knew there were a small number of law enforcement officers who distained bounty hunters and felt that we shouldn't be allowed in Canada. I wondered if Lieutenant Buckingham was one of those.

"We have a rogue Were on the loose who has killed four civilians and one police officer. You appear inside our crime scene uninvited and pull officers away who could be out hunting down this killer but instead have to deal with you. I am sorely tempted to have you charged with interfering with a police investigation. What do you have to say for yourself?" asked the mage calmly.

I couldn't help but notice that the superintendent had nodded his approval at the "pressing charges" part. I also caught that they still believed this was a rogue Were. Normally, after being treated the way I had been—and with the bad vibes I was getting off them—I'd be giving it back as hard as I was getting it. But with a dead police officer and the bodies mounting, I decided to take a deep breath and take the high road.

"I think, before I answer any questions, some introductions would be good. I am Zack Stevens, an Air elemental, formerly known as the Hamilton Hurricane and currently, for the last six years, working as a bounty hunter. I have worked with many EIRT officers before, such as Sergeants Ray Dunham and Bobby Knight. If you call either of them, I am sure they will give me a good reference and can point out a number of times where our cooperation has worked out beneficially to all concerned. For the superintendent, if you call the Hamilton Police, I'm sure they, too, will vouch for me. Now, if both of you would be kind enough to extend the same courtesy to me?"

"Very well. My name is Lieutenant Charles Buckingham the third," said the mage.

"OPP Superintendent Bates."

"Thank you. Superintendent, please accept my sincere condolences on the loss of what I'm sure was a fine officer."

He nodded at that, and I continued. "My team and I have been investigating the earlier attacks, and we have come to the conclusion that your attacker is a demon, not a Were."

Both shot me skeptical looks at my "demon" claim, and the mage spoke up first. "I find that highly unlikely. A person possessed by demon would not have the strength to do the damage that has been inflicted on the victims."

"It is a full demon, not a possession, and in that form, it would easily have the ability to do this sort of damage."

"That is even more ludicrous. There hasn't been a full demon on Canadian soil for decades," argued the mage.

"Yeah, and there haven't been drow on Canadian soil since World War II—except we both know that isn't the case."

The mage's expression turned to one of surprise and then understanding, whereas the superintendent just looked confused. While Olivia had been hunted by the French vampire court, they had sent a team of dark elves—*drow*—out to capture her. We had beaten them, and the Hamilton Police and EIRT had been called in to deal with the cleanup. EIRT had decided to cover up the attack as a "Mexican biker attack" and not let the general public know that it had been drow.

"That is classified information," said Lieutenant Buckingham angrily.

"You are EIRT, and I'm sure an OPP superintendent has the clearance to know something like that. "

"Regardless, just because there may or may not have been drow on Canadian soil doesn't make it any more likely that we have a full demon out there."

It was like dealing with a brick wall, and I decided that I'd had enough. "Look, Chuck, you are a mage. Surely, in your vast repertoire of spells, you have something to detect a demon's presence. At all four crime scenes, the Were and vampire on my team smelled sulfur. The kills also don't fit a Were attack. Weres kill to eat; they don't torture their victims first and then eat them. Lastly, Weres will always go for the liver and kidneys, as those are the richest source of protein, and yet most of the victims still had those organs. All victims were instead missing their hearts. A demon, on the other hand, when using its power, produces a sulfur-like smell as a side effect, they certainly like to torture before killing, and they will always take the heart of their victim, as some have speculated that the heart is where the soul is."

"How did you know I was a mage?"

"How I know isn't important, but I will go one better: Your primary focus is Earth, and your secondary is Ice/Water. You have just enough Fire magic to light a candle and maybe just enough Air magic to blow out that candle. Your other Enhanced EIRT team member is a Tank, who I'm assuming is out in the woods fruitlessly searching for rogue Weres who don't exist. Now, since I have correctly identified your power and your teammate's power, maybe you will realize that I know my Enhanced Individuals, and you can cast the spell to see if I am right or not. Once you have, we can actually get down to nailing this demon and stop more dead bodies from showing up."

By the shocked expression on his face, I knew I'd finally gotten through.

The superintendent glanced over at him and asked, "Is he right about your powers and your teammate?"

Charles nodded slowly.

"Cast the spell if you have one," demanded the superintendent.

We moved closer to the tarped-over cruiser that was the center of the crime scene. To my amazement, Charles pulled out an iPad and began scrolling through it. I'd expected him to have the standard thick leather-bound spellbook and not be using a tablet.

After a minute or two of searching, he started mumbling out the incantation. He did this a few times and then pulled out a small pocket knife. He turned over the iPad and then used the blade to nick his finger. He squeezed out a small drop of blood onto the back of the iPad. He then loudly and clearly began chanting the spell in a language that sounded like Latin. He made a few precise hand gestures as he continued the spell. The blood on the iPad went up in a thick line of black smoke at the conclusion of the spell.

"Shit. It's a demon," said the mage.

I had been, like, 99 percent sure before the spell, but it was nice to have the mage confirm it.

He put away the knife and iPad and unclipped his radio. He called back the search parties from the woods and then clipped up the handset.

"Why are you calling them back? The demon could still be out there?" argued the superintendent.

"Full demons can teleport. Therefore, if we are lucky, then this one is long gone from the immediate area."

"Why would that be 'lucky'?" asked the superintendent, obviously confused.

"If it is still in the area, then we are going to have a lot more dead bodies. A full demon is one of the more powerful monsters out there, and the teams out in the woods are no match for one. This is going to be bumped up the chain, and GRC13 will deal with it."

Now it was my turn to be shocked. GRC13 was EIRT's most elite team. GRC13 was actually two twelve-person teams: one active team of twelve and a second team on standby. A normal EIRT team was six people.

GRC13 was only called into the worst and most dangerous situations, and if Charles was bumping it up to them, then he was taking this demon seriously.

The attitudes of both men toward me had changed too. Both thanked me for bringing the demon to their attention.

"Don't thank me. Just nail this thing," I said.

They both nodded resolutely at that.

I asked if they needed me for anything else and was told it was good and I was free to go. I was escorted out of the crime scene, and I called Blue to come get me. If GRC13 was dealing with it, that meant this was one bounty we weren't likely to collect on, and I figured we'd be going after pixies after all.

Chapter 10

Friday, April 14

"This is complete horseshit!" said Bree as she unconsciously bent the butter knife in her hand damn near in half.

I sighed mentally. I had known that giving up this bounty wasn't going to be well received, and the reactions I was getting around the table were about on par with what I had expected.

"We did the legwork, we found out it was a demon, and now the government just gets to take over, and we get nothing?" continued Bree.

She glared at me, and I said, "I know it sucks, but GRC13 is not a group that we want to mess with. They are an elite team and will take this demon down in the next couple of days. Look on the bright side: Thanks to us and our legwork, GRC13 is involved, and there is a good chance that they will nail this thing before another body appears. That is great news. We have saved lives today."

Bree reluctantly nodded at this, but I could tell she was still ticked off.

Stella's phone made a chiming noise, she picked it up and read from the screen. "The bounty has now been updated to include the information of the slain police officer, but they are still listing 'Unknown Enhanced Individual' as the perpetrator. They have also raised the bounty to $1.5 million."

Bree just growled at this. The extra half million made us dropping the bounty even harder to swallow.

Blue tail bobbed playfully behind her, and she said, "If the bounty is still up and hasn't been taken down then, there is no reason why we can't keep going after it. Zack, your wizard will have the demon-tracking device done tomorrow. Once we have that, why don't we use it to go after the demon?"

I rubbed my temples. Blue had a good point. It was also too late to cancel the order, so we'd be out the $10,000 Walter was charging us. But I still didn't want to tangle with this thing. "My concern is, what if we find the demon and hit it just before GRC13 arrives? If we do that and the demon teleports out, they are going to be extremely unhappy with us."

"That would be unfortunate, but my point still stands. The bounty is still up, and therefore, we can still legally hunt this thing. If the authorities wanted this bad enough, they could have taken the bounty down."

As much as I hated to admit it, Blue had a point. EIRT/GRC13 had the power to get a bounty delisted, and if they wanted exclusive rights on this, they should have done just that. "Okay, you have a point. Once Walter drops off the tracker, we will go after the demon. Do we do this during the day or wait until night and include Olivia?"

That touched off a debate between them, and I decided it was time for another beer. I got up to get one from the fridge.

Once I returned to the table, it had been decided that we'd wait until nightfall tomorrow and go out as full team. The thought of taking on a demon at night had my stomach knotting up in all sorts of uncomfortable ways. I still felt that going after a full demon was a mistake, as it would be too powerful for us, but with the bodies piling up, I really wanted to take this thing down. The extra-large bounty on it didn't hurt either.

"If we are going to go after this demon, we need a plan," I said and got nods from around the table. "We are going to use Stella in her Hyde form as our hammer. The demon, while it is still in its shell form, shouldn't be powerful enough to hurt Stella. I will hit it from the air with Lightning and Air attacks and use one of the Nerf guns with holy water. Bree, Liv, you two need to do hit-and-run attacks. Do not engage this thing in a stand-up fight. Blue, I will leave it to your own judgment on how and when to engage."

Blue smiled and nodded in approval at that, then asked, "What about when we crack its shell and its true form appears?"

I shuddered. "Then we pray and hope for divine intervention or a nuke strike ..."

Bree rolled her eyes. "Stop being dramatic. There are five of us and one of it. We can take this thing."

I had my doubts about that, but for the next hour we kicked around different ideas for dealing with the demon in its true form. I was still nervous about taking it on, but by the end we had a rough plan, and with some luck, we might actually take this thing down.

Our impromptu meeting broke up shortly after that. Stella and Blue were going to call it a night and turn in. Bree asked Blue for a quick trip to the lab to get more food, and Liv piled on, as she wanted another pint of blood from the Food-O-Tron as well.

I had finished my second beer by the time the girls got back from the lab. Bree and Olivia passed me on the way to the living room and were laughing and seemed not to have a care in the world. They said they were going to watch a movie and asked if I wished to join them. I declined, as I wasn't in the mood for a movie at that point. I was tired, but I was also too keyed up to sleep and decided to go out flying to clear my head.

I grabbed my jacket—but not because I needed it for the cold night. With the hint of Ice elemental powers I had, I didn't really feel the cold, but the larger pockets were convenient for my iPhone and keys. I locked the front door behind me and used my Air powers to lift me into the night sky. The takeoff was a touch wobbly. I guessed flying right after a couple of beers hadn't been the greatest idea. Thankfully, it was just past midnight, and there wasn't much air traffic. There were also no kamikaze birds to avoid.

It was a beautiful, clear night. The half moon hung low in the sky, and I flew toward it. The rush of air blasting across my face sobered me up pretty quickly. My thoughts rolled back to the demon again. I really wanted to let GRC13 deal with it, and I wasn't sure if that was fear or just common sense pushing me in that direction. I had a number of rules that guided my life and had kept me alive over the years, and not getting near God-class Enhanced Individuals was certainly one of the top ones. Yet tomorrow, if everything went according to plan, we would be going toe to toe with a full demon.

It dawned on me that I didn't fear for my own life. In my years as a solo hero and bounty hunter, there had been many times I hadn't thought I would live through an encounter. Now, my deep-seated fear was losing one of my teammates. I'd grown quite fond of all four of them and didn't want to picture life with one of them no longer in it. I was also wise enough to know that any of them would be furious at me if I kept us out of a fight because I was afraid for them. They were strong, independent, and bold and were aware of the risks. All of them had been through a number of difficulties that would have brought me to my knees, and yet, all of them had taken those problems in stride and kept going.

I thought, at times, I still saw them as my charges that I was protecting, like when we had first met, and not as my teammates and partners. But things were different from when we'd first met. The biggest difference was that Blue was conscious and not in a coma, but on top of that, we'd been in combat together—first against a Fire elemental and five heavily armed killers, and then taking down a master vampire together, which was something few people still walking this Earth had done.

What if I did convince them to drop the bounty, and GRC13 failed? It was only a matter of time before the demon killed again, and if we walked away, we would be partly responsible for that death. The voice of my dead mother echoed at that moment in my head: "Our powers are a blessing and a gift, and it is our duty to help those less fortunate ..."

Something inside of me clicked, and I knew that going after the demon was the right thing to do. We were going to take this evil bastard down and claim that bounty. Yeah, there were risks, but life was a risk, and if you weren't willing to take a risk, then you weren't really living.

* * * * *

I woke up the next day and checked my phone. I smiled when I saw Walter had emailed about an hour ago and had the tracking spell ready to go. I replied and told him to stop by in an hour, which would give me more than enough time to grab a shower and some breakfast.

When Walter showed up at my front door, I was just a little underwhelmed at his craftsmanship. The tracking device was a two-inch plain-looking metal arrow with a string tied around the center of it.

The expression of disappointment must have shown on my face, and Walter said, "Dude, you gave me a day to make this. What were you expecting? Excalibur? It will work, and it is so simple even you can use it. Just hold the end of the string. If it detects a strong sense of evil, it will pull the arrow clearly in the direction it senses the evil is coming from. If the arrow doesn't react, then the demon isn't within the hundred-kilometer range."

I nodded. He was right: As long as it did the job, it didn't matter what it looked like.

We said our goodbyes, and he told me he would email me his invoice, then he left.

The rest of the day was just a waiting game. We had dinner together—except for Olivia, who was still in her daytime slumber.

Then we geared up, and as soon as Olivia got up and had her glass of pick-me-up, she too geared up, and we were on our way.

We stepped out of the shadows just south of the campsite where the couple had been killed near Armstrong. Armstrong was the most northern and western crime scene. I fished the tracker out of my pocket and let the arrow dangle in the air from its string. It moved around a little from the motion of being unraveled and then went completely lifeless and still.

With Armstrong being a bust, we had Blue take us through the shadows to Nipigon, which was the southernmost point where the bird watcher had been killed. I repeated the ritual, but this time the arrow reacted and tugged gently in an east-northeast direction. Stella got out her phone and the folded paper map we had of the area. She used the compass on her phone to get the exact direction and then drew a line on the map that extended out from Nipigon toward the direction the arrow had been pointing.

We popped out of shadows on the road just outside of Hornepayne, where seventeen-year-old Tamara Lightfoot had been killed walking home from her friend's house. I pulled out the tracker and let the arrow dangle, but it didn't react. That was disappointing, but even the lack of reaction was useful, as we now knew the demon was closer to Nipigon than here.

Our next stop was about 500 meters away from where the OPP officer had been killed near Longlac. There were a couple of cruisers on scene, and they still had the yellow police tape up. Thankfully, this time we didn't end up inside the perimeter.

I felt the arrow twitching in my pocket and thought that was a good sign. I grabbed the string, and this time, the arrow practically jumped out, pointing hard in a south-southwest direction.

Stella took out the map and her phone, and updated the map with another line from our current position. The two lines intersected about twenty-five clicks from our current position and about ninety clicks east of Nipigon.

"Looks like we have found our demon—or something as evil as a demon, at least," I said as we all studied the map.

"How do you want to do this?" asked Blue.

The wind was blowing in from the east; therefore, I wanted to come in downwind from the west. That way, Bree and Liv should be able to scent the demon coming in. I also had no idea how strong the demon's sense of smell was; therefore, keeping downwind from it was probably a smart play. I shared my thoughts with the group, and they were good with the plan.

Blue suggested that we come in a couple of clicks to the west and approach carefully on foot. Without being told, Bree began stripping off her clothes, which would allow her to more easily change into her Were form. Stella stayed in her human form, as it was quieter than her lumbering Hyde form, and unlike Bree, she could change instantly into the Hyde form when needed. Bree handed her clothes to Blue, who stuffed them in a knapsack and then tossed the knapsack into the shadows. That knapsack would be waiting for us at home in the living room.

I kept my back to Bree to give her some privacy. She had become more practical about having to get naked to change and probably wouldn't have said anything if I had turned around, but as we weren't in any danger here, I could afford to be a gentleman.

The sounds of her muscles tearing and bones cracking as she changed put my teeth on edge, and I couldn't even imagine how painful the process was for her. Thankfully, the whole change only took about fifteen seconds.

Once the sounds of the change had stopped, I turned, and Bree was in her standing hybrid Werepanther form. It always surprised me how, in this lethal-looking form, she stood at 6'6" when her normal human height was only 5'3".

"Blue, you and Olivia take point, since you both have the best night vision," I said. "Stella and I will follow, and Bree will guard our backs. We have plenty of time before dawn, so take it nice and easy, and stay alert. I have no idea whether the demon will have planted traps or warning tripwires around wherever it is hiding."

They all nodded, and I handed the tracking arrow to Olivia, so she could lead us to the demon. This also kept Blue free to look for traps.

Blue opened a shadow portal, and we all went through. We emerged in the middle of lightly wooded area that was pitch black. Thankfully, the road way we had been on hadn't been well-lit, and it didn't take too long for my eyes to adjust.

We had barely begun moving toward the demon when two blacked-out helicopters came in fast and low over top of us. They blew by in seconds, and then, after a bit, the low engine noises disappeared.

"Hold up. I am pretty sure that was GRC13 arriving on scene. What do you want to do?" I asked.

Even in the darkness, I could see the looks of disappointment on Olivia, Blue, and Stella's faces. I had no idea what Bree was feeling—in her Werepanther form, her face held its usual snarling feline expression—but I expected she wasn't happy either.

"If they are an elite team, then we should watch them from a distance. There might be tactics we can use ourselves going forward," said Blue.

I knew GRC13 wouldn't be overjoyed to have an audience, but Blue had a point; seeing an elite team do a takedown would be enlightening. As long as we kept well back and out of the way, it shouldn't be a big deal. They were also costing us $1.5 million by taking down this demon, so I figured we should get something for our hard work in tracking it down.

"Agreed, but we need to make sure we keep well out of their way," I said.

They all agreed, and we continued our march through the dark and silent woods. By my estimate, we were a couple of kilometers out from the demon's position on our map. That distance on good terrain should only take about twenty minutes to cover, but with Stella and me stumbling through a wooded area at night, our progress was going to be much slower.

Ten minutes later, we found the helicopters parked in a clearing to our left. The engines were off, and both birds were silent. I could see the pilot's and copilot's outlines in the faint reddish glow of the instrument lights. We moved on from there and kept heading for the demon.

I finally caught sight of a multicolored aura in the distance. It was half red, with two large chunks of green and brown, and two slivers of yellow and blue. That meant the person was a mage whose primary magic was Fire-based with decent Earth and nature magic and the barest trace of Air and Water/Ice. A Fire mage was an odd choice for going after a demon, as they were immune to fire. For an elite team, I wasn't impressed so far by their choices. I hoped the other Enhanced members of GRC13 were better suited.

We approached the area cautiously and ended up hiding behind a cluster of trees that were a good 300 feet from the nearest GRC13 officer. The nearest member of GRC was human, as there was no aura around him. He was hunched over a low tree branch, peering down the scope of a large sniper rifle. He was hard to see from this distance, but the glowing silver-and-white "POLICE" on the back of his black tactical gear stood out clearly in the night.

About 500 feet from us, there was a dark and rundown log cabin in the center of a small clearing. As GRC13 seemed to be moving directly toward it, I assumed that was where the demon was hiding out.

The mage I'd spotted earlier was fifty feet to the left of the sniper and a touch closer to the cabin as well. At least they were smart enough to keep him back; his Fire magic wouldn't be that useful in the initial action. I didn't doubt, though, that his Earth and nature skills would be useful in this upcoming fight.

I caught three other auras closer to the cabin and examined them with interest. There was a rainbow-colored one, which meant fae, with a green-and-brown outline—therefore, a wood elf. Wood elves weren't any stronger than a human, but they were exceptionally nimble and quick. They were also adept at bows and swords, and usually had innate magic that was usually Earth- and nature-related. I hoped the elf's blade and arrow tips were silver or at least silver-edged. I wasn't sure how good an elf would be at taking down a demon, but with his speed, he could be effective if used the right way.

The next aura was purple, so it was a Were. The green-and-brown outline told me it was a Werebear. The aura was a good six inches in size, which meant this person had been a Werebear for about forty years. He was also in an upright hybrid form like Bree was. Werebears were exceptionally tough and strong, and could take and dish out a lot of punishment. This was the best anti-demon fighter I'd seen so far.

The last aura had me puzzled, as it was orange, which meant it was part of the Super class, but it had an outline of grey and gold—I had no idea what that meant. The Super class was an odd one, as a number of their members had unique powers, which made it hard to get a read on some of them. There were common ones like Tanks, fliers, and speedsters, but a lot of them had odd powers. I had met a Super once whose only power was to make it rain, but the rain would only cover her and about eight feet around her. Other than watering a garden, it was a pretty useless power. Probably a good 80 percent of the Super class were like Rain Girl and had odd powers that really weren't much use in combat. I only hoped that this Super was one of the 20 percent who had a useful power.

The Werebear was at the head of the group, carefully approaching the foreboding cabin. Behind the Werebear, there was a human officer, and he looked to be carrying a grenade launcher.

The remaining eight members were in pairs in a diamond formation directly behind the Werebear and the grenade-launcher guy. The wood elf and the unknown Super were paired together on the left edge of the diamond.

The Werebear stopped about fifteen feet from the front door of the cabin. He crouched and held up a massive paw. The entire approaching team got lower and froze. He slowly lowered his arm and then nodded his massive head. The officer with the grenade launcher stepped to the side of the Werebear, lifted the launcher, and fired.

I heard a faint *pop* and then the sound of glass shattering as the grenade smashed through the lone front window of the cabin. I turned my head away from the cabin and closed my eyes at the last second—I knew what was coming.

There was a massively loud *bang*, and a bright light lit up the forest a moment later. I heard Liv, Stella, and Blue cursing as their night vision was suddenly disrupted by the flashbang going off. Bree growled behind us, as well, at the bright light.

I turned my head back and opened my eyes. The assault team charged for the front door of the cabin, and there was another loud crash as the Werebear blew through the front entrance of the cabin like the wooden door was made of tissue paper.

Out of the corner of my eye, I caught the sniper dropping to the forest floor, and I figured he had gone prone to find a better firing position than the low tree branch he had been using. I wondered why he hadn't done that before the assault.

The rest of the team charged into the cabin, and shots started ringing out inside the small structure. I wasn't shocked to see them going in hot; no one in their right mind would try to capture or arrest a full demon.

"Can you guys see anything?" I asked over my shoulder as I continued watching the action in front of me.

"Sort of," "Mostly," and, "Barely" were the three answers I got in reply.

My attention was pulled toward the mage, as his aura suddenly went out, and there seemed to be some sort of black haze surrounding the area he'd been standing in a moment ago. At first, I figured the mage had cast some sort of invisibility spell, but then I realized that even if he had, I would have still been able to see his aura. The black haze began moving toward the cabin, and then I saw the crumpled form of the mage lying on his front, lifeless on the ground, and I knew what had happened.

Chapter 11

Friday, April 14

"Zack, I smell human blood," said Olivia in a worried voice.

"We have a problem—" I started to say when the screams began in the cabin. "The demon wasn't in the cabin; it was out in the woods. It has killed the mage and the sniper who were outside, and now it's in the cabin, hitting the rest of GRC13."

"We have to help them!" said Stella.

Olivia had already turned toward the cabin and was about to go rescue them.

"Freeze!" I said in a firm tone. "We will help them, but rushing in piecemeal is just going to get more people killed." At that, I got nods from the team.

I took a deep breath to calm myself. "We are going to do this by the numbers. Stella, when I am done, change and take point. Olivia, Blue, and I will follow, and Bree will watch our backs. I have no idea whether or not that cabin has a back exit. I don't want the demon doing to us what it did to GRC13. Stella, when you get to the cabin, tear down the side to the right of the doorway to open up the cabin. We aren't going in; fighting in that tight a space favors the demon. Once the wall is gone, Olivia, Blue, and I will open up with our Nerf guns. The holy water will hurt the demon, and hopefully, that will cause it to flee or come out after us. If it comes after us, we stick to the plan we had last night: Stella is the main point of attack, and the rest of us hit and run, got it?"

They all nodded. Stella's small form was instantly replaced by her hideous-but-powerful Hyde form. She turned and began lurching toward the cabin and the screams. Sadly, those screams were a good sign; it meant there were still people alive in there. I clutched my Nerf gun and followed after the three of them. I could hear and feel Bree's hot breath behind me.

As we walked past the dead mage, I looked down and saw him staring lifelessly back at me from a head that had been twisted all the way around to his back. I shuddered and shifted my focus forward.

Holding a toy gun filled with water wasn't making me feel really confident about our chances in the next while. I thickened the air in front of me as a shield as a precaution in case the demon had any ranged surprises.

Stella didn't hesitate and gripped the right side of the door frame, then heaved. Sharp cracking noises filled the air as the wooden logs of the right side of the wall snapped like toothpicks, and with a grunt, Stella tossed the one-time wall away.

The cabin's interior looked like it had been painted blood red, and there were several still-and-broken bodies littered around its small interior. Some of the bodies were moving, so at least some of them were alive. In the center of the room stood a black-scaled demon, and its eyes glowed red back at us.

It locked eyes with me and smiled, showing off its fangs briefly, until all three of us fired our Nerf guns. Three long streams of harmless-looking water shot toward the demon, but when they hit, they were anything but harmless. Its matte-black scales smoked and melted like candle wax wherever the holy water hit. A red pulsing glow appeared in areas where the water had done the most damage.

The demon hissed and threw its right arm out in our direction. The next thing I knew, I was flying through the air with the rest of my team. It had used its telekinetic power to toss us back. My air shield didn't do a damn thing against the wall of force that hit us.

The move caught me by surprise, and I lost my Nerf gun as I tumbled backward. The mental blast tossed us a good sixty feet, and it was a minor miracle that none of us hit any of the trees we went sailing by. I called on my Air power and used it to cushion our falls back to Earth.

We got back to our feet. Olivia and Blue had also lost their Nerf guns, but both drew their swords. Bree's Were form nimbly popped back upright, and Stella and I were the last to get to our feet. The demon stepped out from the cabin and into the clearing out front.

"Everyone alright?" I asked.

A grunt and growl from Stella and Bree respectively, then a nod from Blue let me know they were fine.

Olivia was the only one who actually spoke. "I'm good, but it is time for the demon to meet Mister Slicey!" She didn't even pause before blurring away at top speed with her sword out in front of her.

"Hustle, people. Let's back up the crazy vampire," I said as I lifted myself into the air at top speed.

Flying was faster than running, and I didn't want Olivia taking on that thing alone. I knew Blue, Bree, and Stella would be right behind us.

Olivia flashed by and lopped off its right arm just above the elbow. The demon screamed in pain. Thick black fluid streamed out of the wound, and where the blood touched the forest floor, it sizzled from the contact of the acid-like blood.

I was just thinking, *You go, girl!* when Olivia made her first mistake of the night: She stopped dead about ten feet past the demon instead of staying at top speed, then turned back to go at it again.

The demon recovered almost instantly and lifted its left hand, telekinetically tossing Olivia back into a tree. She crashed hard, but somehow remained standing against the trunk. Her sword fell lifelessly from her hands and hit the ground. To my amazement, the sword shot from the ground and spun, then launched itself blade-first at Olivia. She grunted as the sword went point-first through her chest and buried itself into the tree, pinning her like a butterfly on a display board.

"*NO*!" I cried out and was close enough to fire an arc of lightning at the demon.

The stench of ozone filled the air, and bluish-white jagged arcs of lightning reached out for the demon. It must have sensed them coming, and it jumped out of the way. As it landed and glared at me, it then made a hand gesture as I flew past. An unseen force shot me out of my flight path, and I spun off and went shoulder-first into a sturdy tree. My right shoulder shattered like glass, and white-hot pain flashed through my mind. The agony overwhelmed everything else. I fell in a heap and groaned at the base of the tree.

Why did it have to be another shoulder injury? I thought as another hot poker of pain radiated out from it.

Déjà vu hit me as a flaming sword flashed out of the darkness when Blue stepped out of the shadows, taking her best shot at the demon. The last time I had been lying on a floor with a broken shoulder, Blue's flaming sword had saved the day by decapitating a vampire master from the shadows. This time, however, she missed. The demon nimbly ducked out of the way and managed to keep its head attached to his shoulders.

The demon flicked its hand at Blue, and she flew back and disappeared with a hard crash inside the cabin.

A deep, menacing growl split the night, and Bree's midnight-dark Werepanther form leapt out of the air and tackled the demon. Her claws and teeth flashed as she viciously raked the demon's prone form for all she was worth. Its toxic blood splashed out and over her, and began eating away at her fur. Bree squealed in pain but didn't even pause in her attack; she continued tearing away at the demon, despite the obvious pain.

A scaled hand shot out and grabbed Bree's Werepanther form by the neck, lifting her away from its body. Remarkably, after all the damage she had inflicted, the demon held Bree's 300-pound hybrid form up as if she weighed nothing.

"You will die slowly for that, vermin," hissed the demon in a gravelly voice filled with menace.

It violently shook Bree and squeezed her neck tighter. Her blue eyes bulged out from her fur-covered face, and she desperately clawed at the hand and arm holding her.

I tried to get up to help and almost screamed at the crippling pain in my shoulder. I stopped moving and just stayed still against the tree I was leaning against, praying for my shoulder to go numb. This was my worst nightmare: My teammates were getting hurt, and I couldn't do anything to stop it.

A tree crashed to the ground nearby, and heavy, lumbering footsteps thumped closer, which had to be Stella in her Hyde form joining the party.

The demon whipped Bree toward Stella. Stella brought her massive arm up as if to swat the Were missile away, but then, at the very last second, realized it was Bree and took the impact. Both crashed down in a tangled heap to the ground.

The demon turned toward me, and more than half its body was showing the red glow its true form gave off under the damaged areas of its shell. It paused for a moment, shimmered, and shrank about two inches in height, but it had completely regrown its right arm. Thankfully, the rest of the damage was still showing.

"Zack Stevens, I'd hoped you'd be one of the people hunting me. Any chance Ray Dunham and his team are nearby? I would dearly love to say hi to Benny again," taunted the demon.

Having it know my name was a bit disconcerting, to say the least, but then the rest of its words clicked into place. This must be the same demon that had possessed Benny for six months. Its master must have rewarded it with a true form here on Earth for a job well done.

"I will leave your corpse as a greeting card for Ray and his team," said the demon as it stalked toward me.

A growl and heavy footsteps began heading toward us, but I knew Stella and Bree wouldn't make it in time. I called on my power and started building up one last desperate charge. It was time to find out how good my lightning would be.

A red laser dot danced across the demon's chest. I smiled as the steady thrum of a submachine gun firing started up from the cabin. The demon's body jerked and twitched as the rounds slammed home.

A blue glow surrounded the demon, and it teleported out. I sighed in relief and let go of the power I'd been building up.

Chapter 12

Friday, April 14

Two large forms stopped in front of me, and I was never as happy to see Stella's ugly mug and Bree's fur-covered form as I was at that moment. I did, however, look at Bree in concern; the demon's acidic blood had done horrific damage to her Were form. The area around her muzzle, the flesh and fur, had complete disappeared down to the bone. Her hands were bloody and raw, and she was missing clumps of fur all over her body. Yet even I was assessing her damage, I noticed she was starting to heal. I swore, next to her endless appetite, her healing ability was the most impressive thing about her being a Were.

Stella held out her massive hand to me; I nodded and steeled myself as I reached up with my working arm. I cried out in agony when she lifted me to my feet and, for a moment, thought I'd black out from the pain. Stella held me upright, and after a few seconds, I was able to stand on my own.

"Let's go check on Liv and Blue," I said through clenched teeth as my shoulder throbbed again.

Bree took point, and we headed for the tree Olivia was pinned to. Thankfully, she was fairly alert and seemed more annoyed than hurt.

"Mister Slicey needs to be more careful about who he slices," giggled Olivia as a line of blood leaked from her mouth. Her lower front was covered in blood that was leaking from the sword stuck in the middle of her stomach. It was obvious she had lost a lot of blood.

Stella reached for the sword, and I motioned for her to stop.

"We need to think this out. Liv is going to lose even more blood when we remove that sword."

Vampires were pretty durable: Give them blood, and they would heal from pretty much anything. Stella was in the best shape of all of us, but thanks to the changes Hyde potion made to her DNA, she wasn't a good donor for Liv. Bree had given blood to Liv before, but with Bree's damage, I didn't want to weaken her anymore. That meant I was the best choice. My shoulder was toast, but I hadn't lost any blood.

"Here is what we are going to do: I will get closer to Liv, and then on three, Stella, pull the sword free. Bree, once the sword is out, press your hand hard against the wound to slow the bleeding and keep Liv against the tree. Liv, once the sword is out, feed from the left side of my neck, but do not touch my right shoulder area, okay?"

They all nodded, and I stepped right up against Liv so my left side was pressed against hers. I counted to three, and then Stella jerked the sword free. Liv gasped in pain. I felt Bree's hand press against the wound, and I grunted as sharp fangs buried themselves hard into my neck. Liv moaned happily as she drank from me, and I was praying she only took enough to fix herself and didn't drain me completely.

After what was probably only twenty seconds or so—but felt much longer—she lifted her mouth slightly then licked my neck. I knew that vampire saliva contained healing agents, and the area tingled, but there wasn't any pain. On the other hand, my neck could be on fire and it would have paled against the agony in my shoulder at that moment.

I was, however, a touch lightheaded, but Olivia was back to her usual perky self.

"Oh wow! I can see why Sarah was willing to trade sex for your blood. That was super yummy, and my whole body is tingling," said Liv.

Bree moved back, and I also stepped back from Olivia, who practically bounced off the tree. Stella held out the bloody blade to Liv, who took it and, after wiping it on her pant leg, sheathed it behind her back again. Stella headed for the cabin, and we followed. Or at least, I tried to, but I stumbled and would have fallen if Olivia hadn't caught me. She snuggled up to my left side and slipped her right arm around my waist, and I put my left arm over her shoulder. We walked together, with her supporting me.

When we reached the cabin, Blue was there talking to a large, pale, hairy naked bald man who had an MP5 hanging off his shoulder by its straps. The man was a couple inches taller than me and easily had a hundred pounds on me due to his extremely well-muscled form. I briefly wondered who the hell this guy was and why he was standing nude in the middle of the woods, but his Werebear aura eventually clued me in. Blood loss was a bitch—but I still felt pretty stupid for taking so long to notice his aura.

Bree growled, and she and the man locked eyes for a few moments. To my amazement, Bree lowered her gaze first and submitted to him. I also noted that there seemed to be less bodies in the cabin than earlier.

"You, comrade, are Blue team leaasder?" asked the man in a jovial deep voice with a thick Russian accent.

"Blue team leader" sounded like something from Star Wars, and the Russian accent confused me for a moment too. After a moment, I realized that he was asking if I was *Blue's* team leader, and I nodded.

"I am Dmitri Petrov with GRC13. Thank you for coming to aid. Blue has transported my teammates to base to get healing."

That explained the lack of wounded in the cabin. "Was that you who just blasted the shit out of the demon?"

"*Da*, that was me," said Dmitri.

"Then you have *my* thanks, as well, as that drove the demon off."

He shrugged and added, "Your shoulder is injured. Come to base with me, and healer will fix."

Free healing would have been nice, but there were several GRC13 members who were worse off than me, and they would be first in line. I figured I'd check with Marion and see if she was free; with her, I would get first priority.

My phone was in my right jacket pocket, and I asked Olivia to carefully take it out and call and talk to Marion.

"Your offer is kind," I told Dmitri, "but I am sure your healers have more important things to take care of at this moment. I am curious, though, how a Russian became a part of GRC13."

"At end of Soviet era, I had ... how you say ... falling up with KGB and left Mother Russia. I was outside Soviet area at time, and there were Canadian peacekeepers in area. I walked to their camp and claimed asylum. They brought me back here, and I became proud Canadian. All I have ever done was be soldier and was recruited by EIRT. I am policeman now thirty years. Good weather here, just like Mother Russia, and good hockey, too, but Russian hockey better," laughed Dmitri.

"Marion is available and waiting for you to arrive," said Olivia as she tucked my phone back into my pocket.

"Dmitri, my shoulder is killing me, and I would like to get healed. My Were friend is probably hungry, and my vampire companion probably needs more blood. Do you need us for anything else?" I asked.

"Da, superiors will want to talk to you. Can wait until tomorrow. Give me phone number. I will call you," said Dmitri.

I started to give him my number, but he held up his hand for me to wait. He grabbed a flat piece of wood from the floor and changed his finger into a razor-sharp bear claw, then nodded at me to continue. He carved my number into the wood. That claw dug half-inch grooves into the hardwood like it was butter.

"I'm sorry for the loss of your companions," I said as I looked around one last time before leaving.

I counted four bodies in here, and with the mage and the sniper out in the woods, that brought the total to six, which was half the team. Add to that the five others who were alive but injured, and tonight had taken a terrible toll on GRC13.

"*Spasibo*. I shall miss Glee," said Dmitri, staring at the broken and mangled corpse of the wood elf in the corner.

"Before I go, can I ask one question?"

"Da."

"I know you have four Enhanced Individuals on a GRC13 team. I know about you, the mage, and the wood elf. Who was the fourth?"

Dmitri gave me a hard look, and I realized I'd slipped up. Dmitri had been in his Were form, and there was no mistaking a wood elf, but the mage had never used his powers—therefore, I shouldn't have known he was a mage. I also realized that under Dmitri's large, friendly exterior, there was a keen mind.

"Magda was our fourth. She can manipulate metal—make it stronger or weaker, call it to her, and reshape it."

That explained the greyish metal color on her outline. It also hit me that Magda wouldn't have been that useful out in the middle of these woods with little to no metal around.

There hadn't been a good mix of Enhanced Individuals for this mission. The Fire mage and the metal manipulator would have been next to useless; a wood elf in an enclosed environment would give up its biggest advantage of speed. Dmitri, as a Werebear, was probably the only one suited to this mission. I hoped the alternate GRC13 team was better suited for the next time they took on the demon.

"Would you like Blue's help for transportation for the others?" I asked, gesturing to the bodies.

"*Nyet*. I will carry to helicopters. Go, get your shoulder healed. I call you tomorrow."

We said our goodbyes and stepped through the shadows, then popped out into the lab. The lab as the first stop made sense so that Liv and Bree could get food. Blue then gently grabbed me back into the shadows, and she and I emerged in Marion's hallway.

I knocked on Marion's door and almost laughed. Judging by her clothes, she had been in bed before Olivia's call. She was wearing a long tie-dye cotton nightgown and pink bunny slippers. Her long grey hair was all over the place; usually, she wore it in a braid. Her keen silver eyes were magnified by her glasses, and she studied me with concern. Her gaze focused on my busted shoulder.

"C'mon, let's get you fixed up," she said, shaking her head at me.

"Zack, call me when you need a lift back, okay?" asked Blue.

I nodded, and Blue disappeared into the shadows as I entered Marion's apartment. She led me to a chair and had me sit down. I gritted my teeth as she reached for my shoulder, but she only touched the area outside the damage. A moment later, I sighed in relief as the whole area went numb.

"I deadened the nerves around the wound just long enough so you can get your coat off without passing out on me," said Marion with a smile.

I took off my coat and tossed it on the table beside us. My T-shirt had to come off next, which was going to be a bitch, but Marion returned with a large pair of scissors and said, "How attached are you to that T-shirt?"

"Not enough to try and take it off," I said. In my line of work, I had long since stopped wearing higher-price clothes. Most of my clothes were from Mark's Work Warehouse, and this particular T-shirt had probably cost me less than $10. Replacing the shirt for that type of money made it a no-brainer.

Marion went to work and cut the right side of the T-shirt from the sleeve to the neck, opening up the whole area where my broken shoulder was.

"Damn, Zack, you really did a number on that shoulder. This is going to hurt—and going to cost you," said Marion, shaking her head again.

An hour later, we were both exhausted—me from the pain of Marion fixing me, and her from the amount of magic she had used to fix me up. The area tingled, but my right arm and shoulder were both fully working again.

"The area is going to be tender for the next couple days. Make sure you eat and sleep a lot, as your body is going to need it. Take it easy on your shoulder during that time as well. I will email you my invoice," said Marion.

I thanked her and called Blue for a ride. In less than a minute, I was back at the lab. The healing and the night had taken a lot out of me, and I was starving. Thankfully, Bree had already eaten, and the Food-O-Tron was free. I ordered myself a hamburger and fries, and once they were done, I used the machine to get a Coke as well.

I joined the girls at the table. Bree's hair was wet, but I was happy to see that none of the damage she had taken in her Were form was showing. The skin around her jaw and hands, though, was a pinker color than the rest of her skin.

"I took a shower to get the stench of sulfur off me. How's the shoulder?"

"Good. I'm supposed to take it easy, but it should be fine. How is everyone else?" I asked, looking around the table.

"Between your blood and a couple of pints from the Food-O-Tron, I am back to being my usual perfect self," said Liv with a smile and playful pose.

"I have cracked ribs, but they will be healed tonight while I rest," said Blue.

"I didn't take any damage," added Stella.

"My skin itches a bit, but other than that, I am good," finished Bree, stealing one of my fries.

"Well, we fought a demon and lived. That, to me, is one in the 'win' column," I said.

The ladies all nodded at this but still seemed down. I couldn't blame them; tonight, six good people had died, and the demon was still out there. On the upside, though, we had hurt it some. It probably had already healed the damage we had done, but that meant it would use up some of its energy. The one weakness demons did have when on Earth was they couldn't get any stronger while here. They could eat human hearts and blood, but that only sustained their current levels, and the energy they gained from the killing was sent back to their sponsor in Hell. That meant every time we hurt it, it weakened a little. The problem was, they were so damn powerful, all of tonight's effort might have been akin to scratching the paint off a Sherman tank.

"Zack, I'm sorry. I didn't fully believe you when you mentioned how strong a full demon really was. I figured there were five of us and that we'd be able to handle it with no issues. We hit it hard tonight, and it just shrugged off the worst we could do to it," said Bree.

She looked down at the floor and went quiet. I could sense the doubt and worry coming off her by her body language. A small part of me itched to say, "I told you so," but I pushed that down. We were at a pivotal moment here, and there was only one thing to do. "Do you want to vote on continuing to take down this demon?"

Bree nodded, and I looked to the rest of them. Stella gave a small nod, and Blue and Olivia both shrugged.

"All right. All in favor of continuing to go after the demon, raise your hands," I said and put my hand up instantly.

It was funny: Until tonight, I had wanted nothing more than to go hunt pixies or something else instead, but now it was personal. This demon knew me, Ray, and his team, and there was no way I was going to ignore it now, as I feared it would come after us. I wasn't going to spend the rest of my days glancing in fright over my shoulder. I also didn't have a lot of faith in the alternate GRC13 team doing any better than the first one. If the best Canada had to offer couldn't take this thing down, then it looked like we might be the only ones who could stop it. Whether we'd survive taking it down was a whole other matter.

Olivia's hand went up first after mine, and she said, "Mr. Slicey and I need some payback."

I smiled at this and turned my attention to Stella and Blue. Stella seemed torn, but then reluctantly put her hand up, and I wasn't shocked to see Blue follow her lead. I shifted my gaze to Bree, who was looking at me like I was crazy, but then shrugged and raised her hand too.

Bree frowned and asked, "What the hell? You have been trying to get us to move on to another bounty the whole time, and now, after we get our asses kicked, you want to hunt this thing?"

I explained my reasons to her, including how it was the same demon that had possessed Benny, and then added, "This thing has killed eleven people and needs to be stopped. It also has a $1.5 million bounty on it. It wouldn't surprise me if, after tonight, EIRT either revokes that bounty or ups it, and I'm guessing it will be upped. $2 million to $2.5 million is a good chunk of change. That is a lot of pixies we'd need to hunt to make up that kind of money."

The mood around the table had picked up. I watched shoulders straighten and spines stiffen, and knew a sense of purpose and determination had set in.

"Since we are going to keep hunting this demon, let's look at what went right tonight and what we can do better the next time we hit this thing," said Blue.

We spent the next hour breaking down the fight and analyzing it and our mistakes. By the end of that hour, though, I was yawning—and wasn't the only one. Blue shadow-traveled us all back to the house, and at that point, she, Stella, and I headed up for bed while Bree stayed up to keep our sunlight-sensitive friend company.

Chapter 13

Saturday, April 15

The next morning, there was a text on my phone from Dmitri, stating that I needed to come to GRC13's base to be debriefed. After a quick shower and breakfast, I had Blue transport me out to the base. She and Stella were going out shopping for supplies, since all three of our holy water Nerf guns had gotten broken last night. She was going to get replacements, and Stella had an idea for a weapon she wanted to make. This intrigued me, and I asked for details, but Stella just smiled and shook her head, and said it was a surprise.

Before I could probe anymore, Blue said, "Call us when you need a lift," and they disappeared back into the shadows.

After popping into that crime scene a few days before, I thought it would be best not to have Blue warp us into the middle of a secure government base. Instead, she dropped us in the woods outside the base. I searched around to get my bearings and could just make out the guardhouse to the base around a hundred feet to the east, and I headed for it.

As I stepped out of the woods, the troops manning the gates were on full alert. I assumed they had either spotted me in between the trees or had sensors in the woods. There were more automatic weapons being pointed in my general direction than I was generally comfortable with; my ideal number of big-ass guns being pointed at me was zero. The 5.56-mm automatic rifles the soldiers were carrying didn't concern me too much, as I had instinctively thickened the air around me to stop those from hitting. The scary-looking .50-caliber machine gun on the back of the light-armored vehicle parked beside the main gate, though, was another matter.

I slowly put my hands up to hopefully show I meant no harm and yelled, "My name is Zack Stevens! I am here to see Dmitri Petrov!"

Dmitri's name instantly had an effect, as a couple of the soldiers lowered their rifles slightly, and I was overjoyed to notice the gunner on the light-armored vehicle relax his grip on the trigger of the .50 caliber a bit.

"Keep your hands up where we can see them and approach the main gate slowly. Do you have any weapons on your person?" asked the sergeant in command of the gate.

I shook my head and said clearly that I had no weapons. The sergeant nodded and made a "Come here" motion with his hand. I examined the sergeant's uniform closer and saw "Davis" on the name-patch on the front. As I almost reached the main gate, Sergeant Davis made a "Stop" motion with his hand, and a corporal came forward and patted me down. He removed my iPhone and my keys from my coat. He examined the keys for a moment and then put them back in my pocket but kept the phone. He stepped back and gave the sergeant a nod.

"You can put your hands down, but please don't make any sudden movements. This base is a restricted area, so cameras and smartphones are prohibited. We will return your phone when you leave. Corporal Mathis will write you up a claim ticket. We have contacted Mr. Petrov, and he will be up shortly to escort you onto the base."

The corporal headed off to the main gatehouse, and the rest of the soldiers, except for the sergeant, resumed their posts. Thankfully, none of the guns were pointed in my direction anymore. I released the air shield.

The gatehouse was impressive and formidable. A couple of feet in front of my current position, there were raised three-inch metal tire spikes, and fifteen feet beyond that, there was an imposing-looking three-foot tall retractable thick steel barricade. There were two gatehouses on either side of the barricade with solid steel doors and barred glass. I had no doubt the glass was bulletproof. The light-armored vehicle was parked beside the right gatehouse. On top of each gatehouse, there were half-height sandbag-covered walls with a couple of soldiers behind them. There were at least three dark Plexiglas bubbles that contained CCTV cameras and sensors that I could see—and there were probably many more I couldn't see.

On either side of the gatehouses, a pair of ten-foot-high metal fences ran from the entrances as far as the eye could see. The inner fence that was five feet back from the outer one had several black-and-yellow lightning-bolt signs, indicating it was electrified. I could sense the juice coming off it from where I was standing.

There were several signs on the outer fences warning that this was a secure government location and that trespassers found on the grounds would be shot on sight.

Beyond the main gate, there was a decent-size parking lot that was half full and a large aircraft hangar behind the lot. There were three Blackhawk helicopters sitting just outside the hangar on the edge of the runway, but other than that, there wasn't much to see. I wondered if the main building on the base was behind the large hangar and that was why I couldn't see it.

The sergeant's voice pulled me from my musings. "Can I ask why you were walking through the woods?"

"My teammate is a shadow-traveler. She can reach anywhere in the world instantly via the shadows. It is quicker and easier than driving. We picked the woods, figuring that appearing in the middle of your base might not be well received."

The base was a good fifty kilometers outside Ottawa and in the middle of nowhere. Driving here from Hamilton would have taken at least six hours—more if the traffic around Toronto was bad, and it usually was.

" 'Teammate,' eh? You a superhero or something?" asked Sergeant Davis with an amused smile.

I was about to answer when I spied Dmitri's large and imposing form emerge from the right gatehouse, with the corporal who had taken my phone in tow.

"Comrade Zack, good to see you, my friend!"

I had only met Dmitri less than twenty-four hours ago, but despite that, I too was glad to see him again—especially now that he was dressed. He was wearing a loose-fitting grey track suit and flip-flops, with a lanyard around his neck with his photo ID on it.

I shook hands with Dmitri.

The corporal handed me my own lanyard that was bright pink and had "Visitor" written on it in large black letters, plus a receipt for my phone.

"Captain and director are anxious to talk to you, but both are tied up for a bit. I will give tour," said Dmitri.

He led us into the right-side gatehouse. Inside, there were a couple soldiers monitoring screens. There was an elevator toward the back of the gatehouse and an exit door. The elevator had a keypad and a fingerprint scanner where you would normally find a button. It dawned on me that's why I couldn't see the main building I had been expecting: The main base was underground.

Dmitri, though, kept going, and we left the gatehouse via the rear exit door. From outside the gatehouse, the hangar didn't look that impressive.

Once we crossed the parking lot, though, I realized it was much bigger than I had thought. It was actually three large hangars connected lengthwise from the road. I'd only seen the side of the first hangar.

I was almost nose-blind, as my sense of smell was terrible, but even I picked up the faint smell of aviation fuel in the air, which was getting stronger as we approached the hangar.

"My comrades who weren't killed last night made full recovery thanks to healers. We are down half our people on team—and offline until replacements are found. At least there is still team, and I thank you and *your* team for that. How is shoulder?" said Dmitri as we walked.

I actually had forgotten about it and moved it around to test it. "Tender, but fully functional."

"That is good. I am sad comrade Blue not joining us."

I stumbled for a moment when it dawned on me that Dmitri was attracted to Blue.

Dmitri looked at me with concern and added, "She is not your woman?"

I stopped walking completely at that point, as I needed to take this in. I had never even remotely thought of Blue as a "woman" and as a possible romantic partner—probably because she was a blue-skinned alien with a tail and a mouthful of pointed shark-like teeth, and towered a good five inches above me. I stepped back in my thoughts of Blue and pictured her again. She did have a lovely feminine figure, and her purple eyes were both exotic and attractive. She was honorable, loyal, and determined in whatever she did. She had a good sense of humor, though it was a little strange at times what she found amusing. Looking at her from Dmitri's point of view, the height wasn't an issue, as he was as tall as she was. She was sturdy and strong, so Dmitri's large size and strength wouldn't be an issue for her. The pointed teeth probably didn't bother him, either, since he turned in a freaking bear. All in all, Blue had a lot to offer for him.

I shook my head and said, "She is not my woman, just a friend. You like Blue?"

Dmitri's face lit up with a smile. "Da, she is all woman and all warrior. I would like to make many beautiful blue babies with her. She is single?"

"She is single, but maybe start with coffee first." Dmitri laughed at this, and I added, "I will mention to her that you would like to get to know her."

Dmitri was also probably grateful to Blue for shadow-traveling all his wounded teammates back to base to get immediate help. Blue's quick actions had probably saved the lives of at least two of the survivors.

Parts of the battle last night came rushing back and reminded me of one of the things that had been nagging at me about the assault: the makeup of the GRC13 team. Other than Dmitri, the other three Enhanced Individuals who had made up the team hadn't really been suited for taking down a demon in a forest. I wondered what the other GRC13 team's makeup was and decide this was a good time to ask.

"Eh? The other team has Werewolf, Water/Ice elemental, Tank, and mage. Why?" asked Dmitri.

"Is that mage a Fire mage, as well?" I said, ignoring Dmitri's question for the moment.

"Nyet. Earth, with Water/Ice as his secondary focus."

I stopped dead in my tracks, and Dmitri looked at me with concern. I said, "Why the hell wasn't *that* team sent?"

The second GRC13 team was almost designed to hunt a demon with that roster. Any Were could take and dish out a ton of damage, though I'd probably take Dmitri as a Werebear over the Werewolf. Werebears were stronger and could take more damage, but Werewolves had better speed, which meant I was just being picky. The Water/Ice elemental would be useful against a demon. A demon didn't normally feel the cold, but the extreme cold that an Ice elemental could produce would hurt it and slow it down. A Tank would be a perfect opponent for a demon, as there wasn't much it could do to hurt the Tank, and if the Tank got a hold of the demon, the Tank could do some awesome damage. A mage with Earth and Water/Ice spells would also be effective: an Earth golem spell, opening the ground under the demon, erecting stone walls to box it in, or Odin only knew what other useful battle spells the mage had.

Dmitri looked down, kicked a rock on the ground, and said, "Budget issues. Our team was on duty when call came in. If they used other team, like captain wanted, it would cost more in overtime pay. Director made call to use our team."

I clenched my fists and felt the vein in my right temple begin to throb. Fucking bureaucrats were always trying to save a shortsighted penny, which ended up costing much more in the long run. This director had probably managed to save a few bucks by using the team on duty, but six people were dead. The cost to train the replacements for those six would probably be in the millions.

I recalled that up to about seven years ago, the director of GRC13 had been promoted from within the ranks of GRC13, EIRT, or the RCMP. That had changed after a Native protest over a proposed pipeline that would have crossed Native lands had gone badly. Some of the Native protestors had been Weres, and when a couple of them had changed into their beast forms during clashes with police, GRC13 had been called in. As a few regular police officers had been injured in an earlier clash, GRC13 had come in hard and fast, and eleven protestors had been killed. An official inquiry had been held, and several recommendations had come out of that inquiry. One of them had been to appoint a civilian director for GRC13. The then-Conservative government had done just that. I assumed that the current director had probably been appointed shortly after the currently Liberal government had come to power two years ago.

Last night's fiasco had been a direct result of a civilian director being in charge. A director who had been promoted from within the ranks would have known the dangers that fighting a demon entailed and wouldn't have been trying to save a few pennies, risking the lives of his men and women in the field.

"You think bureaucracy bad here, you should see in Mother Russia," said Dmitri, as if sensing my thoughts.

In the end, I took a deep breath and exhaled, then tried to let it go. It was in the past, and what was done, was done. Nothing could change that now.

We reached a secure side door to the hangar, and Dmitri punched in a code, then placed his finger on the scanner. The red light above the pad changed to green, and a distinct *click* could be heard. Dmitri opened the door, and we entered the hangar.

I was staggered by the sheer size of the place, as on the outside there were three sets of large hangar doors, making it look like there were three separate hangars—but it was just one big hangar. There were two blacked-out Hercules transports just in front of us. The first one had one of its engine cowlings off, and there were three technicians working on it. At the far side of the giant hangar, there was a small Learjet parked in the corner. Even with the three planes in the hangar, it was less than a quarter full.

"Is this an RCMP base or a military base?" I asked as I spied a number of Canadian Armed Forces personnel walking around the hangar.

"Both. We share base since 1950s. Military handles security, but we handle any Enhanced Individuals that threaten base. All aircraft are maintained and piloted by Canadian Armed Forces. Outside, hangar, and first level underground are common area shared by both, but after that, they have own levels lower down, and we have ours."

As we walked deeper into the hangar, I pondered Dmitri's last statement. If this base had been built in the late forties or early fifties, I was willing to bet that it had been designed in case of a nuclear attack, as it was only fifty kilometers from Ottawa. I was also going to guess that deep underground, there were probably living quarters meant to house the prime minister and his cabinet. This would allow the government of Canada to continue in the event the unthinkable happened.

This shocked me a little. I knew the US government had underground bunkers for the government to retreat to in the event of a nuclear attack, but I had always assumed that Canada didn't. I had figured the cost of a hardened underground facility would have been too expensive for them to spend money on.

That was assuming, of course, I was right and that was what this place actually was. But the location and time period seemed right. Also, why would you waste the money to build everything underground if that hadn't been the purpose of this place?

As we walked across the puke-green-colored floor, I noticed that it had been painted over several times without stripping off the old paint first. I was starting to get a slight headache. Whether from frustration at the team selection earlier or the now-almost-overwhelming stench of aviation gas, I couldn't say, but figured it was probably both.

Dmitri stepped up in front of a small terminal that came up from the floor on a thick pole to about waist height. His large finger daintily punched in a code on the pad. For such a large, muscle-bound man, he was impressively quick and nimble when he wanted to be.

There was a deep hum of large machinery, and the floor under us started to vibrate slightly. A deep clunking sound echoed around the hangar. After a few seconds, the section of the floor we were standing on began to lower slowly into the ground. This was an elevator, like the aircraft elevator on a carrier.

After about five seconds, my eye level was lower than the original floor of the hangar. In front of me was a massive and solid-looking steel wall. The wall directly behind me was the same imposing steel. The side walls were reinforced concrete. We kept going down, and there was a good fifty feet of steel and concrete walls above us, until the shaft finally opened up into a cavernous underground room.

As the platform descended the last thirty feet in the chamber below, I had an awesome overview of the whole room. To the right was obviously the Canadian Armed Forces equipment, as there were four main battle tanks, a dozen light-armored vehicles, and eight heavy-duty transport trucks all parked in rows. The left side was the RCMP side; there were four police-marked cruisers, two marked SUVs, eight black unmarked SUVs (that I was used to seeing EIRT teams use), a large RCMP-logoed RV, and two armored assault vehicles with battering rams on the front. I also noticed, deeper in the RCMP side, there were half a dozen snowmobiles, two sport bikes, and two pickups that had been modified for off-road use.

There was a loud rumbling above us, and I glanced up and watched the two massive steel walls closing up. Just after the platform touched down, a loud resounding *boom* occurred when the two metal walls came firmly together, sealing us down here like in a tomb.

We stepped off the platform, and I noted the floor here was painted in the same awful green as the floors above, but with the walls they had opted to go with a dull-grey color instead. This chamber was probably half the size of the massive hangar above but was still impressive in its size.

The armed forces side had a bunch of techs working and maintaining four of the vehicles on their side, whereas the RCMP side was deserted and there wasn't a soul to be seen. Dmitri headed toward the RCMP side, and I followed quietly beside him.

"This is our vehicle storage area. We take other elevator to reach captain's office," said Dmitri.

Other than the occasional noise of hammers and power tools deep from the armed forces side, the only noise down here was the rhythmic *clip-clop* of Dmitri's flip-flops as we walked.

On the far wall of the chamber were two elevators. Dmitri stepped up to the left one and entered a code, then placed his finger on the scanner. A *ding* sound filled the air, and we stepped aboard the elevator. I noted that there were fifteen buttons on the elevator panel, but none of them were marked. Dmitri hit the middle one on the second-to-last row from the bottom. The car lurched alarming down for a moment, then steadied out to a more gradual descent.

I must have had a concerned look on my face, because Dmitri said, "No worries, my friend. Elevator is good. Been working for over fifty years. Besides, if it fails, neither of us be around to complain, da?"

He chuckled at this, which made me laugh too. His warm, deep bellow was infectious.

A vision of my deceased mother popped into my head as I started to sense a warm, fuzzy feeling in my being—somewhere in this complex was another Air elemental. That sensation had memories of my mother flooding back to me. She had been gone sixteen years, and there were times I could go weeks without thinking of her, but then something like this or a certain song playing would happen, and memories of her would come rushing back. The torrent of emotions hitting me was staggering, but I gritted my teeth and forced myself to focus on the here and now. I made a promise to myself to spend some time thinking about her when I was done with this bounty.

The ride down was surprisingly long, and I idly wondered just how deep underground this complex went. The comforting feeling of another Air elemental also got stronger with every passing second as we traveled down.

The base was pretty cool, but I probably would have been more impressed if I'd seen it before meeting my teammates and spending time in our own secret underground hideaway. This place had been built in the fifties, whereas Sir Reginald's mad-scientist laboratory had been built before the 1900s. Add in the Tesla coils, the interdimensional power tap, the Food-O-Tron, the walking automations cleaning his lab 24/7, and the rest of his invented goodies, and this place paled a little by comparison ...

The doors finally opened, and we stepped out into a long, wide hallway. The feeling I'd experienced in the elevator got stronger, so I asked, "Is there Air elemental on this level?"

"Da, the captain."

Learning this, I was more intrigued about our upcoming meeting. Other than Mom, the only other Air elemental I'd encountered since she'd passed had been a female assassin I'd taken down during my hero days. I had never asked my mother if the ability to see auras was an Air elemental trait or another power from our mixed genetic background.

I obviously wasn't going to ask an assassin, but a captain of GRC13 would be someone I might be willing to trust with the secret of my ability to see auras.

I took a moment to take in the hallway we found ourselves in. The walls had once been white but were now more of an off-yellow color, thanks to the nicotine stains. I rolled my eyes at the newer "No smoking" sign on the wall. Nice thought, but with decades of people smoking down here, it would take a lot more cleaning and paint to erase that history.

There was a picture of Queen Elizabeth the Second, but it was an earlier portrait, as she looked to be in her twenties, rather than the distinguished older matron I was used to seeing. On the opposite wall, there was a much newer portrait that had our young, Liberal prime minister's handsome smiling face on it. I was surprised the portrait didn't have him holding a smartphone and taking a selfie, as that would have been a more realistic painting of our PM in action. There were also a couple of large, dusty fake plants sitting against the walls. The carpet looked much newer than everything else, but it was your standard institutional-blue color that was only ever used in offices and didn't do much to improve things.

We proceeded down the hallway and passed a number of closed, unmarked wooden doors until Dmitri stopped at one on our left and opened it. I figured the lack of numbers on the elevator buttons and the unmarked doors were for security, to make life harder for intruders attacking this place. It made a certain kind of sense to me, but it must have made life brutal for rookies joining GRC13.

We enter a medium-size reception area that was sparsely furnished. There was a large, plain wooden desk with an older lady behind it who looked even more imposing than the armed gatehouse up above. She examined us critically with sharp, keen blue eyes peering above the bifocal glasses resting on her nose.

"Mr. Petrov, you are late, but the director hasn't arrived yet, and the captain is still busy, so I guess no harm is done. You and your companion can take a seat."

"Nice to see you, too, Agnes," said Dmitri with a put-on smile.

She rolled her eyes and *hrrphed* at us, then went back to typing and ignored us.

There were three cheap stainless-steel-frame armless black pleather chairs lined up against the wall that wouldn't have been out of place as a high school teacher's chair. Dmitri lowered his massive form onto the closest one to the captain's door and made it look like the chair had been meant for a small child. I grabbed one closer to the door we had come in from.

I soon got bored of sitting there doing nothing. I studied Agnes. With her dated hairstyle and conservative attire, she would have fit in nicely in a 1970s office typing pool. But while Agnes might be stuck in the '70s, her equipment wasn't. There was a modern and attractive-looking twenty-seven-inch flat-screen monitor on her desk and a Cisco IP phone. Her mouse and keyboard were both wireless. I wondered how long this equipment had been here and was willing to bet that it had replaced an old rotary phone and probably a monochrome CRT monitor or an electric typewriter. Governments and banks were funny that way: They were slow to replace equipment, but when they did, they ended up going top-of-the-line and going with cutting edge on technology.

The minutes ticked away, and I started getting restless and annoyed. I had no doubt that the director was playing office politics: "I am going to make you wait to show you how important my time and I are." I also had no doubt he or she would show up, offer an insincere apology for their tardiness, and name-drop someone from up above who had delayed them from this meeting.

As more time went by, my patience ran out, and I decided to have some fun. I slowly leaned over and tapped Dmitri on the leg when Agnes had her back to us for a second.

He looked at me with questioning look, and I winked at him, then said in a loud, clear voice, "Thanks for the porn link you sent me. I never would have imagined that such a petite lady could take that many men ..."

Dmitri's eyes went wide at this for a moment, and then he caught on and suppressed the grin that was coming to his face. "Da, she truly skilled and very flexible!"

I noted with amusement that the clicking of Agnes's typing speed had suddenly slowed right down. For the next ten minutes, Dmitri and I kept one-upping each other and getting more vulgar and graphic with each passing minute. The hardest part was not bursting out laughing. Toward the end, Agnes had stop typing completely, and I had no doubt she was hanging on our every word.

I had just finished a monologue describing a made-up site that featured four men and ample-chested 300-pound women moments before the director walked in. I was grateful for his arrival, as I was tired of waiting around, and if Dmitri had topped my last story, I'm not sure I would have been able to top his.

The director was a lean man of average height with glasses and was in his late forties or early fifties, with fair-colored hair that had noticeable amounts of grey creeping in along the temples. The tailored dark-grey suit with a patterned red tie and black shoes shined to within an inch of their lives made me feel underdressed in my jeans, T-shirt, spring jacket, and sneakers. His formal attire and mousey features made me think of an accountant, rather than the leader of Canada's most elite response teams.

"Mr. Petrov and Mr. Stephenson, sorry to have kept you both waiting," stated the director as he held his hand out to me.

The nasally, almost whining tone to his voice really didn't help dispel my "accountant" impression.

I got to my feet and shook his hand. "It's *Stevens*, not Stephenson, but please called me Zack."

"Very well, Zack, I am Robert Smyth, director of GRC13. I am afraid I won't be able to return the same informality, as it is either 'Director' or 'Director Smyth.' My apologies for my tardiness. My call with the RCMP commissioner went longer than I had planned for. Shall we join the captain and get started? Mr. Petrov, please wait out here, as you will be escorting Mr. Stevens off the base when we are done," said the director.

He headed for the captain's door, and Agnes added, "The captain is expecting you, sir. Please go right in."

The director didn't even break stride but did give the receptionist a nod of acknowledgement as he passed. Agnes smiled at him, and once he passed by her, she shot me a glare of disapproval when I went by. I smiled sweetly at her and followed the director into the office, and he closed the door behind us.

The instant impression I got from the captain's office was that he was a man buried in paperwork. There was a row of beige filing cabinets along the left wall, mountains of files on his desk, and organized piles of files on the credenza behind him and on the narrow table running the length of the right side of the office. There were pictures of his wife, kids, and grandkids on the right edge of his crowded desk. There was an engraved silver nameplate on the center of the large, polished wood desk that read "Captain Ben Cooper."

My attention was pulled quickly to Captain Cooper. I sensed him accessing and using his powers, and on instinct, I readied mine. I relaxed as I realized he was just using his Air powers to assist himself from his chair. This puzzled me for a moment until he stiffly walked around the desk to shake my hand. His left arm hung limply at his side, and it dawned on me that both it and his right leg were missing, as his oddly shaped yellow aura gave both of these issues away. There were prosthetics replacing both missing limbs.

The size of his aura was decent, but as it only came out about three inches from his body. I doubted he had command of both air and electricity like I did, and predicted he probably just had mastery over air.

Captain Cooper was a bald man in his early sixties. He was wearing a formal RCMP uniform that was slightly stretched at the seams around his midsection. He stood about six feet in height. His knowing blue eyes were the most striking feature about him; this was a man who had seen some terrible things in his career. I had no doubts that this man, even with his extensive injuries, was a formidable warrior.

He greeted the director first and then turned to me, smiled, and said, "Dmitri said your team was the only reason there still is a GRC13 Team A. I want to thank you deeply for coming to their assistance." His handshake was firm and confident but not crushing.

"I'm just sorry we didn't jump in sooner. You lost some good people out there."

He nodded solemnly and pointed toward the nearest empty chair in front of his desk. The director grabbed the other seat to my left, and the captain took his seat behind his desk again.

As soon as he was seated, the director said, "As you mentioned, we lost some well-trained individuals last night. This is second-worst loss of personnel in the history GRC13. We will be launching a more formal investigation into this incident. Team A is offline until the investigation is completed and they can be brought up to full strength again. For now, as you witnessed the events, we would like you to tell us in your own words what they did wrong out there."

The captain stiffened at the last part of the director's statement, and his whole head went a dark shade of ruddy pink. He was shaking slightly in rage but managed to hold his tongue.

I felt my temper flare as well. The one who had made the biggest mistake last night was sitting beside me. His decision to send Team

A and not spend the extra overtime pay to send Team B had been the screw-up. Now this self-serving worm was trying to find a scapegoat to cover up his fuck-up.

"I'm not going to play this game," I spat out in a soft but clear voice between clenched teeth, then got to my feet.

"Where do you think you are going, Mr. Stevens?" asked the director in an imperious tone.

"I'm leaving. If you wish to learn what went wrong last night, then hold a full *public* inquiry, and I will testify," I said.

"Mr. Stevens, I am ordering you to take your seat and tell us what went wrong out there last night!" said the director.

I laughed bitterly at him. "I don't work for you, Director, so you can't order me to do jackshit. I will tell you exactly what went wrong out there: Some cheap, spineless bureaucrat trying to save a few bucks sent the wrong team. Those six brave men and women who died last night died because *you* fucked up—"

"Now see here," interrupted the director, but I used my power to float myself about a foot off the floor and let showers of blue crackling sparks drip from my hands, which cut off whatever else he was about to say.

"Sitting on the other side of that door is a Werebear who, even in his human form, is powerful enough to tear through that wooden door like it's paper and rip your limbs off. With his enhanced hearing, he can clearly catch every word of our conversation. You are lucky that he is an aged and controlled Were, as a lesser one might have erupted into a bloodthirsty rage upon hearing you trying to scapegoat his team—half of whom bravely gave their lives in defense of this wonderful nation last night—and would have done exactly that."

The director made a worried glance over his shoulder at the door, as if expecting it to explode into splinters, and then looked back at me.

I continued. "Do you even have the slightest clue how powerful and dangerous a full-fledge demon is? With the full fury of my Air and Lightning powers, I could take down Dmitri with ease. I probably could take on everyone in this base and walk out of here without a scratch. Yet, despite all my power, that demon tossed me like a child into a tree and went through your team and mine like we were toys. Yes, we drove it off, but every single person out in that forest, except one, ended up wounded or dead. This is the biggest threat our country has faced since World War II. Stop worrying about the blame and the dollars and cents, and start figuring out how to deal with it. My first piece of advice is to shut your mouth and let the captain and his teams do their jobs."

I lowered myself back to the floor and released my powers. I stood there and quietly glared at the director, daring him to rebut my comments.

After a long silence, he cleared his throat and made a point of carefully adjusting his tie, then said, "Captain Cooper, you have my permission to call upon any resources you or your team need to apprehend or terminate this demon. We will worry about what happened last night after this creature has been dealt with. I shall excuse myself, as I need to make some calls to make sure the resources you might need will be available."

The director got to his feet and calmly left the office, closing the door behind him.

As soon as the door closed, Captain Cooper's face erupted into a huge grin, and he motioned me to sit down. He leaned forward and hit a button on his IP phone. "Agnes, tell Dmitri to get his fuzzy ass in here." He hit the button again to cut off whatever reply Agnes had.

The door opened, and in walked Dmitri's large, bald, imposing form with a happy grin splashed across his face. As Dmitri took over the director's seat beside me, Captain Cooper opened a drawer under his desk and pulled out a bottle of Tovaritch Premium Russian Vodka and three glasses. He cracked open the bottle and poured out a healthy shot in each of the three glasses. The captain put a glass toward each of us.

He raised his glass. "To fallen friends!"

We both echoed his statement and drained our glasses. I am not a hard-liquor fan, and it burned going down the back of my throat, but I managed not to cough or make a display out of myself in the silence that followed … well, other than my eyes watering a bit, but I hoped neither of them noticed.

Captain Cooper picked up the bottle and poured Dmitri another one, then raised an eyebrow at me. I shook my head, and he poured himself one, then he and Dmitri had another. He put the cap back on the bottle and put it back in his desk.

"Dmitri, we will have another one—or four—once this demon has been taken down. As of now, GRC13's only focus is on this; we will be doing no other assignments. Team B has been out trying to track the demon using the same spell we used yesterday to find it, but so far they are having no luck. This means it has either left the area or has found a way to block the spell. They are widening the search pattern, and we will see what happens. I am also reassigning you to Team B until this demon has been taken down. I know you have seniority, but Jack stays as team leader, and you are second in command. If the demon is found in an urban environment, I will also assign Magda to Team B, but if it stays in the wilderness, she is not to be used. Any issues with this?"

I wondered who Magda was, but then remembered the metal manipulator who had survived last night's attack, and it all clicked into place.

Dmitri shook his head, and the captain turned his attention to me. "Dmitri briefed me on last night's events, which means you don't need to go over it again, as I trust his account, but is there anything you want to add?"

I pondered this and mentally went over last night's action, then groaned. "One thing: The demon knew me. It was the same one who possessed Benny Sidana a few months ago."

"Shit," said the captain as he instantly clued in to the issues.

"Who is Benny Sidana?" asked Dmitri.

The captain looked at me and indicated he would explain. "Benny is a telepath on one of the EIRT teams. Before that, he worked with the UN on their special counterterrorism team. He was possessed by a demon for six months—three under the UN job and three under EIRT."

Dmitri cupped his forehead and muttered something in Russian. He, too, seemed to understand what the issue was: Demon Benny would have had access to all the EIRT tactics, which were the same ones GRC13 used. This meant that on any type of assault, hostage rescue, takedown, or whatever, the demon would know their playbook. That was probably another reason why the assault on the cabin had gone so badly: The demon had known exactly what GRC13 would do and had planned around it.

"Jack and I have been working on new tactics. We were planning on trying them out at next GRC13 cross-team training. We will do run-through of them as soon as team is back," said Dmitri.

Captain Cooper nodded and turned his attention back to me. "Any other surprises?"

"Just one, but I need both your words that what I am about to tell you stays in this room?"

"As long as it doesn't have any security implications, you have my word it will stay between us," stated the captain, and Dmitri gave a solemn nod.

"Can you see auras?" I asked.

The puzzled look on the captain's face gave me my answer before he answered, "No. What does an aura tell you?"

"Around any Enhanced Individual, I see a colored aura. Depending on the color and size of the aura, I can usually tell what their power is and how powerful they are."

"That is how you knew Mark was mage, even though he didn't cast any spells," said Dmitri.

I nodded and noticed the captain was giving me a look that was a cross between intrigue and doubt.

"You are an Air elemental," I said, "which, even without my aura ability, I would know, as elementals sense each other. Your aura, though, is a decent size but not huge, which tells me that you have mastery only over air and not electricity."

Captain Cooper's eyes widened at this, and he said, "Interesting. I could see where having this aura-seeing ability would be useful. I am assuming you asked me because you are wondering if this is an Air elemental trait or not?"

I nodded, and he continued. "It might be, but it might be like electricity for me—that I am just not powerful enough for the aura ability to have manifested. If you like, there is an FBI captain in Arizona I have known for years, and he is far and away the most powerful Air elemental I have ever met. I could ask him. I would keep your name out of it, of course, but that would answer your question, because if he doesn't have the ability, then I doubt it's an Air elemental trait."

I kicked around the risk of him asking and decided it was worth finding out, then asked him to talk to his friend.

"You have also solved another mystery for me today," the captain said. "I read the report on Benny's possession and wondered how Ray Dunham knew Benny was possessed. His report was extremely detailed on everything else, but it was quite vague on that point."

The phone rang, and the captain answered it, then listened for a bit. "Thanks, Agnes," he said, then hung up. "Team B is low on fuel and coming back in. They have had no luck finding the demon, even with the wider search pattern. I don't think it has left the area, and it is probably doing something to block the tracking spell," said the captain.

I asked, "Why do you think it hasn't left the area?"

"When the demon returned from Hell, it could have been sent anywhere on Earth, but it chose here for some reason. Whatever it came back for, I doubt that it would give up that easily on it."

I couldn't fault that reasoning. "After this meeting," I said, "I will go out with my shadow-traveler and see if the device we used still works or not, and let you know."

"I'd appreciate that. As far as I'm concerned, you and your team have earned that bounty, Zack. I owe you for your help last night. I would like us to work together on this. If we find the demon, Dmitri will let you know, and you can join the assault team as backup. If we take it down, we will fudge the report a little so you get credit for it. If *you* track down the demon, do the same for us? If you find it, you can let us take it down, and we will give you credit, or you can take it down but have the GRC13 team standing nearby in case you run into issues. Does that sound fair?" asked the captain.

That was more than fair and extremely generous on the captain's part. I was more than happy to take him up on his offer and quickly agreed.

He smiled at that, then turned to Dmitri. "I owe you an apology, my friend. I should have fought harder with the director to get Team B sent, and for that, I am sorry."

"Director was in charge. My team knew risks. But thank you for apology."

With that, we ended the meeting, and Dmitri and I thanked the captain for his time.

Just as I was about to leave the room, the captain said, "Zack, one last thing. As much as I enjoyed your dressing down of the director, it will come back to haunt you. He is a small, petty man, and right now, it is in his interest to take a backseat until the demon is dealt with. But once it's gone, he will try and get back at you. It will be nuisance items, like Canada Revenue auditing you every year or your property tax getting reassessed or by-law ticketing you for anything ... He has many connections in all levels of government. Just wanted to warn you."

I shrugged and followed Dmitri out. I wasn't too concerned about the director's revenge; compared to a full-blown demon, a bit of annoying red tape didn't even register.

Chapter 14

Saturday, April 15

I was back at our underground lab less than thirty minutes after my meeting with the captain, enjoying lunch with Stella and Blue. They had bought more Nerf guns and acquired more holy water in the time I had been gone. There were ten 19L giant plastic water bottles—the type used for office water coolers—lined up against the wall. I wondered how the heck they had procured so much holy water, and I speculated that there must be a Holy Water Depot that I'd been unaware of.

They had also been working on their mysterious project while I had been gone. It was hidden under a tarp on a nearby workbench. This project was why we were having lunch in the lab, rather than back at the house. My curiosity was killing me, but neither of them would budge on telling what it was.

Stella had a pair of magnified brass-framed goggles perched on her head. Combine the goggles, her long, braided pigtails, and her youthful appearance, and you instantly had the world's cutest-looking mad scientist.

I brought them up to speed about the meeting at GRC13, and both were pleased about us working with GRC13 for the bounty. The news got even better when Stella informed me that the UN bounty site had upped the bounty from $1.5 million to $2.5 million US.

They were both concerned that GRC13's spells didn't seem to be able to track the demon anymore. Blue agreed to take me out to all the kill sites after lunch. We would try to use Walter's tracking device and see if it picked anything up.

Blue frowned and asked, "Any chance that the demon has left the area completely?"

I shook my head and told Blue about the captain's theory on why the demon was still around.

This demon bothered me more than I wanted to admit. They lived for chaos, misery, and carnage. Normally, they couldn't resist giving in to those base urges, but for six months, this one, when in possession of

Benny, had controlled itself. It hadn't done that because it was a nice, gentle demon that just wanted to get along and sing campfire songs with people. No, there was a reason behind that control. The fact that it had been rewarded and sent back as a full demon so quickly meant it had a powerful sponsor in Hell who had been pleased with its work.

The demon knights and lords who ran Hell usually spent most of their time fighting with each other for power, territory, and position. Earth and its people were more of a minor attraction, rather than their main focus, as they were usually busy keeping a wary eye on each other. Demons on Earth were usually sent here to gather souls and kills, which would be transferred back to Hell as power to continue the war there. This meant whoever had sent the demon to possess Benny had power to spare and was looking at a longer-term goal.

It was that unknown long-term goal that had me worried. There were only two goals that I could think of being worthy enough: opening a permanent portal from Hell to Earth and allowing the legions of Hell to invade, or creating an event on Earth that would cause massive loss of life, where the souls and power of that loss could be harvested and sent back to Hell. Either one of those goals was a nightmare scenario that needed to be stopped.

I found that I suddenly wasn't as hungry as I had been and prodded Blue to hurry up and finish her meal. I wanted to get out and try the tracking device.

About fifteen minutes later, Blue and I stepped out from the shadows at the campsite where the young couple had been killed. The site in the daytime was just as beautiful as I'd imagined. The sun was out, reflecting off the clear water of the lake, and the birds were tweeting happily in the trees. The trees were still leafless and bare, but this spot really was a little slice of paradise.

I fished the metal arrow out of my pocket. I held its string, letting it dangle in the air. The arrow wobbled around for a few moments and went disappointingly still. We tried the bird-watcher's site near Nipigon, the seventeen-year-old's murder site near Hornepayne, the road east of Longlac where the OPP officer had been killed, and the cabin where the demon had been found ... All of them netted the same result of a lifeless arrow.

Blue marked up her map with circles that were scaled to a hundred-kilometer range. We traveled to another five sites that were outside the circles to widen our search, but they, too, were a bust. Either the demon had left the area or had done something to block spells from finding it.

Blue and I studied the map after she had updated it with the last circle. Our search area had been pretty extensive. My heart rate picked up a bit as I noticed something on the map. We were close to the Minnesota border, and I wondered if the demon had teleported across that border. That would have taken it out of GRC13's jurisdiction, but it would still have been close enough that it could teleport back in whenever it wanted to hunt. I mentioned this to Blue, and she agreed that the demon might have done this. We examined the map and decided to go to Hibbing, Minnesota. Its location was central enough that the tracking device's range should cover most of the Ontario-Minnesota border.

Blue shadow-traveled us to the northern edge of Hibbing. I pulled the tracking device out and let the arrow dangle. Unfortunately for us, it just hung there once again, lifeless and still.

"Good thought, but no luck. Michigan and Wisconsin are both close enough to be in range, too," offered Blue, handing me the map.

We studied the map and picked Iron Mountain, Michigan, as our next destination, as that would cover most of the southeastern section of the Ontario-Michigan-Wisconsin borders.

This, too, was a bust. I kicked a loose rock on the ground in frustration. The demon hiding in the US had made sense to me, and I'd been sure that was what the demon had done.

"We could try farther south?" said Blue.

I considered this, but ruled it out for a couple of reasons. It cost the demon more effort to teleport farther, and any farther south would probably be too far out of its range. The other reason I didn't want to try was that the tracker had been designed to point to sources of great evil—and not the demon specifically. It would be just my luck that a state senator would be home from Washington, DC, on a break and the tracker would pick him up instead ...

I had Blue take us home. She dropped me off back at the house. Our timing was good, as our resident Were had just woken up and was looking for food. Blue took her to the lab to get some food, and I went to my office to think.

I called Walter the wizard and brought him up to speed on what had happened. I asked if he had any way of getting around the blocking spell the demon might be using, but he couldn't think of anything. He told me he would think about. He also promised to make some calls to other wizards and mages he knew and let me know if he came up with anything. I thanked him and ended the call.

I emailed the captain and Dmitri to let them know that our tracking device had also been unsuccessful at tracking down the demon. I included the range of the device and the locations of all the stops we'd made, then sent off the email.

I spent the rest of the afternoon searching the internet, hoping to find something that would let us track a demon. I also searched for strange phenomenon that had occurred in northern Ontario; a demon's presence was so evil that it could disrupt nature at times. Most of the stuff I came across wasn't helpful or was completely wrong. There was a lot of crap on the internet. Spells were the most common way to track down a demon, which didn't help me. There also wasn't any mention of dead frogs, plagues of insects, or anything else that would indicate a demon in the area.

I did find one piece of information that might be useful: It seemed that demons could track other demons. This was similar to how elementals could sense other elementals. At first, I didn't think it would be that useful; summoning another full-fledge demon killing-machine to track our demon didn't exactly seem like the most helpful idea. After thinking about it, though, I wondered if all demonkind could sense each other. If that was the case, then maybe a lesser demon like an imp or a succubus might do the trick.

After sunset, we all gathered at the dinner table for dinner. Blue, Stella, and Bree were in good moods, as it seemed the secret project was ready to be tested after dinner. They still wouldn't tell me what it was, but did let me know it had been made for Olivia. This, at least, let me have some fun guessing what it was.

"You invent something that will stop her driving like a maniac?" I asked with a hopeful smile.

"Sadly, no," said Blue.

Liv rolled her eyes at this but didn't say anything, since she was currently drinking her pint-mug of blood.

"You built her armor to prevent her from getting stabbed by her own sword?" I said.

This time, Olivia just flipped me the bird, and Blue shook her head.

I ate a few more bites of my hamburger and pondered my next question. One came to me, but it took me a minute to compose myself. With mock horror, I said, "Oh my God! You figured out a way that Liv can be up during the day, so we can 'enjoy' her company 24/7!"

Bree snickered between the brief window when she wasn't stuffing her mouth with food. Blue shook her head, and Liv simply said, "You should be so lucky!"

I tossed a couple more mocking guesses out and got negative replies from Blue each time. I was about to ask another one, when Olivia cut me off.

"Before you make another guess, I really enjoyed your elemental blood last night. One more annoying shot, and I will drain you of the rest of it ..."

Liv finished this statement by giving me a smile, and I noticed that her fangs had descended and were on full display. I decided to behave myself and brought her up to speed on my GRC13 visit and our unsuccessful attempts to track the demon. I then brought up my find on the internet about demons being able to sense other demons.

"I don't see how another demon isn't going to make our problems worse," said Bree.

"That was my first thought, as well, but there are lesser demons like imps, incubi, or succubi. If we can grab one of those, they may be able to lead us to the demon."

Ideally, an imp would be best; many mages used them as familiars, as they were handy. An imp looked sort of like a hairless cat with wings. They had hands and could fly and, therefore, were useful to fetch things and run errands. A succubus would work, too, but having a super-sexy demon trying to seduce me for my soul might be a bit distracting. An incubus would work, as well, but a hunky beefcake trying to seduce the ladies would be equally distracting ...

The table had perked up at my suggestion, and Stella said, "I will contact Sarah, as she might have an idea or a contact that could get us a lesser demon."

Sarah, in her position as the enforcer for the English vampire court, would probably have the contacts to get us an imp. The English vampire court had dealings with most of the Enhanced communities, and if they couldn't get us one, then no one could.

Stella got up from the table with her smartphone and headed to the living room. I presumed she was making that call now.

We had all finished eating at that point—except for Bree, who was just finishing off her third or fourth meal (I had lost count by this point).

"Other than your big surprise for Olivia, what is the plan for this evening?" I asked.

I groaned to myself as Blue gave the table a pointy-teeth-filled smile, and I knew what she was going to say.

"Training, my soft, pudgy friends, and we are going somewhere warm, so dress for that."

Sometimes, it sucked being right. Worse, it was going to be hot, and I hated heat. My touch of Ice elemental power was great for cold weather, as it made me nearly immune, but it was so weak that I couldn't use it to cool myself off. I knew I would be sweating buckets shortly and went to fetch a bottle of water, as I knew I'd need the hydration.

Stella returned just as I was coming back to the table with my prize.

"Sarah is going to make some calls tonight. She said to stop by tomorrow at sunset. Did you want to go, Liv?" asked Stella.

I wasn't surprised to see Liv nod at this, as sunset in England was 1:30 p.m. our time. This meant Blue and Stella would take Olivia's corpse with them, and she would get a few more hours of up time tomorrow.

"Bree? Zack?" asked Stella.

I shook my head. I didn't really feel like playing politics at the English court tomorrow.

Bree quietly debated whether she wanted to go with them and also decided to stay home. This meant Bree and I would be on our own tomorrow.

"Hey, Bree, there is a new all-you-can-eat Chinese place in Burlington that just opened. We could go there tomorrow?"

Hamilton had three all-you-can-eat Chinese restaurants, but Bree had visited them already—and had been asked not to return. Burlington, too, deserved to be tormented by my favorite bottomless pit.

Bree smiled and nodded. It was always funny watching restaurant owners look on in horror as Bree put the "all" in *all*-you-can-eat.

"Get changed. We are going training after this," said Blue.

Bree, Liv, and I headed upstairs to get changed. Stella didn't get up from the table, as she would just wear her usual white *Little House on the Prairie* dress that she was currently wearing. This might have seemed odd to some, but something about the magic of the Hyde potion kept her outfit pristine and perfect. If the dress did get dirty, ripped, or worn, all Stella had to do was change into Hyde and change back to restore the dress. The always-perfect dress bothered me, as it made no logical sense why it could do this, but I had long since given up trying to figure out how it worked.

Blue also stayed downstairs, as she would just wear her scale-mail armor that she always wore.

I ditched my jeans and put on a pair of black shorts in a light material that breathed well. I left on my white cotton T-shirt but changed my full socks for some half-height ones and found my sneakers. The socks and sneakers might have been overkill for a hot climate, but I had made the mistake of wearing sandals once on one of Blue's workouts, and that had been a very bad idea; she always picked spots with brutal terrain, and appropriate footwear was essential.

Once we all had our weighted knapsacks, Blue opened a portal in the shadows in the corner of the basement, and we all stepped through. We came out in the main area of the lab. I noticed there was still a tarp covering their secret project.

We all dumped our backpacks and headed over to the table. I went to peek under the tarp, and Stella slapped my hand, then said, "As the Nerf guns with holy water did decent damage to the demon, Blue and I decided that something more powerful would be even more useful ..."

Stella nodded at Blue, and Blue lifted the blue tarp with a flourish.

I studied the contraption on the table in confusion for a moment. The first thing I noticed were the two 19L plastic water cooler bottles. They were strapped together and mounted on a stainless-steel frame. The steel frame had harness straps on the front of it. The bottom spouts of the two water bottles were both connected to a wide pipe. On the right side of the pipe was an electric motor. I realized the electric motor was actually a motorized water pump. From the pump ran a garden hose that was three feet long and ended in a trigger mechanized with a three-inch barrel. It sort of looked like a flamethrower, and it pretty much was the same idea—but with water.

"Oh, gimme! Gimme! Gimme!" said Liv, practically bouncing in excitement.

It dawned on me why this had been made for Liv: Out of the three of us who used the Nerf guns, she was the only one who had the strength to carry this thing without being slowed down too much. The two water bottles probably weighed about a good hundred pounds. Add in the frame, piping, and pump, and this water cannon was probably close to 130 pounds.

Liv turned, and Blue and Bree lifted it off the table, then secured it to her back. Liv clipped the front of the harness together in the center of her chest. The harness had a quick-release button where it was attached that would allow Liv to be free of this thing in less than a second once she had used up the water.

Olivia grabbed the trigger in her right hand and said, "Turn it on!"

"Not here. Let's move to the hangar to test it," stated Stella firmly.

Liv gave a pout at this, and we all headed to the main hangar. Olivia stood in the center of the cavernous hangar, and Stella turned her so that she was pointed away from the rest of us. Stella started explaining the features of the water cannon.

The operation was pretty simple: Flick the switch on the water pump, give it a second to spin up, and then squeeze the trigger. Stella added that the water pump was powered by a lithium-ion battery, and it drained the battery pretty quickly, but if the battery was fully charged, it had enough juice to empty both tanks.

Stella was about to say something else when Liv reached back and flipped the switch. A low whine echoed in the hangar as the water pump powered up. Stella beat a hasty retreat back to the rest of us.

"Bath time, filthy demon!" exclaimed Liv as she squeezed the trigger.

A powerful stream of water erupted from nozzle and easily traveled the sixty feet to the far wall. Liv sprayed down the wall for a few seconds and let her finger off the trigger.

She turned toward us and had a beaming smile on her face. "That demon is going to have a very bad day when we meet again. How much water did I use up?"

Liv flipped back around, and we looked at the water levels remaining in the two tanks. She had barely used 10 percent of the water. Stella told her this, and she nodded and turned back toward us. The twinkle in her eyes and the mischievous smile dancing on her lips clued me in to what was coming.

"Liv, don't you dare!" screamed Bree.

Blue dove away from us and disappeared into the shadows. Liv squeezed the trigger, and I thickened the air directly in front of me, which saved me from getting drenched. Bree and Stella weren't quite so lucky. Both tried to run away, but Liv nailed them and soaked them to the skin. Once they were both looking like drowned rats, Liv turned her attention back to me.

This was a mistake on her part, as I was now better prepared and used my powers to not only thicken the air in front of me but also drive the water back at her. Olivia got a full blast of her own medicine dumped right back on her. She gave off a small, surprised shriek and stopped firing.

Liv looked around and laughed in delight at the carnage she had brought to the hangar.

"You are a wicked girl!" scolded a dripping Stella, which just made Liv laugh harder.

I had to admit that the test had been successful; the hangar was drenched in water, and if there had been a demon in here, that much holy water would have done some real damage to it. I was about to praise Stella on her creation when I noticed two things that left me speechless. First, it was extremely obvious that Liv wasn't wearing a bra under her white halter top; it was completely soaked and clinging to her like a second skin. Second, as Bree stepped forward to lecture Liv, her own white T-shirt and white sports bra were also well and truly soaked through.

"If I had known we were going to have a wet T-shirt night, I would have brought some beer!" I said with a smile.

Bree looked down her shirt and instantly went red, then covered herself with her arms. Liv just laugh harder at this and ignored the fact that she was giving me even more of a show than Bree had.

Stella took the opportunity to sneak around Liv and hit the switch that turned off the pump. Blue cautiously peered around the corner from the far access tunnel and stepped out into the hangar again.

"Despite the unorthodox testing methods, the water cannon is a success," said Stella as she ignored Liv's giggles and gazed around the waterlogged hangar.

I couldn't help but agree. The water cannon putting out that much holy water was sure to hurt the demon—if we could ever find it again. The weight of the device would have slowed me to a crawl, but since Liv trained with a 500-pound pack on her back, I was sure a mere 130 pounds would barely slow her down. If she could sneak within sixty feet and hit the demon with a solid blast, it might be enough to actually crack its shell and release its true form. The true form would be huge and terrifying, but the demon would lose both its ability to teleport and its telekinetic powers. At that point, we could kill it for good and end its time on Earth.

We retreated back to the main area of the lab. Blue helped Liv get the water cannon off, and Stella plugged in the battery to recharge it. They would replace the two empty bottles later, since Blue wanted to get on with the training. She offered to take us back to the house to allow Liv and Bree to change into dry clothing, but to my surprise, they both declined.

I groaned as I lifted and secured the fifty-pound pack on my back, and the rest of the team put on their packs as well. Blue opened a portal, and we stepped through.

It was like stepping onto another planet. The muggy wall of humidity was thick enough that it felt like you could cut it with a knife. The din and chorus of insects and wildlife echoing around the darkened jungle was louder than I had imagined it could be. The smell of rotting vegetation hit me like brick, and I almost gagged. The worst part was the bloodthirsty bugs, which swarmed us like someone had rung a dinner bell.

"Alright, you lazy, soft-bellied maggots! Get moving!" said Blue as she disappeared into the darkness down what might have generously been called a trail.

I felt something biting me. I pushed out with a field of low-voltage electricity and zapped every bug within a one-foot radius. Liv quietly jogged after Blue, followed by Stella and me, with Bree covering the rear.

As we slogged through this hell on Earth, the sounds of wildlife in the distance were disconcerting. Thankfully, we were in no danger of anything attacking; animals would sense Bree's Were nature and would flee as we approached. It was too bad the bugs were too stupid to do the same. I made a habit of turning myself into a human bug zapper every ten or fifteen seconds, which kept me from being eaten alive. This helped me, but I felt for my teammates, who couldn't do the same.

I focused on keeping one eye on Stella ahead of me and the other on the ground directly in front of me. There was barely enough light to see the trail, and roots and debris were a constant tripping hazard.

As the minutes dragged by, my suffering got worse as the hot, humid air made it difficult to breathe when jogging like this. I longed for the cool, crisp air of Canada in April. I was also sweating in places I didn't even know could sweat.

The sting of salty sweat dripping into my eyes as we continued was just another annoyance to be endured as our death march continued. Blue continued to verbally encourage us by throwing out insult after insult about our lack of physical prowess. Even though some of the barbs were quite vulgar and offensive, they became background noise. I just focused on putting one foot in front of the other.

As much as I hated every step and everything about this place, I couldn't deny that it was a great place to condition and lose weight. I was probably dropping a pound in sweat every ten minutes.

After what seemed like hours of jogging—but was probably less than even an hour—my reserves were starting to falter. I seriously started to consider tapping out. At that moment, the demon came to mind, and I thought about the eleven people it had viciously killed and that it was still lurking out there somewhere. My anger flared at these thoughts, and I channeled that helpless rage to push me on.

To my amazement, Stella was the one to tap out first. In all our time training, Stella had never quit first. It was usually me, but Bree and Liv had both given up a few times.

"I am done with these bloody bugs. Take me home" was Stella's exact quote.

Blue opened a portal, and we all gratefully stepped through, back to the lab. Stella's face and arms were covered in angry-looking red bug bites. Seconds after we got back to the lab, she changed into her Hyde form and back again in the span of about three seconds. The bites were gone, and Stella's face was back to its normal pale complexion. Bree looked fine, as her Were healing would have healed the bites almost instantly. Liv didn't have a mark on her either. Whether that was due to her vampire healing or the bugs not touching another bloodsucker out of courtesy, I wasn't sure. Blue seemed fine, as well; I guessed her alien blood didn't hold the same appeal for the bugs.

Liv had blurred over to the Food-O-Tron, with Bree hard on her heels. I assumed Liv was getting a pint-mug of blood and Bree was getting herself a snack. Blue, Stella, and I wandered over to one of the tables, as there was an open case of bottled water sitting on it, and we each grabbed one.

I killed half the bottle in one swig. Rarely had something tasted as good as that room-temperature water at that moment.

Stella looked at me with a puzzled look. "How did you manage not to get eaten alive?"

"Easy—I was using my powers to zap them whenever they got close."

"That is cheating, which means you can get whatever punishment Blue is dreaming up for me," countered Stella.

Blue had made me swear that I wasn't allowed to use my Air powers to lighten myself or my fifty-pound pack during physical training; for combat training, that restriction wasn't in place, of course. She had also made Stella swear that she wasn't allowed to change into her Hyde form during training, which was why she had waited until we were back at the lab to change. Bree wasn't allowed to change into her Were form either. Blue hadn't, however, said anything about using my Electrical powers, and I was about to point this out to Stella when Blue came to my defense. She explained that I had been within the rules, since there were no restrictions on my Electrical powers.

"For tapping out, you get fridge clean-out," said Blue.

Stella nodded with a grumpy look on her face, and I said, "That one is easy; just open the fridge and call Bree, and half your work is done."

"I heard that!" yelled Bree from the Food-O-Tron.

Stella smiled at this, and we all quietly finished our waters. After Liv finished her mug of pick-me-up-juice and Bree killed a Philly steak sandwich and fries, Blue transported us back to the house.

There were text messages waiting for me on my phone. Because Blue took us all over the world to train, we only took Stella's phone, as the out-of-country roaming fees added up quickly; therefore, the rest of us left our phones at home. Stella's phone, though, had an international plan on it, which helped. I swore that Stella's phone provider must have been scratching their heads when they analyzed her calling patterns and locations ...

"Dibs on one of the showers," said Stella, and Bree instantly claimed the other one.

I was ticked, as I would have killed for a shower at that moment and was about to teasingly ask Bree to share, but the text I was reading stopped me dead. "I'm afraid the showers are going to have to wait. There has been another demon attack. Dmitri wants us on scene now. Gear up, people."

Chapter 15

Saturday, April 15

After changing into other clothes and gathering up our weapons, Blue used the shadows to take us to the site. We left the water cannon at home, but Liv, Blue, and I were carrying our Nerf guns with holy water. Bree and Stella stayed in their human forms for now. The text had come an hour ago, which meant the demon had killed its victim and was probably long gone; showing up at the crime scene with Bree in her Were form and Stella in her Hyde persona would have caused more grief than it was worth.

I had gotten out my hero ID before even stepping through the shadow portal. This time, Blue put us well outside the crime scene. As we walked the hundred or so feet to the edge of the perimeter, the two officers manning it came to full attention. One dropped his hand to his holster but didn't draw. He relaxed when I held up my ID.

"We are consultants, here to see Dmitri Petrov with GRC13. My name is Zack Stevens. Can you let him know my team is here, please?" I said.

The taller of the two OPP officers nodded and unclipped his radio from his vest. A few seconds later, the response was an order to escort us in. The shorter officer lifted the yellow police tape, and we followed him.

The officer eyed Stella critically and asked, "Isn't your companion a bit young to be here?"

I laughed. "She is actually the oldest of us all by close to a hundred years. It's a long story, but she isn't the ten-year-old she seems."

The cop gave me a look like I was pulling his leg, and I didn't blame him.

"Hold up a second," I said. "Stella, show the nice man why you are here."

We all stopped, and Stella transformed into her Hyde form.

The cop simply said, "Holy shit," and hastily stepped a few feet back from Stella's massive form.

Stella changed back, and I said to the open-mouthed officer, "I believe you were leading us to the crime scene?"

The rest of the walk to the kill site was quiet and uneventful, though it amused me that the officer kept glancing at Stella like she was a walking nuclear bomb that he expected to go off at any moment. If I was him, I would have been more nervous about Liv; he might be able to out-run Stella's lumbering Hyde form, but Liv would be able to kill him before he even realized it. I kicked around pointing this out to him, but decided to hold my tongue.

We reached a line of OPP cruisers as we got closer. I glanced up the line of emergency vehicles and saw an 18-wheeler with an open trailer full of huge logs parked at the side of the road with its blinkers on. I assumed the rig belonged to the victim. I was more surprised to see two unmarked Blackhawk helicopters landed farther on down the road; GRC13 must have sent out a full team in response.

As we approached the truck, Bree gagged, and Olivia made similar sounds.

Liv said, "Sorry, sulfur stench ..."

At least that confirmed it had been the demon. My attention was pulled to Dmitri walking toward us.

He said, "Looks like our friend hasn't left area."

I nodded, and Dmitri added, "It left you message. I hope you not eaten recently."

That sounded ominous.

He turned and walked toward the cab of the truck. Even my nose-blind self had picked up the coppery smell of blood and the sulfur stench of the demon. The driver's door to the truck was open, and at first, I thought the window on it was tinted. Then I realized that it wasn't tint coating it; it was blood.

Even in the near-darkness, the care and love the driver had had for his truck was obvious. The chrome tanks, bumpers, and mirrors all gleamed in the moonlight. The glossy black paint job covering the cab was immaculate. The silver lettering of "Earl's Transport Inc." on the side of the cab jumped out at me in the night. I idly wondered if it was Earl in the truck or one of his employees.

"What take you so long to get here?" asked Dmitri as we got closer to the cab.

I explained about Blue's out-of-country training and that we had only taken one phone due to international roaming costs. At the mention of Blue, Dmitri looked at her and gave her a shy smile. He nodded but pulled out his phone and asked for Stella's number, which she gave to him in case he needed to reach us again.

I pointed to the cab, and Dmitri again nodded. I used my Air powers to lift me level with the driver and got my first look at the cab—then wished I hadn't. The driver was still sitting in his seat, and the whole interior had been splashed with blood. As I examined the body, I was confused at what I was seeing, as the whole posture looked wrong. The bile rose in my throat as I figured out what I was looking at. Thankfully, I managed to choke it down and not puke all over the crime scene.

Clawed into the burly driver's hairy back was "Catch me, Zack." The demon had snapped the driver's lower back and shattered both his knees to pose him in the opposite way a body was supposed to sit. He had also twisted the guy's head around 180 degrees and, worse, ripped open the sides of his mouth in an upward direction, giving him a creepy permanent grin. My stomach lurched again, and I barely managed to keep its contents down. I used my Air powers to quickly push me back from the truck and landed on the other side of the road.

I immediately turned and lost my dinner in the ditch. As I heaved several times, I sensed someone beside me.

"You okay?" asked Liv with concern.

I dry heaved one last time, and then nodded and stood up. Liv handed me a bottle of water, which I gratefully took from her and rinsed my mouth out. As I stood there getting my legs back under me, I felt a slight tingle go through my body and knew there was an Ice elemental somewhere nearby. I recalled that one of the alternate GRC13 team members was an elemental.

Dmitri strolled over and stopped just in front of us.

"I see terrible things while in service to Mother Russia, but this up there," said Dmitri.

I nodded. What bothered me most about the scene was that the driver had probably been alive through a good chunk of it. Not an easy way to go. The back thing puzzled me, too, and I wondered why the demon hadn't written its message on the guy's front. I then remembered about demons always taking a victim's heart and figured that is what had happened. It had ripped out the heart through the chest and ended up using man's back, as there probably wasn't enough writing space left on the front.

I explained my thoughts to Dmitri, and he said, "Da, that my thought too. Now you have seen body, techs will examine it."

I realized the whole writing-on-the-back-versus-the-front thing really didn't matter. The demon had still been in the area, and it had killed again; those were really the only two important facts. I looked over to the cab as Blue raised Stella on her shoulders and stepped closer to it. I was about to warn Stella not to, but I was already too late, as she had seen everything. She didn't react, but just coldly analyzed what she was seeing and wisely kept her hands away from the cab, as to not disturb the evidence. Thanks to the early horrors in her life, Stella seemed to possess a remarkable talent for being able to shut down her emotions and just deal in pure logic and reasoning.

Once Blue lowered Stella back to the ground, Bree used the bar on the side of the truck to step up and take a look. She went perfectly still for a few seconds, like she was trying to puzzle out what she was seeing. When she figured it out, her whole body went tense, and she gripped the bar so hard I was surprised she didn't bend it. I swear I could hear her growling in anger even though she wasn't in her Were form.

Liv cocked her head. "Your team is returning, Dmitri. They had no luck finding the demon."

Dmitri stared at Liv for a moment, as if trying to figure out how she knew this, but then nodded. Were hearing was impressive, but vampire hearing was downright scary.

In the distance, I saw the GRC13 team heading to the helicopters. I picked out the solid-blue aura of their Ice elemental and was impressed by the width of it. She was quite powerful. I was glad she was on our side; this was one lady I wouldn't want to fight in a duel. Behind the Ice elemental was an orange aura with red-and-white checkers around it, which meant Tank. The Tank's aura was decent in size, but smaller than the Ice elemental's—and even Stella's when in her Hyde form. The height of the Tank amused me; she was barely five feet tall. Despite her small size and fairly small aura, this woman wouldn't be an easy opponent to take out. I pitied anyone who made the mistake of underestimating her abilities.

The last two auras emerged from the woods. The first was the purple, brown, and silver of a Werewolf. His aura was a decent size, and I guessed he had been a Were for a good fifteen to twenty years. The Were headed to the helicopters with the rest of the team.

The last aura was without question that of a mage, who turned and headed toward us. The mage's aura was impressive, as more than half of it was brown and green, which meant his primary focus was Earth and nature magic. A quarter of it was blue for Water/Ice magic, and the remaining 20 percent was equally split between Fire and Air. His aura radiated out from him a good nine or ten inches, which made him one of the more powerful mages I'd ever run across.

I had to admit I was impressed. What really impressed me was the size of the Fire and Air parts of his aura. While they were only about 10 percent each of his power, he would be able to do much more than just light a candle or blow it out with what he had. Most mages usually focused on the primary element and their secondary one, and ignored the other two. The fact that this mage had that much power in those neglected areas meant he was an extremely capable magic user.

I smiled to myself as he got closer, as he was also an old-school mage by his appearance, with a long grey beard that Santa or Merlin would have been proud of. He also carried a seven-foot-tall oak staff and wore the traditional dark-blue robes with silver trim. I gave him credit, though, for passing on the pointy wizard's hat. He was probably only 5'8" in height, and by the way his robes protruded around his waistline, I guessed he liked his food as much Bree did.

Stella, Blue, and Bree joined us just the mage arrived, and Dmitri introduced us to Jack Latour. I then turned and introduced him to my team.

His silver twinkling eyes focused on Blue, and he said with a slight French accent, "I have never encountered someone like you before. I am being presumptuous in assuming you are from another realm?"

Those silver pupils really stood out in the dark. There was warmth to them but also deep wisdom. He looked like he was in his sixties, but I had no doubt he was much older than that. Mages and wizards had much longer lifespans than normal humans, and I was willing to bet he was over 200 years old.

The faint French accent also had me betting that "Jack" had actually been born "Jacques."

"I am from a world called Willetta. As far as I know, I am the only one of my kind to walk on this planet, so I am not surprised you find me unique," said Blue.

"Portal?"

Blue nodded, and he added, "Simply fascinating. I do love meeting people from the Alien class and hearing about their worlds and cultures. I hope we can meet again after this nasty demon business has been concluded, as I would love to learn all about you."

Blue actually preened at this, which took me back a bit, as she was usually quite stoic. I hadn't thought she would be one for flattery. I guessed if I thought about it, it made sense—for a scary-looking blue alien with a mouthful of pointy shark-like teeth, excitement at meeting her probably wasn't the usual reaction she got.

"Dmitri has our contact information. Please give me a call after this is done. I'm sure I can arrange some time to answer your questions."

He beamed at Blue's answer and then studied the rest of our team. "The captain informed me that you are an Air elemental with both Air and Electricity powers. Quite impressive." He then focused on Liv and added, "Nosferatu," to which Liv got a confused look on her face. He grinned and said, "Vampire." He then turned to Bree and asked, "Were?"

"Yes."

"May I ask which type?"

"Werepanther."

Jack's eyebrows rose at this. "Oh my! Tonight is fast becoming a bounty of exotic Enhanced Individuals. This is wonderful! I hope you will also indulge me at some point after this business is done?"

Bree agreed, and I was floored by how astutely he had guessed or figured out that Liv and Bree were vampire and Were. I wondered if Jack had an ability or spell to detect auras, like I did.

His luck ran out, however, when he studied Stella. "You, young lady, have me puzzled. I currently have a spell that shows heat signatures. I was using it to try and spot the demon in the darkness. That was how I knew about the vampire and the Were, but your temperature is perfectly normal, and I'm honestly baffled as to what you are. I'm assuming Zack would not be crass enough to drag a ten-year-old girl to a murder scene?"

The heat signatures would have been a dead giveaway for Liv and Bree. Vampires were around ten degrees cooler than humans, and Weres ran about five degrees warmer.

Stella eyed the mage warily. "I am probably the oldest one here with the exception of you, my good mage, as I have no doubt that you are quite a bit older than your appearance indicates ..."

Jack nodded at this, and Stella continued. "I believe your night of exotic Enhanced Individuals is about to continue. I can show you what I am if you wish?"

"Please do."

A moment later, Stella changed to her Hyde persona and stood looking down at Jack in all her hideous glory.

"My God, a Hyde! I thought these creatures had been extinct for over a hundred years now. This is truly amazing. You have also managed to control the anger and rage that is common with the Hyde form?" asked Jack.

Stella changed back. "Yes, I am fully in control of the creature when I am in that form. I had to change back to answer your question, however. Other than grunting, I lack the ability to talk in that form."

"I hope I can also persuade you for some time after as well?"

Stella nodded unsurely, and Jack turned his attention back to me and said, "You have a formidable team here, Zack. I will admit, I was apprehensive at the thought of working with civilians on something as dangerous as a full demon, but your team seems aptly suited for this job. I look forward to working with you and your team. The biggest issue we have now is tracking this tricky devil. It is obviously still in the area and has found a way to block our tracking spells. There is a lot of ground out there, and tracking the demon down isn't going to be easy," said Jack.

Stella was about to speak up, but I subtly waved her off and said, "We are working on some ideas, but at the present, we have nothing solid. If we find a solution, we will be in touch. I'm assuming there was no trace of the demon on your search?"

"None. It must have teleported out as soon as the killing was done," said Jack.

We chatted for a few more minutes, but with the demon gone and us currently having no way of finding it, there wasn't much more to say. So we said our goodbyes, and Dmitri and Jack retreated for the helicopters. I had Blue take us home.

As soon as we shadow-traveled back to the living room, Stella asked, "Why did you not share about us getting a lesser demon to track this demon?"

"Two reasons. One, obtaining a lesser demon—or any demon—is illegal in Canada, so sharing with law enforcement that we are going to do that is probably a bad idea. Second, as jolly as Jack is, I don't fully trust him. Mages play politics like the vampire courts, and I didn't want to tip our hand just yet."

Stella pondered this for a moment and then seemed to accept my reasons. She announced she was going to have a good, long hot bath and headed for the stairs. Blue told Liv that it was time for sword practice in the basement, and they exited the room, leaving just Bree and me.

"I can finally get that shower now!" exclaimed Bree.

Without even thinking, I said, "I can join you. I will happily soap up those hard-to-reach places and make sure you are nice and clean."

Bree gazed at me with a look of pure hunger and desire on her face. The expression was so wanton that I actually got butterflies in my stomach, as I worried that she was going to take me up on my harmless flirt. Her eyes glowed for a second, like when she was changing or accessing her beast powers, and my nervousness instantly turned to concern.

She shook her head like she was coming out of a daydream and simply said, "I will let you know when I am done with the bathroom," then walked away.

That was odd. Usually with Bree, if I made a flirtatious comment, she would gently scold me but with an amused smile on her face. Her initial silent response to my comment just now had had some serious sexual heat to it, but with every passing second, I wondered if I had just imagined it. The monotone "I will let you know" had been weird too.

On the other hand, it had been a long day. Between the brutal exercise and the gruesome crime scene, maybe she was just tired. Hell, I knew I was exhausted.

In the end, I stopped worrying about it and headed for bed.

Chapter 16

Sunday, April 16

The next day, I crawled out of bed just before 10:00 a.m. I found Blue and Stella having tea together in the kitchen. I made myself a bowl of cereal, then joined them.

"I got a text from Sarah. There will be a gentleman who deals in demons at court tonight. He is willing to negotiate for providing us with an imp," said Stella.

I hastily swallowed my mouthful of Cheerios and said, "This is for cash and not for something like your souls, right?"

Stella laughed at my concern. "Of course. Do you really think Sarah would set up a deal that involved our souls?"

It was early, and I still wasn't awake. Any guy who sold creatures of evil might not have been the most upstanding character, so I didn't think my concerns were totally off base. On the other hand, Stella was right—Sarah loved them both too much to get them involved in anything that dark, and I should have known that.

"How much?" I asked.

Stella shrugged. "Fifty thousand dollars is his initial asking price, but Sarah assured me that there would be room to haggle on that price."

I coughed, as I had almost choked while swallowing my cereal at the figure. Fifty grand for a hairless cat with wings and a bad attitude? That was insane. What was worse was that there was no guarantee the imp would be able to track our demon; that had just been speculation on my part. Spending that much money for something that might not even work was a touch disconcerting. However, if it did work and we managed to take the demon down, $50,000 was pocket change when talking about a tax-free $2.5 million US bounty. For that type of money, I was willing to roll the dice. "Hopefully, you can knock that price down. Do you need money?"

Stella shook her head. "Blue and I have a line of credit with the English court. We will use that. I will use the company account to reimburse the court later."

It sounded like Stella and Blue had this well in hand, and I decided to leave them to it. I had a quick shower, and I retired to my office. I wasn't even sure if I could call it *my* office anymore, as Stella and Blue tended to spend just as much, if not more, time in here doing computer research, looking up bounties, and dealing with our company finances. Thankfully, this was one of those rare times where they hadn't taken it over. I checked my email and spent more time doing fruitless web searches about demons, trying to find something to give us an edge.

I lost track of time until Stella's crisp British accent cut the air from downstairs. She yelled up to let me know that they were leaving for the English vampire court. I was stunned to see it was already after 1:00 p.m. on the computer clock. I wished them luck and said to call if they needed anything.

An hour later, I felt the weight of someone's eyes on me. Bree stood at the threshold of my office. Her shoulder-length blonde hair was disheveled and sticking up in random places, but it looked good in a funky sort of way. I began noticing other small details, like her cheeks were flushed and there were thin beads of perspiration around her hairline. Her blue eyes darted around nervously, and I swore I caught a slight glow to them. This had me concerned, as that usually was a sign her beast was lurking close to the surface. The full moon was more than a week away, which meant the beast shouldn't be doing this.

Her hand shot out and gripped the doorframe for support as she staggered slightly. I jumped out of my swivel chair and closed the distanced between us. A cracking sound filled the air, and my eyes were pulled to her white-knuckle grip on the doorframe. Bree was clutching it so tightly that the wood was buckling under her fingers.

"What is going on?"

She ignored me and asked in a weak and desperate tone, "Where are Stella and Blue? They aren't answering my texts or calls …"

"They are at the English vampire court, remember? They are probably in negotiations for our tracking demon right at this moment."

The English court was old-school and used cell jammers in rooms where negotiations took place. They felt interruptions were poor protocol.

Seeing someone as strong as Bree like this had me near panicking. Weres didn't get sick. I racked my brain, trying to think what was causing her to act like this, but nothing jumped out at me.

"I think it's the Heat ... Oh God, why did it have to hit now? ... If they're gone, I can't get to the lab to lock myself up ... I can't hold off the beast much longer ..."

Oh shit. It couldn't be the Heat! That didn't kick in until at least nine months from now at the earliest ... That timeline, though, was for Weretigers and Werelions. Maybe for Werepanthers it came earlier. Or maybe Bree being sired by an alpha had sped it up ...

I realized that *why* it was happening didn't matter; the important thing was what we were going to do about it now. With Blue out of reach, we couldn't get Bree to the lab to lock her up.

"There are chains and restraints in the basement. I will get them."

"No time ... Remember our discussions at the lodge ... You are my plan B," gasped Bree.

"But ..."

Her eyes flashed, and she stood straight up, releasing her grip on the doorway. In a deep growl, she said, "Keep your promise!"

Before I could even say a word, she reached out and yanked me by my arm out of the office. She pulled us to her room and closed the door behind us.

I knew where this was going, and my body was answering the call much quicker than my mind was. There were times when my mind went to strange places, and this was one of those times. Instead of focusing on what was happening—and that Bree and I, or at least Bree's beast and I, were going to have sex—I was admiring her room. To be fair, this was the first time I had been in here since she had moved in. Since my room was at the top of the stairs and the main bathroom and my office were beside it, I'd had no reason to pass or see her room, which was farther down the hallway. I had made it a point to respect her, Stella, and Blue's privacy, and had set this part of the house as off limits in my mind.

As I had never needed the extra space, this room had been almost empty until Bree had moved in. Seeing it filled with furniture and decorated caught me off guard. There were oil paintings of landscapes on the walls. I wondered if the wide-open views they represented were soothing to her or to her beast. There was a desk off to the side with her MacBook open but off. In the center of the room was a queen-size bed. The large, comfy-looking white comforter was bunched up to the side, and there was a white lace skirt that ran along the bottom of the bed. The bed somehow seemed more girly than I'd expected Bree's bed to be.

"Kitty," the plush cat sitting beside Bree's pillow on the bed, certainly didn't do anything to dispel that girly impression either. The black-colored toy cat had these big Bambi eyes that stared at me in perpetual wonder. Kitty had been a gift from Liv that she'd given to Bree after returning from one of her many shopping trips. Liv had commented that it reminded her of Bree's panther form, and she thought Bree would enjoy having a "Mini-Me" to keep her company …

A growl to my left pulled me from my musings about Bree's design tastes and back to the here and now. My eyes widened, as Bree had completely stripped down and was now standing there as naked as the day she was born. With Bree being a Were and having to get naked to change forms, this certainly wasn't the first time—or even the thirtieth—I had seen her like this, but the look of raw hunger and desire in her glowing blue eyes made this time completely different than any previous time. While my mind was confused and not sure what to do, my body didn't have the same issue, and I felt myself responding to Bree's lovely form.

She moved closer to me and pressed her warm body against mine, then kissed me deeply. On instinct, I wrapped my arms around her and fell into the kiss.

This felt good, but wrong. I knew Bree, and this wasn't her; this was her beast in control at the moment. I knew that when she regained control, she would be mortified that this had happened. I racked my brain, trying to figure out an alternative to what was about to happen. I probably could have used my Air powers to pin her against the wall and hold her there, but with her Were-enhanced strength, it would have been taxing. I probably could have kept her in place for an hour at most, and then my powers would have been drained. If I did that, though, I worried that her beast's demeanor would change from lust to anger, and once my powers ran out, I would be at the mercy of a pissed-off Werepanther.

Stella and Blue would return as soon as they got Bree's messages, but did I want to gamble that they would be back before my powers gave out?

I decided, as I had no idea how long Stella and Blue would be, that it wasn't worth the risk of using my powers to restrain Bree. In the end, I'd made her a promise to be there for her, and that was what I was going to do.

She broke the kiss to lift my T-shirt up and over my head. She dropped it to the floor, and in moments, her hands were tugging away at the top button on my Levi's.

"Too slow," growled Bree, and to my horror, her hands transformed into razor-sharp claws. Before I could call on my Air powers to defend myself, those talons slipped under the waistline of my jeans, and the sounds of denim tearing filled the room. She had completely torn apart the front of my jeans, and I blinked stupidly as gravity took hold of them and they dropped down my legs to the floor.

To my amazement, as she reached for my underwear, her hands were already back to the usual dainty human ones I was used to. If I'd had any doubts that the beast was in control, they would have vanished at that exact moment. Bree couldn't transform that quickly on her best day.

Bree stepped back into me, and I was instantly aware of the heat of her body against my bare skin. The extra warmth of her being a Were made it feel like I was wrapped up in a toasty blanket on a cool winter's day.

I barely had started getting into the kiss when she broke it and slipped her hands firmly just under my armpits. The next thing I knew, I was flying through the air. I landed on my back dead-center in the middle of her bed.

Great. I finally get to have sex with Bree, and I don't even get to be the man. Figures.

My minor emasculation was quickly forgotten as Bree crawled onto the bed and slinked toward me.

She straddled my waist and sat up above me, lightly running her hand down the center of my chest. The image of her proudly sitting above me in all her naked glory would be burned into my memory for the rest of my life.

I was about to make a quip about the lack of foreplay, but I just moaned instead.

Bree fell forward, and our lips met as we kissed deeply again. Bree slowly started riding me, and I let my hands explore her body.

In my years of involuntary sexual abstinence, I had almost forgotten how damn good sex felt, but it was certainly all coming back to me now. That lack of sexual activity had also been at the root of another problem … as I felt myself getting *close* already. This really was starting to feel like I was losing my virginity all over again.

I didn't want to climax yet. This all felt too wonderful, and I wanted to savor it for as long as I could.

Bree picked up the pace with a deep moan and rode me faster. This wasn't helping. I tried my best to think of non-sexy things and did everything in my power to not lose control, but having an extremely hot blonde riding me with hunger and determination, I was fighting a losing battle. I needed to slow the pace down.

I called on my Air powers and lifted both of us into the air by a few feet. I flipped us around so I was on top, then gently lowered us back to the bed. I shifted so I was on my knees. I reached down and grabbed her ankles. I pulled them up and hooked them over my shoulders. In moving around like I had, I almost slipped out of her, so I corrected this by firmly thrusting forward.

Bree matched me and arched her hips up hard at the same time. I groaned as that one firm stroke broke the last of my willpower, and I climaxed hard. Unfortunately, I hadn't fully released my Air power, and I lost control. A hurricane force gust of wind shot from me as I continued making my O face.

The entire house groaned as the wind rocked it to its foundations. I cringed as I heard the shattering of glass behind me and wood splintering, but I was too far gone in the throes of passion to do anything about it. Anything not nailed down was flying up and around the room. There was loud *crash*, and the bed partially collapsed. By the angle we were now on, three of the four of legs had given out. Even in my climactic daze, I was aware of the cool winter's air that had come rushing in, and I realized that I had blown out the window to Bree's room as well.

As my climax finished, I managed to regain control of my Air powers. I opened my eyes to see Bree staring up at me with an amused look on her face. Her hair was completely blown back, and heat filled my cheeks. It had been many years since I'd lost that much control of my power. Thank God she had been on the bottom, as Odin only knew where she would have ended up if she had been on top ...

Tonight's top story: A naked woman was seen entering orbit this evening. Witnesses report a pale blonde woman streaking toward the heavens ...

Bree tapped me lightly on my back, and I took the hint and carefully and—thanks to the angled bed—awkwardly climbed off her. She rolled out of bed to the low side and walked around the one remaining corner that hadn't given way. Bree leaned over and reached under the bed. A sharp *crack* filled the room as she snapped off the remaining post and the bed crashed fully to the floor. She tossed the wooden leg over her shoulder and got back into bed.

That afternoon, we ended up having sex twice more after my not-so-impressive first time. I was pleased that for those times, I managed to make a much better accounting of myself. We might have gone for a fourth time as we lay there snuggling under the blankets trying to keep warm in the breezy room and playfully making out, but two things happened.

First, a strange buzzing noise caught our attention. We emerged from the blankets and looked around, then spotted Bree's iPhone shaking back and forth in the drywall. It shook itself free and fell to the floor with dull *thud.* Thankfully, Bree was a prudent girl and had a heavy-duty protective case on the phone, or my windstorm would have killed it.

It dawned on me that it was probably Stella or Blue calling, and I dove out of the bed and managed to answer it before the call ended.

Stella asked, "Zack, why are you answering Bree's phone? Is she okay?"

I could clearly hear the concern in her voice. I was about to answer when Bree said, "Give me the phone."

I turned around, and Bree was holding out her hand. I handed the phone to her and realized that the glow was gone from her eyes. This was second reason our tryst ended: Bree was back in control. She took the phone and pointedly turned her back to me, and I suddenly felt exposed, standing there naked.

I caught Bree's side of the conversation, and she was doing her best to convince Stella that everything was fine now and that she had just overreacted with her earlier panicked texts and voice mails to them.

The room was a disaster. Besides the new hole in the drywall where her iPhone had hit, there were a couple of other items embedded in the wall. Her MacBook's screen was now laced with a spider web of cracks across its surface. The blinds and white-lace curtains that had covered her window were gone, as well as all the glass of the window. The sliding doors to her closest were pushed inward and half off their tracks. I spotted my T-shirt in the corner of the room, but all the rest of my and Bree's clothes were nowhere to be seen.

I hastily grabbed my T-shirt and put it on. It barely covered my dangly bits, but it was better than nothing. I caught Bree wrapping the blanket self-consciously around her nude form as she continued to reassure Stella that she was okay.

I ended up at the window and groaned as I surveyed the backyard. It was littered with debris. There were book pages scattered and blowing all over the brown grass. It actually cheered me up a bit when I saw the torn cover of *Twilight* lying there; at least one good thing had come out of my loss of control.

I spotted Kitty, the plush toy, in the walnut tree at the end of the yard. It was wedged upside down in the fork of a branch, and its Bambi eyes were staring at me with an accusing look.

I instantly forgot about Kitty when I spotted Bree's black bra hanging from another tree branch. Somehow, both straps had gotten snagged on the branch, and the bra was hanging with the cup sides pointing toward the ground. I giggled to myself; if I poured some seed into them, those large cups would make a great birdfeeder. Heck, they would make two great nests for a family of sparrows ...

Bree finished convincing Stella that she was fine and ended the call. I turned to face her, and she ignored me, focusing on brushing off the drywall dust from her phone.

"I'm sorry." It sounded lame, but I felt it needed to be said. I knew Bree was unhappy with what had just happened but hoped that we could resolve it.

"Don't be. You did what I asked you to. Thank you for that," said Bree in a quiet voice.

To my utter amazement, she glanced around the room and then let out a deep belly laugh. I was confused, and it must have shown on my face, as Bree tried to explain but couldn't compose herself and just laughed harder.

It took her a good minute, but eventually, she said, "Dude, you really *blew* me away with your performance earlier ..."

She burst out into giggles again, and I groaned. While the beast had been in control, Bree would have been fully aware of everything that had happened. I should have expected some sort of shot at my complete lack of control. I smiled at her amusement; it was better than her being pissed at me since I had wrecked her room, her bed, her laptop, and Odin only knew what else. Her hair was still blown back due to the wind blast, which made her mirth even funnier, and I found myself laughing with her.

She finally got control again and said, "That whole lifting us into the air to switch positions was super cool and pretty hot, but whatever style points you earned doing that ... *went out the window* right after that."

Bree chuckled again, and I shook my head. I was glad that she was finding this amusing. I knew her well enough to know that under that laughter, there was a lot of pain and embarrassment. She had been through enough having her entire world ripped away the night she was attacked. The amount of control she needed to have to keep the beast's rage in check was almost unimaginable to me. Then, after starting to get her life in order, the Heat comes along and messes everything up again. Now she had another thing to worry about.

"Rather than stand here and get mocked, I'm going to go get dressed," I said and reached for the door, then realized I had another problem: I tried the door, and it was stuck. The frame around the door had cracked, and the door was wedged hard into the frame. I pulled hard on the knob, but it wouldn't budge. I sighed, as I knew I wouldn't be able to open it; this was a job for a big, strong Werepanther, and I knew it. I felt like a little old lady with a pickle jar I couldn't open, in need of a strapping young lad to help me.

"Uh, a little help here?"

Bree gave me a puzzled look, and I explained, "The door is wedged into the frame ..."

An expression of pure amusement danced across her features. She wrapped the blanket around herself more and got to her feet. I moved out of her way. Bree braced her feet on the carpet and, with one hand, casually yanked open the door. I thanked her and retreated to my room to get changed.

Chapter 17

Sunday, April 16

A couple of hours later, a window-repair guy had been by and fitted a wooden board to the window frame. I could tell he was curious about what had caused all the damage, but thankfully, he was an older guy and had probably seen worse in his time and didn't ask. He said the replacement window would be about a week, and he'd call me when it was in.

Bree was showered, changed, and more importantly, fed. I had called a pizza guy before even calling the window-repair guy. I had also had the yard cleaned up, and Kitty was no longer stuck in a tree. I put it back in its rightful spot on Bree's bed. I swear it gazed at me with a total look of disapproval, but that might have just been my guilty subconscious talking.

I made a few more calls. I arranged for a general contractor to come by in a couple of days to fix the doorframe, patch the drywall, and take care of any other damage I'd made to Bree's room. We'd have to hit an Apple store to get a replacement for the MacBook, but Bree didn't seem overly concerned about it.

She had been quiet, and I knew she was dwelling on the whole Heat thing. I asked if she wanted to talk about it, but she shook her head and said she needed a bit of alone time. She retired to the living room and turned on the TV.

I wanted to cheer her up, and there was only one way I knew to do that. I told her I was going out for half an hour.

I returned to the house with bags of groceries, as the one thing that always cheered Bree up was food. I was going to cook her favorite: rare beef tenderloin with baby potatoes, green beans, and Béarnaise sauce. The TV was still blaring in the background, and I assumed Bree was still watching it. I knew she had finished an extra-large meat-lover's pizza only an hour and a half ago, but I also knew that wouldn't stop her from enjoying this dinner.

I had plated everything and was just about to call Bree when she popped her head out of the living room and asked, "Do I smell steak?"

Her face lit up when she saw the two plates in my hands. She grabbed the one from me that was heaped to the heavens and kissed me on the cheek. She sat down at the table as I opened a good bottle of California Cab to accompany the meal. I poured us both healthy glasses and joined her at the table.

The meal was quiet, as we both sat there eating, alone with our thoughts. Other than cheering Bree up with her favorite meal, I also needed to talk to her before the others returned. I wanted to know where we stood. Was today just a one-time thing or might it lead to something more? I knew that it hadn't been Bree per se, as we'd had sex when her beast was in control, but she would have experienced everything that had happened. At a minimum, I wanted to clear the air between us and make sure we were still friends and teammates. We still had to work together in possible life-or-death situations, and the last thing we needed was tension or awkwardness between us.

Out of the blue, Bree said, "I'm sorry."

"Huh? For what?"

"I shouldn't have laughed at you about losing control. You were a real friend today. You stepped up when I needed you to, and I repaid that by making fun of you. That wasn't fair on my part."

I shrugged in response; someone laughing at me was something I could deal with. It would have been much worse if she'd broken out into tears once she'd regained control. I wouldn't have been very good at dealing with that.

I stayed quiet, sensing that Bree had more to say.

She had another couple of bites of steak and then added, "I hate losing control like that. The feeling of not being in control of your own body is just wrong on so many levels. It also caught me by surprise, since I didn't even know if Werepanthers actually would get the Heat ..." She snickered a bit and said, "I guess we know the answer to that now. I also want to thank you for forcing me to go to the Barrie pack meeting. At least when the Heat hit, I knew what it was, thanks to Sabina. It would have been much worse if we hadn't known what was happening."

I thought about that and realized she was right. If we hadn't known about the Heat, I am not sure how I would have dealt with Bree throwing herself at me. I got the feeling her beast wouldn't have taken rejection well.

"You doing okay?" I asked.

Bree nodded, swallowed her food, and said, "Yeah, better than I thought I would be. At least with the Heat, it is just overwhelming lust and not rage. The worse that could happen is I end up hooking up with random strangers and having sex, which, while it isn't ideal, it's at least better than tearing them to pieces."

That made sense to me. I knew her biggest fear was losing control of her beast and killing someone by mistake. Weres were immune to diseases, which meant she couldn't pick up an STD, and even if she got pregnant, it wouldn't survive when the full moon forced her to change. That last thought was exceptionally cold, but that didn't stop it from being true. She would still have to deal with memories of the encounter though.

Bree looked at me. "Spit it out."

"I wanted to chat with you before the others got back. I wanted to make sure we were cool. I also wanted to know if this meant anything."

I instantly regretted that last line, as Bree's eyes went wide, and she sat back like I had hit her. Her reaction told me my answer.

I jumped in before she could say anything. "Ignore my last comment. Are we good?"

Bree took a moment before answering, then said, "Yeah, we are good ... Did you want today to mean something and be more than just an afternoon fling? I would have thought you would have been happy with it just being casual."

"I don't know. I love you, but more in a friend/sister sort of way, though a part of me wonders if starting a relationship from a strong friendship is such a terrible thing. You are smart, funny, strong, compassionate, and caring, and I enjoy being around you. The sex was awesome, and part of me was curious if we could build something off that."

Bree paused like she was considering her words, and I felt extremely vulnerable at that moment.

The silence lingered between us uncomfortably until finally Bree said, "You are a great guy, and I enjoy spending time with you as well. I'd be more interested if I was actually looking for a boyfriend, but with this Were thing still being reasonably new, this new career, and now with the Heat being yet another complication, I'm not sure I want to make any commitments. I really feel like I have to get myself in order before I am ready to take that step. Also, I shouldn't be telling you this, but it will probably come out in short order anyway ... Liv already claimed you."

Olivia "claimed" me? What the heck is that supposed to mean? I suddenly felt like a piece of luggage. Then it dawned on me what she meant … I remembered my own guy friends back when they were single. If one of them liked a girl, they called dibs on her, and the rest of us put that girl off limits. I assumed women had a similar system.

Oh shit! Liv wasn't going to be happy when she got home and found out what had happened. It really hadn't been our fault, as it had been the Heat and Bree's beast that had done everything. The problem was, would our slightly crazy and impulsive resident vampire see that, or would she lose her shit? If I had owned a magic eight ball, I'm pretty sure it would have read, "Outlook not so good," at that moment.

"You know, if you would have just had that threesome I offered, we wouldn't be in this situation."

Bree laughed and shook her head at me. "There is the pig I know and love. Romantic, caring, relationship Zack was a bit weird."

I nodded. "Since I am back, I might have picked up a triple-chocolate cake for dessert, and I am willing to trade slices for sexual favors."

Bree threw her napkin at me. "You already got the favors, so where's my cake?"

We cleared off the dinner plates, and I served up the chocolate cake—"served up" meaning I cut myself a piece and handed the rest of the cake over with a fork to Bree.

"So, Liv called dibs on me, eh?" I said.

"Oh, don't be so smug about it. It really wasn't dibs—more like we drew straws, and she got stuck with the short one. She is just very serious about her commitments. We figured that if you didn't get laid soon, one of us would have to step up for the good of the planet. Girl Guides don't even come to this house anymore, as your horny aura scares them off."

"Yeah, it's *me* scaring off the Girl Guides and not the freaky Werepanther who would eat all their cookies—and might not stop at just cookies," I countered.

Bree stuck her tongue out at me and probably would have made another shot, but thankfully, the cake distracted her.

I couldn't get the fact that Liv had called dibs on me out of my head, but there was one thing I needed to know. "Can I ask when Liv called dibs on me?"

Bree narrowed her eyes at me. "Why?"

"I'll tell you … right after you answer my question."

"It was the night Liv and I went hunting when we were all on the run with you. She woke me up just before sunrise and told me that you were hers. I said fine and went back to sleep. I figured something must have happened between you two, but she would never talk about it."

I smiled at the answer; that night had been our first flying date.

Bree gave me a curious look, and I said, "I wanted to know when, because she fed off me, and I was worried she called dibs after that …"

Bree's expression softened. "You were worried she claimed you because you were a tasty snack and not because she liked you …"

I nodded, and Bree added, "You know, under that confident exterior and hidden behind your piggish comments, there is a lot of insecurity lurking there."

Bree hit the nail on the head, and I didn't argue. I knew she was waiting for me to make some sort of reply, but I didn't really want to go deeper with this discussion, so I changed the topic. "Speaking of our favorite perky vampire, how are we going to deal with Liv?"

Bree swallowed her mouthful of cake, smiled, and said, "I have a plan …"

Chapter 18

Sunday, April 16

Bree's big plan was for me to take a shower and hide in my office until she broke the news to Liv. It wasn't much of plan, but it did keep me out of the firing line, which was a plus.

The ladies returned from the English court around ten o'clock. Fifteen minutes after that, Liv appeared in my doorway with her arms crossed and a pout on her face.

"You owe me! I want two flying dates and one feeding from you, and you are off the hook for tapping my best friend."

I thought about it and said, "If I do this, then you, me, and Bree are all cool?"

She nodded, and I simply said, "Deal."

I wasn't a big fan of being an Olivia snack, but if it kept the peace, it was worth it. The two flying dates weren't an issue, as I had enjoyed the last one. There was something entertaining about tossing a crazy vampire into free fall at 10,000 feet and debating whether I would catch her or not …

"Come downstairs and meet Stinky," said Olivia.

Before I could ask about Stinky, Liv had already blurred off. Vampire speed was so annoying.

Stinky turned out to be our new imp. It seemed that the imp had to be bound to someone, and for some reason, Stella and Blue had chosen Liv. I was guessing they had picked Liv because she thought the hideous little devil was cute. He looked like a humanoid-shaped hairless cat with small wings and was ugly as hell. He was currently perched happily on Liv's shoulder, and she was rubbing his chin. The disturbing part was he was currently sporting wood, and Liv either didn't notice or didn't care. Stella was pointedly looking away, and Bree was just staring opened-mouthed.

He also reeked of sulfur.

"Liv, why don't you take Stinky for a drive? While you are out, stop at Walmart and buy the dude some clothes. Also, see if you can find something to make him smell nicer."

"Driving and shopping! Oooh, good idea!"

"Leave Stinky in the car. Do *not* take him into Walmart, understand?" I added.

Liv nodded and was gone. I went to the nearest window and opened it and a few others. I also turned on the vent fan in the bathroom and the one over the stove to air the house out. Just as I finished turning on the fan over the stoves, the sound of squealing tires let me know Liv was out of the driveway.

I joined my remaining teammates at table. "How much did the flying rat cost us?"

Stella looked sheepishly at me for a moment and softly answered, "$30,000." Then, after a reluctant pause, she added, "US."

I did a quick calculation in my head and figured the real cost had been about $37,000 Canadian, then winced. I should have assumed that the original $50,000 was also in US dollars, but for some reason, I had assumed it was in Canadian. Stella and Blue had actually done a pretty good job getting the price dropped from $50,000 to $30,000, but that was still the price of a pretty decent car.

Stella smiled. "We did find out, though, that an imp can track other demons."

That little tidbit cheered me up immensely. It would have really sucked if we had dropped all that money and it couldn't track our demon.

"You both did good. We now have a way to find the demon, and if we can take it down, the money we just spent is trivial compared to the bounty."

Stella and Blue both seemed relieved that I wasn't more upset about the expense. Bree didn't seem to care one way or the other, as she was focused on the Philly cheesesteak in front of her.

"Do we go after the demon tonight?" asked Stella.

At this, Bree did look up from her food to focus on my reply. I stifled a yawn and shook my head. "No, it has been a long day. We will go hunting tomorrow right after sundown."

Blue nodded. "Bree informed us that you did your duty this afternoon ..."

My cheeks tingled, and I blushed as Blue's words hit home. She continued, oblivious to my discomfort. "If you trained harder, you would have better stamina. She also told us about your lack of control."

Jesus, Bree! was my first thought at the "lack of control" comment. I figured that she had been talking about my lack of sexual control. The heat in my cheeks now could probably have cooked a roast ...

It eventually dawned on me that Blue had been talking about my lack of control with my *powers*.

"Is this something we need to do more training on, as well?" finished Blue.

Bree avoid looking at me and hid her amusement behind the large pint-mug of lemonade she was currently taking a long time drinking. Stella had turned away, and her head was bobbing as she, too, suppressed her own laughter at my expense. Blue was just staring at me with concern, waiting for my reply.

I was about to blurt out "Unless I am banging a sexy Were during combat, it won't be a problem," but managed to not spit that out. I realized that Blue was just being conscientious in her role as team trainer and wasn't making fun of me. I took a deep breath and considered my words carefully. "This was a special circumstance that is unlikely to occur during team combat, so I don't think we need to be concerned. It has been a good fifteen years since I lost control of my powers during combat, and I don't believe extra training will be necessary."

Blue gave me a satisfied nod, but then added, "While it is unlikely to occur in combat, it is still a concern. What if, instead of Bree, that had been a normal human woman? You released enough Air power to shatter a window, crack a door frame, and collapse a sturdy bed. A normal human could have been seriously injured in that."

I really wanted this line of questioning to end, but Blue had brought up a good point: What if that had been a normal human woman? Thankfully, with the way my anemic social life had been going, it would be highly unlikely that there would be a normal woman in my bed for the next decade or so. That would cut down the risk significantly.

Another thought popped into my mind, which I was much more enthusiastic about. "You bring up a good point. I believe that I do require *specialized* training that Bree could provide. I believe that after nine or ten *close* sessions with Bree, I would be confident that I would be fully in control of my powers ..."

Bree choked and coughed up the lemonade as I shot her a leering grin. Blue nodded at this and turned her attention to Bree.

Stella mumbled, "You're terrible," between smothered laughs.

"In your dreams!" said Bree once she recovered her power of speech.

I was about to make a smart-ass reply to that, but Blue beat me to it. "I do not understand your reluctance in this matter, Bree. Zack was there for you when you needed him. Now, when he needs you to help him, you are not willing to return the favor? That is quite dishonorable."

I was about to burst out laughing at Blue's serious tone, but Bree's look of utter annoyance kept me from losing it. I got up from the table to hide my amusement and decided it was time for a beer. Stella was rolling in her chair in laughter, and Blue was giving her a puzzled look, as she couldn't figure out what Stella was laughing about.

"Honor has nothing to do with it. He is just being a pig and using this as an excuse to have sex with me!" exclaimed Bree.

I popped the cap off my beer. "I'm shocked—shocked that you would think that. Blue brought up a valid safety concern, and my only thought was the best way to address that issue. I think more *personal* training with you is a logical way of dealing with that issue."

I sat back down at the table and took a long, satisfying swig of beer, then winked at Bree. A loud *crack* filled the room as the tabletop Bree had been gripping in frustration split. She looked down in horror at the six-inch section that had broken off in her hands.

"Bree, find your happy place," said Blue with concern.

Bree sighed and dumped the broken piece on the table. "I'm going to my room …" She abruptly left the table.

I knew she was upset and realized I had pushed things too far. I decided to head up and talk to her. I excused myself from the table.

As I left the room, Blue said to Stella, "I do not understand why Bree got upset."

Stella answered, "We have had these talks about human sexuality and relationships before and your trouble with grasping the nuances of it …"

I reached the bottom step of the stairs and chickened out. If I was going to comfort a pissed-off Werepanther, I need to go in armed. I grabbed my house keys and headed out …

My trip was uneventful, but I was now adequately supplied and ready to face the music, so to speak. I dragged my feet up the stairs, as I wasn't looking forward to this.

Bree's door was partially open, and I could hear her crying inside her room. The door probably was only open because, with the split door frame, it couldn't be closed. The sounds of her sobs tore at me like nothing else in the world could, and I felt terrible about my comments earlier.

I knocked on the door. "Bree, it's me."

"Go away!"

This was the answer I had expected, which was why I had come prepared. "I have ice cream."

"What kind?"

"Chunky Monkey ..."

This was her favorite, and my concern deepened when I got no reply. Just as I was about to give up and leave her in peace, she said, "You can come in, but if you are lying about the Chunky Monkey, this room is about to get a whole bunch more wrecked ..."

I took that as permission and opened the door, which decided its time on this Earth was done and fell off its hinges. I caught the door in my free hand and awkwardly propped it up against the wall.

I turned to Bree, who was sitting on the bed with her back against the wall and her blanket protectively wrapped around her. Her eyes were red, and tears were running down her cheeks, which caused my stomach to knot. I sheepishly held out the ice cream and a spoon, and was immediately rewarded with a small smile.

"I'm so sorry," I said. "I didn't mean to upset you like this ..."

Bree took the ice cream from me and in seconds had both the top and the plastic white protective cover off. She dove in and carved out a healthy-size spoonful. That first mouthful got a moan of pure pleasure out of her, which hurt my ego a bit; this afternoon, while I'd thought I was rocking her world, none of her moans matched the intensity of this one.

After that first mouthful, she shook her head. "It's not you. Normally, I would find that funny. I thought I was good with the Heat, but I guess I'm not as okay with it as I thought I was ... I'm sorry I ruined your table."

I snorted at that. "I needed to replace the chair Olivia Ginsued earlier. At least now I can replace both on the same trip. The table isn't important. Do you want to talk about it?"

I sat down on the edge of her bed, giving her plenty of space between us.

"It's just that I finally thought I was starting to get my life under control. I can control the rage part ... Well, when I'm not turning tables into kindling or getting into dominance duels with my teammate. I was really excited about this new bounty career and then underestimated how hard it would be to take a demon down. This was our first bounty, and with all the death and pain this case has caused ... It's not going the way I thought it would ..."

"Hey, this bounty by far is the most challenging one I've done in my six years. They are usually more straightforward than this. It will get easier, I promise."

Bree nodded and seemed to be gathering her thoughts, so I just stayed quiet and waited for her.

"The bounty isn't my real problem; the Heat is. I'd hoped that if it happened, Blue would lock me up in the cell in the lab. That way, I could fight with the beast for control like I do with the rage. I think we are both feeling a little embarrassed and awkward about what happened this afternoon. Don't get me wrong—I am grateful that you kept your promise, and I didn't end up in an alley with strangers like Sabina did. Explaining to Liv and the others what had happened wasn't fun, but with my frantic phone messages and the damage you had done, it wasn't like I could hide what had happened ..."

She paused and had another spoonful of ice cream. "I'm tired of all these surprises my condition brings. Every time I think I have things under control, something else pops up and screws things up. Now I lost my temper and am sitting here like a blubbering mess ... I'm so weak ...," sobbed Bree.

I laughed at her last statement, and the noise of my laughter instantly stopped Bree from crying, and she glared at me.

"I'm sorry. I am not laughing at you; I'm laughing about your 'I'm so weak' comment. You and Liv are, like, the strongest people I know."

Bree looked at me like I was crazy, and I explained, "Any Enhanced Individual struggles learning to use and live with their powers. I got mine when I hit puberty. So on top of boners, zits, and emotions all over the place, I could have easily killed people if I lost control of my Air or Electrical power. The difference was that I'd known from birth I would be an elemental. My mother had spent every day of my life preparing me for that. Once the powers showed up, she spent her time teaching me how to control them in a safe way.

"You and Liv, on the other hand ... One day you are working, trying to bank some coin for college and living normal human lives, and then the next day, you have these new scary powers. You didn't have a pack to show you the way, just like Liv didn't have a master around to teach her either. You were ripped from your families and ended up in a secret lab with a little girl who is half monster and a blue alien as your only friends and guides. Despite those disadvantages, you both came through with flying colors. Do you know how rare it is for someone in your situation not to kill someone or go insane? You are anything but weak. I have no doubt that you will deal with this just like you have dealt with everything else—and come out stronger for it."

Bree sat a little straighter as I finished my pep talk. She had another bite of Chunky Monkey and then said, "You're right. I need to stop feeling sorry for myself. Today, I had mind-blowing sex … or, at least, *window*-blowing sex. Plus, you made my favorite meal, and I got ice cream. How bad can things really be? I have also decided that once Liv gets back, the two of us are going for a drive. I am the mood to hunt for some yummy venison."

The last part of her statement made me feel better. Liv and Bree, once a week or so, would head out to some woods that were about an hour's drive away and hunt. Bree would change into her panther form, and the two of them would tear through the woods, hunting deer. I knew she loved the thrill of the chase and the freedom of running through the trees in the moonlight. This usually put her in a great mood for days afterward.

We chatted about lighter, less important things after that. It was terrific to hear her laughter as we talked and she finished her Chunky Monkey …

A loud screeching of tires let us both know Liv was home, though I was willing to bet that Bree, with her Were hearing, had heard Liv approaching long before that.

We bumped into Liv at the bottom of the stairs as she was coming in the front door. My eyes watered as the wave of fruit, driftwood, and moss aromas hit my poor nose. I realized that Liv had doused Stinky in Axe Body Spray to hide his sulfur odor. I wasn't sure at this point, as I was practically choking on the artificial scent, if it had been an improvement or not.

What *was* an improvement, though, was Stinky's new look. Liv had dressed him in blue-denim overalls, a small black knit cap that she had cut two holes in the top of to accommodate his tiny horns, and a thick gold chain around his neck with an "S" medallion hanging from it. The whole thug-life look on Stinky amused me to no end.

Liv made a proud "Tada!" as she presented him and his new look to us.

"Oh my God, Liv! He is adorable!" gushed Bree.

Olivia beamed at this for a moment, but then she must have noticed her friend's red-rimmed eyes, as her face immediately changed to one of deep concern, and she said, "What's wrong?"

"The stress of the day caught up to me. It's nothing, but I need to hunt ... You up for it?"

"Sure, but we need to take your truck. Stinky had an accident on the way to the Walmart, and my passenger seat is still drying."

"What happened?" asked Bree.

To my surprise, Stinky answered, "Stinky peed," in an ashamed, cackling tone. That small statement had me liking the little fellow.

"Don't worry about it, buddy. I did the same thing the first time she took me out in her death mobile ... You know, Liv, you really should just wrap that seat in plastic, since your driving tends to induce bladder-control issues," I said.

She just flipped me the bird in response, then turned to Bree and said, "Grab your keys and let's go!"

Bree scooped her keys out of the bowl by the door, and before I could even open my mouth, both were out the door. I stood there stunned, with Stinky looking as confused as I was and surrounded by Walmart shopping bags.

"C'mon, little buddy. It looks like it is just the two of us," I said as I headed for the kitchen to grab a beer.

Stinky flapped his little wings and flew happily beside me. I grabbed a beer from the fridge and a saucer from the cupboard as Stinky hovered beside me. I had no idea what the little devil ate or drank but figured it would be rude not to share my beer with him. We retired to the living room. I turned on the TV and found a hockey game to watch. I put the saucer on the coffee table and poured some of my beer into it.

Stinky landed on the floor just in front of the saucer. He looked over his shoulder at me on the couch and said, "Stinky's?"

I nodded. "Yup, that is for you, bud."

His long lizard-like tongue licked his tiny lips, and he went to town on the beer.

I was only half paying attention to the game. I was a little bothered about Stinky being spellbound to Liv. The binding had been done to keep Stinky loyal and not have him wander off the first time we were out. The problem was, that type of binding went both ways and enhanced the emotional connection between the two of them. The problem with that was that Stinky would be here long after the demon was gone. I'd assumed that we'd get an imp, use it to find the demon, and then sell him back. Now we'd have Stinky in our lives for the foreseeable future ...

He turned out to be a pretty good sports companion, as he didn't say much. We both sat and just enjoyed the game and beer. He went through his beer before I was even half done with mine, so I topped him up again.

Stinky and I killed a lot of beer that night, and I awoke on the couch to a pissed-off vampire yelling at me for getting her "baby" drunk. There were a shitload of empties sitting on the coffee table and a half-eaten pizza on the coffee table. *Wow! I don't even remember ordering that.*

Liv finished her rant, glared at me, and pointed at a passed-out Stinky on the couch beside me. The little guy was lying on his back, with his long pink tongue hanging out, snoring up a storm at this moment. There was tomato sauce all over his face and a half-eaten piece of pizza lying on his chest.

Bree opened the pizza box and scooped out a slice for herself with an amused smile dancing across her face.

Liv was tapping her foot and had her arms crossed, waiting for my reply. I tried to answer but had the worst dry mouth in history. I was also still quite drunk. I spied a half-empty bottle, snatched it up, and took a long swig. Warm beer sucked, but at least it cured the dry mouth.

"Liv, chill. Stinky was born and raised in the eternal fiery and damned pools of Hell. I am sure a little beer and pizza isn't going to hurt him ..."

I think that might have gotten through to her. Her body language softened a bit.

"Besides, you just dumped him on me and left. You didn't leave me any instructions. I could have just gone to bed and let the little guy fend for himself. But I stayed up and kept him company. That has to count for something?"

"Oh ..." was her one-word answer, as she realized that she *had* just taken off and left us to our own devices.

The room was spinning a little bit, and I realized I needed more sleep. "Would one of you be nice enough to help me to my room? I'm not sure my legs are working quite right at this moment."

"You help him, Bree. I am going to clean Stinky up," said Olivia.

Bree finished her slice of pizza in one giant bite and hauled me off the couch. I slipped my arm around her, and we mostly walked to the stairs.

"You know, pretty lady, you remind me of this super-hot girl I had sex with today, or is that now yesterday …"

"Less talkie-talkie and more walkie-walkie, or I'll drop you right here, and you can sleep this off on the kitchen floor."

Bree got me up the stairs and dumped me into my bed. I wished her a good night and closed my eyes, then heard her cuss under her breath. The last thing I vaguely remembered was Bree undressing me and then tucking me in under the blankets before I passed out again.

Chapter 19

Monday, April 17

The next morning—or I guess should say *afternoon*—was a beautiful spring day. The sun was shining, and the birds were merrily tweeting away in the yard. I so wanted to fry all the chirping bastards; each little tweet rang like a gong in my aching noggin. A dimmer switch for that big ball of fire in the sky would have been nice too.

In retrospect, maybe getting blind, stinking drunk the night before going out to hunt one of the more dangerous things on the planet might not have been the best plan ever ...

The next hour consisted of me downing a bottle of water, killing a cheeseburger and fries, and popping a couple aspirin. Then I went back to bed for a couple of hours.

This time when I awoke, my miracle cure of hydration, grease, and pain killers had all kicked in nicely. My head was now just a dull throbbing that was more livable than earlier. One hot, steamy shower later, and I was ready to face the day.

The house was strangely quiet as I headed downstairs. I wondered where everyone was. Liv, of course, would still be in the sleep of the damned at this moment, but the rest of them should have been up and about. It was late enough in the day that even Bree should have been up.

I found Blue sitting at the kitchen table, quietly doing her needlepoint. It always amused me when Blue did this; it seemed an odd hobby for a big, strong warrior. I mean, here she was, daintily working the needle in and out of the white cloth while wearing her scale-mail, her sword sheathed on her back, and enough daggers and objects of death strapped to her to take on a marine battalion. On the other hand, I was a thirty-three-year-old guy who liked building model aircraft ... so "glass houses," I guessed.

I found a pot of coffee that was still warm and helped myself. As I was pouring it out, I noticed the sound of water running from upstairs and figured it must be Bree in the shower.

"Where's Stella?"

Blue glanced up from her work as I sat down and said, "She is at the lab, working on her latest project. She'll call when she needs me to pick her up."

I idly wondered what Stella was working on this time. She wasn't really a mad scientist, but she was bright and handy, and usually, her projects turned out to be useful—like Liv's new water cannon.

Blue seemed to be entranced in her needlepoint, and as it seemed like it was hobby day, after checking my phone for messages and the internet to make sure there hadn't been another demon killing, I decided to waste a couple of hours in the basement, working on my own hobby.

My nose twitched at the smell of Axe Body Spray as I descended the stairs to the basement, and I figured Stinky must be sleeping with Liv in the cold cellar. At least that scent would be drowned out shortly by the smell of my enamel paints.

I sat down in front of my workbench and checked out the undercarriage I'd painted a few days ago and was pleased with the results. I glanced over the plans and decided to work on assembling and painting the cockpit on the Mosquito next. I turned on my phone, found my model-building playlist, and hit play. The sweet sounds of Glenn Miller's "American Patrol" issued from my Bluetooth speaker, and I lost myself in paint and glue for a while …

Vera Lynn's "White Cliffs of Dover" had just started when I heard Liv say, "C'mon, boy. Let's get some breakfast." Stinky make a little happy noise in response.

Time certainly flew when you were having fun … I was shocked to see I had been at it for two and half hours. Liv's timing was good, as I had just put the final touches of paint on, and I had finished the cockpit assembly. I cleaned and rinsed my brushes and turned off the music. Once I had packed everything up, I headed upstairs.

I bumped into Blue as I exited the basement. She took my dinner order and disappeared into the shadows. Liv was seated at the table in the chair that was missing a back. She was halfway through a glass of plasma, and I saw Stinky on the floor beside her. He was lapping away at a saucer of blood on the floor.

I wondered if feeding a demon human blood was the best plan. But then, most demons drank it, so why should Stinky have been any different?

I quickly found out that imps were basically flying garbage cans and would eat just about anything. At dinner, after getting through two full saucers of blood, he also enjoyed numerous French fries from Stella's plate, which she kept giving to him. He scammed some broccoli from Blue, and once I was done eating my Cornish pastie, I put my cast-iron pan down for him. He gobbled down the remaining pastie I'd left and licked every drop of HP Sauce up as well.

At the end of dinner, the only one still eating was Bree, and Stinky tried cadging food from her, but she just growled at him, and he wisely skittered away and hid behind Liv's chair.

"Don't be mean to my baby," said Liv.

Bree swallowed her mouthful of fries. "My food. You need to teach him table manners."

Liv picked up Stinky and sat him on her lap, rubbing his chin. He seemed happy at this but kept looking longingly at Bree's plate.

Ten minutes later, Bree was done, and it was time to get to work.

I took a deep breath, crossed my fingers, looked at Stinky, and asked, "Where is the demon?"

He turned his head toward me and gave me a confused look.

Liv leaned down and said, "Can you point to where the demon is?"

He bobbed his head and pointed east for a moment, then southeast, and then in three other directions.

I groaned, but Liv once again came to the rescue and asked, "Which one is the strongest?"

Stinky went still for a moment and pointed almost due north. I smiled at this; it seemed we could use the little guy for more than just being a garbage disposal after all.

"Looks like we are in business. Gear up, folks. We have a demon to hunt!" I said.

In short order, we all were geared up and ready to roll. Liv had the water cannon strapped to her back, with two full tanks of holy water ready to ruin any demon's day, and she was carrying Stinky. Blue and I had our Nerf guns filled with more of the same. Bree had changed into her standing hybrid panther form. Stella was just as she always was, as she could change into Hyde in an instant and had elected to stay in her normal form for now.

We decided to start at the campsite near Armstrong where the couple had been killed, and Blue opened a shadow portal. We stepped out into a light rain, with the clouds blocking most of the moonlight, leaving the area forebodingly dark.

"Too close!" said Stinky, and he darted behind Liv.

Shit! I blasted off the ground with my Air powers like I was on fire. Stella changed into her Hyde form as I took off. The ladies went into a defensive circle with their backs to each other. My heart hammered in my chest as fear and adrenalin kicked in. I hovered thirty feet in the air, cursing to myself and slowly turning, trying desperately to find the evil son of a bitch, but my eyes hadn't had time to adjust to the near-darkness yet. I felt blind and helpless.

What were the odds that we would have popped in almost directly on top of the demon? If it weren't for bad luck, I would have had no luck at all ...

"Point to where it is, Stinky," whispered Liv from below me.

I could just make out Stinky's tiny arm shaking and pointing east-southeast. I desperately searched out from the center of the makeshift circle below me, trying to spot the demon, but I couldn't see anything. I started calling on my Electrical powers and began building up a charge. I could shoot out a lightning blast about sixty feet, and its radius would widen out the farther it went from me. I still couldn't see anything but figured at least tossing it out was doing something.

I hesitated, as I knew a flashy blast of lightning would mess up everyone's night vision. Even though that would be the case, it might also blind the demon.

I was about warn everyone to close their eyes before I let out the massive charge when Liv cried out, "Everyone stop for a moment!"

She blurred out of the circle in the direction Stinky had been pointing. She disappeared from my view in less than a second as she ventured out into the night. I figured she was going after the demon solo and flew after her.

I found her standing about 300 meters from where we had started. I still couldn't see that well, but I was able to easily spot Liv's blood-red colored aura in the darkness. She stood dead-still and hadn't turned on the pump for the water cannon either.

Trying to spot the demon's pure-black aura at night was challenging, but if it was down there, I should have been able to see at least the distortion of the aura as it moved.

"False alert. I can't smell, hear, or see the demon anywhere nearby," said Liv below me.

"You sure?"

"Yeah, I was nose-blind with Stinky so close, but I am far enough away from him now that if the demon was near, I'd be able to smell it, but I'm getting nothing."

"Let's head back."

Liv blurred away, and I flew back to join the group. It dawned on me that Stinky's idea of "too close" could be miles away from us. If I was a tiny, almost defenseless imp, even being miles from a full-blown demon would probably be too close.

By the time I returned, Stella was back in human form again, and the group had a much more relaxed posture. My heart rate was beginning to return to normal, and it had stopped trying to pound its way out of my chest.

"I know you are scared, but we will protect you. If the demon gets close, Blue will open a shadow portal for you to jump into, and you will be back safe at the house in an instant, okay?" said Liv.

She was crouched over, stroking Stinky's quivering head and talking to him softly in a reassuring tone. It took her a good five minutes, but Stinky seemed to calm down and was again willing to help us find the demon.

We had two choices at that point. The first was that we could start walking in the direction Stinky had pointed and hope that "too close" meant a couple of kilometers away. I suspected it meant more like fifty kilometers … We opted to go with the second choice, which was to shadow-travel to the other kill sites. At each site, we would have Stinky point to where the demon was and then add that line to our map. Once we had hit four sites, wherever the lines intersected should be where it was hiding.

We popped out of the shadows near Hornepayne where the seventeen-year-old girl had been killed. Stinky's head started frantically shooting around, and his whole body shook. This was freaking me out a bit, but Liv seemed calm and unconcerned, which meant the demon wasn't close by. Bree seemed almost bored, as well, which reassured me even more.

Liv got Stinky to point, and he pointed almost back in the direction of Armstrong again.

Longlac, which was going to be our next stop, was between Armstrong and here, and you could almost make a straight line with the three points. I was a touch concerned that Longlac might be too close to where the demon actually was.

I mentioned this to the girls, and Blue suggested that we go to Nipigon next instead. This made sense, as it was well south of everything. If Stinky could point to where the demon was, it would give us a more perpendicular line to the Armstrong-Longlac-Hornepayne one and should let us pin down the area where the demon was.

Stinky was still a bundle of nerves but pointed north-northeast this time. Blue updated the map, and the lines intersected near Onaman Lake. We Google-Mapped the area and looked at the satellite images, as well, and the area seemed remote and uninhabited. We studied the area on Google where the lines intersected, but there was nothing of interest to note. I suspected the demon must be in an old abandoned cabin or a cave in the area.

"Should we call in GRC13 now?" asked Stella.

I shook my head. "I know we are supposed to call them in as backup, or even to let them handle it, but that was before we illegally brought an imp. We are on our own for this one."

Stella nodded unhappily at that, and we all did a quick check of our gear, as things were about to get very real in the next few minutes.

"Do we bring Stinky?" asked Liv.

"Nope, the little guy has done his job. Blue, open a portal to the house and send him home."

Seconds later, our cowardly little friend was back safe at the house, and we were ready to take down a demon. With Stinky out of the picture, I was tempted to call GRC13, but then realized that I wouldn't be able to explain how we had found the demon. This battle was just going to be us versus the demon.

Chapter 20

Monday, April 17

We stepped out of the shadows, and I heard some large wildlife go skittering off in the distance. Bree perked up and looked longing in the direction the noise had come from; I assumed it was deer, and she wanted some venison snacks.

I turned to Liv and quietly asked, "You smell anything?"

She went still, sniffed the air, and pointed east.

Bree bobbed her snout up and down in agreement. The wind was blowing from the west, which meant we were downwind from the demon. At least one thing was going right tonight.

"Bree, take point and lead us in."

She marched off, and the rest of us followed. As Blue's night vision was just as good as Bree's, Blue took up the second spot in our line. Stella, in her Hyde form, and I were next, and Liv was taking up the rear.

I had put Liv at the back of our line. I had two reasons for this. The first was to prevent the demon from sneaking in behind us. The second was that once we did engage the demon, I wanted Liv to take off, get in behind it, and hopefully surprise it with the water cannon.

The next twenty minutes in the near-pitch-black woods were nerve-racking, but uneventful. Finally, Bree stopped and held up a hand—or, to be more accurate, I guess that would be *paw*. We all stopped, and Bree motioned us closer. We huddled up, and she pointed just off to her left. I tracked where she was pointing, and my stomach instantly knotted up. The darkened open maw in the rock face was an entrance to a cave. The opening wasn't that big, but the real problem was I had no idea how deep the cave ran or if there was another exit. I cursed under my breath; this was going to truly suck.

There was no way we were going in there. Fighting a demon in a confined space would get most of us killed. It did favor Stella; in her Hyde form, she was nearly indestructible, and the demon would have trouble getting away from her. I seriously considered sending her in to either take it out or flush it out. The problem was, the entrance to the cave was narrow, and I doubted her larger-than-life form would even fit in there.

I studied the cave and decided we needed to draw the demon out. I started thinking about how to do that. We could make noise, but that would give up our element of surprise. I kicked around sending Liv to hose the cave opening down with holy water, which was tempting. The problem was, I didn't know how deep the cave was or if it went straight back. If there was a turn or a twist past the entrance, the water might not even hit the demon, and that would piss away our new secret weapon for nothing.

In a flash of inspiration, it came to me. I leaned over and whispered to Blue, "Take us back to the lab."

She nodded and opened a shadow portal. We all stepped into it and emerged into the lab a moment later.

Stella changed back to her human form. "Why are we here?"

The others were looking at me, too, probably all wondering why I had pulled us out.

"The cave presents a problem. Going into it is suicide, so we need to draw the demon out. I'm praying it didn't hear us, and our element of surprise is still intact. I was going to have Liv hose the entrance down, but what if the cave goes deeper or there is a bend just past the entrance? That water cannon could be deadly against the demon, and I don't want to waste it. So, plan B."

Blue groaned. "What is plan B?"

"Do we still have any grenades left from our assault on the French vampire court?"

Blue flashed me a pointed-tooth-filled grin and nodded.

"Grab one and come back here."

I walked over to the case of bottled water sitting on one of the tables and took out four bottles. I emptied them out in one of the bathrooms and returned just as Blue came back with a single grenade. I had Liv help me pour holy water from one of the spare big jugs into the bottles and then sealed them back up. Blue grinned as she handed me the grenade, as I suspected she knew what I was up to. Half a roll of duct tape later, and my holy-water grenade was ready.

A couple of minutes later, we were back in the sparse woods outside the cave. We hung out and crouched down behind a few trees, watching the entrance for the next fifteen minutes to get our night vision back. This was really just for Stella and me; the other three could see perfectly in the dark.

"Okay, it's time," I said in a soft voice, and they all nodded.

I grabbed Liv's hand, and I used my Air power to lift us both into the air. I flew us up and over the cave mouth and landed softly on the rocks above it. I left Liv there and returned to the air. I got myself in position above the mouth of the cave.

Liv moved over about twenty feet to the left, so she wasn't directly above the cave entrance, as we were worried the blast from the grenade might collapse the rocks. With Liv in a safer spot and me hovering a good fifty feet in the air, I held out my right arm and made a thumbs-up gesture with my hand.

My vision in the near-pitch-black still wasn't that great, but thankfully, each of my teammate's auras stood out like beacons in the night. Blue's shimmery aura suddenly appeared about ten feet in front of the cave mouth below me. It just as quickly disappeared again.

I covered my ears and closed my eyes, as Blue popping back into the shadows meant she had tossed the grenade. There was a loud, dull thumping noise, and I was buffeted slightly by the concussion of the blast. I opened my eyes and looked down. Below me, smoke and dust billowed from the mouth of the cave.

A dark aura of distortion shot though the haze, and the demon roared as Stella, in her Hyde form, and Bree emerged from behind the copse of trees.

"You will die for that!" roared the demon.

It raised its hands toward them, but then screamed as its back was hit directly by the stream of holy water. Its dark scales dripped off its body like melted candle wax, and it writhed in agony as Liv continued hosing it down.

Bree was rapidly closing the distance to the demon, as well, and Stella was hot on her heels.

I was just starting to feel optimistic about our chances when things went to shit. Without any warning, I was hit by a wave of invisible force and shot off into the air in an out-of-control spiral. In the pitch black, and being in a rapid spin, it was nigh impossible for me to even figure up from down. I tried to regain some sort of control, but I was too disoriented.

Thankfully, a nice, sturdy tree caught me—and by "caught me," I mean it shattered my right shin bone off its main trunk. I bounced off branches all the way to the ground until I splashed down in the mud puddle at the base of the tree.

I blinked my eyes open and regained consciousness, then realized I must have passed out for a moment or two. The smell of damp moss with a slight undertone of blood brought me back to reality. I tried to get to my feet, as the demon was still out there, but a blinding shock of pain from my lower right leg had me quickly rethinking that plan.

The pain dulled as I stopped trying to put weight on it, and I giggled to myself that at least it wasn't another shoulder injury. I wanted to just lie there and quit, but my teammates were out there battling a demon without me. I focused and carefully used my Air powers to lift me off the ground; I couldn't walk, but at least I could still fly. The shattered shin protested even this movement, and the pain almost caused me to lose control of my Air powers, but I managed to regain control before I hit the ground again. I gritted my teeth and gained more altitude.

I was on the edge of a full-blown panic attack. I had no idea where I was, where my teammates were, and more importantly, where the hell the demon was. I rotated in the air and almost cried in relief as familiar auras showed up off in the distance, and I flew toward them.

They were a good 300 meters away, which gave me a pretty fair idea of how far I had traveled before crashing into the tree. The trees in a hundred-meter radius where all down and pointing outward from the cave like a bomb had exploded there. I also couldn't see the aura of the demon anywhere. My teammates all converged on the center of the blast area where the demon had been.

It dawned on me that the demon must have sent out a wave of telekinetic power to escape from Liv's relentless stream of holy water, and we had all gotten hit by that wave.

"You're bleeding!" said Liv with concern as I hovered a foot off the ground in front of them.

"Where is the demon?" I asked, ignoring Liv's statement for the moment.

"Gone. It must have teleported out," said Blue.

We must have hurt it, and that wave of telekinetic power had probably drained a good chunk of its reserves too. At that point, it must have decided to fight another day. I was ticked, as it meant we would have to chase it down again. A part of me, though, was relieved; I was in no shape to continue fighting.

Blue's left arm was hanging limping at her side, which concerned me. "What happened to your arm?"

"Broke it on a tree when I flew back from the demon's blast. I am unhurt other than that."

"How is everyone else?" I asked.

Stella had changed back to her human form and simply said, "Fine." Olivia answered she was unhurt, but the water cannon had smashed to pieces when she'd landed. Bree couldn't say anything, but I gave her a quick look-over, and I didn't see anything wrong with her.

My head throbbed. I reached up and found my forehead was wet. I checked out my hand, and there was blood on it. I must have gotten a gash from one of the branches on the way down.

Liv stepped closer to me and grabbed my head in her hands. "Let me help," she said. She leaned closer and licked my head.

I found this odd for a moment, then remembered vamp saliva had healing agents in it.

After a few seconds, Liv let go of my head, stepped back, and asked, "Better?" as she licked her lips.

Strangely enough, I did feel much better. The gash on my forehead tingled a little, but the throbbing had gone away. "Yeah, thanks."

"Do we get Stinky and go after it?" asked Stella.

"Yeah, but not tonight. Blue and I need to heal, you need to fix that water cannon, and we need to regroup …" I paused as a random thought hit me and filled me with dread: What if the demon had someone in that cave? We'd tossed a grenade in there and had probably killed them.

I told the group my concerns, and Liv said, "The only blood I smell is from you—nothing from the cave."

I was relieved at that, but figured the demon had been holed up in there, and I wondered why. I asked Liv and Bree to check it out.

"Be careful though. I'm not sure if the blast has made the cave unstable."

The two of them left, and I turned to Stella. "Can you call Marion and see if she is up and available for some healing? Blue, you want her to fix you as well?"

Blue shook her head. "I just require sleep, and my own healing trance will fix my arm. I will retire after transporting you and the team."

Liv blurred up and said, "The cave is empty, but there are weird symbols painted on the walls of it in blood."

I unzipped my pocket and was overjoyed to see my phone was still intact; heavy-duty protective cases for the win! I handed it to Liv. "Take pictures. After that, grab the parts from the water cannon, and then we are out of here."

Liv disappeared again as Stella disconnected her call and said, "Marion is up and waiting for you."

A couple of minutes later, Liv and Bree returned, carrying the mangled water cannon. Liv handed me back my phone. Blue opened a shadow portal, and we hit the lab. Bree began changing back, and Liv made a beeline for the Food-O-Tron. Stella dropped the remains of the water cannon on the table she used as a workbench. I flew up to the Tesla coils and sucked up some electricity to give my flagging spirits a boost.

Once my powers were topped up, I returned to my original spot, and Blue opened another portal. The two of us stepped through—well, Blue stepped while I held onto her and hopped on my good leg—and came out in the hallway of Marion's floor.

I knocked on the door, and Marion opened it. I smiled as I saw her outfit: a brightly colored Mexican-style poncho and faded bell-bottom jeans with a large peace sign on each leg that had been drawn on with black marker. The outfit was completed by long white socks with big yellow happy faces on them.

Marion's eyes were magnified by her glasses, and the eyes narrowed as she checked me out from top to bottom. "Nice. A leg injury and a minor head injury for a change. I was getting bored of shoulders."

"Har har," I said as floated myself inside.

"Call me when you need picking up," said Blue as she opened another shadow portal.

"I'll fly home. Get the team home and get some sleep, okay?"

Blue nodded and disappeared into the shadows. I carefully settled into the examination chair, and Marion began examining my wounds.

"If you keep showing up at my door this often, you may just want to put me on your payroll; it will probably be cheaper for you in the long run," teased Marion as she grabbed a large pair of scissors.

She cut open the right leg of my jeans from the base of the leg to expose the wound.

"I didn't see you as the corporate type ..."

"I'm not. I was kidding. You couldn't afford my price anyway."

Thirty minutes later, my lower right leg tingled but was in one piece again. I was relieved to find that I could walk gingerly on it. The gash on my forehead was just a shiny patch of new pink skin. Marion had also found bruises and other small cuts on my arms, back, and legs, which she had dealt with as well. I couldn't run a marathon or even handle one of Blue's physical training sessions at the moment, but I was in one piece.

Just as I got up from the chair, my phone buzzed. I fished it out of my pocket and answered it without looking at who was calling.

"We tracked your phone to a remote location to an area the demon could be, and now you are at your healer. If I didn't know better, I would assume you went after the demon without calling us first for backup."

It took me a second, but I realized I had a pissed-off Captain Ben Cooper from GRC13 on the phone.

"Demon hunting?" I asked. "Blue was just taking the team out for training, and I tripped and sprained my ankle—"

"Bullshit. My office tomorrow at 10:00 a.m., and don't be late." With that, the line went dead.

Marion smiled. "Making friends, I see."

I nodded, and she continued. "Take it easy on that leg for a couple of days. I will email you my bill."

I thanked her and left her apartment. I headed for the roof of the building. As I flew home, I was concerned about my meeting with the captain tomorrow; he certainly wasn't happy with me at the moment. I was also a bit pissed that they had tracked my phone without telling me they were doing it. I was probably more annoyed at myself, though, as I should have realized they were government and did shit like that all the time …

The flight home was uneventful, and I still didn't have a clue how to deal with GRC13 tomorrow, but figured I would deal with them then. I just wanted a cold beer and then bed. The TV was on in the living room, which was probably where Bree and Liv were hanging out. Stella and Blue would both be in bed and asleep by now.

I twisted the cap off the beer and tossed it in the recycling.

"Beer! Stinky like beer!" said a wheezing voice from behind me.

I turned and found Stinky flapping his little wings and hovering in front of me. Liv had changed his outfit again. He was in a pair of baggy, shiny blue athletic shorts that ended up being more like pants on his small frame and a white muscle shirt, with his gold chain and its big "S" medallion hanging off it prominently displayed above the shirt, plus a backward tiny black baseball cap. I was amused that Liv had kept to her thug-life theme with Stinky. With Liv, you never knew; it wouldn't surprise me if tomorrow Stinky was dressed in a pink tutu with a tiara.

I grabbed a saucer and was about to pour some beer out when Liv's voice rang out from the living room: "You had best not be giving my little guy beer!"

"He was a brave trooper and has earned a beer," I said in a normal voice, knowing her hyper vamp hearing would catch every word.

"One—and I mean *one*—saucer of beer, and that is it!"

I poured out the saucer of beer and put it on the counter. Stinky landed and began lapping it up. I retired to the kitchen table, pulled out a seat, and plunked my butt in it to enjoy my beer.

About halfway through my beer, Stinky held up the saucer from the counter in my direction with a hopeful expression, and I shook my head.

"Stop trying to get more beer, and come see Momma!" yelled Liv from the living room.

Stinky's little shoulders slumped. He put down the saucer and flew off back to Liv. I laughed as I spotted the Raider's logo on the back of the cap as he flew away. I finished my beer and headed off to bed. Tomorrow was going to be a long day.

Chapter 21

Tuesday, April 18

Blue slept in later than usual due to her injuries, which made me late for my meeting. The captain's mood hadn't improved since last night. If anything, it had gotten worse. He spent a good five minutes ripping me a new one.

"And what pisses me off the most is the director has given me the full resources at our disposal, and despite cooperation between the Canadian military, the RCMP, and God only knows how many federal and provincial agencies, we still can't locate this damn demon. Yet five bloody civilians seem to be able to do it. How is that possible?"

I stayed silent, as I was between a rock and hard place here. We had found the demon by doing something illegal by importing Stinky, and heaven help me if the captain found out about the grenade we had used to flush the demon out of the cave ...

We sat silently staring at each other in a test of wills for what seemed like forever until he finally dropped his gaze with an audible sigh.

"Look, Zack, you have been straight up with me to this point. You even trusted me with your aura secret, which means that if you aren't saying anything, I'm guessing you are doing something in a grey area to find this demon. There have been times in my career that I have done things that aren't on the up-and-up to solve a case. I am not proud of those moments, but I was pleased with the results. If you are doing something illegal to find this demon, spill, and I will keep it between us, okay?"

I kicked his offer around and weighed the pros and cons. This demon needed to be dealt with, and last night, we had gotten the drop on it and still gotten our asses kicked. Sure, we had hurt it a bit, but the bottom line was it was still out there, and if I didn't cooperate and it killed again, that was on me.

I decided to roll the dice and trust the captain again. "We imported an imp."

To my surprise, he laughed. "You are a genius and an idiot. I'm guessing that demons can sense other demons?"

I nodded, and he continued. "That was the 'genius' part. The 'idiot' part was not telling me sooner. I know that demons are illegal to summon or import, but that act also takes into consideration how dangerous the creature is. An imp is about as dangerous as a house cat, which means the very worst I could do would be to fine you and confiscate the imp. I'm assuming, then, you managed to track the demon?"

I did feel stupid for not telling him about the imp, as it would have been nice to have a GRC13 team as backup last night. I told him about tracking the demon and the battle, such as it was, conveniently leaving out the grenade part.

"Sounds like you at least hurt it. I am also not sure how much having a GRC13 team nearby would have helped. Once the demon sent out the wave of telekinesis that took out your team, it teleported out right after that. You said the cave had runes painted inside of it?"

"Yeah, I have pictures on my phone. I will send them to you once I get it back when I leave."

The captain nodded at this. "Thanks. I will turn them over to our mages. Maybe seeing what runes the demon is using might let them figure out a way of getting around them and let us track the demon by magic again."

He picked up the phone and dialed someone, then said, "Get a chopper in the air and try using spells to locate the demon. It was flushed from its warded hiding spot last night, so we might get lucky."

He hung up the phone. "It probably has another spot warded, but you never know. If the spells still don't work, how soon can your team be ready to go with the imp?"

My ankle throbbed at that moment, as if warning me that it wasn't ready to be tested. Blue had her arm in a sling this morning, and she said that she needed another night of healing to be 100 percent. I hated the idea of pushing this off another day, but so far, the demon had kicked our asses, and going in injured would be suicide.

"Tomorrow night," I answered.

"No sooner? Any chance you could lend us the imp, so we could go after the demon?"

I shook my head. "My team took injuries last night, and we need another day to get back to full health. As for loaning you the imp, that isn't going to happen. It is bound to our vampire. I won't send her out alone without my team to back her up."

The captain went quiet for a moment. "What if tonight your team just locates where the demon is, and then we go in after it? If we take it down, we will give your team full credit, so you will get the bounty."

I really couldn't argue with this deal; they did the work, and we got the money. Blue, though injured, would have no issue shadow-traveling us around, and Stinky just had to point, which meant there was no real risk. Despite all that, I didn't like it.

"That is a pretty sweet deal, but I don't like it. There has already been one GRC13 team that fared poorly, and the demon has kicked my ass twice now. It seems like a bad idea to split our forces. Can't you wait until tomorrow when we can hit it together?"

Captain Cooper shook his head. "The pressure from above on this doesn't allow me to wait another day. There is also the bigger issue of what if this thing kills someone tonight due to us waiting. At least if we hit tonight, we may not beat it, but that will probably keep it at least distracted from killing an innocent."

I still didn't like it, but he had a point. In the end, I agreed we would locate the demon for them. He and I spent a few minutes working out logistics and hashing out a couple of details on how this evening would work.

Afterward, as I got out of my chair, the captain said, "By the way, I talked to my Air elemental friend down south, and he doesn't have your aura ability, nor do any of his clan members."

That was interesting for a couple of reasons. First, it confirmed that the aura ability was probably not an Air elemental trait and just an odd quirk of my genetic background. It was also interesting that his friend was in a clan. Mom had told me that elementals of the same element often lived in a clan structure. It made sense if you were looking to keep a strong line going; a couple with the same power having kids had a much better chance of passing that power on, versus an elemental having a kid with a norm. It also allowed you to learn your power better, as you had a number of people you could learn from. This was also the first time outside of Mom telling me about elemental clans that I'd come across one.

I thanked the captain for his time, and he called Dmitri to escort me to the front gate.

Once outside the gate, I emailed the pictures of the runes from the cave to Captain Cooper, then called Blue to pick me up.

Blue arrived, and I pretended to be busy on my phone, as Dmitri wanted to chat with Blue. After a couple of minutes, Dmitri came away smiling and said he would see us both here at 8:00 p.m.

Blue seemed amused, too, which was nice to see. She took us back to the lab, allowing us to hit the Food-O-Tron for lunch.

As we stepped out of the shadows, I wasn't shocked to see Stella working at her table. I wandered over to see what project she was working on. She was actually just fixing/rebuilding Liv's water cannon from our ill-fated adventure last night.

Stella cursed as she hooked up the dented water pump to the battery and nothing happened. "It would probably be easier to build another one from scratch than to fix this one."

Blue shrugged and said, "After lunch, we will go out and get more parts."

Stella sighed and tossed the broken pump on the table.

Over lunch, I brought Stella and Blue up to speed. We'd be going out tonight and using Stinky to point and plot out the demon's new location on the map. Once we figured out where it was hiding, we'd head over to the GRC13 headquarters and pick up the strike team. We'd drop them a kilometer downwind from the site and be on standby in case they needed assistance. If the fight with the demon went bad, our job was to extract the team. Blue, Bree, and I would pull the GRC13 team out while Stella and Liv distracted the demon. Once the GRC13 team was out, then we'd get our whole team out of there too.

"Only the two of us are taking it on?" asked Stella between bites of her sandwich.

"Yeah, you are to keep charging at the demon. It will probably keep tossing your Hyde form away by telekinesis, as there isn't much it can do to actually hurt you. Liv will only make high-speed passes, slicing at it with her sword as she goes by. If things go bad for GRC13, our goal is just to keep the demon busy while we get the wounded out, not to take it down. Once everyone is out, Blue will grab you and Liv and get you both out of there. Hopefully, GRC13 will kick ass and all we will have to do is come in at the end to sign the bounty forms. Hope for the best, but prepare for the worst and all that ..."

We discussed a few different scenarios and exit strategies while we finished our lunch. After lunch, Blue dropped me off back at the house before she and Stella went shopping for water cannon parts.

It was just past noon, and I really had nothing to do until after sundown. There was some housework I probably should have been doing, but with my ankle, I didn't want to push it—well, that, and there was an unfinished 1/72-scale Mosquito that was calling my name. I happily headed for the basement and groaned as I opened the door and got hit by the stench of Stinky's cologne. I used my Air power to glide down the stairs, rather than putting weight on my ankle.

The smell of Axe got stronger as I descended, but once I was past the cold cellar that he and Liv were sleeping in, it faded. The pungent odors from my model area soon made the sweet, sickly smell of the cologne a distant memory.

I hit play on my phone, and the soothing sounds of the 1940s were coming out of my Bluetooth speaker as I examined the finished cockpit I had worked on last time. I smiled at how good the small details I had painted in looked, then got down to business. My next step was adding a few parts to the interior fuselage and then painting it. Artie Shaw's "Stardust" started playing, and I found myself humming along as I cracked open the Testor's model glue and began assembling the main body.

An hour later, Bree came down looking for Blue and Stella, as she was hungry.

"They are probably still out shopping for parts to fix Liv's water cannon."

"Oh. I guess I'll find my own breakfast then," said Bree with a slight growl to her tone as she stomped away.

Weres were grumpy when they woke up—and hungry. The sound of the front door slamming a minute later let me know that Bree was gone. I hoped that whatever fast-food place she hit didn't dick her around, or some pimple-faced minimum-wage jockey was going to have a very bad day.

I got a text from Captain Cooper shortly after Bree left. They'd had no luck tracking the demon by magic. This meant the demon had another warded hidey hole somewhere.

The rest of my afternoon was uneventful but productive, as I got the interior fuselage painted and assembled. A quick dinner once Liv was up, and we were off demon hunting again.

We started in Armstrong, as it had been the most northern attack spot. After calming Stinky down, he pointed southeast. Stella marked the direction on the map and hit the next two spots, repeating the process. Our three lines bisected an unnamed island in the northeast part of Lake Nipigon. Mission accomplished—we'd found where the demon was hiding.

I checked my phone. It was five minutes to eight o'clock, and I pointed this out to Blue. She opened a shadow portal, and after dropping Stinky off at home, we stepped out of the shadows just outside the main gate of the GRC13 base. The team was assembled and ready to go. Dmitri was already in his stand-up Werebear form. There was a big-ass grey wolf beside him, which was the Werewolf in his beast form. Jack was standing at the front of the assembled group in his mage's robes, holding his staff. The two Enhanced female members blended in better with the rest of the GRC13 human members, as they were in full tac gear and armed like the rest. The blue aura of the Ice elemental and the red-and-white-checked aura of the Tank, though, gave them away.

Stella handed me the map as we approached the group, and she fell back behind Blue. Jack and I exchanged greetings, and I handed him the map. He passed it off to the nearest human GRC13 officer, who was a taller man with "Johnson" on his uniform. Johnson stepped away and pulled out a phone, taking a few pics and then saying something into his mic.

"Dan will send the pictures to base," said Jack. "They will task a satellite to get a better look at the island. If we are lucky, it might pick out a structure or something that will give us a better idea where the demon is hiding."

I nodded at that, and he added, "Before I forget, the captain passed along those runes you sent from the cave to our research scholars. They only managed to translate a few words, but what they've found out so far doesn't bode well. The first part of the runes seems to be some sort of blocking spell, which we suspected. The problem is, there seems to be a second part to the runes' purpose. The scholars have only translated two of the words to that part: 'energy' and 'portal.' "

My stomach knotted at those two words and what they could mean. "You are thinking that the second part has something to do with opening a portal to Hell?"

Jack nodded grimly. "The captain, just after your meeting, sent an investigation team back to the cabin where we first encountered the demon. Under the floorboards, they found more runes. Those runes are only half the length of the ones found on the cave wall. That was how we figured out the cave runes were two parts. The good news is we have destroyed and sanctified the runes in both locations."

I studied Jack for a moment. "For someone who has just given me good news, you don't seem happy. What am I missing here?"

"This is just speculation on my part, but I think the runes aren't the actual location of where the demon is trying to open a portal. I think the runes just act as relays for the energy, and they pass it on to the site where it is trying to open one."

"Shit. Getting rid of the runes stops any new energy from being sent from them to the portal spell, but the kills that have happened so far have already been sent. As we can't find the demon through magic, then it at least has another set of runes wherever it is hiding, so if it kills again, more energy will be sent to that portal spell."

Jack nodded and was about to say something when a deep, low growl split the air. The Werewolf bared its teeth and raised its hackles. It was pointed directly at Bree. The GRC13 team went on alert, and most were reaching for their weapons. Bree made eye contact with the wolf, and in less than a second, it whimpered and moved behind Dmitri's large form.

"Bree! Leave the puppy alone," I teased.

"Puppy needed to learn its place. We are all good now," said Bree while she rolled her head to stretch out her neck muscles.

The troops stood down, their weapons were lowered, and a few nervous laughs echoed from them. Many of them were eying Bree with newfound respect—or at least a wariness of my short blonde friend.

I turned my attention back to Jack. "How many kills does the demon need to open a portal?"

He shrugged. "It depends on how big and how long the portal needs to last. Blood rituals like these generate a lot of magical energy, but thankfully, portals need massive amounts of energy to work. The demon could be a couple of kills away, or it could take thousands of these kills to open one ..."

At that point, one of the GRC13 officers approached Jack with a question about the mission. Jack excused himself, leaving me with my thoughts.

Northern Ontario being so vast and remote had several advantages—and disadvantages—for a portal. The biggest advantage was you could probably bring an army of demons through a portal out here and no one would be the wiser. Another advantage was that the chances of someone stumbling onto the portal by accident were next to nil.

One disadvantage was that the sparse population meant there weren't a lot of places to achieve a large kill count, which meant it was harder to open a portal.

My thoughts went back to Jack's statement about how big and how long the portal needed to last. I doubted the demon would be able to kill enough people to open a large, permanent portal due to the sparse population in the area, but what if that wasn't the plan? What if the demon was just trying to open a portal long enough to pull another couple of demons across? If those three demons scattered to Manitoba, Quebec, and Northern Michigan and started doing the same thing our demon was doing here, the numbers could grow exponentially. Heck, they didn't even have to scatter. We were having enough trouble dealing with one demon; trying to take on four of them would be impossible.

The bottom line was, we needed to stop this demon soon before it could open a portal ...

Twenty minutes later, there was a murmur from the GRC13 team.

"Command has spotted a small structure at the south end of the island, which is close to where your lines intersect," said Jack.

Blue stepped forward, and the three of us looked over the map.

"Can you get us here?" asked Jack as he pointed to the far southeastern edge of the island.

Blue studied the map for a moment, looked up to the sky, and said, "There is enough moonlight, so there should be some shadows close to that area I can use."

We spent a few minutes going over the plan and got the details sorted out.

"Alright, listen up!" yelled Jack. "Blue, here, is going to transport us to a spot about one click east of the target. This puts us upwind from the demon. We will march overland and scope out the structure. We will determine what to do once we know exactly what we are dealing with. Stay alert and keep your eyes peeled. This thing is tricky; it knows our tactics and has already gotten the drop on Team A. Keep checking your six. If you spot it, go weapons hot. This is not a capture mission; we are going to put it down. Any questions?"

The group was silent, and then Jack turned to us and said, "Stella, can you change so they can see your other form? If things go south, I don't want them shooting at you when you are there to rescue them."

Stella nodded, and in less than a second, her dainty form changed into its monstrous alter ego, which got more than a few murmurs from the group.

"Zack and his team will be on station to render help if we get into trouble," said Jack to his squad. "This lovely lady is a friendly and will not be amused if you take a shot at her, got it? Also, as you may have guessed by Todd's earlier reaction, this other young lady is a Were—a Werepanther, to be exact. Do not shoot the large black cat, as she, too, is friendly. Let's move out!"

Blue opened a shadow portal, and Stella went through first. The rest of us lined up and then stepped through in an orderly manner. I was one of the last to go through.

On the other side, it was much darker than the area outside the GRC13 base, and it took my eyes a bit to adjust. Thankfully, as nine of the seventeen people were outlined in an aura, it was easier to get my bearings.

The GRC13 team formed up with Dmitri in the lead and the female Tank directly behind him. The human element followed in a double line behind them, with Jack and the Ice elemental as the last pair in the line. Todd the Werewolf was alone in the trail position.

They headed west and soon disappeared into the darkness. I could faintly make out their auras for a little while after that, and then those, too, were swallowed up in the blackness. My stomach knotted as they vanished from sight, and I hoped that was not an omen of what was to come.

Chapter 22

Tuesday, April 18

Once the GRC13 team had left the area, Bree began peeling off her coat and the rest of her clothes. Normally, I would have made a funny comment about this, but standing there on that cool, dark, and foreboding shore, it didn't seem right.

Bree stuffed her clothes into the knapsack she'd been carrying and wordlessly handed it off to Blue. Blue opened another shadow portal and tossed the pack into it.

It hit me that I was standing there staring at Bree's naked form, but for a change, I wasn't checking her out sexually. For some reason, her nudity didn't even register with me; either I was getting used to it, or more likely, I was too worried about Dmitri and his team to be distracted.

It was an odd feeling standing around while someone else went to confront the danger for a change. I didn't like it at all. This was even more nerve-racking than heading into battle. At least when I was charging into danger, I was doing something, and that kept my mind from focusing on the fear. This standing around waiting sucked.

Loud cracks of bones snapping echoed like gunshots through the still woods and pulled me from my musings. Bree's body sprouted black fur and began to contort in odd and painful ways. The wet sounds of muscles tearing and reforming put my teeth on edge. I might have been getting used to her naked human form, but I doubted I'd ever get used to seeing her change.

A few seconds later, Bree let out a low growl and stretched out her new elongated limbs for a moment before going still. She sniffed the air to the west and let out another soft growl. It worried me, but I was beginning to understand Growl: I knew that last one had meant "Something I don't like that way, but not too close." Considering that Bree in her beast form could only growl or roar, it was impressive how many different tones and intensities she could express.

Oddly enough, Stella changed back out of her Hyde form just after Bree switched to her new form. Blue raised an eyebrow at her, and

Stella said, "Relax. Bree or Liv will scent the demon if it gets close, and I can change back in a second. It was getting hard to calm my Hyde side; it wanted to go fight."

Liv was strangely quiet and just stayed dead-still in a way that only vampires could pull off. She was staring off to the west. The whole team seemed to be feeling the strain of waiting for the other shoe to drop.

"They will be fine," I said. "Dmitri is a pro, and there is no way he will let that demon get the better of him a second time."

I got a few nods in response, but no one seemed to relax their rigid postures in the slightest.

My ankle was acting up again, so I used my powers to lift myself off the ground by a foot, and it immediately felt better.

Time seemed to drag by, and then a loud *bang* and a bright flash in the distance split the night. It was quiet again for another thirty seconds, and then the sounds of automatic weapons cooking off filled the air. The steady thrum of shots from their MP5s continued, occasionally punctuated by the louder *boom* of a high-caliber sniper rifle going off. The gunfire continued nonstop for a good two minutes, though the volume lessened as it went on. Normally, I would think that someone or something was getting a world of hurt laid on them, but I doubted the demon was just standing around soaking up bullets.

A few last bursts filled the air, and everything went eerily quiet and still again.

We all looked at each other as if wondering if we should rush over to the area and help. An unfamiliar ringing filled the air, pulling our attention to Blue.

She hit a button on the satphone GRC13 had given her and answered it. She nodded, then hung up. "The demon teleported out, but they have wounded," said Blue as she opened a portal.

We stepped out of the shadows and into a small clearing surrounded by leafless trees. The smell of sulfur and cordite hit us like a brick to the head. Someone off to the right moaned in anguish and was clearly in pain. Liv headed off in that direction, and we followed her.

I spotted the female Tank's aura ahead. She was crouched down and rendering aid to someone on the ground. As we closed in, I recognized Johnson from earlier, though the large chunk of wood lodged in his gut was new—that last thought was too flippant, and I realized I was still nervous and worried about what we'd find.

The Tank looked up as we approached—first in concern and then, seeing us, her expression changed to relief. "Can you open a portal direct to our med bay?"

Blue nodded and had one open before I could even blink.

"Hang on, Johnson. This is going to hurt, but we have to get you to the healers," said the Tank.

She slipped her short, muscular arms under his large frame, and he groaned. His mouth opened in a silent scream as she effortlessly lifted him off the ground. They disappeared through the shadow portal moments after that.

"Someone else is bleeding heavily over there," said Liv.

We turned and followed her through the trees. I spotted Dmitri's aura when we got closer. Another human member of GRC13 was on the ground. His face was covered in blood from a nasty head wound, but his chest was moving steadily up and down. He was still bleeding, so he was alive.

Dmitri's large brown furry head lifted as we approached. He gave us a nod and was surprisingly gentle as he slipped his massive paws under the downed trooper and lifted him. Blue opened a portal, and he and the wounded trooper were gone.

Liv led us to two more wounded GRC13 members. The female ice elemental was cradling her busted right arm, and a human officer I didn't recognize was on the ground with his lower left leg sticking out at an awkward angle. Two other GRC13 troopers helped him up as Blue opened another portal, and all four of them went through.

They had been wounded, but at least no one had been killed. I gave a small, silent prayer of thanks for that.

I saw Jack's large multicolored aura off in the distance through the trees and said, "Jack is over there. Let's go find out what happened."

We joined Jack in a clearing. In the center of the clearing were the remains of a small shack that had been flattened. The remaining GRC13 troops dug through the debris while Jack looked on.

Jack turned his attention to us and said, "HQ said that you got our four wounded to the healers; it sounds like all of them are going to make it. Thank you."

Blue waved his comment off, and I asked, "What happened?"

"We found the shack, and Dmitri signaled that the demon was inside. We surrounded it from a distance and fired a flash-bang into it. We sent Sheri, our Tank, and Dmitri in at a full clip to level the shack and hopefully flush the hellspawn out. They went through that old shack like a knife through butter, and it collapsed as they blew through the other side, but no demon. It was dead quiet, and nothing happened. Johnson stepped out from the trees to get a closer look. As he approached, the demon suddenly popped out from under the shack and used its power to toss the debris outward. Johnson was hit and flung back into the trees. Dmitri and Sheri were hit, too, but both shrugged it off. After that, the team opened up, and the demon fought back. Sheri closed in and exchanged a few blows with the demon. It used its power to toss her into the woods, but then decided it had had enough and teleported out."

"Found it, sir!" yelled one of the GRC13 members as Jack finished.

We got closer, and under the debris, there was a small boarded-up hole. Painted in dried blood over the boards were the same runes we had found in the cave. Jack took out his phone, as did a couple of the GRC13 officers, and they all snapped a few pics.

"Tricky bastard," mumbled Jack as he put his phone back into one of the many pockets of his robe.

Jack turned his attention to me again and said, "One piece of good news: Team A reported that when they hit the demon, it was over six feet in height. When it was fighting with Sheri, it was the same height as she was, and she is only 4'11" on a good day. I also noticed that I could see a faint red glow under all of its skin."

"It's using its mass to repair the damage we have inflicted on it, so it's getting smaller. If you are seeing the glow, we are getting close to cracking its shell, as well," I said.

"Exactly. It won't be fun once its true form emerges, but at least we won't have to worry about the telekinesis and teleporting away anymore and can end this thing for good."

It would have been nice if they could have ended it tonight, but at least Jack's report let me know we were grinding it down.

"You want us to grab Stinky and locate the demon again?" I asked.

Jack rubbed his chin and shook his head. "My team needs to recover. We will all go after it tomorrow night. Hopefully, we hurt it enough that it will hide tonight and not hurt anyone else. Can Blue take us back to base? I would like to check on the wounded and make sure they are doing okay."

I nodded in agreement.

Jack whistled, and Todd came bounding through the trees like a big excited dog, rather than the four-legged killing machine he was. Blue opened a shadow portal, and we deposited Jack and his team at the front gate of their base.

We exchanged goodbyes and then headed to the lab.

Chapter 23

Tuesday, April 18

After a quick stop by the lab to get Bree some food and Liv a pint of blood, we were home. I'd planned just to grab a coffee and curl up with a book, but quickly found out that wasn't going to happen.

"I want to go out," said Liv.

Bree shook her head. "I want to have a nice long, hot shower. After that, I plan on vegging on the couch in front of the TV."

Olivia gave Bree a pout. Then she looked at me and smiled. "I want one of the two flying dates you owe me."

I groaned. The last thing I wanted to do tonight was go out, and I tried to get out of it. "I'm supposed to be resting the ankle."

"If we are flying, you aren't putting any weight on it, so suck it up, buttercup."

She had me there, and I reluctantly nodded my agreement.

"Great! Let me get Stinky, and we are out of here."

Like magic, Stinky, at hearing his name, flew down the hallway toward Liv like a missile. She laughed as she caught him. "How is my brave boy? We are going to do something fun now," said Liv as she rubbed his chin.

Stinky's eyes got wide with excitement, and he asked, "Beer?"

Liv shook her head, and Stinky took another stab at it. "Pizza?"

"We are going flying!" said Liv.

Stinky gave her a look I can only describe as "What is the crazy vampire talking about?" But Liv didn't seem to notice.

Liv headed out the door, and I followed. She tossed Stinky up into the air, and I used my powers to lift us up too. We climbed, and Stinky flapped his tiny wings frantically to catch us. I flew south; once you got out of Hamilton, it was mostly rural area in that direction, and there was less chance of us being spotted.

"I want to free fall!" yelled Liv over the wind rushing by us.

I nodded and took us higher. Once I got to about 10,000 feet and we were over farms and woods, I stopped.

Stinky caught up to us and asked, "How is Mama flying?"

"Zack is using his Air powers to lift us both. If he wasn't, this would happen," said Liv as she pushed off from me.

I took the hint and dropped the Air beneath her, and she began plummeting toward Earth like a stone.

"Mama, no!" cried Stinky in his squeaky voice.

"Save me, Stinky!" yelled Liv, followed by a not-so-dramatic "*WHEEEEEEE*!!"

Stinky tucked his wings and dove like a falcon after Liv. I had no idea if the little guy had enough power to actually save her or not, but I had to give him credit for trying. I flipped myself over and shot off after them both.

The wind screamed by me, as I used my power to give myself some extra speed. I had to admit that this had been a good idea. The fresh air was invigorating, and it was a beautiful, clear spring night.

Stinky caught Liv first. She wrapped him up in a hug and whispered something in his ear. He was freaking out as, in the hug, Liv had pinned his wings, and they were both still tumbling through the air. I decided to give the little guy a break and used my powers to catch them both, even though there was still a good 4,000 feet to go before the ground.

As they sat suspended in the air, Stinky stopped panicking but had a confused look on his face.

"It's okay, little one. This is just a game Zack and I play. He lets me fall but catches me before I hit the ground," said Liv, cuddling Stinky and rubbing his head.

"Mama crazy," murmured Stinky.

"Yup! Take us up, and let's do it again! And this time, don't cut the ride short," said Liv, looking at me.

I nodded and rocketed us back up in the sky. I stopped at around 10,000 feet again. Liv let go of Stinky, and he flapped his wings and hovered beside us.

"I'm going to try something different this time," I said.

Liv nodded that she was game.

I concentrated and released a massive burst of wind directly under Liv. The blast shot her straight up, and I heard her giggling as she shot upward. Stinky and I hovered there with our necks bent upward, watching the crazy vampire shoot up above us. She probably ended up a good 500 feet above us before the momentum of the blast gave out. She slowed, stopped, and then gravity took over, and she began dropping back toward us.

A few seconds later, she swooshed by us, laughing. I gave her a ten-second head start and dove after her.

"Save Mama!" said Stinky as he flew behind me.

"You sure? We could let her drop and then go for a beer?" I yelled over my shoulder as we shot after her.

He was quiet for a moment and then, in a determined voice, said, "Save Mama!"

I poured on the speed and left Stinky behind as I raced after the tumbling vampire. I caught her with a good thousand feet to spare. She pointed up, and I did as I was told.

On the flight up, I wondered if a fall from 10,000 feet would actually kill her. I figured it probably wouldn't, unless she happened to impale herself on a tree through the heart or something similar. I had no doubt it would probably hurt and break most of her bones, but as long as she fed shortly after the impact, she'd probably be fine. Not that I had any intention of finding out …

We did five more free falls, a few loop-the-loops, and some other aerial acrobatics. The strain of using my power this freely started catching up with me. I flew farther south and landed on the end of Port Dover Pier. The pier, at this time of night, was deserted. I grabbed a seat on one of the wooden benches facing the lake. Lake Erie was fairly calm this evening, but there were flashes of lightning way out over the lake. My body tingled a little, which let me know the storm was coming our way.

We must have tuckered Stinky out, as he just curled up on the other end of the bench, put his head down, and went to sleep. Liv was dancing around in front of us, giddy with excitement.

"How's the ankle doing?" asked Liv.

To my surprise, it was fine. I was sitting, so there no weight on it, and the flying earlier had also put no strain on it. "It's good."

She nodded and gave me an odd look. It caught me off guard, as she seemed nervous. Liv had expressed many emotions since I'd know her, but I couldn't ever recall her being nervous about anything. She bit her lower lip and moved closer to me. She straddled my lap, and her green eyes sparkled with mischief.

"Liv, what are you up to?" I asked.

She smiled and tilted my head slightly back with her hand. "This is a date, right?"

I nodded, and she added, "What is a date without a kiss?"

She leaned forward, and our lips met. I was stunned and didn't respond for a moment, but quickly got more into it, and the kiss deepened. She wrapped her arms around my shoulders as we continued. Almost on their own accord, my hands slid around the slides of her lithe waist. My fingers found some bare skin in the small area that the bottom of her top didn't cover, just above the waist of her black yoga pants.

The kiss got hungrier and more intense as we continued. My body had become extremely aware of her on my lap. I moaned as she rolled her hips and grinded herself into me. My hands became bolder, too, as they slid down from her waist and cupped her shapely cheeks.

Stinky made a snoring noise beside us, and we both laughed as we continued making out like a couple of love-struck teenagers. I tried to remember the last time I had done something like this with a woman in public. It hit me that the last time would have been with Rebecca, when we'd first started dating. I pushed that thought aside; it felt wrong to think of some else at a time like this.

Liv broke the kiss and leaned in closer. She whispered in my ear, "I'm going to collect on the other thing you owe me ..."

In my lust-induced fog, it took me a second, but I remembered I owed her a feeding as part of the deal. "Go ahead, but go easy. I still have to fly us home."

Liv pushed my jacket down over my right shoulder and yanked my T-shirt collar to the side. I moaned softly as her tongue and lips flicked over my exposed neck. A faint pinprick of pain cut through everything for a moment. Liv moaned deeply as she drank from me, and a head rush of euphoria went through my body. I moaned, as there was something deeply satisfying and sensual about her feeding this time. I was puzzled why this felt so good, as the other time she had fed from me, it hadn't been like this.

She stopped feeding from me and licked the area she had been using. My neck tingled where she had been, but there was no lingering pain.

Liv sat up and gazed into my eyes. Her own emerald eyes almost seemed to glow at this moment. She slowly licked her lips, and the sight of that was one of the hotter things I'd ever seen in my life. I was very aware that she was warmer now as well. She leaned into me again and said, "If Stinky wasn't here, I would take you right here on this bench ..."

My body reacted instantly to her statement, but thankfully, my mind knew better, as I was pretty sure she was just teasing me. "I can probably hit him with a large enough blast of air to send him at least most of the way home."

Liv giggled. "Tempting, but that would be mean. He is sleeping so peacefully at this moment."

I smiled. "But, honey, our sex life hasn't been the same since we had our child."

"I promise, next weekend. I will get my parents to look after him. We can go to that quaint inn on the water that we went to when we were dating."

"The one where you wore the sheer little black number and we tried, um, *you know* for the first time?"

Liv said, "That's the one, and this time you can have the riding crop …" With that, she burst out laughing and hugged me warmly.

We stayed in that embrace and just let the fresh air and the sounds of the waves wash over us for a bit …

A distant rumble of thunder ended the moment. Liv released me, sat back up on my lap, and faced me. "I think that is a sign that this wonderful evening is coming to a close."

I nodded, and Liv nimbly dismounted my lap. The storm was coming in over the lake but was still a ways off. I tried to stand, but my ankle protested, so I used my Air power to help me to my feet. I was a touch lightheaded, and my power reserves were on the low side. I had enough juice to get us home, but I would be totally drained once we got there. A peel of thunder in the background gave me a solution.

"I'll be back," I said to Liv and, before she could even reply, lifted off into the air. I bobbed up and down a few times, as I wasn't totally focused on flying at this moment, but managed to stay aloft and not go swimming in the lake.

The storm got louder, and my body tingled more as I approached the dark, ominous clouds. The rain began pelting me as I hit the edge of the storm.

My ears rang as a huge blast of lightning went off just in front of me. I barely noticed it, though, as my body absorbed the immense amounts of electricity in the air. In seconds, I was brimming with power again. My erection had faded on the flight over, but it was back now. There were times when I thought I liked thunderstorms just a wee bit too much.

If Olivia hadn't been waiting for me, I would have hung out in the center of the storm, soaking up power for a lot longer. I sighed and turned toward shore.

As I landed, Liv gave me a look, and I said, "Sorry. Needed to get some gas for the ride home."

"C'mon, Stinky. Time to go home," said Liv.

Our imp cracked one eye open but didn't move. "Stinky tired."

Liv rolled her eyes but leaned over and scooped him up. She cradled him in her arms, and I lifted all of us into the air.

As I had power to burn, we made it home in short order. I had mostly dried out from my earlier soaking, though there was a little ice around the bottom hem of my jeans.

Liv tossed Stinky into the air as we came in the front door. He flapped his little wings and made a beeline for the kitchen.

Liv leaned in and gave me a quick peck on the cheek. "Thank you for a lovely night."

"You're welcome. I had fun too."

Liv laughed. "Of course you did; you were with me." She then strutted off after Stinky.

I stood there watching her go ... Well, to be totally honest, my eyes were fixed on the amazing curves of the skin-tight black yoga pants. She disappeared into the kitchen, which broke the hypnotic spell I had been under. I shook my head to clear it and decided to call it a night.

Sleep didn't come easy to me that night. My mind kept going over our "date." I wondered if this was the start of something or if it was Liv just being Liv. The main thing that made her exciting and fun to be with was her unpredictability, which, strangely enough, also made her annoying and frustrating at times. I already cared for her deeply as a friend; I felt that way about all my teammates, as I really enjoyed having them all in my life. They made my life chaotic, but fun, and I would take that over ordered and lonely any day of the week.

There were problems with a long-term relationship with Liv, though, the biggest being that vampires couldn't have kids. If I went down this road, my dreams of having a big family would be gone. I guessed we could adopt kids, though seeing Liv in a motherly role actually made me shudder: "Go to sleep, kids, or I will drain you until you pass out. Mommy has a craving for veal ..." I had a feeling those imaginary adopted kids would cost me a fortune in therapy as they got older.

There was also the problem of working together in dangerous situations. Would I hesitate in sending Liv into the fray if we were a couple? Would I be distracted in watching out for her, not focusing on what I was supposed to be doing? That inattention could easily get someone killed.

Lastly, there were the issues of her being a vampire. Long, sunny walks on the beach weren't ever going to happen. Doing things during the day, like normal people, would be out.

I lay there kicking around thoughts like that over and over again. In the end, I realized I was being silly. Knowing Liv, by tomorrow, she would have mostly forgotten tonight, and it would be like the date had never happened. To her, this had probably been just a fun night—a way to kill some time—and nothing more than that.

Sigh.

Chapter 24

Wednesday, April 19

The next morning, things were looking up for the health of my team. Blue's arm was fully healed when I joined them for lunch—well, *their* lunch, my breakfast, as I'd slept in due to being out late with Liv.

I hadn't even thought about my injured ankle until Blue asked how it was. It felt a little stiff, but there was no pain or soreness, which meant I was in good shape for tonight.

Stella had also gotten the water cannon fully repaired/rebuilt that morning. It and both Nerf guns were topped up with holy water and ready for action. There was also a text from Dmitri, saying that all wounded officers from last night would make a full recovery. They would have a full team ready to go for tonight.

I was feeling optimistic about tonight. We were going to hit the demon with us and GRC13 combined, and in my gut, I felt this was going to end—one way or another. I just hoped it ended with us living through the experience.

After lunch, there wasn't much to do until sundown when Olivia was up and able to join us, so I took the opportunity to go work on the Mosquito. As I sat down and looked at the completed parts, I took satisfaction in how this project was turning out. This was always an odd time when building a model: You were so close to finishing it that there was a temptation to rush the last steps to get it done. The problem was, you could ruin hours of work and botch the whole thing up. I forced myself to be patient and started working the nosecone and canopy sections as my 1940's playlist hummed away in the background.

By dinnertime, the Mosquito was fully assembled, and I had the clear plastic parts masked off in preparation for painting. It looked dull in the mainly unpainted grey plastic, but I was pleased by how it was turning out. There were a few painted spots, like the undercarriage, the cockpit interior, and the props, which made it easier to visualize the final version. The last steps would be to paint the rest of it and decal it.

I tidied up the desk, gave the unfinished Mosquito one last admiring glance, turned off the reading light, and headed upstairs. I just hoped I would be around to finish it …

* * * * *

We stepped out of the shadows and arrived at the campsite in Armstrong where the couple had been killed in the second attack. Stinky seemed a little calmer this time and pointed east-northeast without being asked.

"You sure?" I asked.

Stinky nodded firmly and pointed in the same direction again. Armstrong was the most northern attack site, which was why I had confirmed the direction with Stinky. He was pointing north, which meant the demon was outside its normal hunting ground. This might be a good sign, as maybe it was hiding out outside the perimeter of the previous attack sites to avoid being found.

We shadow-traveled to two more spots. The lines on our map intersected about eight kilometers from Little Current River Provincial Park. Little Current River Provincial Park sounded much grander than it was; from Google Maps, it looked like a lake in the middle of nowhere. Googling the park barely brought up much information at all. It was the sort of place a die-hard nature lover would go to get back to nature without having another human around for miles.

Its remote location, though, fit with my theory that the demon was trying its best to remain hidden. The site was well outside the area it had been hunting in.

With the hiding spot located, our next stop was GRC13's base. After dropping off Stinky at home, we shadow-traveled directly into the enormous hangar. This had been prearranged under an agreement that we wouldn't take any pictures or record anything on our phones.

There was a portable screen set up with a projector. There were folding chairs set up in front of the screen. The bulk of them were already filled with heavily armed GRC13 officers. Jack and Dmitri greeted us, and I handed over our map. Jack passed it to a tech who was waiting nearby. The tech fed it into a scanner attached to a laptop.

"Tim will upload that to Control, and they will get a better image of the area from the satellite. While we are waiting for those pictures to come in, take a seat, and we will brief you on how tonight is going to work."

I noticed there were five empty chairs in the front row waiting for us.

After we were seated, Jack started his briefing. "Tonight's operation has three phases. Phase one is to find the exact location of where the demon is hiding and to flush it out into the open. Phase two is to take on the demon and crack its shell. Phase three is to take down the demon in its true form."

He paused for a moment and then added, "Tonight, we are going to take down the demon no matter what it takes. If we take casualties in the first encounter, our two healers onsite will deal with them. As soon as we shadow-travel out of here, the choppers will head to the site and be on standby to evac any wounded. The rest of us will re-form. We will use the imp to locate the demon and hit its new location. We will keep doing this until we are all dead or wounded, or the demon has been banished."

My gut knotted up as the reality of what was about to happen sunk in. Tonight, one way or another, was going to be for all the marbles.

Jack started going over each of the phases in detail. The thing that surprised me was that he was splitting up my team and integrating it with GRC13. He had Liv and Dmitri on point, with Sheri the Tank and Stella in her Hyde form directly behind them. Bree and Todd would trail the group to watch our backs. In the main group, Jack and Ariel the Ice elemental were in front, the human GRC13 members were in the middle, and Blue, the two healers, the two medics, and their two armed escorts were at the back. The escorts were GRC13 members who had been pulled in for the mission from Team A.

Jack had me flying overhead. Blue, Liv, and I were going to be provided communication gear, so we could listen and talk on the main channel.

He had bumped up the number of sharpshooters on the team from one to four. The sharpshooters would provide fire support from a distance, and each would have a spotter. This made sense, as it kept the humans back from the main fight, and the spotters could also provide close support for the snipers if the demon closed in.

For the fight, there were four groups. The first group—the Enhanced melee group—was made up of Sheri, Stella, and Dmitri. Liv would join once she had drained the tanks on her water cannon. The second group was the Enhanced range group, which was Jack, Ariel, and me. The sniper teams were the third group. The last group was the support/

medical group; Todd, Bree, and Blue were not to engage the demon but were to pull the wounded out and get them back to the healers and medics who were on station well back from the main battle area.

The trickiest part of this plan was being careful about the melee group not crossing the lanes of fire from the snipers and ranged Enhanced group. The snipers would be using silver-alloy high-caliber rounds. These would be fatal to Dmitri and Liv if they were hit in the wrong spots. The rounds might hurt Stella and Sheri, too, though it probably wouldn't be fatal to them. As Dmitri and Stella couldn't talk in their alternate forms, Stella had been paired with Sheri, and Dmitri with Liv. Liv and Sheri would announce they were engaging before approaching the target, in order to warn the snipers to hold fire. The spotters would also keep an eye on the wider area to make sure the lanes were clear to avoid friendly fire.

Just as Jack started answering questions and concerns at the end of his briefing, a technician brought up the new satellite images on the main screen. It was quickly evident that there were no human-made structures in the area. Lots of trees, rocks, and hills, though, which meant the demon probably was in a cave again. The good news was that, with all the hills in the area, there were plenty of good shooting platforms for the sniper teams to set up on.

"Okay. The weather is clear in the area, with eight-kilometer winds from the southwest. We will come in from the northeast one click out, so we are upwind of the target," said Jack. He pointed to a sparsely treed area in the northeast section of the image and added, "This area is fairly open and will make a good approach area. Once we get close, Liv and Dmitri will use their enhanced senses to find the demon."

He then answered a couple of questions. When the briefing was over, he had everyone gear up. Dmitri and Todd moved off to an open area. They stripped off the track suits they were wearing and started to change forms. Bree and Stella went to the opposite end of the hangar from Dmitri and Todd. Stella changed, and Bree used Stella's Hyde form to hide behind as she, too, stripped and changed.

My jaw dropped as Dmitri completed his change into his hybrid standing-bear form in less than ten seconds. Todd's transformation wasn't as smooth; he lay on the floor convulsing and screaming in pain, as his body slowly morphed from human to Werewolf. I had to look away.

Thankfully, the techs approached Liv, Blue, and myself, and started fitting us with our throat mics and earpieces. They had Liv and I equipped in short order. We did our com checks, and they made some adjustments. Blue had no issues with the throat mic, but her non-human-shaped ear was giving her tech fits. In the end, he had to use tape to keep it in place, but Blue was able to talk and hear without any issues once he was done.

A loud wolf howl echoed around the hangar as Todd completed his change. Even from where I was standing, I could tell that was one pissed-off Werewolf. He snarled at Dmitri, and Dmitri's large Ursuline form just gazed down at him silently for a moment. Todd whimpered and lowered his head. The two of them strolled over to join everyone else. Stella and Bree were already back and were standing just off to the side. Bree's standing Werepanther form moved over to Blue and handed her the knapsack with Bree's clothes. Blue did her shadow thing, and the knapsack was gone.

"Alright, people, line up, and let's go end this demon!" yelled Jack.

Blue opened another shadow portal. Dmitri and Liv went through first, with Stella and Sheri on their heels. I was the next to go through.

The crisp night air was a pleasant change from the aviation gas-and-oil odors that had permeated the hangar we were just in. The three-quarter moon provided some light, but the area was almost pitch black, and I was waiting for my eyes to adjust. I immediately took to the air to get a better look of the area around us. I hoped I might get lucky and spot the demon's aura in the distance, but no luck.

Jack's voice came through on my earpiece. "We will hold here for fifteen minutes and let everyone's eyes adjust. Liv? Dmitri? Proceed one hundred meters forward and hold position."

"Roger-dodger," said Liv over the channel.

Liv left her mic open, so everyone heard her next line of "Okay, teddy bear, let's go, boy."

I smiled—only Liv would call a 500-pound Werebear that. I caught a few nervous laughs from below.

I was easily able to watch their auras as they headed toward the southwest. They stopped out at about the hundred-meter mark.

"I can just pick up the faintest trace of sulfur on the wind," said Liv over the com.

"Roger that. Hold position," said Jack.

My heart rate picked up. We were in the right area. I strained against the darkness in the distance to try and spot any signs of the demon or its aura, but still couldn't see anything.

I flew in a random circular pattern over the main group below without really realizing I was doing it. This waiting was making me antsy. This was the part of any battle I loathed, as it gave me too much time to think about what might happen next. My mind, at times like this, usually went to the worst-case scenarios, which really didn't help, as the fear for my teammates and my own well-being grew like cancer inside me.

It was a relief when Jack's calm tone came over the com and said, "Alright, people. Let's move out. Slow and steady. We have dug it out of three of its hiding spots already, and it might be getting tired of that, so watch for traps and your six."

While I'd hated the wait, I couldn't deny that I could see much better now. I left my spot over the group and flew ahead, then positioned myself directly above Liv and Dmitri. Nice thing about being airborne was that I didn't have to worry about traps—unless the demon had installed an AA emplacement, which I doubted.

Liv and Dmitri cautiously moved through the sparse tree line and up and down the small, rocky hills below me. The quiet, peaceful night contrasted oddly against the tension and fear I was feeling as we got closer to the target area.

It took a long thirty minutes to close in on the demon's hideout, but we made it without incident.

"There is a cave about fifty meters ahead. The sulfur scent is strongest in that direction," said Liv.

"Roger. Hold position, and we will come to you," said Jack.

I could see the darkened mouth of the small cave ahead. While it looked foreboding, it was dead and still, and nothing was moving near it. I tried scenting the air, but my nose-blind senses couldn't pick up the sulfur that Liv had noticed.

I saw the auras of Blue, Bree, and Todd stop about 300 meters back from my current position; I assumed that was where they were setting up the aid area for the battle. The sniper teams had set up on a ridge about 150 meters back and to the left of our current position.

Jack, Ariel, Sheri, and Stella had reached Dmitri and Liv's position and were studying the cave mouth intently.

"Report in," ordered Jack.

"Sniper teams ready and in position."

The com hissed, and "Med teams in position" followed that quickly.

I touched my mic and said, "Zack in position."

Jack's voice came back on. "Prepare to begin the assault."

Stella and Sheri split left and right of the main group below and moved about twenty meters closer to the cave mouth. I heard the soft whine of Liv turning on the electric water pump on the water cannon.

Ariel's soft voice filled the com. "Fire in the hole. Ten seconds." She slipped something off her shoulder and held a fat, stubby tube-shaped gun in her hand. I was puzzled about this for a moment and then heard a soft *whoomp* and realized it was a grenade launcher. I closed my eyes and quickly covered my ears.

There was a brief flash of light I could see through the skin of my eyelids and then a deep *boom*. The sounds of rocks and pebbles raining against the ground below followed. I opened my eyes, and a large cloud of dust and smoke streamed from the cave. I reached for my Electrical power in anticipation of the demon coming out of the cave.

The seconds ticked by, and the dust and smoke thinned out, but everything remained strangely still and quiet. I frantically searched for the demon or its aura below me, but there was nothing. I looked beyond the cave mouth, wondering if the cave had a back exit or not, and flew forward over the hill. The other side was completely undisturbed. Surely, if there were a back door, there should be smoke or something coming out of it, but there was nothing.

"Zack here. I am over the back of the hill. No sign of a back exit."

"Roger that. Stand by."

I flew in large circles around the cave, searching for any sign of the demon. Was it playing possum inside the cave? The fire of the blast wouldn't have hurt it, but the shrapnel and the rocks flying around in the confines of that small area certainly would have. The grenade wouldn't kill the demon, but I couldn't see it wanting to take another one.

"Fire in the hole in ten," said Ariel over the com again.

I heard the launcher and closed my eyes again and covered my ears. After the blast, I quickly opened my eyes and went around the back side of the hill, looking for smoke again, and there was nothing.

After thirty more seconds of silence, Jack's voice came over the com. "We are sending Sheri in to take a look. Stay alert, people."

I flew back to the front area and watched Sheri's red-and-white-checkered aura move toward the mouth of the cave. She paused at the mouth and turned on a flashlight, which messed up my night vision a bit. Her aura disappeared into the cave a moment after that.

A few long seconds ticked by, and a new voice came over the coms. "This is the right place, as there are blood runes on the walls, but no sign of the demon."

"Roger that. Take some pictures and keep your mic open. Let us know if anything changes."

Other than Sheri's breathing and a few clicks as she snapped some pictures, her feed was quiet. Sheri strolled out of the cave and headed back to the group. I flew down and landed just outside the main group as Sheri returned.

"The cave is about twelve feet deep. The floor and walls are solid rock, so there is no place to hide. The demon isn't here," said Sheri as she returned.

"The smell of sulfur is fading, and I can't hear or sense anything nearby," said Liv.

The demon was gone, but what worried me was that the only reason I could think of for it to leave its hidey hole was to go hunting.

Chapter 25

Wednesday, April 19

We pulled back to the area where the med team was. The healers were packing up the support area and getting ready to move again.

Jack wandered over and said, "We'll need your imp to find the demon's new location."

I nodded and turned to Blue. She didn't answer, and just opened another shadow portal without a word. Liv was the first through, and Blue disappeared behind her.

"It bothers me that the demon isn't here. We only pinned this location down less than an hour ago. If it is on the move …," I said to Jack.

"You're thinking if it isn't here, it is out hunting again?"

I bobbed my head, and he added, "We couldn't have missed it by much. Hopefully, we will find it again before it adds another victim."

I prayed Jack was right; this thing had killed too many already. I clenched my fists as I thought the demon could be slaughtering someone right now, and for the moment, there wasn't a damn thing we could do about it.

To my relief, Liv, Blue, and Stinky stepped out of the shadows not a moment later. The little guy seemed scared at first. His head darted around nervously, but he relaxed a bit at seeing there was no immediate threat. He pointed almost due south without even being asked. Blue got out a map and drew a line on it.

"We'll take him to a couple of spots to get a fix," said Blue.

She opened another portal, and they were gone.

There was a sense of nervousness in the air. I glanced around and noticed that everyone was alert but also trying to stay calm and relaxed with this unexpected downtime. Todd, Bree, and Dmitri were all making laps around the outside of the perimeter in case the demon returned. A couple of the GRC13 officers were smoking off to the side of the group.

The med team had finished packing up their stuff and were ready to go. Jack was on the phone with the base to get the choppers turned back to refuel and be ready to go for the next location.

I caught myself pacing and realized it was due to frustration. I silently willed Liv and Blue to hurry up and get back. The sooner they did their job and found the demon, the quicker we could get back to going after it and stopping it for good.

"Relax, Zack," said Stella in her crisp British accent beside me.

I nodded and took a deep breath.

"They'll be back soon."

I checked my watch and shook my head, as it had only been five minutes since they'd left. It seemed longer; the adrenaline that had pumped through me earlier was starting to fade …

It was a huge relief to see Blue, Liv, and Stinky pop out of the shadows, but with the grim look Blue had on her face, my initial relief instantly turned to worry.

She handed the map to Jack, and he frowned.

"The demon is on the western outskirts of Terrance Bay near the Trans-Canada Highway," said Jack.

I wasn't sure why Blue and Jack seemed upset, and I asked, "Is Terrance Bay an inlet or something?"

"It is a small town of about 1,500 people on the northern shores of Lake Superior," said Jack.

A deep knot formed in the pit of my stomach, as 1,500 people translated to 1,500 possible victims. A small town like that wouldn't have much in the way of a police force, and whatever they did have wouldn't be enough to even slow down the demon. The Hell portal loomed in my mind, too—more victims meant more chance of it opening.

Jack yelled out, "Alright, everyone, form up! There is no time to waste. The demon is near a populated area, and we are going to stop it now."

"Blue, open a portal, and we'll drop Stinky back at the house," said Liv.

Blue nodded and was about to open a portal, when Jack said, "Belay that. The imp comes with us. If the demon is on the move, we'll need the imp to track it."

I could see Liv wasn't happy and wanted to argue. She let out a frustrated sigh, but then reluctantly nodded. Blue opened a shadow portal. Stella and Sheri went through first, and the rest of us followed on their heels.

We emerged on the south side of the Trans-Canada Highway. The road was deserted, with not a single car or truck to be seen. I could see the lights to Terence Bay off in the distance; it was probably a mile or so away. Other than the small noises we were making, it was eerily calm and quiet.

Liv softly reassured Stinky that everything would be okay and asked him to show where the demon was. The little guy was shaking like a leaf. His tiny hand trembled almost violently as he pointed south-southeast into the woods.

The woods were dark and foreboding and were made up of a thick group of bare, skeletal-looking trees with the occasional pine tree mixed in. My fight-or-flight response started kicking in, and I tamped it down. Those woods looked like something out of a horror movie, and the smart thing to do would be to stay the hell out. Too bad we didn't have that option.

"Alright, people, form up and take it slow and steady. Keep your heads on a swivel. Watch for traps and watch your six," said Jack.

Liv, Dmitri, and Stinky took point, with Sheri and Stella right behind them. Stella instantly changed back to her Hyde form. The rest of us followed. I stayed on the ground for now to save energy. Bree, Todd, and Blue stayed at the back of the formation with the healers.

We hadn't gotten more than a couple of hundred meters into the forest when Liv said, "I smell sulfur. It's close."

A few seconds after that, Stinky suddenly shot forward. At first, I thought he'd done this on his own, but his flight was odd; he was flapping frantically but in the opposite direction he was heading.

Liv cried out, "Stinky, come back!" Then she started going after him.

I started to surge forward, but then stopped as the demon stepped out from behind a tree that was about twenty-five feet ahead of us.

"So this is how you have been finding me," said the demon as it looked at Stinky. It had its left hand wrapped tightly around Stinky's neck, and Stinky was still flapping his wings, trying to break free.

The demon had used its telekinesis to pull Stinky to it. I studied the demon and could see the soft red glow under the thin layer of black scales covering it. It was much shorter than I remembered. We had hurt it, and it was time to finish this. I called on my lightning power and began pulling the power needed for a good blast. I couldn't fire, as Stinky would be hit, too, and I didn't think he would survive the blast.

"No matter," said the demon, and a sharp *crack* filled the air as it snapped Stinky's neck.

Stinky's lifeless corpse dropped to the pine-needle-covered floor, and Liv screamed in a rage.

A glow began to surround the demon, and I realized it was opening a portal.

Not this time, fucker! I extended my hand and shot a ferocious blast of lightning in its direction. A split second behind that was a wave of ice spears that Ariel the Ice elemental must have launched. The demon screamed as the lightning crashed into it and the ice spears slammed home.

To my relief, the blue glow of its portal winked out as well. If it got away, we had no way to track it.

A steady stream of water shot toward the demon and hit it dead center. Liv hosed it down while Sheri and Stella charge toward it from the flanks.

A loud *crack* like thunder went off, and the demon was surrounded by a blinding ball of bright-red light. A moment later, a wave of force knocked me clear off my feet, and I wondered what the hell had just happened. Sheri and Stella's Hyde form both went tumbling through the air too. They crashed into some trees off to my right.

The ground trembled from the direction of the demon. The blinding red glow was fading, and my eyes widened as a massive dark form lumbered out of the glow. A loud roar of anger bellowed from the giant horned form, and it raised its fists to the sky and shook them with rage.

We'd cracked the shell; now the real fun began.

Chapter 26

Wednesday, April 19

The forest floor actually vibrated as the demon's massive true form stepped out of the fading red glow. I swallowed with dread as my brain frantically tried to take in what I was seeing. The demon's new form stood among the tree branches. It had to be fifteen feet tall, and I didn't even want to guess its weight, though it would probably be in described in tons, rather than pounds. Heck, one of its muscular arms was probably bigger than my entire body.

"Now you die," rumbled through the woods as the demon opened its maw.

Its face was pig-like with an upturned nose, two deep-black beady eyes, and two massive tusks protruding from its lower jaw. It had two ram-like horns on the side of its head. The demon's hands and feet had wicked-looking claws at their tips that probably could have diced an Oldsmobile. Its broad chest was as imposing as the front of a Tiger tank.

Even with its muscles, claws, and huge size, the most impressive thing had to be the three-foot-long barbed schlong hanging between his legs. That thing had a girth larger than my thigh, and I was pretty sure it could bludgeon someone to death. I made a mental note to avoid getting near its waist; getting knocked out by a giant dick would give my teammates ammo to torment me until the end of time.

"This is for Stinky, asshole!" yelled Liv as she went to town with the water cannon.

One of the two water tanks had been split open and was empty; I assumed this must have been when we were all tossed back, and Liv must have landed on it. The other tank, though, was still half full.

A sizzling sound filled the air as the holy water hit the demon's chest, and it roared in pain. It turned and yanked a good-size pine tree clean out of the ground and tossed it at Liv. I hastily called on my Air power. I pushed the tree up and over Liv with a powerful gust of air, as she continued Ramboing out with the water cannon. The tree flew over and crashed down harmlessly in the woods. I also used my Air power to get myself upright; now was no time to be lying around in the dirt.

The stream of water ran out quickly. Liv popped the release button on her harness and let the whole thing fall off her. It was a shame she didn't have more in reserve; the demon's chest smoked and bubbled, and thick lines of black blood dripped down it.

It roared again when a couple of silver-alloyed .50 caliber rounds slammed into it. The deep *booms* echoed in the woods as the sounds of the snipers' rounds caught up to the shots.

Liv drew her sword, but strangely stayed where she was and looked off to the side. I followed her line of sight; Stella and Sheri were up again and charging full-tilt at the demon. Sheri's sub-five-foot frame leaped into the air. To my absolute amazement, she grabbed the shaft of the demon's schlong in her left hand and delivered a massive uppercut with her right, straight into the demon's balls. I winced in sympathy, and the demon made this odd yelp-like cry. It curled over in pain, but on instinct, swung down with a hard right and hammered Sheri. She flew off into the trees like a rocket.

Stella's Hyde form, which was usually imposing at its nearly seven-foot height, slammed into the demon's right leg but looked a like a small child trying to tackle an NFL linebacker. The demon actually got pushed back a couple of feet from her blow. Stella began throwing powerful punches at its knee. The demon roared and kicked forward with its left foot. Stella was launched into the air, and she crashed down hard about twenty feet away.

I caught a blue glow out of the corner of my eye and saw Jack moving his staff in precise motions, and I realized he was casting a spell. I shot forward using my Air power and grabbed Liv before she went charging in.

"What the hell, dude?" asked Liv as we shot into the air.

"Jack is casting. Didn't want you to get hit."

We both looked down as a deep rumble filled the air. A sizeable chasm opened directly beneath the demon, and it sunk a good eight feet straight down into the ground. The earth around it shook and closed, half burying it.

The demon roared in anger and grabbed another tree. It yanked it out of the ground and tossed it at Jack and Ariel. Ariel's hands shot out and erected a huge barrier of ice in front of them. The tree managed to crack the ice, but it held, and the tree deflected off, landing harmlessly behind them.

"Get me down there. I want some more payback," said Liv.

I nodded, and the demon bellowed in rage as more sniper shots slammed home.

"Check fire! Check fire!" I said into the com as we dove toward the ground. I released Liv like I was a Stuka dive-bomber, then pulled up.

I swung around to bring the demon into view again and noticed it was completely missing its left horn, which had been sliced clean off by Liv's sword. There was also a deep, oozing gash running down the left side of its back, and Liv was nowhere to be seen. I assumed she had blurred off into the woods after dismounting the demon.

Stella lumbered back into the fray and came with a powerful right hook that landed right on the demon's pig-like snout. The demon swayed and might have fallen back if it hadn't been braced upright in the ground. She followed up with a left to its chin, but that seemed to wake up the demon again.

He grabbed Stella and tossed her at Sheri, who was coming in from the left with a head of steam. Stella grunted as she flew through the air and crashed into Sheri. They both went down in a tangled heap of limbs.

The demon roared in pain and jerked its right arm up. There was a long, deep gash in it. I spotted the blur of Liv's deep-blood-red aura disappearing into the woods again.

Dmitri's imposing bear form shot out of the woods behind the demon and jumped on its back. He sunk his mouth into the broad neck and raked the demon's back with his claws. The demon shook itself violently, trying to dislodge Dmitri, but he hung on like he was a lion taking down a zebra. The demon reached back and grabbed Dmitri and, in a cloud of black gore, tore him free. It tossed Dmitri's snarling form away.

I directed some wind under Dmitri's sailing form, and he landed softly just before he would have crashed into a group of trees. He looked around in confusion, as if trying to figure out what had stopped his fall. His bear-like face turned toward me and gave me a nod of thanks.

My elemental senses tingled, and I glanced over to see Ariel launching a wave of ice at the demon's head. The hell-spawn blocked this with its left arm. Thick sheets of ice formed over the arm and froze it in a massive block of ice.

With its free hand, the demon tossed a boulder that had to be at least two feet in diameter at the Ice elemental. This time, Jack came to the rescue and, with a flick of his wand, brought up a thick berm of earth in front of them that absorbed the rock with a ground-shaking *thump*.

Dmitri, Stella, and Sheri were all charging back in, and the demon roared again as another sword gash appeared on its side as Liv blurred by.

I stayed in the air and watched as the three of them dogpiled onto the demon and pounded away at it. The ice-encrusted left arm was hampering the demon in some ways, but it used it as a club to swat Dmitri and Sheri away.

Stella followed next. She had landed a couple of vicious blows, but the demon connected with a hard right that had her sailing away again.

The massive beast roared in frustration as more sniper shots slammed home.

We were hurting it; it had wounds in numerous places now, but it still seemed like it had plenty to give. So far, no one had been hurt too badly, but that would change if the fight continued. We needed to end this.

A large cracking noise filled the air, and the demon roared as it used the ground to break its left arm free of the ice. Worse, it planted both arms firmly on the forest floor and attempted to pull itself free.

"Don't let it get out of there!" said Jack over the coms.

"Stand back! I am going to hit it with lightning. Liv, as soon as I'm finished, bury your sword in its back and try and stab it in its heart."

I swiftly landed about twenty feet in front of the creature, and I had been calling on my Electrical power, building up a massive blast of lightning. I raised my right hand toward the demon and released an arcing bolt of almost pure-white lightning at it.

The demon screamed and twitched as the electricity coursed through its massive form. I poured it on and kept dumping more and more electricity into its convulsing body. My nose started to bleed from the strain, and all I could smell was blood, ozone, and sulfur.

I completely drained my reserves and collapsed in a heap on the pine-needled forest floor again. I blacked out for a few seconds but came to as Bree was lifting me over her shoulder in a fireman's carry. She sprinted us off, away from the fight.

I was lightheaded and barely conscious. I vaguely heard noises in the distance. I realized the noises were cheers, and I blacked out after that.

Chapter 27

Wednesday, April 19

I awoke on a cot facing up toward the stars. I struggled to recall where I was. Slowly, in pieces, it started coming back to me. The image of the big-ass demon flashed into my mind. I tried to leap out of the cot but was as weak as a kitten. I reached for my Air power, but there wasn't enough left to even blow out a candle.

"Welcome back," said Blue.

I turned my head, and the world spun a bit. Blue's purple eyes were staring back at me, and she had a grin on her face.

"Help me up. I need to help with the demon."

"Relax. It has been vanquished," answered Blue. "You have been out for about ten minutes. You drained yourself electrocuting the demon, but your gamble paid off. You stunned it long enough for Liv to get on its back and kill it. Wasn't the prettiest piece of sword work, but she got the job done."

I exhaled with relief, but panicked a bit when another thought hit me. "Did anyone else get hurt?"

Blue smiled and shook her head. "No, a few bumps and bruises, but no one is seriously hurt."

Movement of a heavily armed GRC13 officer nearby caught my attention, and I called out to her.

The tall women stopped and looked over at me. "Good job stunning the demon."

"Thanks. Can I ask a favor?" I spotted a name on her uniform that said "Barclay" as she nodded. "Can you fire that Taser you are carrying at me?"

Officer Barclay looked at me like I had lost my mind. She glanced up as Blue said, "It is like Red Bovine to him. Go ahead."

I weakly giggled to myself, as Blue hadn't quite got the brand name right …

Officer Barclay must caught the gist of what Blue meant. Her eyes widened, and she shrugged, but thankfully reached for the Taser. She pointed at my left thigh and asked, "You sure?"

"Oh yeah. Do it," I said.

She squeezed the trigger. The two barbs sank into my jeans, which stung a little, but then the sweet burst of electricity followed, and I just sighed in pure pleasure. After a good five seconds, it ran out of juice.

"That hit the spot," I said as I sat up and pulled out the ends of the Taser from my jeans.

"I can get another one from my partner, if you need more," said Officer Barclay with a smile.

Before I could even speak, Blue jumped in and said, "We are trying to cut him down to one a day ... That is enough to give him the boost he required."

"Spoilsport!" I said.

I hopped out of the cot and thanked Officer Barclay. Blue was right, though; the Taser had given me enough power that I was back to normal. My power levels were maybe at 20 percent, but after being on fumes, that was enough to feel good again.

"Shall we find the others?" asked Blue.

I nodded, and she opened a portal, and we came out near the battleground. The demon's headless corpse was still half-stuck in the ground. The ground around its body was smoking and hissing as its acidic blood burned into the earth around it.

A couple GRC13 officers were snapping pictures. Liv was off to the side, dutifully cleaning her sword. Stella was back in her little girl form and standing with Bree near Liv.

Jack intercepted us as we headed over to link up with the rest of our team. "Nice work, Zack. After EIRT and OPP get here to secure the scene, we will head back to base and write up the paperwork for the bounty."

I nodded and headed over toward Liv. As we passed close to the body of the demon, I noticed a flash of something in the moonlight. I leaned over and picked up the large "S" Stinky had been wearing on his gold chain. The "S" was bent slightly, and the top curve had been eaten away a little by the demon's blood. There was no sign of the chain or Stinky's body.

Liv was frantically scrubbing the blade of her sword with a cloth, even though it looked clean to me. She had pink-tinged tears streaming down her face as she worked. I glanced over at Stella, and she just shook her head.

"C'mon, Liv. The sword is clean," I said gently, but she didn't look up. I moved closer and pulled the "S" from my pocket and held it out to her. "I thought you might want this ..."

Liv stopped as she saw the gold "S" in my hand and went dead-still for a moment. She reached out and took it from me. Liv clutched it tightly in her hand like it was the most precious thing in the world. Her katana tumbled to the ground as she sprang to her feet and wrapped her arms tightly around me. She buried her face in my neck. The sounds of her deep, muffled sobs filled the air, and her lithe body trembled against me.

"I'm sorry, Liv," I said as I stroked the back of her head.

The hug grew as Bree in her Were form stepped closer and hugged both Liv and I against the coarse fur of her arms. To my surprise, Stella's small form piled in, and Blue did too. Our whole team was surrounding Liv in a group hug.

I found my eyes, too, were getting a bit moist. I hadn't had deep feelings for the little guy, but Stinky hadn't deserved to die like he had. I hated seeing Liv like this.

We just stayed like that for a couple of minutes, but then I was finding it hard to breathe. Liv, in her grief, wasn't as aware as she usually was about her vampire strength, and a "gentle Werepanther" was an oxymoron.

"Blue, take Liv and Bree home. Bree can get changed, and Liv will be more comfortable. We'll come back tomorrow and have a ceremony for Stinky."

To my relief, the pile split apart, and Liv reluctantly let go of her death grip on me. I tried to be subtle as I sucked in much-needed oxygen as we parted; I didn't want to upset her more.

Blue opened a shadow portal. Liv reached down and sheathed her sword. Bree took her hand after that and led Liv through, and then they were gone.

Sirens were approaching in the distance, which meant the regular cops were coming, and we could head back to base and do the paperwork.

"You think she will be okay?" I asked Stella.

Stella shrugged at first, but then nodded and said, "Yes, she has been through worse than this, and I'm sure she will be back to her normal self in no time."

We walked over to the corpse of the demon. I got out my iPhone and snapped some pictures. Usually, I felt remorse when I had to kill a sentient creature in a battle, but not this time. This thing had deserved to die; my only regret was that we hadn't killed it sooner. At least no one else would die by its hand now. I also doubted that it would be sent back to Earth in my lifetime. It took an immense amount of power to send a true demon from Hell to Earth, and I doubted it had been here long enough or collected enough souls to justify its mission. I smiled as I realized that whoever its master was would be very unhappy with the demon at this moment. I hoped that its master would spend years showing the demon its displeasure in long, painful sessions ...

My Taser boost was starting to wear off, and I yawned. It would have been nice to go home, take a long, hot shower, and crawl into bed, but there was still the small matter of bounty paperwork to take care of first.

Blue popped out of a shadow nearby and joined us.

"The bards of my world would write songs about this battle," said Blue as she examined the monstrous corpse with a critical eye.

I smiled at this. I had to agree that slaying a fifteen-foot-tall demon was certainly a memorable occasion and one I wouldn't be forgetting about anytime soon.

Sheri showed up and asked to speak to Stella. Stella and her wandered off a bit deeper into the forest. I wondered what Sheri wanted to talk to Stella about. I figured that they were both female Tanks and had fought together, and it might be related to that. Maybe Sheri was just happy to find another woman with similar powers and wanted to keep in touch after all of this.

"Liv okay?" I asked Blue.

"Her and Bree were quietly sitting on the couch in the living room eating ice cream—or drinking blood, in Liv's case—when I left them. She was still upset, but Bree is with her, and I'm sure with time she'll be okay."

It took another thirty minutes, but an EIRT team and the OPP came on scene. After they secured the area, Blue opened another shadow portal, and we all went though.

I was hit by the overwhelming smell of aviation fuel again as I stepped out of the portal and into the GRC13 hangar. The human members of GRC13 said goodbye to us and left to go stow their gear. Dmitri and Todd moved off deeper into the hangar and started changing back. Jack ordered a tech to find the paperwork for the demon bounty.

The director and the captain exited an elevator on the far left of the hangar and approached us. The captain floated just behind the director. I caught Sheri nudging Ariel as she noticed the director getting closer and murmured, "Oh shit!"

"Nice working with you, but we really need to store our equipment now," said Ariel.

She and Sheri beat a hasty retreat for the elevator but took a wide approach to avoid the director on their way.

Jack smirked at his teammates' quick exit, but he didn't seem too concerned about staying and dealing with the director. As a team leader, I was sure he'd had to deal with the director on a regular basis. I was also sure that as an elder mage, the politics of dealing with a jumped-up bureaucrat was child's play compared to the Mages' Council.

Dmitri joined us seconds before the director arrived. Out of the corner of my eye, I spied Todd making a beeline for the elevator. I really was starting to get the impression that the director wasn't popular with the troops on the ground …

"Good work out there, Mr. Petrov and Mr. Latour!" said the director. His eyes widened as he spotted Stella hiding behind Blue and Jack. "Why, pray tell, is there a child in a restricted area?"

I smirked and said, "Stella, show the nice man why you are here."

Robert Smyth went pale as Stella transformed into her Hyde form. I smiled again to myself as he hastily stepped back a couple of steps.

"She is part of my team and was an essential part of the battle tonight. I'm sure Jack and Dmitri will confirm this," I said.

He didn't take his eyes off her as he replied, "Oh, I see. Nevertheless, this is a secure facility, and as you are civilians, you shouldn't be here. Jack, please get the paperwork done ASAP and escort them to the gate. I will also remind you that anything you have seen here is covered by the Official Secrets Act, and as such, you are forbidden to discuss this facility with anyone, or you will be incarcerated. Understood?"

I nodded, and he took a deep breath and made an unpleasant face, then added, "I do believe that I owe you and your team my thanks for your assistance in this matter. Now, if you will all excuse me, I must call the prime minister's office and let them know this issue has been resolved." With that, he turned and rigidly walked back toward the elevators.

Out of the corner of my eye, I caught the motion of Stella changing back into her human form again. We all stood there until the director was well out of earshot.

"I hope you three get paid extra to deal with that little twit," I said.

Captain Cooper chucked and added, "Captains and team leaders are paid much better than regular GRC13 officers."

"Still probably not enough."

The tech Jack had been dealing with appeared with a stack of papers, which were our bounty forms. Jack thanked the tech and produced a pen, then started filling out the forms.

A random unpleasant thought hit me, and I asked, "Do we need to be concerned about more demons showing up to finish what this one started? Or that with time, the portal to Hell might open on its own?"

Jack laughed and shook his head. "Portals to Hell don't open on their own. As to more demons coming through in the future, I doubt it. The energy that was sent to the portal spell will fade completely over the next few months. It cost someone in Hell a lot of energy to send that demon. I'd be shocked if they sent another one so soon after that expenditure."

Jack's words flooded through me in relief. I had no urge to take on another demon anytime soon.

Fifteen minutes later, I had the forms and a receipt in my hot little hands. I was kind of in awe that I was holding what would lead to $2.5 million US.

With the demon banished, the paperwork done, and GRC13 safely back at their base, our work was complete.

Jack reminded Stella and Blue that he wanted to get together with them in the future to discuss their backgrounds and abilities for his research, then wished us all goodbye. Dmitri shyly asked Blue if they were still on for their date Friday, and Blue smiled and nodded, to which Dmitri brightened considerably.

"Zack, it was good working with you. I want to thank you and your team for bringing an end to this menace," said Captain Cooper. He then added, "And watch your backs. The director is a small, petty man, and he will hold a grudge against you."

I smiled and replied, "I'm not too concerned—$2.5 million buys a ton of good legal and financial help."

He nodded at that, and Blue opened a portal, then we headed home.

Chapter 28

Thursday, April 20

I filed the paperwork with the UN bounty site the next morning. I knew it would take at least a week for them to process it and pay it out, but I wouldn't have been shocked if it took double that time due to the size of the bounty. We weren't hurting for cash, so I wasn't overly concerned how long it took, as long as we eventually got paid.

Walter's bill for the tracking device was in my inbox, as was Marion's bill for the healing. I paid both of those electronically and sent the funds we owed the English court for Stinky, as well, which wrapped up most of the expenses we had incurred during this bounty hunt.

I logged off and shut down the computer, but just sat there for a moment. I pondered this last case and figured it was a miracle that we had all survived—well, other than poor Stinky. This certainly had been one of the more challenging cases of my career. I was pleased at the large bounty we'd earned but hoped that our second bounty case together would be much more routine than this one had been. After this one, pixies really didn't sound so bad after all …

After joining Blue and Stella for a late brunch, I retired to the basement and spent the afternoon painting the underside of the Mosquito and putting on a base coat for the topside two-color camouflage.

Dinner that night was a somber affair, as Liv was still down about losing Stinky. After dinner, we shadow-traveled to the spot where Stinky had been killed.

The demon's head and body were gone, and the hole where it had been stuck had been filled in as well. There was no vegetation in the immediate area where demon had died, as its toxic blood had burned it all away. There was just a patch of darkened soil and rocks. We stood in a circle around that, and each of us said a few words.

"I didn't get to know Stinky very well," I said, "but in our short time together, his little beer-loving form did brighten all our lives. His life was cut much too short, but his death means that our world is now a much safer place, thanks to his sacrifice. I hope he can rest easier, knowing that we avenged his death."

I stepped forward and twisted off the cap of the beer I was carrying. I poured out about half of it for him. I stood there quietly as the frothing white bubbles sank into the ground. I think I half expected his little form to shoot from the ground and start lapping up the spilt beer. Unfortunately, the ground stayed lifeless and still.

I moved back, and Blue stepped forward and said a long statement in her native language, which sounded like an odd mix of Japanese and French. Her tone had a slow, almost musical quality to it. When she was done, she raised her right fist to the sky and yelled something that sounded like "Ah-kig!" She lowered her head and stepped back.

We were all looking at Blue with curious expressions, and she said, "It was the Warrior's Farewell Prayer from my home world. As Stinky died in combat, it seemed appropriate. Did I do something that is offensive in human death rituals?"

Liv shook her head and said, "No. It was beautiful. Thank you."

I glanced at Stella, and she said, "I will miss the creature known as Stinky, as it was lovely not being the smallest one in the house for a change." She paused as a couple of us laughed, then added, "My time with Stinky was limited, but in that short time, he seemed like a loyal member of our team, and without his help, that evil creature would still be out there killing innocents. For that, he died a hero."

The group was quiet for a moment, until Bree stepped forward and added, "My first impression of Stinky was that he lived up to his name, and with my enhanced sense of smell, that wasn't easy getting used to. I also found him a bit creepy, but he made my best friend happy. Seeing Liv light up when Stinky was around, and how protective and caring she was of him, brought out the best in my friend, and for that, I will miss his presence."

We all glanced at Liv, who was staring at the ground motionless, with pink tears streaming down her face. She shook herself and stepped forward. "A mother's first duty is to protect her young, and I failed at that, Stinky, and for that, I am so sorry. You deserved better than how things ended." She paused, clenched her fists, and continued. "I may not have protected you, but I sure as hell made sure I avenged you. Mama sliced up that son of bitch until it dropped. That won't bring you back, but at least I made sure the demon wouldn't hurt anyone else. Take care, little guy. I'll miss you ..."

As Liv stepped back and went quiet, my eyes started to water a bit. I must have gotten some dust in them or something ...

Stella stepped forward again and placed a small bronze plaque in the dirt. It simply read, "Here lies Stinky, who bravely gave his life so others didn't have to."

* * * * *

We retired to back to the house after our funeral for Stinky. Liv and Bree hung out in the living room watching *Legally Blonde*, which was one of Liv's favorite movies.

Once the movie was finished, I tried taking Liv out on another flying date, hoping to cheer her up. I talked her into it, but it quickly became apparent that she wasn't into it. There was no loud "Wheeeeeee!" when I dropped her in free fall, and she barely smiled. We flew around for another twenty minutes, but then I decided to take her back home.

In my desperation to cheer her up once we got back, I offered to let her feed from me.

"It would be a waste right now ... You are just offering to cheer me up, and I don't want to take advantage of you." With that, she headed back to the living room to hang out with Bree.

Her rejection, more than anything else, worried me, as I couldn't remember a time when she wouldn't have jumped at that offer. I wanted to make things better for her, but I realized that what she needed most was time.

I decided to call it a night; I was tired and not really in the mood to do anything else today. I had been feeling wiped all day from draining myself during yesterday's battle, and it had caught up with me.

* * * * *

The next morning, I was up just after dawn. Liv was down in her death trance in the basement, and Bree was sound asleep. I wasn't surprised to see Stella and Blue up, and joined them for a small breakfast.

Liv's grief was still weighing heavily on my mind, and as I ate my Cheerios, I wondered if there was anything else I could do to cheer her up.

Stella pulled me from my musings. "Now that the demon bounty is over, we should look for our next one. I checked the bounty site this morning, and the pixie bounty is still listed."

My first reaction was to say, "Pass," but then a wonderful idea hit me, and I started making plans ...

A couple of hours later, I had Blue open a shadow portal to Burlington. The three of us stepped though the portal and out into the noonday sun. I smiled as I spotted the small rainbow auras flittering through the trees in front of me. I placed the large slab cake I had bought earlier on the ground, along with the large water cooler filled with human blood that I had filled using the Food-O-Tron. Blue and Stella in her Hyde form stood behind me.

My hands were already sweaty, and my stomach rolled at the thought of what I was about to do. Pixies were fae and, as such, were tricky to deal with. All fae could tell when someone was lying. They were also incapable of lying themselves but were masters of half-truths and deception.

Liv's moping image flashed into my mind, and I steeled myself for what I was about to do.

"Oh, mighty pixies, I bring tribute and wish to parley!" I said.

The auras instantly stopped moving, and I sensed a bunch of invisible eyes upon me. Long seconds ticked by, and nothing moved.

I whispered over my shoulder, "Back up and hang out across the road. I will call if I need you."

I caught the sound of Blue's hard-soled boots and Stella's Hyde's lumbering gait as they crossed the road behind me. I got on my knees and prostrated myself, facing toward the trees.

"I bring offerings of sugar and blood, and only wish to talk," I said loudly.

I noticed a couple of the pixie auras moving in the trees. They were invisible to human eyes unless they wished to be seen, but my aura ability let me see their outlines. The movement was around the pixie with the largest aura, and I assumed that must be their queen.

Five pixies flew out from the trees and hovered in the air a few feet in front of me. A feminine voice cut through the air and asked, "What do you want, elemental?"

I caught the scents of cinnamon, lilac, and baked bread, and glanced up. A purple-haired pixie holding a small sharpened stick was the speaker. The tips of her pointed ears peeked out from the silky strands of hair. She was nude, save for a red ribbon sash and a beer cap tied down on her head as a helmet. The other four pixies dropped their glamour, as well, and they, too, had tiny spears, ribbons, and beer-cap helmets, and flanked the speaker, two on each side. Two of the four had purple hair like the speaker, and the other two had shimmering green hair.

Pixies were normally nude; their elemental natures meant that weather didn't bother them. The ribbon and helmets were significant, as that meant all five pixies were part of the queen's royal guard.

"I come in peace. I wish to discuss business with your queen. I ask only for her to hear my proposal, and whether she accepts or not, the tribute is hers."

"Do not move. I will return."

The speaker darted off. The four pixies in front of me gave off a buzzing noise from their wings as they hovered in place. The noise was disturbingly like an angry swarm of wasps.

A couple of minutes went by, and my knees were starting to get sore from being pressed against the partially frozen ground.

The buzzing got louder, and I saw the entire swarm emerge from the trees, and my mouth suddenly got very dry. I was seriously rethinking my plan at that moment. I had known that if I ran into trouble, Stella's Hyde form would be over in an instant, and there would be many dead pixies after that, but I stood to take a world of hurt before she made it here.

More scents filled the air as I inhaled: roses, pine, cotton candy, and fresh-cut grass, to name a few.

A small whistle cracked through the air, and one of the pixies said, "All bow, for you are in the presence of Queen Kileeanna and Prince Grog!"

I pressed lower into the ground and remained dead-still. The buzzing got louder, and I started to sweat more, despite it being a cool spring day. The image of a swarm of pixies stripping a human to the bone in under twenty seconds like they were flying piranha was weighing heavily on my mind at this moment.

"You may rise to a sitting position, but no sudden moves," said a voice with a sultry feminine tone that was slightly deeper than the previous ones.

I lifted my head from the ground and slowly shifted to a sitting position. Hovering about four feet in front of me at eye level was a plump pixie with long golden hair. She was seated on a throne made of sticks and covered in foil and shiny candy wrappers. The throne was held aloft by four struggling pixies who were holding supports that ran under the throne. She had two red ribbons that were worn as crossed sashes that met between her ample cleavage. In the center of the two sashes was a small clear diamond. On her head, there was a small crown of gold.

From pixie lore, even without the dual sashes and the crown, I would have known this was the queen by her weight. Pixies lived to do two things: eat and fornicate. They had low birthrates, and less than one in a hundred were born male. If a pixie had a son, the current queen would pick ten other pixies and send her, the baby, and those pixies off to find another area to begin another swarm. The mother of the boy was automatically made queen. As she was the mother and wouldn't be fornicating in the future with her own son, she was granted first bites on any food the swarm procured. She would have her fill, and the remaining food would be shared equally among the swarm. Most pixies had figures like mini Barbie dolls; the plump one was always the queen. Her aura was also three times the size of any of the other pixies.

To the right of the throne was a male pixie with the same golden hair as his mother. Unlike his mother, he was in peak physical form. He was about seven inches tall, which made him about an inch taller than most of the female pixies around him.

"You may speak," said the queen.

I took a deep breath and gathered my thoughts. I had one shot at this and wanted to get it right. "Thank you for seeing me, Your Majesty. I bring tribute of cake and human blood, and only hope both are worthy of your greatness."

She smiled at this and then nodded her head for me to continue.

"I have two things I wish to propose. The humans have become aware of your mighty swarm here, and they are afraid. They have put up a large reward, and the call has gone out to many great warriors to gather for battle. I, too, am a warrior, but I am also a peacemaker. I wish to avoid bloodshed and propose an alternative, if you are interested, Your Majesty."

I was laying it on a little thick and *just* keeping on the side of truth. I also noticed that when I mentioned "many great warriors," the queen and prince both blanched. She narrowed her eyes at me and studied me quietly for a moment.

"I would be foolish not to hear your alternative. Whether I choose to go with it or not is another matter."

"Thank you, Your Majesty. My blue companion over yonder is a shadow-traveler. She has the ability to travel anywhere in the world via the shadows. We have recently become aware of an island north of here. It is free from humans, and the game on the island is plentiful, as well as there being good fishing around the island. If we moved your swarm there, the humans wouldn't be able to find you, and bloodshed would be averted."

She eyed me as she rubbed her double chin. "This island free from humans is intriguing, but you mentioned *two* things you wished to propose. What is the second?"

Here was where things got tricky. I centered my thoughts. "My companions and I employed an imp"—the pixies all hissed at this—"who we used as a scout. He is no longer with us. I felt that a pixie would be much better in this role and wished to add one to our ranks, Your Majesty."

She frowned at this. "All my subjects are precious to me, and I would be reluctant to part with one."

"I understand, Your Majesty. The warrior prowess of pixies is legendary, and as such, I would be more than content with even your weakest or the one who had displeased you the most ..."

The queen glanced over to her son, and they both winked at each other, as if being in sync at who they had in mind. Her son mumbled, "Alteea," under his breath, and I assumed that was the name of the pixie they both wanted to get rid of.

"Very well," said the queen. "I believe we can come to some arrangement. Now let us work out the details ..."

It took another hour of negotiations, but we came to a deal. At the end of it, I was instructed to rise and hold out my right hand. The purple-haired speaker from earlier came forward and pricked my finger with her spear; I hoped this one wasn't poison-tipped.

The queen rose from her throne and flew over to me. She bit her tiny forefinger with one of her fangs and then placed her finger on mine where I was bleeding. "I, Queen Kileeanna, swear to uphold my side of the deal with the elemental known as Zack Stevens by oath of blood."

I repeated the oath, but in reverse, and with that, she leaned forward and tickled my finger with her tongue, cleaning up the blood.

"Waste not, want not," the queen said as she licked my blood from her lips. "Summon your companions over."

I waved Blue and Stella over as the queen flew back to her throne, stopping to grab a large handful of cake on the way.

I explained to Blue what I needed, and she opened a shadow portal to the island on Lake Nipigon where the demon had had one of its hideouts. She, Stella, and about half the swarm went through.

I knew it would take a bit of time for the swarm to scout the island and make sure it was suitable. I had one pressing question on my mind from our deal. I turned toward Queen Kileeanna and said, "Your Majesty, I beg a moment of your time in private, as I have something to discuss that is for royal ears only."

The queen looked up at me and, after stuffing the rest of the cake in her mouth, nodded. "Take the cake and blood back to our nest, but I have not yet finished my sampling. Grog, remain here," ordered the queen.

The buzzing of wings got louder, and they descended on the cake and the large container of blood, and both lifted from the ground and headed for the trees behind us.

"Now, elemental, what is it you wish to discuss?"

"Are we safe from prying ears?" I asked.

The queen made a rapid gesture with her hand, and I felt the air tingle around us. "That will ensure our privacy."

"The pixie known as Alteea who I bargained for: I'm assuming she has been a thorn in your side? I wished to know why and didn't want to hurt her feelings."

The queen and prince laughed, and the queen said, "You needn't have bothered with all this privacy, as she is quite aware of our disappointment with her. She is unnatural. We pixies love two things: the hunt and its spoils, and the pleasures of the flesh. Alteea barely cares for either. Her only love is to learn. She finds humans fascinating and wishes to learn all she can about them. Instead of hunting for food, she gets distracted and spends her time observing them; most times, she comes back from a hunt empty-handed. A pixie who doesn't contribute to the swarm is a burden. If her dear, departed mother hadn't been my closest friend, I would have banished her many moons ago."

I was flooded with relief at the queen's answer. I'd inherited a pixie nerd! This actually worked out well, as she wouldn't miss her "time" with Prince Grog like most pixies would.

"This looks like it works out well for both of us. You lose a problem, and we gain a pixie who will be happy living among humans. You are a wise queen."

The queen preened at this, and I was really starting to understand that the queen liked flattery. She waved her hands, and the air no longer tingled. Then she bellowed out, "Alteea, attend me!" For her small size, the queen had an impressive set of pipes on her.

Nothing happened, and the queen sighed. "Grog, go find Alteea and bring her here."

Grog nodded and darted off. A good ten minutes went by, and Grog and another pixie emerged from the trees and shot toward us. Grog stopped and hovered to the right of his mother, and a red-headed pixie flew in front of the queen and bowed.

Her funky red hair, which was sticking out in all directions, was the first thing I noticed. The rest of the pixies I had seen all seemed to have paid great attention to their hairstyles. This pixie looked like she had just gotten out of bed. Despite the lack of care, her hair certainly added a lovely character to her. She also had these amazing deep-green eyes. She was totally nude and, in that department, seemed as stunning as most of the pixies were.

Without raising her head, the red-headed pixie asked, "You wish to see me, Your Majesty?"

"Where have you been?"

"I was observing the human young in their place of learning over yonder, Your Majesty."

The queen sighed. "Of course you were. Alteea, this is Zack. He is an elemental, and we have made a deal for the good of the swarm. He will help us relocate, as he has brought to my attention news of an imminent threat. His price for his services is the service of one of our kind. I have selected you to be our representative. Once we have moved, you will go with him and follow his orders as if they were from me, understand?"

Alteea seemed shocked at this, but was, by her expression, more intrigued than anything else. "Yes, Your Majesty."

"Good. I have tribute to sample and will leave the two of you to get acquainted while we wait for Zack's companions and our scouts to return." And with that, she and Grog flew off to the trees.

Alteea eyed me with a curious expression. I noticed her rainbow aura had deep streaks of red in it and assumed her affinity was Fire.

"Hi, Alteea. I am sorry for pulling you from your home like this," I said.

She smiled. "No worries, master. I have never really fit in here. What services will I be required to provide?"

"First, please call me 'Zack.' You will have two main roles. One of my companions is depressed, as she was close to an imp"—Alteea hissed; I was starting to realize that demons weren't popular with pixies—"who was part of our team. He gave his life in a battle when we slayed a true demon."

Her eyes went wide at this, and she gave an approving nod.

"Since the battle, she has been missing him a great deal, and I was hoping your company might cheer her up."

Alteea ponder this for a moment. "Is she an elemental like you, master Zack?"

"Just 'Zack,' and no, she is a vampire."

The tiny pixie trembled with fear and said with a stutter, "W-w-will she d-d-drain me, master?"

I laughed at this, then quickly added, "No, she is house-trained," which got me an odd look. "No, you will be quite safe, I assure you. She has an ample supply of blood and would have no interest in drinking from you."

Alteea seemed a bit better at this. "And my other role, master Zack?"

"You don't need to call me 'master.' 'Zack' is fine. Due to your invisibility and size, we may use you to scout locations and our enemies."

She seemed enthusiastic about the scout role, but said, "Her Majesty assigned me to you. Therefore, by her royal decree, you are my master. Not using the term 'master' would be disrespectful to her and to you, master."

I made a mental note that once we were away from the swarm, to try and get Alteea to drop the "master" bit.

We spent the next half hour going over different things about her roles, the team, my house, and me, answering the plethora of questions she had. She certainly was an inquisitive little thing and, by the end of our talk, seemed genuinely excited about her new role.

A portal opened, and Blue, Stella's Hyde form, and a number of pixies emerged. Alteea and I headed over and joined everyone in the trees. The purple-haired pixie made her report to the queen and mentioned that she had scented demon on the island. This threw the whole swarm into chaos for a moment until I explained that we had defeated that demon, and it would not be returning. This settled everything down, and the purple-haired pixie gushed about the wildlife and the island in general. The queen was happy with this, and in short order, Blue opened another portal, and we spent the next half hour moving their meager possessions to their new home.

I filmed the whole thing on my phone. I figured that while we hadn't killed the pixies, we had moved them to an area where they would no longer be a threat to humanity, and that might be enough to claim the bounty. It was worth a shot anyway.

Alteea said goodbye to the swarm, but no one really, including her, seemed to care that much. The queen reminded me of the remainder of our deal: I was to visit the swarm on each new moon and bring cake. I nodded, and with that, our work was done. I had Blue portal us home.

Epilogue

As we stepped out the shadows and into the hallway of our house, we were greeted by Bree. By "greeted," I mean she grunted at us and said, "Food, now!"

By her bedhead, I assumed she had just woken up and was looking for "breakfast." Stella danced around Bree and headed to the kitchen. Blue closed the portal we had just used and opened a new one.

As she and Bree stepped into the shadows, Bree asked, "Why do I smell cinnamon and roses?" Then they were gone.

Alteea buzzed out from behind me, dropped her glamour, and became visible again. "You live with a beast, master?"

I took me a second to understand who she was referring to before I replied, "That is Bree. She is Liv's best friend and a member of our team. She is a Werepanther, and I would strongly suggest that you do not call her a 'beast' to her face; she has a bit of a temper."

"But, master, we were taught that beasts eat anything that moves."

I smiled. "You are not far from wrong, but Bree won't eat you. At your size, you are barely worth the effort ... Just don't ever try and take food from her plate."

Alteea nodded solemnly in response, and I felt a little bad about teasing her.

Stella was already making herself a cup of tea when we entered the kitchen. I grabbed a Coke from the fridge and considered Alteea, who was just hovering in front of me. I opened the cupboard where I kept aspirin, vitamins, and cold medications, and I glanced around. I surveyed it for a moment and spotted a tube of ChapStick that had been in there forever. I popped off the cap and tossed the tube in the garbage. I rinsed out the cap in the sink. I dried it off and headed for the basement with Alteea in tow.

She pointed at the cold cellar door where Liv was "sleeping" and asked, "Is that the vampire's lair, master?"

I hardly thought it should be called a "lair," but couldn't be bothered to argue with her and just nodded. We went deeper into the basement and reached my model-building area. I grabbed a few of my smaller model boxes and arranged them so one worked as a seat for Alteea, then propped my iPhone up against a couple of boxes in front of the "chair."

"Have a seat," I said.

Alteea gracefully landed on the desk and planted herself on the edge of the box.

"Your queen said you like to learn, so I thought you might enjoy this …" I then showed her the pin code to my phone, opened up the browser, and went to Wikipedia. I asked her for a topic, and she answered, "Vampires." I hit the vampire page on the site, showed her how to scroll up and down and where the box to do another search was, and left her to it. My little friend took to it like a duck to water and was instantly transfixed by the content on the screen.

I opened my can of Coke and carefully poured some out into the plastic white lid I'd washed out earlier. I offered the cap to Alteea, who took it from me with her tiny hands. She sniffed the dark liquid and then took an experimental sip.

"This is yummy, master. What is it called?"

"Coke."

She nodded and took another sip and then placed the "cup" carefully beside her and went back to reading on my phone.

With Alteea settled, I turned my attention to the Mosquito, as it was time to do the camouflage pattern on the top of it. I opened the plans for reference and, in pencil, started lightly outlining the pattern I needed to paint.

It took me close to an hour, but I had the entire pattern penciled out on the top of the model. I figured that by now, Bree had some food in her, and it would a good time to introduce her to Alteea.

"Okay, let's take a break and go meet Bree."

Alteea glanced up from the phone and nervously nodded.

"Relax. You are perfectly safe. If anything, Bree will adore you."

We found Bree in the living room, lounging on the couch. She looked up as we entered, and her eyes widened as she saw Alteea.

I introduced them, and both of them stared, fascinated, at each other for a bit, until Bree turned her attention to me for a moment and shot me a stern look.

"Alteea, why don't you head back to the basement and use my phone again, and I will join you shortly," I said.

She nodded and darted off.

Bree crossed her arms and said, "Okay, you pervert, why is that pixie naked?"

"It's my idea for our new team uniform ..."

Bree didn't say anything, but just glared at me harder.

"That wasn't my doing. Most pixies are nude; they have elemental affinities and don't feel the heat or the cold. They are also not the most modest race you'll meet. Actually, after seeing their setup, I'm hoping in my next life I come back as pixie male," I finished with a leering grin.

Bree rolled her eyes. "Okay, nudity aside for now—as I'm not 100 percent sure you are telling me the truth—why do you have a pixie?"

"On the nudity front, ask Blue and Stella, as they were there with me today when I got Alteea. As to the why, I thought Alteea might drag Liv out of her grief ..."

Bree's expression instantly softened as I mentioned Liv. "I'm sorry, Zack. That is so sweet of you. I'm sure Liv will love Alteea. I just focused on the nudity and figured this was one of your usual perverted things ..."

"I am wounded that you think that poorly of me. This is difficult on Alteea, as she is used to being around all her pixie friends, so if you could try and make her feel more welcome, that would be nice."

"Oh wow, I didn't even think about how much of an adjustment it must be for her. What do you suggest I do to make her feel more welcome?"

I grinned internally at Bree's statement and said in a serious tone, "Well, maybe we could try and make our house feel a little more like home for her."

Bree nodded, and I continued. "So, tonight at dinner, it would probably be best if you and Liv stripped down, so she doesn't stand out as much."

Bree groaned, and I ducked as she tossed a cushion from the couch at me. "Get out!"

I laughed as I beat a hasty retreat to the basement.

* * * * *

I'd finished applying the brown camouflage a good hour before dinner. At about the same time, Alteea had pointed out the low-battery warning on my phone. We moved the party upstairs. Everyone, except Liv, was seated around the kitchen table.

Alteea started asking each of them questions. She was tentative at first but became more comfortable as it went on. Blue seemed to be her main target for questions, as she was absolutely enthralled with Blue talking about her home world.

Time flew by, and before I knew it, Liv emerged from the basement. She waved half-heartedly at us as she made a beeline for the fridge to get her glass of blood that was chilling there.

Liv reached for the fridge door and stopped. Her head turned in a flash toward us and instantly focused in on Alteea.

"Liv, this is Alteea. She will be living with us from now on. Today, while you were asleep, Stella, Blue, and I relocated her swarm from Burlington to a safer place up north. As a reward for our services, their queen gave us Alteea."

Liv went dead-still in the way that only vampires can and studied Alteea. We all held our breath, waiting for Liv's reaction.

"Oh my God! She is adorable! Why is she naked? Zack, is this you being a perv again? Oh, we will just have to go shopping! This is too much. I need breakfast first, and then we'll go shopping. What does she eat? Where will she sleep?"

She grabbed her pint of plasma from the fridge and blurred over to the table and sat down. "C'mon, little one—oh, maybe I shouldn't call you 'little one,' as that might be offensive. Is it offensive?"

Out of the corner of my eye, I caught Blue, Stella, and Bree all smiling as they watched Liv and Alteea.

Alteea fluttered over toward Liv and said, "I do not find the term 'little one' to be offensive, as it is accurate, mistress."

"*Squeeeeeeee*! You talk, and you have a lovely voice!"

Alteea smiled at Liv. "Thank you, mistress." She stared longingly at Liv's glass.

"Oh, I am being rude. Would you like some of this?"

Alteea gave a small nod, and Liv blurred out of her seat. Cupboards rapidly opened and closed, and in less than three seconds, Liv was back with a shot glass. She poured some blood out for Alteea and handed it to her. Alteea took the shot glass awkwardly from Liv, as it was a bit too big for her. The two of them drank, and we all just quietly watched them. Both glasses emptied in short order, and Liv was on her feet again.

Liv looked at Alteea. "Let's go shopping! Do I need to find something to cover you, so we can go out in public?"

"No need, mistress," answered Alteea, who promptly turn on her glamour and disappeared.

"Oh, that is neat! I know you are still there, as I can smell you and hear your heartbeat, but normal people won't be able to detect you like that. Let's go! We will need to get you clothes, furniture, a place to sleep—maybe a doll's house would work—and probably a ton of other stuff. Should I make a list, or can you remember all of this? Ah, skip it. We'll figure it out!"

Liv blurred for the door, and I watched Alteea's aura lift from the table and follow her.

As if being afraid of breaking the spell, nobody said anything until the front door slammed.

"She's back!" said Bree.

"Yeah, too bad it's all going to come to a crashing end shortly," I said.

Bree gave me a puzzled look. "Why's that?"

"That poor pixie probably won't survive Liv's driving ..."

Bree giggled, then nodded sagely. "We'll cross our fingers and hope for her survival. Seriously, though, that was really nice of you to go to the trouble of getting Alteea to try and bring Liv out of her funk. And she is certainly easier on my nose than Stinky was."

Stella said, "Yes, poor Stinky wasn't easy to be around, even for those us with normal noses. I don't know how you and Liv managed to deal with him."

"That pixie will also be a useful addition to our team," said Blue. "With her small size and that glamour that makes her invisible, she makes an ideal scout. Does she have any other powers?"

All eyes turned to me, and I said, "By her aura, she has Fire affinity. I'm guessing she can toss small fireballs, light things on fire, and probably warm the air around her, but I will make a note to ask."

"I will add her to our training regime," said Blue, and with a pointy-tooth-filled smile, she added, "I will sew her a tiny weighted pack. And speaking of training, we have been slacking during that last case. I have something special in mind for tonight to shake the rust off."

I groaned at this—and I wasn't the only one.

"Training can wait. Dinner first!" said Bree.

Shortly after that, Blue and Bree left to hit the Food-O-Tron, and Stella and I stayed behind to set the table. We finished our tasked in short order, and Stella retired to the kitchen to make tea, leaving me with my thoughts.

Our first case together had been a doozy, and I prayed the next one wouldn't be quite as intense. We had all survived though—well, except for Stinky—and our bank account would certainly look better once the bounty cleared. Taking on a true demon and winning gave me a very positive feeling about the future of our partnership. If we could handle that, then we could handle just about anything together. Though I was seriously wondering if I would survive Blue's training this evening ...